'If poetry was the supreme literary form of the First World War then, as if in riposte, in the Second World War, the English novel came of age. This wonderful series is an exemplary reminder of that fact. Great novels were written about the Second World War and we should not forget them.'

WILLIAM BOYD

'It's wonderful to see these books given a new lease of life [...] classic novels from the Second World War written by those who were there, experienced the fear, anguish, pain and excitement first-hand and whose writings really do shine an incredibly vivid light onto what it was like to live and fight through that terrible conflict.'

JAMES HOLLAND, Historian, author and TV presenter

'The Imperial War Museum has performed a valuable public service by reissuing these absolutely superb novels.'

ANDREW ROBERTS, author of *Churchill: Walking with Destiny*

TO ALL THE LIVING

Monica Felton

IMPERIAL WAR MUSEUMS

First published in Great Britain in 1945

First published in this format in 2021 by
IWM, Lambeth Road, London SE1 6HZ
iwm.org.uk

© The Estate of Monica Felton, 2021

About the Author and Introduction
© The Trustees of the Imperial War Museum, 2021

ISBN 978-1-912423-42-2

A catalogue record for this book is available from the
British Library.

Printed and bound by CPI Group (UK) Ltd,
Croydon CR0 4YY

Every effort has been made to contact all copyright holders.
The publishers will be glad to make good in future editions
any error or omissions brought to their attention.

Cover illustration by Bill Bragg
Design by Clare Skeats
Series Editor Madeleine James

About the Author

Monica Felton

MONICA FELTON (1906–1970) was a feminist, socialist, peace activist, historian and author, and a pioneering proponent of town planning. She attended University College, Southampton, and was awarded a doctorate for a thesis on emigration from Britain between 1802 and 1860 at the London School of Economics. In 1937 she was elected a member of the London County Council, representing St Pancras South West.

During the Second World War Felton served in the Ministry of Supply, on which her publications *Civilian Supplies in Wartime Britain* and her novel *To All the Living* are based. After her time at the Ministry, Felton was Clerk of the House of Commons until 1943. She then worked for the Army Bureau of Current Affairs, lecturing servicemen and women across Britain and the Middle East about world affairs and the problems of post-war Britain. After the war, she became heavily involved in town planning, serving as Chair for the Peterlee and Stevenage Development Corporations. However, she was fired from the chair of Stevenage by Hugh Dalton, Minister of Local Government and Planning, after taking an unauthorised trip to North Korea on behalf of the Women's International Democratic Federation in 1951, during the Korean War. On her return from this trip she accused American troops of atrocities and British complicity. There was a media and establishment backlash, and even accusations of treason from Members of Parliament for suborning American and British prisoners of war. As a result, Felton became increasingly isolated in Britain and moved to India in 1956. Whilst there, she wrote biographies of the Indian statesman Chakravarthi Rajagopalachari and women's social reformer Sister R S Subhalakshmi. She died in Madras (modern day Chennai) in 1970.

Introduction

One of the literary legacies of the First World War was the proliferation of war novels, with an explosion of the genre in the late 1920s and 1930s. Erich Maria Remarque's *All Quiet on the Western Front* was a bestseller and was made into a Hollywood film in 1930. In the same year, Siegfried Sassoon's *Memoirs of an Infantry Officer* sold 24,000 copies. Generations of school children have grown up on a diet of Wilfred Owen's poetry and the novels of Sassoon. Yet the novels of the Second World War are often forgotten, with female voices in particular being overlooked.

Monica Felton's *To All the Living* is one such novel. First published in 1945, it tells the story of life in a shell-filling factory on the British home front. The author's own experience in the Ministry of Supply in the first years of the war inspired this depiction. The Ministry (established in 1939), was responsible for the production of munitions and stores for the Army and later most raw materials were included in its remit. It was also responsible for the salvaging of waste products of all kinds, including domestic salvage. Therefore, as a result of her time in the Ministry, Felton was aware of munitions work, and the bureaucracy and the social issues that were prevalent within it. Indeed, allegedly her brother was an industrialist making parts for aircraft and the novel has been seen as a veiled attack on him. The Ministry was overseen for the majority of the war by the businessman Sir Andrew Duncan, however press baron Lord Beaverbrook was in charge for just over a six month period in 1941–42 and he, or conceivably a mixture of Duncan and Beaverbrook, is quite possibly the model for the Minister depicted in the novel: 'Lord Outrage'. The setting of the factory – Blimpton – is reminiscent of the satirical Colonel Blimp character popularised by the David Low cartoons published in the *Evening Standard* during the 1930s.

To All the Living takes place throughout 1941, during the Blitz. Although the factory is untouched by the bombing raids, they loom in the background of the characters' lives. George Parsons, the

Labour Officer in the factory, is constantly worried about his wife and children in London: 'He thought of his wife, grown querulous with anxiety as she moved from one temporary home to another. He knew that she would not be happy at Blimpton, but he believed that she would be less unhappy there than in London, where the last severe air-raid had shattered her conviction that whatever might happen to other people no harm could ever come to anything that was hers.' Similarly, the factory functions as a microcosm of the wider war. This is exemplified when Germany's invasion of the Soviet Union is addressed on the same pages as the playing of Mozart in the factory – a precursor to the BBC Home Service's 'Music While You Work', which both helped to relieve the monotony of factory labour but also improved production across the country.

Factory work, as depicted in the novel, could be exhausting and repetitive, with workers often receiving low pay. During the First World War, large numbers of women worked in munitions factories. These 'munitionettes' moved from their homes to the munitions areas at a rate of 5,000 a month. Similarly, in the first two years of the Second World War, women moved to hostels and lodgings near the factories. However as this was on voluntary basis, there was always a shortage of labour. Challenges around keeping and retaining workers are debated and discussed throughout the novel, alongside wide-ranging issues such as transport for workers, occupational health and relationships between both the different classes and sexes who all form part of the factory's wide community. In one passage Dan Morgan, the Assistant Superintendent, describes:

> 'But I should explain,' Morgan went on, relaxing a little, 'that the shortages vary from week to week, sometimes from day to day. Dawson will be able to give you a chart showing the main bottlenecks on that side over the past three months. Then, of course, we're short of labour.'
> 'What kind of labour?'
> 'Every grade, almost. Naturally the worst difficulty is in getting unskilled women.'
> 'How many do you need?'

'About fourteen thousand, I estimate.'

Gunn put his notebook down. 'Would you repeat that figure?' he asked.

'About fourteen thousand. Of course we don't need them all at once. But we ought to be taking on about five hundred each week.'

'How many do you get?'

'Fifty to a hundred. Sometimes more.' […]

Otway Dolphin strolled over to the fireplace, displaying well-tailored trousers…. 'In any case,' he pointed out, purring slightly, 'I'm sure Miss Creed would be the first to agree that it's utterly useless to recruit women who won't stay in the factory for more than ten minutes or so… I mean, it's a waste of everybody's time.'

'Who won't stay in the factory?' Gunn asked. His eyes, too, were beginning to gleam.

'Oh, the vast majority, if you take my meaning. They come and they go.' Dolphin paused to fidget daintily with his flowing silk tie. 'I estimate that most of the women we recruit don't last more than two months on the average. Some stay longer, but some just take one look and –' he waved a hand airily, 'home they go… I'm sure Captain Knowles will confirm what I say.'

[…] 'Some stay,' Morgan told him, 'but the figures Dolphin has given you are near enough. Blimpton isn't a place that people like to come to.'

'What's the reason?'

'It's dangerous work, you know,' Dr Maclver said mildly.

'Oh, no, it isn't,' Morgan contradicted, 'we've a much lower accident rate than the average engineering factory.'

Nicholls, the senior chemist, advanced from the other end of the room. 'The work is incredibly monotonous,' he remarked, as if that were the beginning and end of the matter.

'But most girls like monotonous work,' someone reminded him.

'It isn't the work,' Otway Dolphin agreed, 'it's the conditions.

You've only got to take a walk round the factory to see why the workers won't stay.'

These shortages were mirrored in all factories at the beginning of the war. Consequently, Ernest Bevin, Minister for Labour, introduced the Essential Work Order in March 1941. Although he gets an unfavourable mention in the novel – the Superintendent declares he 'can't stand him' – 'that chap, Bevin' was instrumental in resolving the labour crisis. After the introduction of the Essential Work order, no person is allowed to leave or be dismissed without the consent of the Ministry's local National Service Officer and the problems of bureaucracy in the factory are rife (as reflected in the large cast list of characters provided by Felton at the start of the book).

Bevin also introduced conscription for women in December 1941 to help stem the problems of recruitment for factory work. Of a population of 48 million, 6.7 million women were contributing to the war effort by 1945, with a further 2.5 million in the voluntary sector. Only the Soviet Union mobilised a higher percentage of women for the war effort. Extremely large numbers of women worked in factories during the war: at the peak (in June 1942), over 320,000 women worked in the explosives industries, outnumbering the number of men in the industry until 1944. In South Wales, for example, the three Royal Ordnance Factories at Bridgend, Hirwaun and Glasgoed employed 60,000 workers, three quarters of whom were women. Felton herself was passionate about the contribution of women towards the war effort, recalling her memories of the First World War in later life, 'I remember a violent quarrel with a boy cousin who told me that he was going to be a soldier and then went on to tell me, when I declared that I would be a soldier, too, that girls were not good enough to fight and that I would have to be a nurse and look after the wounded.'

Social divisions usually persisted in the factories, rather than the more harmonious relations depicted in the 1943 fictional film *Millions like Us*. For instance, when Norah McCall is promoted to assistant forewoman, she still feels inferior to some of her colleagues. Griselda Green – whose own background is rather different –

struggles to understand why this might be the case:

> *The other trainees, both men and women, were better educated*
> *than [Norah] was, and at first she was often discouraged by*
> *their casual, off-hand manner, by their chatter about the*
> *importance of their peace time jobs and, above all, by the*
> *ease with which they put pen to paper. When they went into*
> *the canteen she would sit rather apart from them, and she*
> *preferred to spend her leisure with the girls she had begun to*
> *know during her first few days in the factory rather than with*
> *strangers who seemed to her to be snobbish, cold and stupid.*
> *[...]*
> *'But why do you make such a fuss about all these silly little*
> *people?' Griselda persisted. Her grey eyes were extraordinarily*
> *clear as she watched the other girl with puzzled, friendly*
> *interest.*
> *[...] 'I suppose,' [Norah] continued after a brief pause, 'it's*
> *the way they talk about their homes and their families and the*
> *holidays they used to have and the sort of cars their boyfriends*
> *used to drive – '*

Felton's own political views on class division were partially shaped by early memories of her own grandfather, who made his fortune making straw hats. In 1954 she recalled, '[He] told me the stories of Dickens' novels and Shakespeare's plays. We were halfway through *Oliver Twist* when he asked if I would like to visit a workhouse and see for myself how Oliver was brought up. I still remember the stark, grey building, the women dressed in grey uniforms... my stately grandfather explain[ed] to me that these people were not to be pitied, because people were only poor because they were wicked and idle... I wondered, and stared and could not altogether believe him.'

Snobbery is prevalent towards people like Parsons, being deemed not 'our kind of person' and 'not quite one of us' by the factory hierarchy. Class-consciousness is apparent at all levels, with Dan Morgan, who comes from the Welsh valleys, remarking to Griselda

Green that she has 'the sort of face that belongs to the ruling class'. Moreover, Morgan derides Blimpton and middle-class garden cities as having no sense of community. However, in spite of all this, a feeling of comradeship and togetherness does manifest, especially in times of danger and tragedy.

There is a lot of criticism (both implied and overt) of the bureaucracy seen in the factory and the Ministry – we see the 'hero' Morgan coming up against this with the Superintendent and others, including some questionable dealings over the awarding of a contract. Indeed, this early passage may elicit a wry smile from the reader:

> THE SUPERINTENDENT OF Blimpton scribbled his signature for the forty-fifth time that afternoon. The rule that no civil servant earning less than £2,000 a year is allowed to endorse a document with his initials only was strictly observed by every employee of the Ministry of Weapon Production.
>
> The Superintendent of Blimpton, who earned (or at any rate was paid) £1,200 a year, had not been a civil servant for very long and had tried during his first few weeks at Blimpton to ignore a rule whose observance seemed to him to involve not merely a waste of time but also a rather serious derogation of his dignity. His attempt had failed. Initialled documents, the Principal Clerk had admonished him, had no validity inside the factory [...] So now the Superintendent wrote his name on every letter, minute and odd scrap of paper that was allowed to leave his office. 'D W Brown,' he wrote for the forty-fifth time, and drew an imposing but meaningless flourish underneath. Then he rang the bell for his secretary.

As Monica Felton had worked in the Ministry of Supply and was a member of the London County Council, she was used to the bureaucracy of government, which forms a recurring motif in the novel. She also wrote a pamphlet for the Ministry of Information at the end of the war entitled *Civilian Supplies in Wartime Britain* in which she states that the ministry was 'staffed by both permanent and temporary civil servants, and while there have been among the former men and women with a wide experience of the problems of public administration, the latter have included experts with previous business experience or academic knowledge of the subjects they have been called upon to handle'. *To All the Living* includes both types of civil servant, and reflects petty rivalries frequently arising between them, especially since they are living on top of each other. After her time at the Ministry, Felton was Clerk to the House of Commons until 1943. She then worked for the Army Bureau of Current Affairs, lecturing to servicemen and women across Britain and the Middle East about world affairs and the problems of post-war Britain. After the war, Felton was heavily involved in town planning until the early 1950s.

To All the Living is almost forgotten as a Second World War novel, perhaps as a result of Monica Felton's unauthorised trip to North Korea in 1951 and her criticism of the American troops and British complicity during the Korean War, which culminated in her becoming a national pariah (Felton felt that it was her duty to take this trip, and said later that this story had to be told 'not only for the sake of the Korean people, but for the sake of all humanity'). The novelist Paul Scott, in a letter to *The Times* after she died in 1970, remarked on her physical and moral courage. He also noted that if she had visited Vietnam in late 1960s rather than North Korea in the early 1950s, the establishment's reaction might have been altogether different. The novel is one of the best depictions of factory life from both a top down and bottom up perspective, and arguably more readable than the fictional reportage of Inez Holden's *Nightshift* (1941) and *There's No Story There* (1944), as well as Diana Murray Hill's *Ladies May Now Leave their Machines* (1944). Both *To All the Living* and Monica Felton deserve to be better known to a new generation of readers and historians.

Alan Jeffreys
2021

For to him that is joined to all the living there is hope.

Ecclesiastes IX, 4

CHARACTERS

The Superintendent	D W Brown
Assistant Superintendent	Dan Morgan
Principal Clerk	Gittins
Chief Medical Officer	Dr MacIver
Deputy Chief Medical Officer	Dr Gower
An Assistant Medical Officer	Ruth Aaron
Progress Officer	Dawson
Chief Chemist	Nicholls
Senior Labour Manager	Captain Knowles
Chief Woman Labour Officer	Miss Creed
Senior Assistant Labour Officer	George Parsons
Junior Labour Officers	Sebastian Bates,
	Freda Elliston,
	Phoebe Braithwaite,
	Pamela Grant
Entertainments Officer	Miss Hopkins
Public Relations Officer	Otway Dolphin
Transportation Officer	Finch
The Warden of the Hostel	Miss Marshall
The Superintendent's Secretary	Miss Gadd
Workers	Griselda Green,
	Kitty Baldwin,
	Norah McCall,
	Rose Widgery,
	Doris Chandler,
	Winnie Poulton,
	Ma Venning,
	Nellie Dimmock,
	Mrs Baker,
	Bob Roberts,
	Whitey,
	Sid Peachey,
	Harry Foster,
	Mrs Foster and shop-managers,
	foremen and others
The Permanent Secretary	Sir John Lentill
The Minister's Personal Representative	A E Gunn
An Official of the Ministry	Colonel Jervis
The Manager of the Dustborough Employment Exchange	Wood
The Editor of the *Dustborough Echo*	Meakin
The Proprietor of the White Lion	Little
His daughter	Mavis
An airman	Tom Walton

ONE

BLIMPTON IS SO far away from anywhere as to be, for all practical purposes, nowhere. As far as the ordinary, everyday things of life are concerned – such as paying a visit, or sending a letter, or ringing up on the telephone, or delivering a thousand tons of cordite – the place might almost as well not exist. Almost, but not quite. It is true that you can telephone to Blimpton, but only when you have induced one of the thirty-thousand-odd officials of the Ministry of Weapon Production to give you the number; and only then if the number is not changed, as it very probably will be, between the time when you put down the receiver at the end of one call and pick it up again to ask for another. You can, too, send a letter; but the whereabouts of Blimpton are so shrouded in secrecy, even within the confines of the G P O Sorting Office, that anything you put in the post is likely to arrive, if it arrives at all, only after going to Brompton and Brimpton and Brighton and Blisworth and fifteen or twenty other places whose names begin with the letter B or look as if they might.

It is also possible to go to Blimpton; but this is the most difficult undertaking of all. It is true that nearly twenty thousand men and women go there every day unless they happen to be attending a football match or going to the cinema or staying at home to do the shopping or to have a baby. These twenty thousand, however, would not willingly do anything to lessen Blimpton's happy obscurity. Some of them come from Scotland, a few from Wales and a good many from Ireland; the others come from almost every county in England, and it is said that those who do succeed in arriving at Blimpton find it extraordinarily difficult to get away. If Blimpton is the last place in the world that you want to go to, and if your innocent ambition is merely to keep on with whatever job you have been doing since you were first thrown out upon the world to earn your living, if you are one of the people who know that they ought to be doing something about the war, and can't think quite what, then, for such is the way things are ordered, if you haven't been sent to Blimpton yet the probabilities are that you will find yourself there before the war is over.

The nearest railway station (apart, of course, from the Halt which has been made just recently, and the great sidings at either extremity of the factory) is at Dustborough, fifteen miles away. Dustborough is the county town of Dustshire, but it is not, as you might perhaps imagine, an open-faced country town with a wide row of Georgian houses, a market and a few good shops selling the leather trappings of horses. It is a town which the Industrial Revolution came to, saw and conquered some hundred and fifty years ago, and subsequently left. Dustborough still lives, or did until a year or two ago, on its legacy of unproductive mines and decaying, but still not quite dead, industries. An enormous gothic Town Hall, a somewhat less enormous but even more gothic pair of railway stations (originally built to serve competing lines which have long since amalgamated) and uncounted streets of narrow black houses remain as a memorial to the great days of Dustshire. Two trains stop every day to put down and pick up passengers at the North Station, and three, or maybe four, at the station which is still known as Grand Trunk Central. Several hundred passengers arrive by these trains in the course of a week and most of them, though this would not be generally admitted, are on their way to Blimpton.

On a grey and frosty afternoon in January 1941 a young woman was the only passenger to get out at Dustborough North Station. She was, if anything, almost too inconspicuous, of medium height, slender build, and dressed in worn clothes of a type which the unsophisticated mistakenly believe to be simple and cheap. She looked up to smile at the soldier who handed out her heavy cardboard suitcase, and her face, aloof yet friendly, was so unusual as to make the anonymity of her dress appear slightly ridiculous, like an over-elaborated disguise. Her dark hair was swept loosely away from a broad forehead with an effect of deliberate, carefully achieved carelessness. Her grey eyes were large and extraordinarily expressive, mocking, humorous and then suddenly, inexplicably, serious. Shadows ran under her cheeks, emphasising the curve of her long mouth, giving her an air that was both intense and ironical, an air so contradictory that it seemed that her features had grown up to a pattern of behaviour which she had now lost. Yet her bearing was confident and, in spite of the pinched look of cold about her nostrils, almost gay.

The soldier closed the door of the compartment and put his head out of the window. 'Could I look you up if I'm round this way?' he asked.

She smiled again, her lashes veiling a faint look of amusement, and nodded.

The engine gathered steam noisily.

'Gosh!' the soldier shouted above the noise, 'I forgot to ask you your name!'

The train was already moving. 'Griselda Green,' she said, speaking in a light, clear voice that he might, or might not, have heard.

'Griselda Green,' she repeated to herself as the last coach disappeared around the bend. Then she looked up and down the platform. The station seemed to be empty. She left her luggage and climbed the stairs to the bridge. There was not so much as a ticket collector visible anywhere.

She looked for, and found, the booking office, which was closed. The silence was absolute. She stepped outside and looked around. Across the road stood a crenelated hotel, a relic of the great days when Chambers of Trade outrivalled each other in splendour and when the passing of Municipal Corporations Acts was celebrated with all the food and drink that civic pride could swallow. The hotel now advertised 'Busby's Entire', and its doors were closed.

Two cars and a lorry stood unattended in the road. There was nothing to connect them with Blimpton, but Griselda Green stood and looked at them for a minute or two.

Presently a man came out of the side door of the hotel, crossed the road and got into the older and shabbier of the two cars. As he closed the door the girl took a step nearer. 'Isn't there ever anyone here?' she asked.

'Isn't there ever anyone here?' the man repeated in a slow and wondering tone. He was an odd-looking person, hatless and shaggy-haired. 'What kind of a person would you be looking for?' he asked.

'For someone to take me to Blimpton.' Her eyes widened as she stared at his clothes, and more especially at the peculiar dirty-white flannel coat which looked like a cross between the uniform of a

London dustman and that of a convict on Dartmoor. 'Have you come to fetch me?' she asked. She had the manner of one accustomed to command and unused to being kept waiting.

'And what would you be going to Blimpton for?' The man looked her up and down, resenting her air of authority, slowly taking in every detail of her appearance from the clumsy, expensive country shoes to the casual line of the knitted cap. A lock of hair fell forward like a dark smudge against the pallor of her face, and suddenly she shivered.

She squared her shoulders and thrust her hands in her pockets. 'To work.'

'Ah,' the man relaxed a little now, 'so you're going to work. Well,' he looked again at her clothes, her bearing, at the great eyes set wide apart beneath fine level brows, 'well,' he repeated, 'it takes all sorts to make a world.'

He started up the engine.

'Wait!' Griselda took a step back. 'I left my luggage in the station.'

'Your luggage!' The man's grin had a touch of malice, but his eyes were friendly. 'You didn't think I'd come here to fetch *you*?' He paused, but she did not attempt to speak. 'Well,' he said, 'I believe you did! Well, well,' he paused again, 'I wouldn't mind taking you, either, though it's against everything that's ever been done. Only, you see I have to go over to the other station to fetch three A F Ws... what's an A F W? Haven't you ever worked in a factory before?'

'No, I haven't.'

'Well, you'll soon learn your way around... a nice girl like you... an A F W is an Assistant-Forewoman. You might get to be one yourself if you lay off those la-di-da airs. Well, I must buzz...'

He was gone.

Griselda Green watched until the car disappeared. Then she crossed the road and went into the hotel. The huge, smoke-coloured hall smelled mustily of stale beer and long-extinguished cigars. Portraits of mayors with heads like cows and heads of deer with faces like defeated town clerks looked down at her from the panelled walls. There was not a living soul to be seen. She crossed the room

4

and opened a door at the far end. It led into a corridor, chocolate-coloured and smelling of cabbage. At the end of it was another door, and this too she opened, to find herself in a kitchen. A stove gave out a pleasant heat. Beside it, with his back to the door, sat a man in a chef's cap, his feet on the fender, snoring.

The girl paused for just so long as it took to see the whole picture. 'Where do I get tea?' she demanded then, in a loud commanding voice.

The man in the chef's cap stopped snoring but did not open his eyes. 'Eh?' he murmured.

She repeated the question.

This time the man sat up with a start and turned to see her, slender and angry, framed by the open door. 'Not here, you don't,' he lifted himself out of the chair. 'And what's more, if you don't get out – pronto – I'll have you reported to the C O for breaking and entering.'

She stood her ground. 'This is an hotel, isn't it?' she demanded. Her voice was cold, but her eyes were bright with rage. 'If you'll tell me where the waiters take their afternoon naps I'll order tea in the usual way.'

'That's enough!' The man, who was extremely fat, had now succeeded in getting on to his feet. 'You won't get any tea, not here you won't. And why? Because, my lady, this hotel has been taken over by the military, as you could see if you'd got half an eye in your head and didn't march round with your nose stuck up in the air. No chance meals. And that means you, whoever you are.' He began to advance towards her. 'So get out. Get out, or I'll – '

She did not wait to hear the end of the sentence.

Outside in the street the emptiness was absolute. She went into the station. There was still no one to be seen. Her luggage stood where she had left it, and now she saw that this was just outside the refreshment room. She tried the door, and found it locked. Through the frosted windows she could see the shape of the long marble-topped counter, and beyond a dim light burning in an inner room. She banged on the door with a gloved fist. Nobody came. She continued to knock, but with decreasing vigour, until after a few minutes her hands made little more noise than if they had been quietly drumming the table at a rather boring dinner party. Then she stopped altogether. As she turned away a porter emerged from a door a few yards away. He was an oldish man with a straggly walrus moustache.

'Anything up?' he asked. His face, if perhaps rather vacant, indicated no positive ill-nature.

'I was just wondering whether I could get a cup of tea.' The girl's voice had lost some of its confidence.

The man shook his head. 'They don't do teas any more, not for a long time now. You a stranger?'

She nodded.

'Going to Blimpton?'

A hint of a smile showed about her mouth. 'Trying to,' she replied.

'Thought so.' The porter took a half-smoked cigarette from his waistcoat pocket and lit it. 'That's where they all go now. And leave. Talk about leave! They go nearly as fast as they come, and that's saying something... there's another young person for Blimpton in the Ladies' Waiting Room now. Been waiting since this morning, she has. I put a fire in there for her not an hour ago... might go and see how it's burning up,' he finished absently.

They walked the whole length of the vast platform in silence. As the porter opened the waiting room door a vast cloud of smoke rushed out to meet him. Through the fog a girl could be dimly seen, half-sitting, half-lying on a long leather-covered bench. 'I wondered when you were coming to look at that fire,' she said indifferently, speaking with a strong north-country accent.

'Ah!' the porter breathed up the smoke with relish, and then sneezed loudly, 'we'll soon have a fire for you. You'll see. It takes a bit of time to warm up, but by tonight we'll have a fire for you that really is a fire. Ah!' he sneezed again, getting down on his knees and putting his head into the thickest of the fog. 'It didn't ought to be like this, but you wait.'

'I hope we shan't have to wait much longer,' Griselda Green observed, addressing the porter but glancing at the other girl whose features it was still impossible to distinguish.

'Wait?' The porter shovelled sticks under the coals. 'You don't know anything about waiting, not until you've been to Blimpton, you don't. Blimpton,' he rolled the word on his tongue, savouring every consonant, 'Blimpton's just another word for waiting... I've seen girls wait here all night, and not so long ago at that, either...'

The smoke was already dying down, and the two girls were now able to see each other. Griselda Green was standing very erect, her hands in her pockets, her head thrown back. Her face showed amusement, anger and a controlled impatience. 'I think I'll go and telephone,' she said at last.

The porter looked up for a moment and remarked: 'The phone's out of order.'

'Oh!'

The second girl got up and crossed the room. She was tall, untidily built, with blonde hair darkening at the roots and a face so bedecked with cosmetics that it was impossible at first glance to see the kind of features she naturally possessed. She moved stiffly, with an air of exhaustion that might well have been posed for the photograph of a woman who had not yet learned to use the most widely advertised brand of some ordinary household necessity. 'Have you got a cigarette?' she asked. Her eyes were red and swollen, though whether from too much smoke or too much weeping it was impossible to judge.

'Of course.' Griselda took a packet from her handbag.

The porter had put some paraffin on the fire, and a sudden glow illuminated the room. 'I shouldn't be too free with them,' he suggested, 'smokes aren't that easy to get around here.'

'I guessed that,' Griselda held out the packet towards him, 'I've got a few more in my luggage. Have one of these.'

He took one in his blackened hand. 'If you'd like to come along the road,' he volunteered, 'my missus might make you a cup of tea...'

'I don't want any tea,' the blonde girl said. She spoke with a sort of suppressed energy, pulling her thin black coat more tightly around her. 'I've got work to do,' she stared at Griselda. 'Are you for Blimpton too?'

'Mm... my name's Green.'

'Miss?'

After a barely perceptible pause the other nodded. 'First name: Griselda,' she said.

'Funny name, that.' The blonde girl took a long puff at her cigarette. 'My name's Baldwin. Mrs Stanley Baldwin… at least, that's what they used to call me. Better forget it.'

'Why?'

The blonde girl sat down heavily. Her haggard face grew a shade paler beneath the heavy make-up. 'Because Stanley's dead, and now I'm all by myself again, funny old Kitty, the way I always was…' Her voice broke and she began to cry, at first softly, and then with a burst of rough, noisy sobs.

Griselda stamped out her cigarette, sat down and put a hand on the sleeve of the other girl's coat. 'Killed?' she asked. There was no curiosity in her tone, but only an obscure sympathy.

'Mm,' Kitty Baldwin wiped her eyes between sobs, 'all shot to pieces… shot to pieces in France last June, and they wouldn't let him die till Christmas… and all the time he knew he was dying. But that wasn't the worst of it… Oh my God!' She stiffened, sat up, her swollen, indeterminate features tense with some indescribable memory. A shudder went through her, and she relaxed, leaning the weight of her shoulder against the other girl's out-stretched arm. 'He wasn't himself,' she went on slowly. 'They killed him in France, but he couldn't die. He didn't even have a proper face any more – ' she broke off.

'Had you been married long?'

'Two years… I used to go to the hospital every week. Sometimes oftener. He didn't speak much. I think he went mad sometimes…'

'And now you think you'll go mad?'

'No, I'm not the sort.' For a moment Kitty Baldwin turned and looked into Griselda Green's face. 'That's a funny thing to say,' she remarked, 'but you're quite right. Sometimes I just want to scream my head off.' Her tears fell quietly now. 'But screaming won't help.'

'It might.'

'That only shows you don't understand.'

Griselda's face was expressionless. 'I think I do.'

'How can you if you're not even married: And besides – '

'Well?'

'You don't even know me – '

'If I did you wouldn't be able to talk to me like this.'

'That's right.' She seemed to settle into a sort of numbed despair. The porter had disappeared and for some time they sat in silence. Presently Griselda Green disengaged her arm, and the other girl sat up. 'His real name was George,' she said. 'He used to get mad when people called him Stanley.'

'Why?' Griselda was staring into the fire and did not look up.

'I dunno... well, I suppose I do really. He was that keen on politics... anything else he'd make a joke of, but not politics...'

'Did he admire Mr Baldwin very much?'

'Admire!' The blonde girl broke into hysterical laughter. 'If George could've heard you say that! He always said if it hadn't been for Mr Baldwin and Lord Outrage and that crowd we'd never have got into this war... anyway, George is dead and Mr Baldwin's still kicking around – or isn't he?'

At this moment the porter returned.

'Say, mister,' the blonde girl asked jauntily, pulling out a lipstick, 'is Mr Baldwin still alive?'

'Well!' The porter propped the door open with one hand. 'Of all the – ' he gaped for a word that seemed to be escaping him. 'Now, look here, miss,' he began again, 'you'd better stop that. There's a lady from the factory down at the booking-office now. I'd come along quietly if I was you – '

The blonde girl jumped up and grinned at Griselda, a hint of mischief lurking in her tear-distorted face. 'Come along quietly!' she echoed. 'What does that remind you of?'

TWO

THE SUPERINTENDENT OF Blimpton scribbled his signature for the forty-fifth time that afternoon. The rule that no civil servant earning less than £2,000 a year is allowed to endorse a document with his initials only was strictly observed by every employee of the Ministry of Weapon Production.

The Superintendent of Blimpton, who earned (or at any rate was paid) £1,200 a year, had not been a civil servant for very long and had tried during his first few weeks at Blimpton to ignore a rule whose observance seemed to him to involve not merely a waste of time but also a rather serious derogation of his dignity. His attempt had failed. Initialled documents, the Principal Clerk had admonished him, had no validity inside the factory; and the admonition had been followed by practical steps to ensure that initialled instructions were invariably ignored. So now the Superintendent wrote his name on every letter, minute and odd scrap of paper that was allowed to leave his office. 'D W Brown,' he wrote for the forty-fifth time, and drew an imposing but meaningless flourish underneath. Then he rang the bell for his secretary.

The secretary, who was decorating her face in a distant cloakroom, did not hear the bell. Brown pushed back his chair and took a turn or two across the room, pausing as he passed the bookshelf to examine his reflection in the glass door. He was below the middle height and protruded in too many places, so that his dignified gait was apt, when he forgot himself, to degenerate into a waddle. (It was perhaps for this reason that he was sometimes referred to as 'Donald' or even 'Ducky' Brown, and these nicknames, though not altogether apt, at least served to distinguish him from Brown, the managing director of the building contracting firm which had erected Blimpton, from Brown the senior night-watchman, Brown the canteen manager and Brown the local Member of Parliament.) But now, peering into the glass he seemed pleased with what he saw: his hair was still thick and dark above the heavy, important-looking face. The face itself, rather red and with features too small for the vast expanse of flesh in which they were embedded, was given character by a remarkable pair of jutting eyebrows. When he spoke he used his eyebrows as other people use their hands, to add to or subtract from the meaning of the words he used. Raising, lowering, beetling, the ordinary motions connected with these features, were only the small beginnings of the vast range of expressions which Brown, his face otherwise immobile, could command. Sometimes, indeed, it would seem to the fascinated onlooker that not merely each eyebrow, but every hair, was capable of independent and significant movement. This afternoon the total effect was one of boredom faintly tinged with anxiety. He smoothed one or two stray hairs back into position, returned to his desk and rang again.

By this time the secretary had slipped on her fur coat and was on her way to the Staff Canteen to have tea with the Deputy Assistant Public Relations Officer, or, if he should not turn up, with the Junior Assistant Accountant for Small Tools. Brown rang once more and then, when there seemed to be no hope of attracting any attention, pressed the buzzer for the Principal Clerk.

The Principal Clerk's firm but suitably subordinate knock was rapped on the door almost before the buzzer had stopped, and no sooner had he knocked than he had entered, crossed the carpet, and placed himself in the exact spot at which he always liked to stand, a foot or so away from the Superintendent's desk, yet near enough to be able to read anything that was left lying around and marked 'Secret'. (This was not because he had any special curiosity about secret documents; most of the correspondence that came to Blimpton was marked 'Secret' and it was an important part of his duty to know, and even to understand the contents; but these documents had a way of disappearing and it was useful to be able to remember where they had last been seen, if only because it then became relatively easy to trace them to one or other of the vast steel cupboards which lined the corridors of the Administration Block.) His shoulders were bent from many years of peering at the litter on other people's desks and his grey suit hung loose and shabby. His hair, also grey, had grown thin on top and its recession gave height to a face which might once have been round and hopeful. Now, furrowed and humorous, it wore a perpetual faint smile which served admirably to conceal whatever he might be thinking.

The Superintendent pretended to be searching for something in his pocket diary, and a slight pause was allowed to elapse before he looked up. This was one of the important ways in which he exercised his sense of authority.

Gittins took off his spectacles and cast an expert eye over the Superintendent's desk. Apart from the forty-five documents which had just been signed, there seemed to be nothing fresh.

'Where's Miss Gadd?' Brown asked when the silence had lasted about a minute. 'Why isn't she ever here when I want her? Sit down.'

Gittins sat down gingerly on the edge of the green leather armchair, and rubbed a hand over the bald patch at the back of his head. He was, like the Superintendent, a man who never felt at his best when seated. Nevertheless, when told to sit, he sat.

The Superintendent did not seem to expect an answer. 'Where's Colonel Jervis?' he asked next.

Gittins appeared to consider. His manner was that of a man who had always known what he wanted and, pitching his ambitions moderately and with care, had usually been satisfied, though only just. The war was the first gratuitous piece of good fortune which had ever come his way, and at times, thinking back over the fifty years of his working life, he acknowledged a sort of gratitude to Hitler for having saved him from death-dealing retirement in 1939. But his sixty-four years sat on him lightly, and his brown eyes were alert, missing nothing.

'Jervis?' he answered slowly. 'I'm not sure. He was over at South-by-North about an hour ago.'

'South-by-North? The place is empty!'

'I think that's what's worrying him,' Gittins began, filling his pipe with an air of extreme concentration.

'Well, that's the Ministry's affair,' the Superintendent interrupted in a more confident tone, his eyebrows settling back into position. 'If the Ministry choose to keep half my factory empty it's no concern of mine... Thank God for that,' he added after a slight pause.

'Did Colonel Jervis say anything about putting some grenade filling down there?' Gittins asked.

'Grenade filling! I never heard such nonsense! Grenade filling, indeed! They'll be asking us to fill petrol bottles next... Who told you that?' he demanded sharply, his face taking on a deeper shade of red.

'I'm not sure,' Gittins lied with a beautiful air of mild hesitation. 'One hears so many things... Would you like me to find out where Jervis is now?'

'Yes, I wish you would. I'd better go and see what the old boy's up to... ' The Superintendent pushed back his chair, then changed his mind. 'No, I'll see him later. He's coming to dine with me at Mowbray Lodge. Come along, Gittins, get your hat.' He looked wildly around the room. 'These letters should have gone out hours ago.'

'I'll speak to Miss Gadd,' Gittins reassured him. 'I've got one or two things to do before I leave, anyway.'

Brown slipped on his overcoat and felt in his pocket for his torch. At the door he stopped. 'By the way,' he commanded rather than invited, 'you might look in for coffee, say about eight. And bring the missis – we don't want to talk shop all night... Hand grenades! and they call this a filling factory.'

Gittins' smile widened. He was proud of the factory. He had spent all his life at the Great Arsenal and had been sent to Blimpton right at the beginning, before the builders' men had begun to pull down the gates and tear up the hedges around the fields. He had seen the harvesting of the last crop of oats on Blue Bottle Farm, where East-by-South now stood; and when Members of Parliament and other visiting dignitaries asked questions, as they still did, which implied that the best of the wheat had been ploughed into the earth in a spring-time panic to get the factory up, the Principal Clerk was ready with the answer. He had seen the first road laid, and the first railway siding. He had watched the weekly change of plans, and the fortnightly change of architects. He knew the strength and weakness of every building contractor and of every contractor's foreman. He knew exactly how many millions the place had cost, and exactly why nobody else was ever able to find out. He had hidden in his office when the first batch of Operatives arrived, and had stood discreetly in the background when the first Superintendent greeted the first

Minister of Weapon Production on the perilously new platform at Blimpton Halt. He rarely asked questions, and was always ready to reply to those asked by others. It was generally believed that he knew everything that was to be known about Blimpton. It was his factory. It had its teething troubles, and sometimes it seemed as if it would never get over them. People from the Ministry were constantly rushing down, tearing up this, reconstructing that, re-organising something else, changing their minds and changing their plans, rushing back to London and then hastily returning to Blimpton because they had had a better idea while they were in the train.

Now he stood there, an elderly civil servant trying not to laugh. 'They'll be asking us to fill bully-beef tins next,' he observed.

The Superintendent frowned the famous, thoughtful frown which everybody in the factory knew. 'I shouldn't be surprised,' he agreed. 'There's nothing old Outrage isn't capable of… why on earth the PM should make him Minister… really, I sometimes wonder… of course I lost touch with Churchill a good many years ago… but still… Outrage…' Muttering to himself, eyebrows writhing, he wandered off.

As soon as the door had closed, Gittins switched off his smile and picked up the telephone. 'Get me the Staff Canteen,' he asked, then, as the call came through, 'will you ask Miss Gadd to come over to the Superintendent's Office immediately? Immediately.' He began to look through the documents on the Superintendent's desk, his face thoughtful.

Meanwhile, the Superintendent was groping his way along in the dark. His torch had, as usual, mysteriously switched itself on while it was lying in his overcoat pocket and now the battery was exhausted. He wished he hadn't forgotten to order a car to take him home. He wondered whether to go back and wait for one, and then decided not to. He was in no hurry to have dinner with Colonel Jervis at Mowbray Lodge. He would probably be late, anyway.

He was.

Mowbray Lodge was built about a hundred years ago by a Dustborough manufacturer who had made enough money to set up as a country gentleman. Its exterior has (allowing for the

14

small scale on which it is built) much of the neo-gothic splendour associated with St. Pancras Station and Dustborough Town Hall, and its interior reveals more than average contempt for the comfort of those compelled to inhabit it. The hall is baronial, but too draughty to be put to any practical use, and the rooms intended for living, sleeping and eating are dark and badly arranged. When the government purchased the estate on which it was situated (together with portions of other and larger properties in the vicinity) for the erection of Blimpton, its owners succeeded in persuading the Ministry that the house would be needed too. But for some time nobody could think of any use to which it could be put. The grounds adjoined the boundary fence that skirted the factory site, but the nearest of the factory gates was two miles away, and the Main Gate still further. Mowbray Lodge, its face to a by-road that no one used, its back to a magazine not yet required, was, for a time, forgotten. Then someone – though who it was no one could ever remember – suggested that it should be used as a place of residence for the senior staff. Gittins, perpetually haunted by fear of criticism by the Comptroller and Auditor General, received the suggestion with relief and, after much difficulty and months of negotiation, persuaded the Ministry that the house ought to be occupied. A housekeeper was appointed, a scale of charges drawn up, furniture was moved and the more valuable pieces transported to South Kensington for safety. Competition for the fifteen or so bedrooms was keen, and Gittins derived, it was thought, an excessive pleasure in selecting the inhabitants and in filling such vacancies as occasionally arose. But however they were chosen, and however much they grumbled at the discomforts of the place, those who lived at Mowbray Lodge were, and knew themselves to be, members of a privileged class.

This evening when the Superintendent arrived the residents had already gone in to dinner, and Colonel Jervis was sitting alone in the drawing room, turning over the pages of the Journal of the Royal Statistical Society. His neat, elderly face wore an expression of extreme boredom, and his eyes, when he looked up, were blank with disappointment. He had been looking forward to dining with the inhabitants of Mowbray Lodge, and could not understand why the Superintendent should have asked him to dinner nor why, having done so, he should not have entertained him in his own house where, Jervis had been told, there were two well-trained servants who took pride in being able to cook. To dine at Mowbray was to get the worst of both worlds: Mowbray's food and the Superintendent's company.

Brown had, in fact, invited Jervis to dinner because he had nothing better to do that evening, and had asked him to Mowbray Lodge because it was cheaper than entertaining him at home; also, since Jervis was staying at Mowbray, the Superintendent could leave when he liked instead of having to go through an elaborate ceremony of whiskies-and-sodas and increasingly long-drawn yawns.

The dining room was crowded, but a table near the fire had been reserved for the Superintendent and his guest. The former glanced around, grunted one or two good evenings, and then began to tell his guest a story. This left Jervis free to study his neighbours, while paying the minimum of attention that courtesy demanded. There was nothing stimulating about the company assembled around the tables. Under the window three or four engineers and research chemists made laboured conversation with two Polish officers, a Czech and a Yugoslav. Captain Knowles, the Senior Labour Manager and Miss Creed, the Chief Woman Labour Officer, sat together discussing something in whispers, their noses, as they leaned forward, casting grotesque shadows on the white cloth. Dawson, the Progress Officer, was dining with three people whom Jervis was unable to recognise, but it was obvious that their conversation had been brought to an abrupt end by the arrival of the Superintendent. Dr Gower, the Deputy Chief Medical Officer, had hidden his scowling good looks behind the pages of a learned periodical and was forgetting to eat. Ruth Aaron, his assistant and the only young woman in the room, was sharing a table with grey-haired Miss Hopkins, who organised the factory's entertainments, and Otway Dolphin, the Public Relations Officer. They were an odd trio Miss Hopkins, fluffy and pink-cheeked, Dolphin, neat, worldly yet vaguely bohemian, a young-old man with a flowing tie, and Ruth Aaron: Jervis, who still prided himself on having an eye for a pretty woman, was suddenly struck with the notion that little Dr Aaron was simply thrown away in this dismal corner of nowhere. He squared his shoulders, pulled himself in at the waist, and remembered that what he had been looking forward to all day was a nice long chat with Miss Hopkins about dogs.

The Superintendent seemed to have finished his story. The soup was taken away and a steak-and-kidney pudding placed in front of them. Brown eyed it doubtfully. 'I ought to have asked you to come along to me,' he said as he helped himself to boiled potatoes, 'but you know how difficult servants are nowadays, even refugees... but next time you come I'll get Madame Dubois to make you a real dinner – lobster mornay, a chateaubriand and perhaps one of her soufflés... ' He bent to pick a yellow weed from the cabbage, his brows arched with disgust. 'The fact is,' he continued, 'she's very temperamental... but at least she can cook.'

Colonel Jervis was still watching the party on his left. Miss Hopkins was chatting with great animation, and her remarks were punctuated with little bursts of laughter from her companions. 'Funny,' he said, 'I didn't know that girl could laugh.'

The Superintendent turned for an instant. 'Queer girl, Dr Aaron,' he observed, 'very queer indeed sometimes.' His eyes were narrowed and he lowered his voice as he went on. 'Between ourselves, I don't think she's settling down too well... but the Ministry couldn't get anyone else, so of course we had to take her, though I'm not too keen on having foreigners about the place myself.'

'I thought she was English?'

Brown assumed his John Bull expression, red-faced, dogged. 'English! With a name like that! My dear fellow!' He swallowed the last mouthful of steak-and-kidney pudding and looked round impatiently for the waitress. 'Of course,' he continued, 'she's British born of British parents, if that's what you mean; otherwise they wouldn't have sent her to us. But she's no more English than my cook, except that she happens to speak the language – '

'And happened to be born here?'

'Yes, I said that. As a matter of fact I believe her father is quite well known in Manchester or Liverpool or one of those places... but I must say I've no use for the Jews myself, or any other kind of

foreigner for that matter. Of course you have to put up with them
if you want to get food worth eating.' He prodded the apple pie
tentatively with his fork. 'Foreigners, I mean,' he added, and poured
himself another helping of artificial cream.

Colonel Jervis made a vague motion of assent. Miss Hopkins and
Dr Aaron were already getting up from the table, and it occurred
to him that if he and Brown did not hurry they would find, when
they went into the drawing room, that everyone worth talking
about would have disappeared. It was a long time since he had met
anyone with such an intimate knowledge of the habits of long-haired
dachshunds as Miss Hopkins appeared to possess, and he thought he
had never met anyone with such a delicate appreciation of their finer
qualities; so he finished his apple pie with the greatest possible speed
and refused a second helping.

The Superintendent, however, insisted on eating cheese, and,
when it was put before him and the other occupants had left the
dining room, seemed inclined to linger. 'I hear you were looking over
South-by-North,' he observed, thrusting out his chin to conceal his
anxiety. 'I hope the Ministry isn't thinking of putting a job in there
already. The place is nothing like finished. I mean – '

It was difficult to tell whether Jervis was listening. As a matter
of fact, he was. His habitual air of soldierly blankness would
certainly have been absent if he had been thinking about long-haired
dachshunds. He suspected that Brown was leading up to something;
he could not guess what, but thought it his duty to find out. So
he sat still, trying to trace some pattern in the intricacies of the
Superintendent's conversation.

'Of course it's hard for you people to see just what we're up
against,' the latter was saying, 'I don't mean you personally – '

'I'm just a poor soldier,' Jervis interrupted mildly.

' – and I can imagine what you have to put up with from the
civil servants. But still…' Brown's eyebrows were doing double duty
in the effort to express what he wanted to say without committing
himself in words. 'Down here, you know, it gets pretty intolerable
from time to time. It's the pace that kills, as they say. Poor old
Jenkins, my predecessor, you know, has crocked up completely.' His

hand went to his head, stroking the patch from which he had pulled three grey hairs, barely an hour ago. 'It's a wonder to me how any of us manage to keep going, with all this outside interference… I wish someone would tell the powers that be – '

He broke off as the waitress approached, her face distraught. 'The telephone,' she said breathlessly, 'you're wanted, sir.'

He waved her away with an impatient gesture. 'Tell them to ring later. Can't you see I'm busy?'

She was still panting a little. 'It's London, sir,' she persisted. 'He said it was Lord Outrage's personal representative.'

Jervis looked up and smiled. 'Aren't we all?'

But Brown was already halfway to the door, his short legs carrying him as fast as they could go.

After two or three minutes Jervis got up slowly, straightened his tunic, made his way into the drawing room.

The evening was taking its usual course. Most of the men had finished their coffee and disappeared. Dawson had remained because he knew that he was expected to serve as a second line of defence (second to Gittins and Mrs Gittins) when the Superintendent had guests for dinner. He knew, too, that he was only needed when Morgan, the Assistant Superintendent, was too busy or too indifferent to be bothered. Dawson, who was a quiet, mild man, knew that he had little talent for conversation, and guessed, rightly, that many people in the factory thought he had little talent for anything else either. Before the war he had managed a toy factory, and in the last few months he had realised that his experience of filling calico dolls with sawdust did not provide an altogether adequate training for life in an organisation concerned with filling steel with explosives. He was unhappy at Blimpton, and felt that he had lost his independence. To make matters worse, he had not yet succeeded in inducing the Principal Clerk to give him one of the new houses that were being completed for the use of married members of the staff, and the prospect of bringing his children to Dustshire seemed to grow daily more remote.

It was on this subject that he was now trying to sustain a conversation with Ruth Aaron. The effort seemed to exhaust them both, and as soon as Colonel Jervis opened the door Ruth jumped up to offer him coffee. Dawson shrank into a corner, his thin face anxious at the prospect of another two or three hours of his colleagues' company. Meanwhile, Captain Knowles and Miss Creed, who had been sitting on the sofa nearest the fire, finished their conversation and began to take an interest in their surroundings. Gittins and Mrs Gittins arrived, more coffee was sent for, and everyone began to talk at once.

'It's quite a party,' Colonel Jervis observed to Ruth Aaron, and began to brighten up a little, his soldierly appearance taking on some faint traces of individuality. Ruth looked, he thought, exactly like an Old Testament heroine: Ruth, Naomi, Esther? Looking into the fathomless depths of her black eyes he could not be sure which. Later, he realised with impersonal regret, her figure would thicken and she would probably grow stout.

'Ah,' she put down the coffee pot, 'you only see us at our best. You should come more often if you want to see what it's really like.'

'At least you're pretty comfortable here.'

'Comfortable!' She looked at him with scorn, her dark eyes smouldering. 'Comfortable...' she repeated. 'We have hot baths, if that's what you mean. But comfortable!'

He fidgeted uneasily, and spilled a little coffee into his saucer.

Mrs Gittins came to the rescue. She believed, almost passionately, in her ability to say the right thing, to make a party 'go'. She could chatter indefinitely about nothing in particular until her audience would start talking in self-defence. Presently Miss Hopkins came in with her knitting, and Colonel Jervis sat back happily knowing that he would soon be able to start a really serious conversation about dogs.

But before the perfect moment arrived the Superintendent entered. He looked hot and flustered, and for a moment or two he stood quite still. He seemed in fact as if he were trying to regain not so much his self-command as his power of speech. His face was very red, and the contortions of his eyebrows were so violent as to be, for once, meaningless to his audience. They watched him, puzzled, trying once more to find the main clue to his character. He was now about fifty-five years old. He often said that he preferred to work with men who were a good deal younger than himself, yet he frequently, and often violently, taunted the younger members of his staff with their lack of experience. He was, for so talkative a man, remarkably uncommunicative about the experiences he had himself enjoyed. Occasionally, in the Mowbray lounge, or at a party, or even in an expansive moment over a cup of tea in the office, he would give a glimpse of himself planting rubber in Malaya, selling oil in China or buying it in Persia, running a cotton factory in New Zealand or a chocolate factory in Buenos Ayres. From these anecdotes it sometimes appeared that he had been engaged in all these activities simultaneously, and a good deal of time was expended in Mowbray Lodge and elsewhere in trying to piece together the fragments of a life thus exiguously exposed to the gaze of subordinates or casual visitors. The result of these attempts at historical reconstruction was invariably unsatisfactory. It was assumed that someone in the Ministry probably knew something about the experiences which had qualified the Superintendent to order the working lives of twenty thousand men and women and to plan the production of unspecified but doubtless enormous quantities of munitions of war; but whatever was known of Brown in London, at Blimpton he remained a mystery. Gradually a theory grew up that he had never in fact done any of the things to which he laid claim; a rash and perhaps unwelcome visitor once hazarded the guess that he had spent the last thirty years in the seclusion of an obscure laboratory at Cambridge; and this conjecture was added to the legend.

In spite of these stories there was nothing mysterious about either the Superintendent's manner or appearance. Now, after a few moments he collected himself sufficiently to be able to speak.

'Jervis,' he said, stopped, and lit a cigar to steady himself, 'Jervis, did you ever hear of anyone in the Ministry called Gunn?'

'Oh yes,' Jervis began to smile, 'Oerlikon Alf. Nearly everyone knows Oerlikon Alf. Knows of him, I should say.'

'What a lunatic name,' Ruth Aaron observed coldly.

'It suits him though,' Jervis explained mildly, 'you know – but of course you know – that the Oerlikon fires 450 cannon shells a minute. Well, that number may not be quite right, but you get the idea. Only Alf's bursts are always misfiring. He hasn't got a very good aim.'

'But who *is* he?' the Superintendent interrupted. 'He's been on the telephone to me for the last half-hour and now he says he's on his way down. I told him,' he lied with an air of great frankness, 'that I'd never heard of him, that as far as I was able to judge he might be a special emissary of Dr Goebbels, and that I wouldn't have him inside my factory until I got a proper authorisation from the Ministry.'

'Oh, he's all right,' said Jervis, 'he's just one of the boys.'

'Which boys?' The impatient note in Brown's voice was creeping up towards hysteria.

'The thugs. The go-getters, the Outrage circus, whatever you like to call it. I haven't much use for them myself, but then I'm a little old-fashioned in my habits. I don't care for professional ideas-merchants. They run around and stir up a tremendous lot of dust. And dirt. But things settle down again, you know.'

'He's on his way here now,' the Superintendent repeated.

'That's a pity... you'd better get some rest before he comes. From what I've seen of Alf you won't get much chance of sleeping for the next twenty-four hours.'

Miss Hopkins put down her knitting. 'Is this a joke?' she asked.

'Why, no,' Jervis answered at once. He wanted to get this conversation finished. He could never understand why people in the factories were so invariably excited at each incursion into their privacy, nor why they could not settle down and converse like civilised beings. He wished the Superintendent would go away.

Brown, however, had other ideas. Gittins, Dawson and the reluctant Jervis were led into an adjoining room where plans could be discussed in greater privacy.

'Now,' said the Superintendent, when they were seated round a table, 'this man Gunn, or whatever he calls himself, says he'll arrive soon after midnight. I'll have to go up to my house in a few minutes to make arrangements to put him up.'

'He won't want putting up,' Jervis said, 'not in that sense...'

'But what is he coming for?' Gittins asked.

The Superintendent's eyebrows wavered momentarily. 'Some crazy Dutchman has invented a new fuze.'

'So?'

'So we have to fill it, of course.'

Gittins turned to Jervis. 'Does this man carry the authority of the Minister?' he asked.

'I think so,' Jervis replied, 'I'm afraid there's not much doubt about that.'

'As long as there's any doubt – ' Gittins, speaking with quiet confidence, did not finish the sentence.

'Where are they making this fuze?' Dawson asked.

The Superintendent was turning over the pages of a small note book. 'I gathered that... that it isn't in production yet.'

'You mean they're giving us experimental stuff to fill?'

'Uh-uh. They've been knocking them up in a garage in one of those suburban places. Tooting, I think he said. It's ridiculous to ask us to mess about with half a dozen fuzes...'

'It might be interesting,' Jervis remarked kindly. He had no further opinion to express.

'But, I ask you, what do we want to start making new fuzes for?'

'What type is it?' Dawson asked.

'I've no idea... Gittins, could you find out where Morgan is, and get him to come here... No, don't go out of the room, I may need you. Dawson, you get him, will you? Tell him it's urgent. Jervis, you'll have to help us out on this...'

THREE

A QUEUE WAITED at the bus stop. It was raining. The January morning was mild and still. The bus came. The driver put his head out of the window. 'In you come,' he commanded flatly, 'in you come.' The girls seemed, in fact, rather like sheep. Inside the bus the rain began to dry off their coats in imperceptible clouds of steam. They sat in silence, peering now and then through the mist-shrouded windows. Once or twice the driver turned round to offer some jocular remark. Nobody responded and soon he, too, became silent. The journey seemed interminable. Yet they came within sight of the factory after a little more than half an hour. Then they skirted it for another ten minutes. The girls began to be curious. The place seemed to be surrounded by many miles of brick wall and barbed wire fencing. From the bus it was impossible to get more than an occasional mysterious glimpse of the scene inside.

'It doesn't look like anything,' one girl remarked at last.

It did not look like anything that any of them had ever seen.

Nobody could describe it. 'It's like reservoirs,' somebody said. It was not so much camouflaged as built for concealment, half in the earth and with earth heaped up on top of it. Grass grew everywhere, rank, wintry, yellow. Here and there a building stuck up out of the sad landscape; but for the most part Blimpton looked like a geometrical accident that had fallen at random into the wintry countryside and had somehow got stuck. In the misty rain it looked insubstantial, and at the same time frightening.

The girl who had already spoken now addressed the driver. 'Is it really so awful here?' she asked.

The driver did not appear to hear her.

'I say!' she called, 'I say! Driver!'

'Well,' he turned his head a little to one side.

'I said: is it really so awful here?'

'Depends on what you mean,' the driver replied laconically, 'I can't say as most people exactly likes it. But it's a job.'

'Is there any work to do?' somebody asked in a frozen voice.

'Well,' the driver considered the point, 'it depends on what you mean by work. Who's been telling you there isn't any work?'

'Well, nobody,' the frozen voiced girl answered with some hesitation, 'at least, my landlady did say – ' She stopped suddenly.

'Say what?'

'Go on, better say it.'

The girl glanced round the bus. She was small and rather frightened looking. She took a deep breath, swallowed, and then spoke very quickly. 'My landlady did say there are hundreds and thousands of girls here get browned off with not having enough to do. She said she didn't know why they were bringing us here from all over nowhere.'

'Huh,' said the driver, 'don't you take on when landladies say things like that to you. It's only that they don't want strangers coming into the place, eating up the rations. You girls ought to know how it is.'

'Then there really is plenty of work here?' the girl persisted.

'You'll soon see,' the driver told her, 'we're just about there.'

On their left the wall surrounding the factory retreated a little, and between it and the curve in the road was a vast car park, filled with shabby motor-coaches, red, yellow, purple, green, decorated with worn and mud-stained advertisements of trips to Brighton, Scarborough, Southend-on-Sea and Blackpool. It was impossible to believe that so many motor-coaches could ever have been collected together in one place, and the girls stared at them dumbly, filled with vague memories of the half-forgotten days before the war. Beyond the car park the brick wall gave way to a high wire fencing, broken at intervals by police boxes and closely guarded gates, and within the gates could be seen a tangle of huts surrounded by strips of clay that in summer might possibly be flowerbeds.

The bus drew up on the other side of the road, in front of another group of huts. The driver got out. He turned to look at the girls. 'You wait here,' he said, and went off.

Now that they were alone the girls began to talk. There were about thirty of them.

'I wonder why I came here?' said one.

'Looks horrible!' another remarked, and shivered a little.

'Looks!' a third repeated contemptuously, 'who cares about looks, anyway?' It was evident from her appearance that she did not. She was a big handsome girl whose manner gave a rather theatrical touch of shabbiness to her clothes. 'Who cares what the factory looks like?' she asked again, challenging the whole busload of girls. 'Who cares what the job is, either, as far as that goes?' No one answered her, but everyone sat forward, listening. 'Some of us have to be thankful we can get a job at all, indeed we do. And here we are with a job on munitions, where we'll get the big money – '

'There's no big money here,' another girl interrupted.

'Who told you that?' the dark girl challenged.

The interrupter was silent.

'I'll tell you who told you that,' the other continued. 'Your landlady. Didn't she?'

The other girl did not respond.

'Didn't she?'

'All right. Yes.'

'And you heard just now what the driver said about the landladies in Dustborough. They're just trying to frighten us off. Not that I blame them. If I lived in that miserable town I wouldn't want munition workers billeted on me, either.'

'But my landlady was really sweet to me,' the other persisted. 'I'm sure she didn't mean any harm. Really she didn't. But she said you couldn't make any big money here. She said it's hard enough for us girls to keep ourselves, without being able to send any money home. That's what she said.' Suddenly she seemed to recognise that she had an audience, and stopped abruptly, subsiding into her seat with a sort of shrinking motion. She was small and young, scarcely more than twenty, and should have been pretty. Now her pale face looked shrunken and her eyes were red.

Kitty Baldwin, who had been leaning against a window watching the traffic come and go, sat up sharply. 'I think it's disgusting to talk about money at a time like this!' she exclaimed in a loud, angry voice.

Somebody giggled.

'That's all very well,' somebody else said, 'but we have to live.'

'So do the soldiers,' Kitty continued, 'and what do they get? Hardly enough to buy stamps for their letters home… You ought to be ashamed of talking about getting big money when you think of what those boys have to put up with.'

The dark girl who had started the conversation broke in sharply. 'Somebody has to think about money,' she said, 'and it isn't just a question of what we need for ourselves, or whether we have to send money home. It's a lot more than that. We have to safeguard the standards of the working classes.'

'Huh,' Kitty Baldwin looked at her contemptuously, 'that's a fine way to talk. Safeguard the standards of the working classes my eye! Did anyone ever mention to you that there's a war on?' She paused a moment, as if waiting for the other girl to flare up. 'What's your name?' she demanded abruptly.

'Norah McCall, if you want to know.'

'Irish?'

'What business is that of yours?'

'None, if you don't start talking silly.'

'I'm not talking silly. All I said,' Norah McCall spoke as one whose patience was nearing exhaustion, 'all I said is that we have to safeguard the standards of the working classes, war or no war.'

'And you know as well as I do,' Kitty Baldwin persisted, 'that that sort of talk is just a lot of hooey to keep people from getting on with the job. We've come here to fill shells, and if we get enough to live on that's all we've got a right to ask for.'

'That's anti-social,' Norah McCall declared dogmatically.

'Anti-socialist or anti-communist – '

'I didn't say anti-socialist. I said anti-social.'

'Well, what's the difference?' Kitty demanded. 'All you socialists and communists are just the same. Money, money, money, that's all you care about, and to hell with the country.'

Norah McCall stood up and moved a pace or two down the aisle of the bus. Everyone was watching her. Her head was thrown back, and she smiled a slow patient smile, quite out of keeping with the eagerness of her face. 'Socialist and communism have nothing to do with it,' she insisted. 'We've all got a right to as much as we can

27

earn – '

'That's right,' two or three girls murmured, looking around for confirmation.

'But my landlady says we don't earn any too much here,' the timid girl ventured again.

'They told me at the Labour I'd get four pounds a week,' another girl said.

'Where did they tell you that?' someone else asked.

'At home, London.'

'They didn't tell me that,' said another, 'fifty bob, they said. For the start, that is. Maybe three pounds later on.'

'They told me four pounds,' the girl from London persisted, 'and if I don't get four pounds next Friday night I'm going to find out why.'

'You won't get four pounds this week,' somebody said, 'it's Tuesday already.'

'I know a girl,' someone else announced, 'who takes home six pounds every week. And lives at home, too.'

Suddenly they fell silent. A shadow of anxiety hung over them. Until now they had hidden their fears. Most of them had cried a little at leaving home, but they had come of their own free will, or so they believed; and they had come determined to enjoy what they had persuaded themselves they had chosen. In their lodgings the previous evening most of them had been frozen with shyness, and with a sort of horror at the uncertainty of what lay before them. But over their icy fears they had worn a mask of cheerful independence, even of gaiety. A few already had friends or acquaintances from their home towns working at Blimpton, and these had made for themselves an image of what their job was to be, and of what their life was to be like. Most of them, however, knew almost nothing of what lay before them. The Employment Exchange officials who had induced them to come could not tell them what the factory was like nor, except in the vaguest terms, what the work involved, because they themselves had never seen a filling factory and had not the curiosity necessary to enable them to begin to imagine one. To some, the prospect that had been held out had seemed enticing and even thrilling; for others, going to Blimpton was not more than a way of getting a job, of getting out of domestic service, or of becoming disentangled from the complications of an unhappy home. But all of them, as they arrived at Dustborough, had decked themselves in all the self-confidence they could muster, and had cloaked some of their physical exhaustion with an air of cheerful anticipation.

It had not been easy. Some of them had travelled long distances. Half of them at least had never before spent a night away from home. They were taken by officious and indifferent strangers to landladies whose houses were already crowded with the tedious problems of family life, and who agreed to accept them partly because they needed every possible addition to the family income, and partly because of the implied threat, held over them at each previous refusal, that if they did not take Blimpton girls willingly they might soon be compelled to do so. Some of the newcomers were at once adopted into the family, perhaps to replace a son or daughter who had gone to the forces, and a few had been thawed into a brief and natural grief by the kindness with which they were received. But most of them were treated simply as what they were: unwelcome strangers whose contribution to the family budget might before long be outweighed by the trouble and inconvenience they would cause. This hostility would, for many of them, eventually disappear; meanwhile it had helped for a time to preserve a rather precarious gaiety.

Now, in the dirty steamy bus, the gaiety had suddenly disappeared. The girls surveyed one another in silence. Griselda Green, sitting at the back, was shivering a little, but her face wore an expectant and faintly mocking smile. Norah McCall had taken off her hat, and looked, for the moment, defeated. None of the girls had had very much to eat since they had left home, and their faces began to take on a uniformly greenish tinge.

After ten minutes or so, the driver returned. 'All right,' he said, 'you can go in now. They're ready for you.'

Slowly they trooped out, across the beaten mud path, into the nearest of the wooden huts, the factory Labour Office. A uniformed messenger ushered them through a narrow lobby into a sort of hall, furnished with rows of wooden benches and, at the far end, a dais on which was a baize-covered table and a chair. The room seemed to be full, but the messenger led them to the empty rows at the front of the room, where they reluctantly sat down. The fifty or sixty women who had arrived before them were talking quietly, and the newcomers turned round to look at them.

'What are we waiting for?' Griselda Green asked a woman who was seated just behind her.

'The day of judgment, I should think.' She was a shabby little woman, and when she smiled her face seemed to fold itself into a thousand creases. 'Did you ever go to Sunday school?' she asked.

'No. Why?'

'Nothing. Only this is just like it. Not so lively, though.'

'How long have you been waiting?' Griselda asked.

The woman grinned again. 'I wouldn't know,' she said, 'but long enough. Do you think they're getting our elevenses?'

'What a hope!' the girl next to her observed bitterly.

They continued to wait. Once or twice the messenger who had shown them in opened the door, peered around and then went away. Otherwise nobody appeared. Conversations were started only to die away into silence. At one moment everyone was talking. A minute or two later there was a complete hush.

After about a quarter of an hour Kitty Baldwin, who had been seated in the front row, stood up. Everybody looked at her. She began to move out of her place.

'Where are you going?' the girl next to her asked.

'I'm going to find out what's going on,' she replied. 'I don't know about you, but I've come here to work, and I'm going to find out when I start.'

At that moment a young woman marched into the room, bringing with her a brisk air of authority. She strode up to the dais, mounted it, and perched herself on the edge of the table.

'Now, please, everybody sit,' she commanded.

Everybody except Kitty Baldwin was already seated. Kitty Baldwin sat.

'First of all,' the young woman began, 'I'm Miss Braithwaite, one of the Labour Officers. You'd better try to remember my name.'

Miss Phoebe Braithwaite. Miss Phoebe Braithwaite was extremely frightened. She was thirty-four years old, and looked younger. She wore her mouse-coloured hair coiled in plaits round her head, and her foggy eyes looked at the world through thick spectacles. She felt that her hands were shaking, and she could hear the echo of each word as she spoke. This was the first time that she had been entrusted with a party of entrants. She was sure that something would go wrong, and that she would drop some innocent phrase in which these strange girls might detect a hidden ambiguity and start giggling. Even when Miss Creed received the intake in person such things occasionally happened, but they were glossed over quickly; people forgot; and it did not often happen. Miss Creed had the sort of personality that could quell with a look. Phoebe Braithwaite thought she understood how Miss Creed did it, but she was not quite sure that she could do it herself.

But she had to try. She knew that Miss Creed had paid her a great compliment. She had come to the factory barely three months ago after a short course of training at the London School of Economics, and this was the first time that she had ever earned her living. Now she had been entrusted with the week's intake, although there were at least six assistant labour officers who were senior to her and who had never had the opportunity of receiving a party.

'She looks dead scared,' Norah McCall murmured to Griselda Green.

'Silence, please!' Phoebe Braithwaite had caught Miss Creed's intonation exactly. 'Before we go over into the factory there are a few preliminaries that we have to go through. So please pay attention, and if there are any questions you wish to ask I will answer them before you go on to the Groups this afternoon. Now, just one thing before we get right down to business. You must never forget that the work we are doing here is extremely secret – '

'What is the work, anyway?' somebody asked.

'Before you start work,' Phoebe continued, ignoring the interruption, 'you will have to sign a paper pledging yourselves never to tell anybody anything at all about the work we are doing in this factory, nor about anything that happens here. You are making that promise to the Government, and if you break it you will be dismissed from the factory without a moment's notice, and,' she paused with a neat touch of drama, 'and you may even be sent to prison for a long term. If you gave away information that got into the hands of the enemy you might even be hanged.'

A small wide-eyed girl in the front row exclaimed 'Coo!' in a loud tone that might or not have been awestricken. Phoebe took one glance at the interrupter, and then continued. She was not quite word-perfect, but very nearly. She began to hope that she would be allowed, when the party was drawing to the end of the initiation ceremony, to give the final exhortation on risks to life, health and morals.

'Now,' she continued (part of the effectiveness of Miss Creed's style came, Phoebe had observed, from beginning as many sentences as possible with the word 'Now'). 'Now, we have a great deal to do today. Some of you have never worked in factories. Some of you have done all kinds of jobs, and,' she looked round doubtfully, '… and perhaps some of you have never been out to work before. But whatever you did before you came here, you will find that you have a lot to learn at Blimpton. All I want to say at the moment is that you must make up your minds to learn quickly. Someone will speak to you later about the different things you have to learn. Perhaps I will speak to you about them myself. Now we'll get down to business. First of all, we must make sure that every girl has brought all her papers with her. Everybody, make sure. Get out your documents, and we'll check up.'

Handbags were opened. Papers rustled. The first check-up began. Birth certificates, printed foolscap forms covered with life-histories, genealogies, medical case-histories, marriage certificates, green cards from Employment Exchanges, unemployment books, health insurance cards, ration books, identity cards, the whole documentary evidence that each of these individuals was qualified to become a wage-earner, to be given a number, to sew cartridge bags, weigh cordite, pour TNT into shells and bombs and mines, press fulminate of mercury, fill fuzes, and do the thousand and one other jobs about a filling factory – all the evidence of the worthiness of these women and girls to risk their lives in jobs that were dangerous, messy, exhausting or merely monotonous, was produced, ready for examination.

A thin young woman, very neat and pale, left her seat and made her way to the front of the room.

Phoebe Braithwaite looked her up and down. 'Well,' she asked, in a tone intended to indicate a controlled impatience, 'well, what is it?'

'Please, miss,' the woman stood with her eyes cast down, and spoke with evident hesitation, 'please, miss,' she repeated, and though she was scarcely younger than Phoebe Braithwaite her timidity was that of a child addressing an adult, 'I can't possibly stay in those digs. They're not clean. Fifty-seven Patterson Road, Dustborough, it is, and I had to share a bed with two children and their habits aren't clean, miss, if you understand me… I can't possibly stay there. I can't really,' her delicate hands were toying with her gloves, pulling out the fingers one at a time, 'I can't possibly stay there another night. I never saw anything like it.'

Phoebe relaxed. She had heard this sort of story before. She knew the right answer. 'You can't expect to live in a first-class hotel, you know,' she said severely, 'but if it's really as bad as you say you'd better come and speak to me about it later. We've got other things to see to now. And don't forget there's a war on.'

She had spoken loudly, and now a mocking voice came from somewhere in the middle of the room, 'Yes, girls, and whatever you do, don't forget there's a war on.'

A smothered giggle fluttered through the air. Phoebe told herself that such comments were best ignored.

'Now,' she said, when the pale girl had sat down, 'we'll just check up that you've all brought your papers. Hands up those who haven't brought their birth certificates.'

A dozen hands shot up.

'You can't all have forgotten them. Look again.' Pause. 'Once more!'

She counted again. Ten. That was bad. Six had merely left them in their lodgings. The other four had not known or had forgotten that no one could be admitted to the factory without a birth certificate. Now the ten were finished, as far as that day was concerned. They had fallen at the first hurdle, and were dismissed to sit on the cross-bench that ran along one side of the room.

The test continued. Three girls joined the cross-bench because they had forgotten to bring their green cards from their local Employment Exchange, two others because they had failed to produce their ration books. At the end of half an hour the goats had been finally divided from the sheep. Phoebe glanced at her watch, and saw with satisfaction that she had finished that part of the job in average time. Someone else would arrange for the girls who had arrived without their papers to be sent back to Dustborough until such time as they qualified themselves to enter the factory premises.

The main party was ready for the next stage. They followed Miss Braithwaite out into the rain and across the wide road to the factory gate. A policeman counted them. Another policeman checked the count, and the two compared results. The girls were then counted a third time, and then at last found themselves (if found is the right word) inside the precincts of the great factory. They were tired, cold and hungry, too dazed to look around, too confused to be interested in their first entry into this city of death, a city larger than many of them had ever seen, and stranger than any of them could have imagined.

For perhaps ten minutes they followed Miss Braithwaite along a wide concrete road bordered by one- and two-storied buildings, some built of brick, some of wood, some looking like mounds of earth with a door cut in, like huge communal graves newly thrown up and not yet ready for the stone-mason. Presently one girl took a quick step forward and asked: 'When do we come to the factory?'

'This is the factory,' Phoebe told her coldly.

A minute or so later they entered a hut very much like the one they had left, but larger and with tables set out among the benches. Two young women, one round and cheerful with the glazed look of a well-baked dumpling, the other a dimmer and (if that were possible) chillier edition of Phoebe, were distributing along the tables sheaves of forms, small bottles of ink, and pens. Miss Creed, wrapped in a long coat with a fur collar, and with a hat sitting awry on the back of her head, was exercising a general supervision.

Now she came forward to greet them, whispered a word or two to Phoebe, who blushed with pleasure, and, in ringing tones, commanded the party to be seated.

'If I pass this,' somebody said in a loud whisper, 'it'll be the first examination I ever did pass.'

The dumpling-like young woman was standing just behind her. 'But it's not an examination,' she said with a friendly giggle, 'it's just a lot of forms that have to be filled up. And we're here to help you do it. There's nothing to be nervous about: it takes rather along time, that's all.' She giggled again and retreated.

Then Miss Creed took over. It was usual to describe Miss Creed as a woman of vast experience, yet looking at her it was hard to believe that she had ever experienced anything. She was in her late forties, a large faded blonde who might have been described as overblown had it not been so obvious that she had never flowered. It could not even be said that she was withered in the bud, so difficult was it to believe that any vitality had ever budded in her. Very few people had ever liked Miss Creed, but if she knew this she showed no sign of her awareness. She was both bland and fussy. Pamela Grant used to say that she was like the worst kind of headmistress, and this was true. 'Come along, girls,' she would say, 'come along.' The phrase would awaken a thousand uncomfortable memories; the young women suddenly became children, the lovely word 'truant' would spring into their minds, some would think of stacked armfuls of bluebells, and oozy sap spreading down the front of their dresses, of dressing-up in back alleys, of collecting for Guy Fawkes and spending the pennies on sticks of liquorice and newspapers-full of chipped potatoes. When Miss Creed said 'Come along, girls,' the Minister of Labour's nightmare of absentee fifth columnists dissolved into a dangerous, tearful, irresistible daydream.

From this daydream the girls were woken sharply. Miss Creed and her assistants had no time to waste. Their job was to get the weekly batch of newcomers sorted out and distributed to the different parts of the factory with the least possible delay. There were forms to be filled up; then more forms to be filled up; factory passes to be issued; medical examinations to be carried out by Dr Aaron and Dr Gower in the surgery next door; the book of rules had to be issued and explained; arrangements had to be made for the payment of the Ministry of Labour's settling-in allowances, ten shillings now and the rest next week. Travel vouchers for buses and trains had to be distributed; magazine clothing had to be sorted out. At least twenty different stages had to be gone through before the girls could be allocated to the different shops in which they were to work and the different shifts on which they were to start.

The day dragged on. Nobody could follow exactly what was happening. At lunchtime those who had been medically examined were taken to one of the canteens; the others were promised tea and sandwiches, but the promise remained unfulfilled. It did not matter. By this time most of them were too dazed to feel hungry.

And they had begun to feel less lonely. They were getting to know each other. Friendships were beginning to spring up. The party was no longer a shapeless mass. It broke into little groups, with the shy ones and the proud ones still standing aloof. The girls from Scotland, who had travelled together and had then been separated when they were sent to their billets, were now reunited. Girls from London began to recall pleasures that they had all enjoyed. Country girls found each other, and their individual envy of girls from towns became less shameful as they began to talk of the things they had possessed and to forget the things they were all privately certain they had missed.

Few of these friendships would survive the day. Indeed, it was probable that many of these girls would not see each other again. Some of them realised this, but most did not. A few were overcome with disappointment when they were finally given instructions as to when and where they were to start work. Winnie Poulton and Doris Chandler decided that they could not stand it.

They had not known each other until they found themselves sitting on the same bench, but they both came from Oldham and they were both nineteen. Doris Chandler had been an usherette in a backstreet cinema. 'Call me Doreen,' she would say as soon as an acquaintanceship showed signs of ripening. She knew all about films. She was all the stars rolled into one. She read all the fan-magazines, she knew all the secrets of success and all the pitfalls of romance; and she was a little bored with Hollywood. She was neat and smart, except on her Garbo days, and she was thankful to get away from home. To live in a hostel and have a bath whenever she wanted one seemed to her a very fair substitute for Beverley Hills and the Brown Derby.

Winnie Poulton had worked in a cotton mill. For her a job was just a job. She wasn't specially anything. She had a way of looking at people and saying 'Ah' in a deep significant tone that meant nothing in particular. She had no special boyfriend, no notable joys and no real sorrows. There were already hundreds of people like her at Blimpton, and by the time the factory was in full production there would be several thousand more.

She did not know this, and she was determined not to be separated from Doris Chandler. She sat hugging her determination while Doris approached the youngest and prettiest of the assistant labour officers. Doris was doing her Greer Garson act; she was very winning. Pamela Grant was sympathetic, but she was new to the factory and was not sure what she should do. She consulted Phoebe Braithwaite, who knew all the regulations.

'Oh dear,' Phoebe wilted a little; Miss Creed was going to give the Talk herself after all, 'sometimes I think these girls set out to make as much trouble as they can. It isn't as if they were old friends.'

Pamela Grant looked at her. 'They are a little difficult,' she agreed, 'but still – '

She paused.

'I can't worry Miss Creed with a silly question like that,' Phoebe said decisively.

'They're frightfully upset. Look.' Pamela pointed out the two girls. Doris Chandler was holding a handkerchief to her eyes. Winnie Poulton sat beside her saying nothing. She looked deeply aggrieved.

'It isn't as if they weren't both going on contact work,' Pamela continued. 'It would be quite easy to shift one of them over. Nobody would ever know, and those two will have a decent chance to settle down.'

'We can't start changing the girls around without asking Miss Creed.'

'Then ask her.'

'I can't ask her. Don't you see that she's already worn out?'

'Very well, I'll ask her.'

'I wouldn't if I were you.'

'I think I will, all the same.'

Miss Creed was sitting at a table, making jottings in a notebook. 'Quite impossible,' she said when Pamela Grant had finished her story. 'Quite impossible. She looked up, surveying the girl as if she were seeing her for the first time. She noted the set of her hair, the lines of her suit, the matching colour of nails and lipstick. It seemed to her that Pamela Grant looked exactly like an operative who had suddenly had her wages doubled. 'When you've been with us a little longer,' Miss Creed spoke drily, 'that is, if you decide to stay with us' – at that the girl's expression hardened a little, but she did not attempt to interrupt, 'if you decide to stay with us,' Miss Creed repeated, 'you will find that the first duty of all of us in the Labour Office is to fit in with the general organisation of the factory. We should all like to be able to perform these little kindnesses, no doubt. But we have other duties that must come first; and these girls will have to learn sooner or later to act under discipline. This isn't a holiday camp. Now, Miss Grant, I think you'd better help Miss Braithwaite to check over the list of factory passes. Then you can take the girls who are going on the night shift to have a rest in North Canteen as soon as the Talk is over.'

The Talk. As she listened Phoebe Braithwaite reproached herself for ever having dared to imagine that Miss Creed might trust her with this difficult and fascinating task. The Talk was designed to give the newcomers not so much an idea of what their life at Blimpton was to be like as a picture of the sort of death they would meet if they failed to carry out the prescribed regulations. It was true, and Phoebe had been at the factory long enough to know this, that the risks to life and health were commonly exaggerated by the workers; but Miss Creed argued, to those who were important enough to be argued with, and declared, to those who were not, that a wholesome fear was the surest foundation of safety. So every week, as soon as the routine business of reception was completed, Miss Creed talked about the factory rules, hours and conditions in a way that made most of the new entrants decide that they would go home again as soon as they had earned enough money to pay their railway fares.

Phoebe found that she was listening less attentively than usual. It wasn't that she knew the Talk too well, and in fact she had often reproached herself for not knowing it well enough. She knew it as the enthusiastic amateur knows the part of the stage star whom she has watched through half a dozen performances. Here and there she had caught the spirit of it exactly; she knew each phrase, each intonation, each subtle movement of the head or hands...

She leaned forward a little, her hands holding the side of her chair. The sentences dripped into her consciousness, sometimes whole and rounded, sometimes in fragments. 'It is essential that every one of you should become fully acquainted with the rules of the factory. Each of you has a copy of the little yellow book...' A wind seemed to blow across the room as each girl tried to sort out her copy from among the papers she had accumulated in the course of the day. 'You will observe that this book is a confidential document, and everyone is expected to take the greatest care of it. You must never leave it lying about in your lodgings, and you must never, on any account, show it to anyone who is not employed at the factory, or tell any outside person that you have a copy, or even that such a book exists. Remember, Hitler has ears everywhere...'

There was certainly something wrong. Several people in the second row were fidgeting. Phoebe moved her chair a little to one side, taking care that the legs did not scrape against the bare floor. Now she could see a section of the audience. A stout middle-aged woman in the third row was sorting out the contents of her handbag. Two girls at the back of the room were scribbling little notes and passing them to each other. The performance was not getting across.

Miss Creed seemed to sense it; too. The sentences flowed on. 'Where there is dirt there is danger. Never forget that. Many of you will be running serious risks. The work has to be done...' The words seemed to be the same, but the rhythm had gone. The sentences made no impact. A cloud of boredom hovered over the room. The speaker hurried on. She omitted a phrase here and there, Phoebe noticed. The climax came too soon. A few people seemed to be listening, but even they were not really attentive.

When it was over everybody at once started to chatter. They hadn't even noticed that they were being given instructions. They did not seem to have acknowledged the leadership of the Labour Officers. They had not even begun to be part of the factory.

Phoebe got up and began to bustle round. In the passage outside assistant forewomen were waiting to conduct the girls who were going on the afternoon shift to their respective groups. The others were told how and when to return to Dustborough. When she had seen the last of them off, Phoebe saw that Miss Creed had already gone. Pamela Grant and Freda Elliston were clearing up unfilled forms and various odds and ends that had been left lying about.

They looked up as Phoebe approached them. 'What's the matter?' Freda Elliston asked.

Phoebe made a passable attempt at a snort. 'Some of those girls are going to make trouble,' she remarked.

'I shouldn't wonder,' Pamela Grant spoke without looking up, 'I shouldn't be in the least surprised if they did. It's no fun for anyone at Blimpton.'

Freda Elliston finished collecting her pile of papers. 'I don't think I should go as far as that,' she dissented mildly, 'a lot of people manage to enjoy themselves, you know.'

'Do they?'

'Of course they do. Come on, I'm sure it's time we had some tea.'

It was half-past four.

FOUR

MA VENNING WOKE as the clock in the house next door struck six. She got out of bed, dressed very quietly so as not to disturb her husband, and went downstairs, carrying her shoes in one hand and the candlestick in the other. She cleaned the ashes from the kitchen fireplace, lit the fire and put the kettle on. Then she cleared the supper things from the table and began to straighten up the room. When the kettle began to sing she found herself wishing for the hundredth, or perhaps the thousandth, time that They had made the tea ration a little larger. She pushed the thought from her and began to wash up.

At half-past six she called to her husband that it was time to get up. She could hear him moving about upstairs, switching on the electric light, letting the door bang behind him as he went into the bathroom. Presently he called down to her: 'What's the matter, Ma?'

'Nothing?' she called back, 'why?'

'You're not singing,' he said.

'It's nothing,' she told him, 'come along down. Your breakfast's nearly ready.'

As she turned the fried bread over it struck her that she had not even noticed that she had not been singing. She always sang about the house. She sang anything, hymns, old-fashioned songs that her mother had taught her when she was a child, choruses that she had learned during the last war, and scraps of new songs that she had picked up from listening to the wireless, going to the cinema, or from other workers in the factory at Blimpton.

Now, as she finished getting the breakfast, she began to hum a little tune that she had heard on the bus the night before.

Jim was coughing slightly as he came downstairs. This morning he looked thinner and paler than usual. Once or twice recently Ma had noticed that he was beginning to look like an old man. He was in his middle fifties, she a year or two younger.

'Did you go to the doctor last night?' she asked as she began to pour out the tea.

Jim took the cup she held out. His hands were very white, but marked with the blue stains of the coal-miner. It was now nearly twenty years since he had worked at Castle Colliery.

'Well, I did look in,' he replied, 'but there was such a queue outside the surgery that I didn't wait.'

'Better go along early tonight.'

'Ah,' he said, 'I will.' He glanced up at her as she stood at the gas-stove, dishing the sausages on to plates. She looked like a farmer's wife, stout and comfortably made. Her thick grey hair was done up in an old-fashioned bun. Her face, now flushed with the heat from the stove, was still handsome.

'You're not fretting about me, are you, Ma?' Jim asked.

'No,' she said, 'I'm not fretting about anything.'

For the last twenty-five years, ever since she had gone to work in a munitions factory in the last war, everyone had called her Ma. In those days it had been a sort of nickname, a joke that the other girls had made because of the way in which she used to boast about her twin babies. Now the twins were both in the Army; Clarice, who was born in 1917, was married and lived in London, and Elsie, the baby, was a corporal in the WAAF. Ma had gone to work at Blimpton the week after Elsie joined up. At first she had tried to get accustomed to being called Mrs Venning, but in a week or two the girls in the shop where she worked were calling her Ma, just as everybody else did. Now that she was a blue-band, an over-looker in charge of a shop, it was too late for people to learn to call her anything else.

She drank two cups of tea before she began to eat.

'Jim,' she said, 'I was thinking.'

'Ah!' Jim looked at her dubiously. He had learned to be nervous when Ma began a conversation in this way.

'I was thinking,' she repeated, 'it's not right that we should have this house all to ourselves. I mean, it's a good house.'

'It is.' They fell silent, each remembering the dingy little place in Brick Street where they had lived for nearly half their married life. If Jim had not broken down with a second attack of tuberculosis the year after the twins left school, they would not have had the slightest chance of getting a council house, of having a bathroom a garden, and the other comforts which they now enjoyed. When she looked back at her life Ma was often puzzled at the way in which misfortune and good luck seemed to get entangled with each other.

'What are you thinking?' Jim asked at last. He looked at the clock. 'It's time I was getting to work.'

'That's ten minutes fast,' Ma reminded him. 'It seems too bad having both those bedrooms empty,' she said slowly. 'Sometimes I can't help thinking that it seems a shame, when there are decent girls being put into lodgings in some of those back streets downtown.'

'I thought they were building hostels out Blimpton way,' Jim observed.

'So they are. But they're not ready yet. Won't be ready for months, from all I hear.'

'I heard that, too,' Jim admitted, his tone grudging.

'Where did you hear it?'

'At the Town Hall.' For the last few years, in fact ever since the doctor had passed him for light work only, Jim had been doing various odd jobs at the Town Hall. He was now in charge of the Gentlemen's Convenience. He still hoped, though of late the hope had been growing fainter, that one day he would be able to do a real job again.

'I wish the Town Hall people would mind their own business,' Ma spoke in her usual placid tone. 'Anyway, it wouldn't hurt us to take in one or two girls. Just till the hostel's ready. They could have a room each, and then if the boys or Elsie came on leave we could get them to double up for a few days.' Her face brightened. 'It wouldn't be any trouble at all.'

'You couldn't do it, Ma,' Jim wiped his mouth on the back of his hand and looked at her uneasily, 'you've got quite enough to do as it is. Now, if you was to give up going out to Blimpton…'

'Give up!' An ominous twinkle appeared in Ma's blue eyes.

'You know what I've always thought…' Jim got up and took his overcoat down from the peg behind the door. 'It isn't as if we needed the money,' he said as he put his coat on.

As things went in Dustborough they were fairly well off now.

In the last war Ma had worked in a shell factory because her allowance as a soldier's wife had not been sufficient to maintain herself and the children. For many years after the war she had worked, scrubbing bedroom floors at the Duke of Cumberland's Arms, charing at the Vicarage and taking in washing to supplement Jim's unemployment benefit and to keep the children fed and clothed in the long periods when Jim was in a sanatorium; when the children began to earn and Jim at last, with the help of some of his friends, found a settled job she was able, for the first time in her life, to stay at home and look after the family. She had plenty to do, and she enjoyed her leisure. Every Tuesday afternoon she went to the meeting of the Women's Co-operative Guild, and on Thursday evenings she and Elsie generally went to the cinema. Until the war came she found life full and reasonably satisfying. Then, as the children, one after another, left home, she found that she had not really enough to do about the house to keep her busy all day. Besides, she wanted to do some war work.

She was very happy at Blimpton.

'The money's useful,' she said now, 'and we're putting something by. If we don't need it ourselves, it'll help the boys when the war's over. Or Elsie.'

'You couldn't do with lodgers as well,' Jim was now standing at the back door, his hand on the knob, ready to go out, 'not with you on shift work, too. You know I wouldn't cross you in anything,' he said.

'I know, Jim.' She had a lovely smile. 'I wouldn't do it without asking you. You know that.'

'I know.' She had always managed everything. She had always done exactly what she intended to do, but at the same time she had always fostered in both of them the illusion that Jim was the real ruler of their life, that it was he who commanded and she who obeyed.

'Think it over,' she said, 'there isn't any hurry. Only if they start billeting soldiers down this end of the town it'll be too late. I'd much rather have girls than men, whatever other people say.' She got up and began to clear the table. Jim was still standing at the door, waiting.

'All right, Ma,' he said, 'if you really think it's the best thing.'

She was filling the kettle at the sink. 'There isn't any hurry,' she repeated, 'you think it over. I'd only take girls I know. Decent girls who want a bit of home life.' She paused. 'Got your torch?' she asked. Jim was dismissed.

She washed up the breakfast things, tidied their bedroom and dusted the empty rooms. She turned the mattresses over, looked in the cupboards and chest of drawers, wondering where she would store the boys' civilian clothes and Elsie's dresses. She made up the double bed in which Elsie and Clarice had always slept, and put a hot water bottle in to air the sheets. She had no definite plans, but now that she had broken the idea to Jim she wanted to be prepared for anything that might happen. When she had finished the housework she had a good wash in the bathroom, put on a clean blouse and her coat with the fur collar. By the time the shops were open she was ready to go out.

She had a busy morning, standing in queues to do the extra shopping that she only had time for when she was working on the afternoon shift. She met several of her friends during the half-hour or so that she spent at the Co-op, and when she went down to the Market to buy vegetables she found several people she knew standing in line at the stalls. She lingered a little to talk, and then had to hurry back to cook a meal that Jim could heat up for himself when he came home from work. She had just time for a snack before she changed into her old clothes and rushed out again to catch the special bus that passed the bottom of the road at half-past one.

Inside the Main Gate of the factory she had to wait for a second bus that was provided to take workers to the North-West Group, two and a half miles away. The bus was later than usual, and a crowd of men and women were waiting on the icy edge of the road, stamping their feet and waving their arms to try to regain a little warmth. Ma noticed Kitty Baldwin standing a little apart from the rest.

'Cold?' Ma asked.

'Cold! I never was so cold in my life!' Kitty pulled her thin black coat more closely about her; she looked haggard and pale beneath the heavy make-up.

'I hope you had a good dinner before you came out?' Ma asked.

'No,' the girl told her, 'it took me all the morning to get my ration books, and my landlady couldn't get anything in. She said I'd be able to get something in the canteen later on.'

'So you will,' Ma agreed, 'but you oughtn't to come out without anything.'

'Oh, I had breakfast. And tea and toast dinner-time…'

She paused for a moment, and then asked, 'Will we be allowed to start work today?' She and Doris Chandler and Griselda Green had been taken to Ma's shop the previous afternoon, and had spent their first working hours watching other girls weigh bundles of cordite. In another building a few yards away Norah McCall with three or four companions watched another group of girls performing the relatively difficult task of tying up the bundles with lengths of silk thread.

'I know it looks easy – ' Ma began. She knew that it was easy; but she also knew that she dare not run the risk of allowing new workers to perform any operation, however simple, until they had been in the factory at least three days. This rule could only be relaxed if special permission were first obtained from the shop-manager, and such permission was difficult to obtain. So Ma changed the subject rather quickly, and began to chatter about the plan for a Group concert.

She talked for ten minutes, and still the bus did not appear. She suggested that they should begin to walk.

Others straggled after them as it became evident that no bus was likely to run.

'Do we often have to walk?' Kitty asked.

'Oh, yes.' Ma explained that the bus service was so uncertain that in good weather it was better to walk, and even in bad weather it was often worthwhile to get a wetting in order to clock-on at the proper time.

'But why can't they run the buses on a proper schedule?' Griselda Green, who had just succeeded in catching them up, asked.

'Ah,' said Ma, 'they're always having trouble with one thing and another. I suppose they can't help it, what with the war and all that.'

'They ought to help it,' Kitty insisted. She glanced at her watch. 'We could be working now.'

They walked in silence, the two girls looking round curiously at the sparse disorderly huddles of buildings that flanked the main road. Most of the side-roads were still unpaved, and here and there workmen were laying drains or digging up those that had already been laid. The grass that grew between the buildings was rank and yellow, and the buildings themselves, stretching away as far as the eye could see, looked dim and uninhabited. Beneath the flat sky the earth seemed dead. Most of the trees had been chopped down, and lay where they had been felled. Occasionally the remains of a hedge marked the boundary of what had until recently been a field. In this strange landscape that was neither town nor country it was difficult to believe that any life could still continue. Yet behind them and in front were little parties of men and girls, laughing, shouting, grumbling. Now and then a lorry passed, heavily loaded. Once a car stopped and put down two important-looking men outside a windowless concrete building. The girls nearest the car called to the driver to give them a lift, but he shook his head and drove on.

At last they reached the entrance to the North-West Group, and joined the queue waiting to show their passes. Ma had learned that it was easier not to carry cigarettes and matches than to remember to give them up at the entrance to the danger buildings, but she always looked through her handbag to reassure herself. The newcomers giggled a little as they handed over their contraband to the gateman. Most of them were thrilled and a little frightened at the prospect of working among explosives.

The shifting-house was warm, but stuffy with the smells of clothing, of shoe-leather, of bodies made warm by exercise. Over everything hung the curious odours of the factory. Every day when Ma started work she remembered how, when first she came to Blimpton, she had been a shifting-house attendant with nothing to do but keep the place clean and tidy and see that the girls did not steal each other's possessions. If Bob Roberts, the foreman of the group, who was a Labour Councillor at Dustborough and an old friend of Jim's, had not come in one day and recognised her she would still have been sitting about for hours every shift with no one to talk to and nothing to do.

The interior of the building was whitewashed, but so badly lit that grey shadows seemed to be cast over everything, over the long rows of pegs that ran down the room dividing it into three, over the benches where the girls sat to take off their shoes, and over the untidy heaps of clothing that accumulated as they undressed. Halfway down the room a barrier, about eighteen inches high, stretched from wall to wall, right across the aisles, cutting the clean side of the factory from contact with the dirt and dust of the outer world.

Ma undressed slowly. She still disliked having to take off her blouse and skirt in the presence of other people; even now she felt a sort of shame in having to cross the barrier in her vest and knickers, and in leaving her shoes and her outer clothes behind her on the dirty side. Nor had she ever quite reconciled herself to wearing magazine uniform. The thick white material shrank and turned grey after one visit to the Blimpton laundry, and to make matters worse, Ma had never yet succeeded in getting a pair of trousers that were really large enough. Today she gave an extra tug to the hem of her jacket, and murmured her usual joke about the difficulty of making ends meet. Then she hurried out to clock-on.

She liked to be the first to arrive in the shop. She was so punctual that sometimes the girls teased her and said that she was planning to frame her clock-card after the war and hang it over the kitchen mantelpiece, for all the world to see what punctuality meant.

But if the girls were proud of Ma, Ma, too, had every reason to be proud of her girls. They were almost as punctual in their attendance as she was herself; they were seldom absent from work, even in bad weather, and they never stayed away merely to go to the cinema or to do a little shopping. In more than two months Ma had not once had to borrow workers from other shops to make up her team, though she had often had to lend two or three of her girls to other shops that were not so fortunate. The girls liked each other and seldom quarrelled. When, as sometimes happened, disputes arose with the other two shifts that used their shop about the condition in which benches had been left or the misuse of the scales, Ma could be trusted to iron out the trouble with the least possible discredit to those concerned.

Ma had been lucky, too, in being allowed to keep her team unchanged. Workers were moved from one part of the factory to another so often and, as far as they were ever able to understand, with so little reason, that for an over-looker to be in charge of the same group of girls for more than a few weeks was almost unheard of; and, since each of the eight groups into which the factory was divided covered an area that was in few cases less than a square mile, any worker who was transferred to another group was as completely lost to those who remained behind as she would have been if she had been sent to the other end of England.

Now, quite unexpectedly, three of the best workers in the shop had been moved, and Ma did not even know where they had gone; the new girls who had been sent to replace them were not only new to Blimpton, but seemed to be without any experience of factory life. All the other workers in the shop came from Dustborough or from some other town within daily travelling distance of the factory. They talked the same language, ate the same food and enjoyed the same pleasures. The newcomers were strangers, foreigners. Ma was not quite sure how to handle them. They frightened her a little, though she would not have admitted this to anyone.

When she reached the shop Kitty Baldwin and Doris Chandler were already there. They sat on a bench, leaning against a wall, and stared at nothing. Both looked as if they had been crying.

'Feeling a bit strange?' Ma asked. Her tone was so full of kindness that both girls relaxed slightly.

'A bit,' Kitty admitted.

Doris began to cry again. A tear trickled down each cheek, then another, and another. Only at the pictures had Ma ever seen anyone cry like that.

'Homesick, love?' she asked.

Doris pulled out a handkerchief from the pocket of her magazine suit and began to dab at her face.

'It's my girl friend,' she sobbed, 'I told you yesterday they'd took... they'd took my girl friend away from me.'

'You said you'd try to get her friend moved over here,' Kitty reminded Ma.

'I know I did, love. I'll speak to Miss Elliston about it when she comes round.' Ma looked from one to the other. 'I don't say it can be done,' she told them, 'but we'll have a try.'

Doris stopped crying. 'When?' she asked. Her plucked eyebrows gave her face a look of extreme surprise.

'As soon as we can,' Ma promised, 'Miss Elliston's sure to be round later on – '

At that moment the trucker came in, wheeling a load of cordite. Ma went over to look at it.

'When are you bringing the rest?' she asked.

The trucker was a wizened little man with a humorous face.

'There ain't no more,' he said, 'Mr Bealby said you was to make do with that.'

Ma looked again. 'That won't keep my girls busy for more than half an hour. You know that, Whitey.'

'Yes,' Whitey agreed, 'I know.'

Three or four other girls who had come in were standing round the truck, listening.

'Well, get along, Whitey,' Ma insisted, 'and see we get some more.'

'I told you,' Whitey repeated, 'that's all you'll get. That's orders. Go and see Mr Bealby yourself, if you don't believe me.' He looked at her and his mouth framed the words 'Hold-up'.

'Hold-up!' Ma exclaimed, 'who says there's a hold-up? I thought we'd got a rush on for the 3.7?'

'Search me!' Whitey was unloading the stuff with a little help from one of the girls. 'I don't know nothing,' he said.

'That's right!' someone jeered, 'and if you did you wouldn't say.'

'Now, Bessie,' Ma interjected.

'I wouldn't either,' Whitey insisted, 'it's no business of mine.' He looked at the row of watching girls. 'Well,' he said, 'I must be getting along. I see you've got some new faces here.'

Griselda Green smiled suddenly. 'Yes,' she said, 'aren't you going to wish us luck, Mr Whitey?'

Whitey stared at her for a moment or two without speaking. She looked strong and gay and confident. She spoke as if the world were hers.

The little man returned her smile. 'Whitey to you,' he said. 'I'll wish you luck. And more. I'll wish you the guts to stick it here.'

'Why shouldn't I stick it?'

'Most don't,' Whitey told her. 'They come and they go. Sometimes they go quicker than they come. Don't they, Ma?'

Ma was standing very still. She made no sign of having heard.

'I'll stick it.' Griselda Green smiled again. She looked from Kitty Baldwin to Doris Chandler, and then back to Whitey. 'We'll all stick it,' she told him, 'you'll see.'

'They may,' he agreed, 'but you won't. You'll never last out.'

'Why not?' An odd smile played about her mouth. It was difficult to tell whether she was indignant or amused.

'You come from a good home.'

She began to laugh, at first quietly, and then more and more loudly. Quite suddenly she stopped. 'Not so good as you seem to think,' she told him.

Ma took a step forward. 'Now, Whitey,' she said, 'that's enough from you. I'll walk along with you as far as number twenty-three.'

She returned after a few minutes, and the day's work started. The girls worked slowly, pausing now and then as they became engrossed in conversation. Ma did not hurry them, but dawdled a little herself, hoping that another truckload would arrive before the girls had finished with the stuff that White had brought.

She was worried. She knew from experience that if work did not arrive someone would begin to make trouble. The girls were not allowed to bring knitting, or any other work of their own, on to the clean-side and they hated to sit still. So after a short time she went out again, to try to find someone in authority who could help her. She had no luck. She came back, and after another short wait went out again. Most of the shops on the Group seemed to be short of work, and while everyone Ma met had a fresh explanation of the absence of materials no one seemed to know when additional supplies were likely to arrive.

At four o'clock Kitty Baldwin fainted. Ma started to try to bring her round while one of the girls went to the first-aid post to find a nurse. At this point Miss Braithwaite arrived.

'Is everything all right?' She addressed herself briskly to no one in particular, and then paused to take in the situation. Kitty had recovered consciousness, and was lying on a bench while Ma leaned over her murmuring vague sounds of comfort.

'I suppose she forgot to have her dinner before she came?' Miss Braithwaite spoke to Ma accusingly. Fainting in the shops was declared by Miss Creed to be one of the worst forms of malingering.

'I did have something,' Kitty declared in a weak voice and tried to sit up.

'How often have you been told that you must have a proper dinner before you come on the afternoon shift?' Miss Braithwaite, standing over Kitty, seemed to be addressing the whole shop.

'But she's only just come!' Annie Clark struck in.

'And her landlady didn't have anything for her to eat,' Ma added. She was already convinced that the fainting was providential. 'I'll take her home myself tonight,' she added.

'I'll be all right,' Kitty said. She sat up, and fainted again.

Phoebe Braithwaite looked at her with distaste. Kitty's cap had fallen off, and her streaky blonde hair lay in a dank fringe across her forehead. Her face beneath the heavy make-up was paper-white.

The nurse arrived with an assortment of remedies, and ordered everyone to the other end of the room.

Phoebe delivered herself of a brief tirade on the folly of starting to work on an empty stomach. As soon as she had finished Ma asked, 'Where's Miss Elliston?'

Phoebe frowned, and her eyes, behind the thick spectacles, narrowed until she looked as if she could scarcely see. 'She won't be coming today,' she said. She had already been in fifteen shops that afternoon and at every one she had been asked the same question. She told herself that she did not envy Freda Elliston her popularity among the workers, but she could not help feeling a sense of grievance that Freda had been selected to represent the junior labour officers at a meeting of the Dustshire Institute of Psychological Control.

'Is there anything special that you wanted to see her about?' Phoebe asked.

'Well, there was.' Ma hesitated. Kitty, leaning on the arm of the nurse, was being led out of the shop.

'It's about my girl friend,' Doris Chandler said quickly.

'Your *what*?' Phoebe looked at her. 'Oh, you're the girl who was making such a fuss yesterday. Well, I told you then that this factory can't be run for the convenience of any individual worker. You are needed in this shop.'

Doris gave something like a snort, and tossed her hair in a fair imitation of Katherine Hepburn.

' – and your friend is needed somewhere else,' Miss Braithwaite continued. 'Do you think we should ever win the war if the soldiers insisted on fighting beside their friends all the time?'

Doris began to cry again. She shook with great heaving sobs of disappointment. Miss Braithwaite led Ma off into a corner and began to issue instructions.

FIVE

NORA McCALL WAS the last worker to leave the bench when the signal was given for the mid-shift break. She pushed open the swing door and stood for a moment in the darkness, savouring the fresh cold air. All the afternoon she had been growing more and more angry: angry, hot and excited. She had listened while the others talked, and had said nothing. Now the sudden chill of the night sharpened her resolution. The dim lights of torches flickering along the clean-way, the muffled footfalls of workers hurrying to the canteen, the scraps of conversation and bursts of laughter all seemed to tear into her mind with such swiftness that it was as if only at this minute she had begun to live. For perhaps half a minute she waited, and then she too joined the crowds hurrying along in the darkness, all anxious to make the most of the half-hour interval.

Inside the canteen Griselda Green was sitting at a table with five or six girls who had joined the factory on the previous day. At the centre of the party was Kitty Baldwin, still very pale, but determined to spend no more time in the first-aid post. 'That nurse gives me the creeps,' she was saying when Norah joined them. 'I don't believe she's a proper nurse at all. Ugh!' Kitty shuddered at some unspeakable reminiscence.

'Was it about the explosions?' Doris Chandler asked, her face alert, waiting.

'Yes. Partly. And about the rash.'

'What's that?'

'It's what you get from working in the powder,' Kitty explained. 'Hundreds of girls have it.'

'Oh, it's awful!' Gladys Hicks, a quiet little girl from Peckham, could contain herself no longer. 'Didn't you see that girl in the shifting-house when we came in? Her face was all swelled up, something terrible. It was the most awful sight! Honest, it was the most awful sight I ever saw. Blinded, she was.'

'Blinded?' someone asked.

'Yes. Didn't you see her? She couldn't see a thing. Great big spots all over her.'

'I didn't see it!' Norah declared flatly.

'I did.' Rose Widgery, the girl from Devonshire, spoke in a shy and hesitant voice. Her fair hair had fallen out from under her cap and lay like a cloud around her face. She was just eighteen. Her blue eyes were misty, and no one had ever told her how pretty she was. 'I didn't mention it,' she added, 'because I didn't know...'

'Will we get it?' Doris Chandler asked.

'Not unless we're working in the powder,' somebody said.

Doris looked round the table. 'My girl friend,' she said, 'the one I told you, she's in the det shop over on South-East... is that what they call the powder?'

No one seemed to know.

Doris rolled up her sleeve and examined her arm. 'Look!' She pointed to a small red mark just above the elbow. 'Is that it?'

Kitty Baldwin laughed. 'Silly! That's where the sleeve has been rubbing against you. Anyway, it starts on your face.'

'Gosh!' Gladys Hicks looked from one to another, 'I feel scared!'

'It's terribly catching,' Kitty went on. 'If one girl in a shop gets it everybody else gets taken with it sooner or later.'

'Are you sure?' Griselda Green asked.

'That's what somebody in the surgery said... Why?'

'Because it isn't true.'

'What isn't true?'

Griselda seemed to hesitate for an instant. The circle of girls watched, waiting for her to speak. 'It isn't true that dermatitis is infectious,' she said. There was a note of authority in her clear voice, and her grey eyes were sober, challenging.

'But this isn't derma – derma-whatever you said,' Gladys Hicks insisted. 'It's the rash, that's what they call it.'

'It's the same thing,' Griselda told her, 'dermatitis is the scientific name for it. It's not infectious. If people took proper precautions nobody need have it – '

'How do you know?'

'Somebody told me – a doctor.'

'What, here?'

'No, a friend of mine.'

They looked at her with growing incredulity. Doris Chandler put the question that they all wanted to ask: 'What! Have you got a friend who's a doctor?'

Griselda picked up her mug and took a long drink of tea.

'Crikey!' someone exclaimed, 'how posh!'

'He wasn't really a friend.' Griselda looked a little confused. 'He was just someone I happened to talk to. He said that it could be prevented quite easily.'

'Then why don't they prevent it?' somebody asked.

Again they turned to Griselda. She smiled enigmatically and said nothing.

'Because they're inefficient,' Norah said.

'That's right.'

Pause.

Rose Widgery broke the silence. 'Did you know we don't get any pay at all the first week?'

'What!'

'Yes. One of the girls in the shop told me.'

'It must be wrong. They couldn't cheat us like that.'

'It's quite true,' somebody else said, 'my landlady told me.'

'Then how are we supposed to pay for our digs?'

'We'll have to write home for money.'

'I can't do that,' someone exclaimed, 'it's all wrong. I came here just so as I could earn enough to be able to send something home.'

Kitty Baldwin was leaning forward, her elbows on the table, her head bent. Suddenly she looked up.

'I wouldn't mind if we were working,' she said, 'you have to put up with things in a war. Bad digs, and not getting anything to eat, I mean. But I didn't come here just to hang round looking at things… why did they send us here if they didn't have work for us?' She looked around, as if examining each girl: Griselda, sitting very erect, the ugly cap pushed back from her wide forehead, the set of her shoulders bestowing a touch of elegance on her ill-fitting uniform; Rose Widgery, very young, timid and perplexed; Gladys Hicks, pale, untidy and indignant; Doris Chandler, small and pert and ready for anything; Ellen Pusey, worrying more about the troubles that she had left behind her at home than about those that she was beginning to meet at the factory; and, last, Norah McCall, dark and eager, her hands clasped tightly together as if in an effort to subdue some all but irresistible impulse. Kitty watched her intently for a moment or two, and then asked: 'Why don't we do something?'

Several people spoke at once.

'That's all very well – '

'But what could we do?'

'We'd only get into trouble – '

'We just have to put up with it.'

'After all, it's the same for everybody – '

'No it isn't,' Doris suddenly broke in, 'my girl friend – '

'We know about her,' Ellen Pusey reminded her gently.

'I can't afford to lose my job,' Gladys Hicks sighed, 'I was out of work two years.'

'You won't lose your job,' Norah told her, 'not while there's a war on.'

'But what can we *do*?' three or four turned to her at once.

Her hands were still clasped tightly so that the knuckles shone white through the skin. 'I know what my dad would say,' she spoke slowly, the image of her father suddenly very vivid, memories of interminable fierce friendly arguments running again through her mind. 'He'd say we should join the Union and wait for them to act for us.'

'But if we did join the Union that wouldn't get us our pay on Friday night,' someone retorted.

'Unions can't stop you getting the rash,' someone else said.

'Or give you your lu – dinner before you come to work.' Griselda looked at Kitty as she spoke.

Norah seemed to relax. 'I didn't say that's what I'd do,' she pointed out, 'I only said that's what my dad would tell us to do. If you ask me, I think we ought to do something ourselves, right away.'

SIX

IT WOULD NOT be true to say that Gittins was only kept alive by his passion for intrigue, since he was, though past the age at which public servants are expected to retire from active participation in the world's affairs, still possessed of a vitality that is rare even in the young; but this vitality was undoubtedly nourished by the strength of what was, after all, his major preoccupation in life. Love and hate, hope and fear, the simpler emotions which guide or distort the lives of less subtle people, were, in Gittins, subordinated to a ruling interest in which curiosity and a desire for the exercise of the more obscure forms of power were combined in about equal proportions. It was perhaps surprising that a passion so intense and so carefully developed had not lifted him out of the rut and carried him into the highest spheres of politics or public administration. Certainly, his gifts had expanded with the vast increase in the opportunity to exercise them that he found at Blimpton. If his touch was sometimes a little less delicate than it had been in early life it was at any rate no less sure. Sitting in his office he would sometimes seem to those who came to see him to have control of every thread of the vast web that started in the Ministry and came down to every shop, every storehouse, every corner of the great factory.

And now, quite suddenly, he seemed to have gone to pieces. He sat at his desk with a sheaf of minutes in front of him, and a fountain pen in his hand. They could not be dispatched until he had signed them; he had never, in all the forty-five years of his life in the service, signed anything unread; and he could not, he simply could not, summon up the power of concentration necessary to carry him beyond the end of the first line.

He got up, went to the door, hesitated, turned back again, and at last went out. Morgan, the Assistant Superintendent, had an office a few yards down the corridor. He was dictating letters to a slinky blonde stenographer, but he looked up when Gittins entered.

'Could you give me a few minutes?' The Principal Clerk spoke without his usual confidence, and his face looked drawn.

'Surely.' Morgan dismissed the typist. 'Well,' he asked as the door closed behind her, 'what's the matter, Gitty?' His coat was thrown over the back of a chair, and he sat with his shirt-sleeves rolled up above the elbow, his strong arms resting on the desk. Now, as he looked at the other man, he eased himself back, and wiped his forehead with a large white handkerchief. He had, inappropriately, the look of a man accustomed to living out of doors and because of this the room, adequate to its purpose and sufficiently, but sparsely, furnished, looked overcrowded. He was perhaps a little over forty, solidly built, with hair the colour of hay and a skin faded from sunburn to a permanent sallowness. His irregular features were made remarkable by the extraordinary liveliness of his yellow-brown eyes and the quickly changing expression of his wide, humorous mouth. He grinned as he replaced the handkerchief in his pocket, showing white, uneven teeth. 'Well?' he repeated. He seemed to have time for everything though he was, as Assistant Superintendent, responsible for the carrying out of the whole of the factory's production programme as well as for dealing with such problems of policy and administration as the Superintendent would not, or could not, handle.

Gittins had thrown himself into the green leather visitors' chair and sat rubbing a hand over the bald patch at the back of his head. 'Do you know,' he said at last, 'I haven't been able to find out a thing… not one blessed thing…' He glanced at his watch. 'It's after six, and that fellow Gunn has been with the Superintendent since twelve o'clock last night… and I've not had a word. Not even a message… I haven't the slightest idea what they've been up to…'

'Didn't you see Gunn?'

'I *saw* him. Naturally.'

'And?'

'Nothing,' the Principal Clerk averted his gaze from the mockery in the younger man's eyes. 'I wasn't even introduced. I came over last night in case I was wanted and – well, I just happened to be in the hall when this Gunn fellow arrived, but the old man simply carried him off… do you believe that story about a new fuze?'

Morgan shrugged his shoulders. He looked faintly amused. 'Why not?'

'Well…' Gittins got up and began to pace the room, 'I can't see why a man should want to rush down here in the middle of the night just to bring half a dozen new-fangled fuzes. It must be something more than that.'

'I don't see why. He's probably got nothing better to do – and rushing around like that is one way of acting up to the Minister's notion of what a high-powered business executive ought to do.'

Gittins looked thoughtful. 'It might be that,' he agreed after a moment. 'Yes, it might be that. He was a twirpish little chap, Gunn, I mean. Not the sort of person I'd send down to represent me if I were Minister… All the same, I don't like it. There's some funny business going on…'

'But I thought you didn't know anything?'

'That's just it, I don't.'

'Why don't you ring someone at the Ministry?'

Gittins reflected. 'It wouldn't do,' he said, 'it's not the sort of thing one can start making inquiries about… though I did just check up that he really is one of the Outrage outfit… We'll know something about his background in a day or two.'

'But surely he's not staying here?'

'No. I shouldn't think so. But we ought to have the dope about him. You never know when it'll come in useful.'

'You mean *you* never know – '

'Well, after all, it's my duty to keep an eye on what goes on in the factory.' He jerked himself up. 'They must be somewhere about the place. I'll ring round to the shop-managers, one of them ought to know something – ' He hurried out of the room.

SEVEN

AS THE SIX girls stood hesitating in the main corridor of the Administration Block they heard a door open and saw a man in military uniform step out and turn in their direction. Panic, never far behind, suddenly caught up with them.

Norah McCall seized the handle of the nearest door, opened it and led them in.

Dan Morgan finished reading through the last of the letters on his desk, signed it, and put it in the Out-tray.

'Well?' As he looked at them his eyes grew rounder than ever with astonishment, and then he smiled with extraordinary, unexpected friendliness. 'Well, young ladies,' his glance travelled from Norah, standing very erect, her face pale but determined, to the knot of girls that clustered behind her and then to Griselda, waiting with her hand still on the door. 'Well, young ladies,' he asked again, 'what can I do for you?'

Norah took a step forward. Her short dark hair stood out in curls around her head. As she began to speak her face flushed and her voice trembled. 'Are you the person in charge of this factory?' she demanded.

'Yes, I'm – ' he gave her a searching look, 'I am at the moment.'

'Mr Brown?'

'No, Mr Brown isn't around at the moment. I'm Mr Morgan.'

The girls eyed him doubtfully, questioning the rolled-up sleeves, the friendly yet quizzical manner, doubting above all the way in which he seemed to accept this visit as a matter of course, taking them for granted.

'It's important that we should speak to someone in authority.' Norah could hear the echo of her own voice as she spoke, too loud and, at the same time, timid.

'I think you'll find that I've got all the authority that's necessary.' Morgan was serious, business-like, no longer smiling. His solidity offered them reassurance. 'Hadn't you better tell me what it's all about? I think we'd talk more easily if you sat down.' He got up and helped them to find chairs. When they were seated he handed round a box of cigarettes, and though they all refused to smoke they began, as he had intended, to feel more at ease.

'Now,' he glanced at Norah, 'what's it all about?'

She said: 'Mr Morgan, we want to speak to you about conditions in this factory. We've only just come here. You may think we have an awful nerve – '

'We'll decide that when you've finished.' He had a deep, warm voice in which the tones he had first learned in the Rhondda were oddly mixed with accents picked up in Belfast, in London, in Cincinnati. 'Go ahead.' He smiled again, encouraging her.

'First,' Norah checked off the points on her fingers, 'we think we've been brought here under false pretences. We've all of us had to leave home to come here. Some of us came because we had to. Some of us came of our own free will, as you might say. We all come from different parts, but they told us all the same story – I mean at the Labour Exchange – to get us to come. They told us it was important war work, but they didn't tell us what the work was – not that we'd have been put off from coming if they had. They said we'd get good money, decent conditions, that it was a proper war job that they needed thousands of girls for from all over the country. Well,' she paused to glance along the row of girls, as if for confirmation, 'we came to Dustborough on Monday. They didn't expect us. The billets weren't ready or anything. They said if we were lucky we'd be put in a hostel, but now we've got here it seems there isn't any hostel after all. Then it seems we don't get any pay the first week, only the allowance from the Labour. And now we've got in the shops we find out there isn't any work for us to do.'

'That's right,' Kitty Baldwin muttered as Norah paused to take breath.

'And it isn't only ourselves,' Norah continued, 'a lot of other girls came here with us. Of course I can't speak for them but only for us here.'

'But they'd all tell you the same,' Gladys Hicks interjected. The girl sitting next to her gave her a sharp nudge. Gladys blushed and subsided.

'But in a way,' Norah spoke with growing confidence, 'in a way

I'm speaking for them all. And I want to say that it isn't right to bring girls hundreds of miles to a factory when you can't look after them properly and when you haven't got any work for them to do. It isn't fair. It's all wrong, the whole thing.' Suddenly she stood up, fierce and very erect. 'There must be something terrible the matter with this organisation, Mr Morgan.'

She stopped, suddenly frightened by the sound of her own words.

'That's a very sweeping generalisation, young lady.' They could see that he was not angered by the attack, but only Griselda noticed the way in which he had stifled a laugh behind his handkerchief before he spoke. 'Now, if you'll sit down again for two or three minutes we'll just go into the details so that I can make quite sure I've got all the facts right.'

Quickly and accurately Norah went over the story, leaving out nothing that seemed to her of importance, but trying to avoid exaggerations, taking care not to give too much weight to the grievances that were not common to them all. As she talked Dan Morgan, watching the row of girls, saw that the incidents that she described showed in their faces: the fear of loneliness, the horror of a strange place in which a moment's negligence might lead to the loss of a hand, an arm or an eye, the dread of diseases that were doubly terrifying because they as yet had no name. He listened carefully, interrupting only to confirm an occasional doubtful point.

And Norah, as she marshalled her facts, spoke fiercely, yet with restraint, as if she were cloaking some deep passion with an air of moderation, of reason. Norah, with her head erect, her voice under control, seemed at every moment about to break into violence, into some wild poetry. Norah, whose father drove a locomotive and was secretary of his trade union branch: Norah, whose mother loved her family to such a pitch that she was unable to understand that there was any world at all outside it: Norah, brought up gaily in a fighting family of brothers, in a family in which politics were considered to be the only subject worth talking about: Norah who, though she had been working for her living since a few weeks after her fourteenth birthday, had always had what she wanted and scarcely knew what it meant to struggle for anything in vain: Norah, from Camden Town, was like a flower that had suddenly burst open. Morgan listened intently, his gaze shifting from one girl to another, but resting a moment each time he came to Griselda Green, who sat at the end of the semicircle, a little aloof from the others, staring around the room with undisguised and faintly amused curiosity.

When Norah had finished there was a long silence.

'Is that all?' Morgan asked at last.

Norah gulped. 'That's all that we actually came to tell you.'

'And has anyone else got anything to add?'

They shook their heads.

He stubbed out his cigarette and addressed Griselda. 'You?'

'Me?' She looked at him with surprise. 'No, Miss McCall has told you the whole story. There's nothing to be gained by embroidering it.' There was a note of contempt in her light, clear voice which caused him to look at her again. In one sharp instant he saw every detail of her appearance: the dark head set high, the wide forehead, the grey eyes that had at first been full of mockery and were now sober. It struck him that, in her shabby overcoat with the red sweater showing at the neck, she looked as if she were wearing a disguise in which she was not yet altogether at home.

'What brought you to this factory?' he asked.

'I have to work.' The shadows curving upwards under her cheekbones deepened as she smiled.

'I mean,' she corrected herself, 'I have to earn my living.'

'Do you, indeed!'

'Indeed I do!'

'And was this the best job you could get?'

She showed no resentment at the question. 'It seemed to be the thing I was best fitted for,' she replied, withdrawing slightly.

'How very remarkable!'

The others had listened to this interchange with vague bewilderment. Now Norah leaned forward. 'Mr Morgan,' her voice was impatient, 'we don't want to waste your time. But before we go we'd like to know what you're going to do about – about all the things I mentioned.'

He sat back and lit another cigarette. The light from the ceiling shone down on his bare arms, covered with light hairs. The girls sat with their eyes lowered, watching, yet anxious not to appear to stare. They had all, since they came into the room, had a dim sense of having come to the wrong place.

'Well, young ladies,' he said at last, 'it's my duty to tell you that you had no business to come here. You've broken nearly all the rules of the factory to get into my office, and' – he looked round with a lively and encouraging grin at their crestfallen faces – 'I'll have to teach you how to break a few more if you're to get back on to your Group without getting all of us into serious trouble – '

The telephone rang, and he paused to pick up the receiver. After listening for a moment he said, 'All right, Finch, come along over.' He returned to the girls. 'You see,' he said, 'nobody's ever allowed to come and see a big shot like me without making an appointment first...'

They sniggered politely.

'But seriously,' he continued, 'if everybody who was in difficulties rushed straight over to me about them we'd be in an even worse muddle than you tell me we are.'

They looked at one another acknowledging, with some surprise, the truth of this observation.

'You know,' he told them, 'if you'd made inquiries before you came over here you'd have found out that we have an organised way of dealing with all the problems we've been talking about.'

'Trade unions?' Kitty Baldwin asked.

'All that's terribly slow!' Norah broke in.

'I know it is,' Morgan agreed. 'And it's a slow job getting a huge factory like this into running order... Sometimes we have to break the regulations, or at least we think we have to, when we're in a hurry to get a move on. But on the whole it's better to stick to the rules; and if the rules don't help us to get what we ought to be getting in the way of production and so on, well, then we can always change them. Now,' he turned to Norah, 'you want to know what I'm going to do about six or seven different problems... If I told you, and even if I succeeded in putting them all straight within the next few days, you'd still have a big bunch of new troubles by this time next week, if not sooner. And if I wrote down on a piece of paper the main things that will be worrying you next Wednesday, when the time came you'd find that I'd guessed right. I know what's wrong with this factory. I know a great many things that you haven't found out yet, and I know some things that I hope you never will find out.'

He spoke unsmilingly; but as he watched them his doubts were resolved; and they, growing aware that they were being treated not merely as individuals, but as equals, almost as friends, looked at him with a new interest, with something approaching eagerness.

'But I'm going to tell you some of the problems we've got here,' he went on. 'You probably don't know that when the war started this factory wasn't even built. It was built in a hurry. A lot of it that you haven't seen isn't finished yet. Then we had to start filling ammunition before we were really ready. Most of the people who work here have never done this sort of work before – after all, you don't fill tens of thousands of shells and bombs except when there's a war on; and then when you have to start doing it you find you haven't any experience, so you make mistakes – and it's surprising how many mistakes you can make over a simple job like filling a 25-pounder shell... We're learning all the time, and it's tough. It's tough for you, because you see that things are wrong, and you can't always see why. It's tough for those of us who are in charge, because we often do know why a thing goes wrong quite a long time before we can find out how to put it right – and sometimes when we think we've got a job running smoothly we're ordered to pack it up and start making something we don't know anything at all about. And then we have to begin all over again. Before you've been here a week you'll notice some of these things yourselves.'

The girls were sitting forward, their self-consciousness forgotten.

'You know,' he looked again at Griselda, 'we've got a hell of a lot to learn. And we can't learn it all at once. When we started up the factory, a few months ago, everyone was working a twelve-hour shift. Well, we found out that it was a mistake to try to keep people going for such long hours. We still keep the factory running twenty-four hours a day, but we've broken the hours up into three shifts instead of two. It means we have to have more workers, and as we get new people coming into the factory we have to try to get more buses – '

'Ah!' Norah murmured with sudden understanding.

'It's the same with a lot of other questions. As soon as we get one problem solved another one crops up. But we are learning. Before the war's over this is going to be one of the finest factories in the country. And,' he spoke slowly and with great emphasis, 'the sooner we succeed in getting it running efficiently, the sooner the war will be over.'

He got up and walked round the desk so that he stood right in front of them, his arms folded across his chest, his ugly face so vivid that they saw at last what he was trying to show them: a factory which was theirs as well as his, belonging to them but seen through his eyes.

'There's one more thing,' the rich, strange voice held them motionless, 'we're all in this together. It's true that in one way I'm more important than you are: but I couldn't do anything without you. I could sit here planning production all day long, and we'd still lose the war if you decided that it was more important to go to the flicks than to come to work, or if you packed up and went home because you were fed up or lonely or scared of getting dermatitis.'

'We never said we wouldn't stick it,' Kitty Baldwin reminded him.

'Of course you didn't. But a lot of people do walk out on us. And when they do we're put back just as much as when a shipload of cordite goes to the bottom of the sea or a consignment of empties gets blown to pieces in a blitz. We need people who'll stick it whatever happens, people who understand the difficulties we have to face and aren't frightened – '

'I'm not frightened,' Rose Widgery said in a small, shy voice.

'No,' he agreed, 'but you will be sometimes. We all are,' he looked down at her, smiling almost tenderly, 'but we stick it,' he said, 'and so will you.'

'Oh, yes,' she assented, 'of course I will.'

'We'll all stick it,' Kitty Baldwin repeated, 'now that we know what you're after.'

'All of you?' He scanned the row of girls.

'Yes,' they said. 'Yes. Yes.'

Norah got up, facing him squarely. 'Mr Morgan,' she spoke with a new warmth, 'as long as we know that you're doing everything you can we'll back you up. We won't walk out on you.'

'Right,' he spoke to them all, but it was still Griselda who held his attention. 'I'm going to ask you to make a definite promise to stay here for six months.'

'We'll stay for the duration – ' Kitty interrupted.

'I hope you will. But the war may go on for a long time, and I want a promise that I can be certain you'll be able to keep. Six months isn't very long, but it's long enough for a lot of things to happen to you – and to the factory – '

'We'll be here,' Norah assured him, 'we promise you that.'

It was at this exalted moment that Finch, the Factory Transportation Officer, burst into the room. He was a gangling young man who always seemed to himself to be doing the wrong thing. Now, as he saw the Assistant Superintendent surrounded by half a dozen girls, with each of whom he was solemnly shaking hands, it dawned upon Finch that he had done it again. So it was with a sense of considerable relief that he agreed to Morgan's request that he should drive the party back to the North-West Group.

When he returned Morgan had just finished signing his last batch of letters. He greeted Finch with that expression of quizzical amusement which many of his subordinates found even more exasperating than the Superintendent's fussy condescension or Gittins' probing curiosity. Respect for those in authority was not fashionable at Blimpton and even Finch, who professed a number of unconventional opinions, generally tried to conceal the admiration he felt for Dan Morgan.

'How did you like my lovelies?' Morgan asked as the younger man threw himself into a chair.

'Those girls? I couldn't make them out. They didn't speak one word – not one word.'

'That's fine.' Dan Morgan began to put away the papers in his desk. 'They're grand girls.'

'I daresay. As far as I could see they were just girls,' Finch pulled himself up jerkily. 'Look here, Morgan,' he said, 'I don't know whether you've heard that we were three buses short when the afternoon shift came on?'

'Yes. I heard.'

'Well,' Finch took a pace or two down the room, 'I shouldn't really have come to you about it. But it's the second time this month that I've been in trouble over these damn buses. Last time it was because my December order for spares was countermanded. I don't need to tell you that practically every bus we've got is on its last legs. I must keep a reserve of spares in the depot.'

'Of course you must.'

'Well, how can I make sure that when I put through an order somebody on this side doesn't cancel it?'

Morgan stubbed out his cigarette. 'How do you know the order was cancelled?' he asked.

'I found out... Don't we all have to find out for ourselves what's really going on here?'

Morgan did not reply.

'But in any case,' Finch continued after a pause, 'that wasn't the trouble today. The buses were all right – more or less. But three of the drivers didn't turn up. Would you believe it, they'd gone to their medical?'

Morgan frowned. 'What do you mean?'

'Only that they're being called up. It seems that Knowles forgot to apply for their reservation – ' Finch sat down again, with a peculiar collapsing movement of despair. 'Can you beat it?' he asked.

'Are you sure?'

'I spoke to him myself. He wouldn't see me – he said he was too busy. I suppose he was too busy to realise that he'll never get his workers into this place if can't run my buses! What can I do?'

'Are you all right for the night shift?'

'Yes. I made sure of that.'

'Then we'll see...'

'Right. Then we'll talk to Knowles – '

EIGHT

FOR SEVERAL WEEKS Gittins pursued his researches into the antecedents, life history and present position of Mr Alfred Edward Gunn, the personal representative of Lord Outrage. The results of these inquiries were largely negative. Those of Gittins' acquaintances who knew anything about Gunn lived in London and were apparently reluctant to commit their knowledge to paper – or perhaps they found Gittins' questions so oblique that they were unable to realise that they were being asked for information; and Gittins himself was unwilling to leave the factory for so much as a single day in case his absence should coincide with Gunn's second visit.

The Superintendent, too, was not merely reticent but positively mysterious about the whole affair. The shop-managers, foremen, and two or three of the workers on the Group where Gunn's fuzes were being filled were willing to talk to anyone who would listen, but their accounts were so contradictory that it was impossible to glean any sense from what they said. The fuzes were filled. It was understood that they would not be fired on the proof-range until Gunn was able to attend the trials in person. He had – this was one of the few points on which there was general agreement – declared that he would return in three or four days' time and would expect the job to be completed: that if it was not completed to his satisfaction he would report the whole matter to the Minister, who would no doubt arrange for all the senior officials of the factory to be replaced by men who were capable of understanding that a rush job was a job that had to be done in a rush.

The job was completed in record time. When, a week later, Gunn had still not returned the Superintendent ventured to telephone to the Minister's private office, only to be told by a secretary that Mr Gunn was away on important business and had left no message. Brown then tried to think about other things, for he knew that if he thought too much about Gunn he would eventually begin to talk to Gittins on the subject, and Gittins would then find out how little even the Superintendent knew.

But though, or perhaps because, Gunn's visit remained a mystery, a number of rumours began to circulate around the factory. It was said that Gunn was the illegitimate son of an Exalted Personage of unknown nationality; that he was the president of an international cartel controlling the production of poison gas; that he had won the Grand National in circumstances of extraordinary drama; that he had been a governor of the Bank of England at the age of twenty-seven; that he had spent three years in Sing-Sing and six months as the confidential adviser to the president of a South American Republic who had subsequently committed suicide. Those who repeated these stories were generally careful to cast a doubt on their authenticity. But out of them grew – at first slowly and then, as Gunn did not return, with ever increasing rapidity – a belief that he was possessed of the most absolute and unshakable authority, that anyone who had Gunn on his side could obtain anything that it was within the power of the Ministry to give.

And so people began to make their plans. At Mowbray Lodge, when members of the staff sat in the drawing room after dinner drinking coffee and wondering how to spend the evening, someone would begin to speculate on how best to be successful in making use of Gunn if and when he should ultimately appear. The myth began to expand. It became a kind of joke. Otway Dolphin, the Public Relations Officer, would invent a scene in which the managing editor of the *Dustborough Echo* and the proprietor of the *Dustshire Times* were cajoled into an undertaking to print no more rumours about the alleged 'goings on' at Blimpton. Dawson, who declared he was not very good at this sort of thing, would detail, generally at great length, changes in the organisation of four or five government departments designed to make it possible for Blimpton to work to a regular production programme that would not be subject to two or three major changes each week. Miss Hopkins, the Entertainments Officer, would develop, with the utmost simplicity and seriousness, the plans for a factory theatre which she had been working out in secret ever since she came to Blimpton, four months ago. When she had finished she would laugh and say, 'Of course, it's all quite impossible,' and would then get out her knitting. Captain Knowles and Miss Creed usually took no part in these discussions, but they succeeded in looking as if their dreams were concerned with the liquidation of most of their colleagues. On most evenings Dr Gower would gulp his coffee and rush off, sometimes dragging Ruth Aaron with him, either to the small laboratory he had contrived out of a corner of his surgery, or else to pay a surprise visit to the danger buildings. But he, too, had his moments of fantasy, and he knew exactly what he wanted.

When, as happened occasionally, non-resident members of the staff dropped in to dinner the game, which after a week or so had begun to grow stale, would be revived; Miss Hopkins would poke a little gentle fun at the wish-dreams of her younger colleagues, and then those who were so inclined would settle down in corners with the people they disliked least and would discuss the problem of what, in their opinion, was really wrong with Blimpton.

On one such evening, nearly a month after Gunn's visit to the factory, Dr MacIver, the factory's senior medical officer, had been induced by Miss Creed to stay to dinner. Dr MacIver had abandoned the practice of medicine in favour of a villa at Juan-les-Pins when he inherited a fortune shortly after the end of the last war; in September 1939 he returned to England, offered his services to the Government, and then retired to his sister's house in Dustshire until such time as it should occur to someone that he might be of use. His services were called on sooner than he had expected, mainly because the wife of Sir John Lentill, Permanent Secretary of the Ministry of Weapon Production, who was distantly related to the son-in-law of Dr MacIver's sister, happened to remark, when her husband was accompanying his first Minister on a visit to the site at Blimpton, that Dusting Hall had once been a pleasant place in which to spend a weekend. The Minister, who was bored with London in the spring of 1940, agreed that the company at Dusting was, if a little remote, at least simpler and more refreshing than that to which he was accustomed. Thus, when Blimpton was at last ready to go into operation, it was natural that Dr MacIver should be offered the post of Senior Medical Officer.

He soon, however, found that he had lost what aptitude for the practice of medicine he might once have possessed, and since Dr

Gower, his chief assistant, was both capable and hard-working, MacIver thought it best to give the younger man a free hand, and nowadays he himself seldom came to the factory. Since he had refused to accept a salary, and since, also, he enjoyed the prestige which his position gave him in the eyes of his friends, he did not feel it necessary to offer his resignation, but tried to use his influence with the Ministry to get the equipment and additional staff for which Gower was perpetually clamouring. If Gower thought himself entitled to the rank normally attached to the duties he performed he did not say so, and since most people liked MacIver and hoped to be able to make use of him the arrangement was generally popular, except among the junior medical officers, who considered themselves to be overworked.

This evening Miss Hopkins was trying to interest MacIver in her plans for a factory theatre. 'You see,' she argued, putting down her knitting to emphasise the point, 'people here hardly ever get any *fun* – '

'They have the canteen concerts,' Miss Creed objected, 'and ENSA – ' She looked as if the very notion of fun were somehow indecent.

Morgan, sipping coffee, leaned over to Ruth Aaron and asked in a low voice: 'Do you have fun at Blimpton?'

She put down her cup, startled. 'What a queer thing to ask!'

'But do you?' He offered her a cigarette, staring into her dark eyes over the flame from his lighter. Her face was cold beneath the plaited coronet of hair, her eyes brooding and remote.

'How can one?' she asked sombrely.

At that he laughed. 'What a child you are!'

'Of course,' MacIver was saying, 'I agree that the workers must have some relaxation. But we're doing so much already... why, someone was telling me the other day – '

He broke off as the door burst open and a maid rushed into the room. 'It's Mr Gunn,' she stumbled, 'he says he wants to see the person in charge – '

'That's the idea,' a voice behind her said, and Gunn entered, pressing half-a-crown on the girl with one hand and pushing her out of the room with the other.

Alfred Edward Gunn was the sort of young man who would have looked inconspicuous in an identity parade designed to assist in the recognition of an unsuccessful housebreaker. He was of about the middle height, of slim build and fair colouring. Above his beetling forehead his mousy fair hair stood up like stubble in a newly-harvested cornfield. He had narrow eyes which saw everything and, beneath the flattened nose of the professional prize-fighter, the wide mouth of a forceful and habitual talker.

Now, as he stood in the doorway surveying the assembled company, it struck Dan Morgan that Gunn looked more than anything like a bodyguard. Nor was this surprising since Gunn had originally engaged himself to Lord Outrage in that capacity: not that he had ever intended to confine himself to guarding his lordship's person, nor, indeed, had that ever been really necessary. Lord Outrage was as well able to take care of himself as any other peer of the realm who had started life as messenger to a street-corner book-maker and had advanced by the usual methods to the doorstep of the War Cabinet. But Outrage, who prided himself on his originality and on his contempt for those who followed the traditional patterns of social behaviour, was at heart a very conventional man; so when, in the early nineteen-twenties, he found himself obliged to spend a good deal of time in Chicago, he followed the custom of the other members of the circle in which he moved and hired himself a bodyguard. Alf, or Ed as he sometimes preferred to be called, was at that time too young to be more than an inconspicuous hanger-on, but when Lord Outrage returned to England to reorganise the advertising industry and to become the chairman of a bank and the vice-chairman of a railway company, Alf was the only member of the bodyguard whose services were retained.

Since then he had struck out on his own. His first successful venture had been a chain of amusement parlours; later he began to make his own slot-machines and it was this that had chiefly qualified him for his entry into the field of weapon production. But he was perpetually jumping about from one thing to another, making money and losing it, but always making more than he lost, so that although he experienced severe financial crises from time to time, he was able to surround himself with a constantly increasing splendour.

Tonight, finding himself some fifty miles away in a hotel full of unpleasantly familiar faces, he had decided to drive over to Blimpton to see what was going on, and to find out what was what. As he looked round the room a certain bewilderment showed in his face.

But none of his audience could have any doubt that this was indeed Oerlikon Alf. The descriptions that they had heard from Colonel Jervis and from people in the factory suddenly fell together as they stood about in a contused circle, each waiting for everyone else to come forward.

Morgan left Ruth Aaron and prepared to take the situation in hand. 'I'm afraid the Superintendent isn't here,' he said. 'Would you like someone to ring and ask him to come over?'

'No. Matter of fact, I came here because I wanted to meet the bunch.'

Miss Hopkins sat down. The other women followed her example.

'Well, here we are,' Morgan said pleasantly, 'or some of us, at any rate.' He introduced the party one by one. Gunn looked more dazed than ever by the time he had finished shaking hands.

'Have you had dinner?' Miss Creed asked. 'Can we offer you something? Coffee?'

'No. I'd like a glass of water.' Gunn glanced at his watch. 'I haven't much time to waste and I want to talk to you people.' He sat down beside Miss Hopkins. 'I understand you've got quite a packet of trouble in this factory.'

'Quite a packet,' Morgan agreed. There was an unusual note of formality in his voice.

'Then let's have it,' Gunn looked round at his audience. The ten or eleven people present, each of whom was aware of many private and public grievances and most of whom had some simple and frequently announced scheme for putting Blimpton on what they called its feet, seemed suddenly to be drowning in their own reticence.

'I think it would probably be more satisfactory if you would discuss the factory's problems with the Superintendent or the Principal Clerk,' Morgan suggested frigidly.

'I've done that. And I shall do it again. But it's you folks here I want to talk to now. You handle the detail, and that's what I want to get down to. We can't get the set-up on to a proper basis until we've got all the small things straightened out.'

'How true that is!' Miss Hopkins spoke with her usual mild enthusiasm. 'But there are so many small things that we are concerned about here, things that wouldn't strike you as being of the very least importance.'

'Well, let's get down to them.'

'First,' Morgan had taken a moment or two to collect his thoughts, but now he was ready, 'first, we're short of components.'

Gunn pulled a notebook and a gold pencil from an inside pocket. 'What sort of components?' he asked.

'At the moment,' Morgan explained, 'certain natures of shell, of gaines, of twenty-millimetre cartridge cases, of two or three explosives – '

'Hold on a second.' Gunn was scribbling into a notebook. He appeared to write with some difficulty.

'But I should explain,' Morgan went on, relaxing a little, 'that the shortages vary from week to week, sometimes from day to day. Dawson will be able to give you a chart showing the main bottlenecks on that side over the past three months. Then, of course, we're short of labour.'

'What kind of labour?'

'Every grade, almost. Naturally the worst difficulty is in getting unskilled women.'

'How many do you need?'

'About fourteen thousand, I estimate.'

Gunn put his notebook down. 'Would you repeat that figure?' he asked.

'About fourteen thousand. Of course we don't need them all at once. But we ought to be taking on about five hundred each week.'

'How many do you get?'

'Fifty to a hundred. Sometimes more.'

'We had a hundred and seventeen last week,' Miss Creed leaned forward and spoke in a manner designed to indicate that she, and she alone, was qualified to speak on the problem of the recruitment of women workers. 'That's as many as we can handle. We haven't the organisation to deal with an intake of five hundred a week. But,' she added, 'we could do it if we were allowed to increase the staff of the factory Labour Office.'

'But it's no good increasing the staff in the Labour Office if you can't get the labour for them to take on… isn't that right?'

Otway Dolphin strolled over to the fireplace, displaying well-tailored trousers. Those who knew him best recognised the curl of malice in his smile. 'In any case,' he pointed out, purring slightly, 'I'm sure Miss Creed would be the first to agree that it's utterly useless to recruit women who won't stay in the factory for more than ten minutes or so… I mean, it's a waste of everybody's time.'

'Who won't stay in the factory?' Gunn asked. His eyes, too, were beginning to gleam.

'Oh, the vast majority, if you take my meaning. They come and they go.' Dolphin paused to fidget daintily with his flowing silk tie. 'I estimate that most of the women we recruit don't last more than two months on the average. Some stay longer, but some just take one look and – ' he waved a hand airily, 'home they go… I'm sure Captain Knowles will confirm what I say.'

Everyone turned, waiting for Knowles. He was thin, awkwardly made, with a purple face and a moustache which was inclined to straggle at the wrong moments. 'Of course it's true in a way, he admitted in rather a loftier tone than he had intended. 'It's true statistically, I suppose, but it gives quite a false impression of the actual facts.'

Gunn shook his head, as if in denial of some inner thought. 'I don't understand this,' he said, 'either the women stay or they don't. Which is it?'

'Some stay,' Morgan told him, 'but the figures Dolphin has given you are near enough. Blimpton isn't a place that people like to come to.'

'What's the reason?'

'It's dangerous work, you know,' Dr MacIver said mildly.

'Oh, no, it isn't,' Morgan contradicted, 'we've a much lower accident rate than the average engineering factory.'

Nicholls, the senior chemist, advanced from the other end of the room. 'The work is incredibly monotonous,' he remarked, as if that were the beginning and end of the matter.

'But most girls like monotonous work,' someone reminded him.

'It isn't the work,' Otway Dolphin agreed, 'it's the conditions. You've only got to take a walk round the factory to see why the workers won't stay.'

Miss Creed had been sitting back, fingering the row of beads that dangled to her waist. 'As the Senior Woman Labour Manager,' she said now, 'I think I may claim to have more knowledge of this problem than those who are only casually concerned with the handling of female labour.' She looked at Gunn for confirmation and he, staring back at her large white face, nodded to her to continue. 'The real problem,' she spoke as if she were divesting herself of all responsibility, 'is not so much the conditions inside the factory as the difficulty in finding proper living accommodation in Dustborough. My staff have to spend far too much of their time inspecting billets – '

'But I thought you had a hostel?' Gunn asked.

'It's going up,' Dawson explained, 'but it isn't finished yet.'

Gunn consulted an entry in his notebook. 'They told me it would be ready for occupation on the first of February,' his voice took on an accusing note, 'that's two weeks ago. Why isn't it finished?'

Morgan shrugged his shoulders. 'Unfortunately, we don't control the building contractors – or the weather.'

'Well, who does?'

'The Ministry controls the contractors. I'm afraid they can't be held answerable for the weather.'

'No, you're right about that,' Gunn made another entry into his notebook. 'How long would you say it'll take to get the place finished?'

'They tell us another month,' Morgan replied, 'though I shall be surprised if we're able to put people into it before the end of May. There's a tremendous amount to be done.'

'And when it's ready you'll be all right for labour?'

'Oh, yes,' Miss Creed assented gushingly, 'if only the hostel were finished everything would be splendid.'

'You agree?' Gunn turned to Morgan.

'I think that's putting it a bit high,' Morgan told him, 'but it would help.'

'It would be of invaluable assistance,' Knowles rushed to support Miss Creed.

'And first-class publicity,' Dolphin, who usually disagreed with everything the labour officers said, could not refrain from adding.

Gunn stood up. 'Where is this place?' he asked.

'On the road to Addle Hinton. About three miles away.'

'Come on, then. Let's get going. Where did that girl put my overcoat?'

Most of them got up, too, startled to follow very clearly what was happening. 'If you don't mind,' Dr MacIver, who was stretched out comfortably in an armchair, excused himself, 'there are one or two things I must talk over with Gower... but if you'd like to take my car you'll find the chauffeur in the kitchen with Mrs Plum.'

The February night was streaked with fog as half a dozen of them set out. The air raid warning had sounded several hours earlier, and the rays of distant searchlights shot up against the pale full moon. Miss Creed, Knowles and Morgan had squeezed themselves into Gunn's powerful two-seater. Otway Dolphin and Ruth Aaron shared Dr MacIver's limousine.

'There wasn't any need for you to come,' Dolphin told Ruth as he settled a rug over her knees. 'I can't think why I let them drag me along.'

'Can't you?' Ruth's voice expressed an entire lack of interest.

'Oh, I suppose it's just my damned inquisitiveness. I can't bear to be left out of anything, can you?'

Ruth did not reply. It seemed to her that she was always left out of everything. No one had asked her to come on this expedition, and she had joined the party not because she wanted to impress Gunn with her alertness, intelligence and enthusiasm (in all of which qualities she felt herself to be singularly lacking) but because she knew that if she had remained at Mowbray Lodge she would have been expected to join MacIver and Gower in a discussion on the best methods of preventing industrial dermatitis, TNT poisoning, influenza, tuberculosis and various other diseases. The two men, left to themselves, would discourse amiably enough, since MacIver was, at least in private, always ready to admit his ignorance of whatever branch of medicine happened to be under discussion, and Gower, whose knowledge of the health problems of the factory was both profound and detailed, liked nothing better than to harangue an appreciative audience. With Ruth there, the conversation would inevitably have turned to the subject of the research in which she was supposed, in such leisure as she had, to be assisting Dr Gower: and Gower would certainly have discovered how much she had left undone in the past few weeks.

But now, in her attempt to escape one trouble, she had run straight into another. She did not know Dolphin well, but she knew, as no one could help knowing, that he was, after Gittins, Blimpton's keenest and most malicious gossip. Miss Hopkins had warned her that any scrap of information which was given to Dolphin was apt to become inflated, distorted and generally made-over, then handed back to the original informer in some unrecognisable but explosive shape that was calculated to do as much damage as possible. So Ruth decided that, even at the risk of offending her companion, it was better not to talk at all. She was perpetually haunted by the fear first of doing, and then of having done, the wrong thing. She had not wanted to become a doctor, and had adopted the career only because her elder brother, who should have carried on the family tradition, had been killed in a mountaineering accident when she was still a schoolgirl. She had not wanted to leave her parents or to live independently; and, above all, she had not wanted to come to Blimpton, to face the pressure of a strange life among people who regarded her as a foreigner, almost as an enemy. She dreaded the mockery of the workers; their easy jokes, their sudden inexplicable laughter, even the way in which the older women addressed her as 'dear', seemed to her to express a contempt for her youth and for her Jewish origin. The indifference of her colleagues was hardly less unbearable. Apart from Miss Hopkins, she had no friends; and Miss Hopkins lavished her kindliness with such complete impartiality as to make it, at least to Ruth, almost valueless.

Dolphin, piqued by her silence, broke off in the middle of a sentence and appeared to be intent on studying the shifting patterns of brightness in the sky.

When they reached the hostel site they found Gunn's car parked just inside the gate. Gunn, Morgan and the two labour officers were nowhere to be seen.

'They can't have gone far,' Dolphin remarked as he put out a hand to help Ruth out of the car.

The hostel, which was designed to accommodate a thousand workers, seemed to cover an enormous area. In the pale, blueish green light the shapes of the huts stood out sharply against the sky.

'It looks exactly like the factory,' Ruth remarked, shivering a little.

'Except that they've left the trees standing,' Dolphin observed. He pointed out a silhouetted avenue of elms, and then gave a yell as he stepped into a deep pool of water.

The others, hearing the noise, called out from the doorway of one of the dormitory blocks, and in a moment the two parties had joined up. Only Morgan had remembered to bring a torch, so that although the night was exceptionally bright, it was impossible to see more than an occasional glimpse of the interior of the buildings. They tramped from hut to hut, each block identical with its neighbour, peering into half-finished cubicles and into bathrooms that as yet contained no baths. Gunn said very little; Miss Creed, sticking firmly to his right-hand side, kept up a flow of informative comment, interspersed with criticisms of the architects, the building contractors and the Ministry's resident engineer; when she paused Captain Knowles took the opportunity to divulge several of the more shining episodes of his earlier life.

'Of course,' he was saying as they made their way across a wide expanse of mud to the central block where the kitchen, canteens and recreation rooms were situated, 'of course things at Blimpton are particularly difficult for those of us who come from industry. It's not as if we were civil servants.'

'I can imagine that!' Gunn agreed shortly. He seemed not to be listening.

'Your typical civil servant – ' Knowles was about to continue when Gunn turned round to call: 'Morgan!'

Morgan took a step forward.

'Why didn't we call the clerk of the works to come over?'

'He means the resident engineer,' Miss Creed translated.

'He's waiting for us in the kitchen,' Morgan replied.

For the first time that evening something approaching a smile appeared on Gunn's face. 'Not bad, eh?' he remarked to himself, and began to walk more quickly.

Morgan had chosen the rendezvous well. The huge kitchen, already complete but empty of any equipment, was lighted by a continuous window that ran, high up under the steel rafters, the whole length of one wall. The moonlight streaked in, lighting up the whole room, and revealing the dim figure of the engineer who stood waiting in a corner.

'All right,' Gunn turned to the rest of the party, 'I think I'll talk to him alone. Meet you at the gates in ten minutes.'

Slowly the others made their way out.

'I wonder what he's up to now,' Dolphin murmured to Ruth in a low voice. He had already forgotten that she had offended him.

Miss Creed, walking beside Knowles a yard or so in front, turned round.

'I think Mr Gunn is going to be a tremendous help to the factory.' She spoke with chilly superiority.

'You don't mean that he's intending to stay here permanently?' Dolphin asked, trying to conceal his alarm.

'He didn't say so,' Miss Creed replied, 'but he has a lot of influence, as the personal representative of Lord Outrage.'

'Whatever that means,' Morgan, on Ruth's other side, commented drily.

'He's already promised to get us some additional staff for the Labour Office.' Miss Creed had meant to keep this piece of news as a secret between herself and Captain Knowles at least until the new appointments had been approved by the Establishments Division of the Ministry; but the triumph of being the first person to derive a positive benefit from Gunn's visit seemed to her so overwhelming that she forgot the need for discretion.

'I wonder what Gitty will say to that?' Dolphin speculated.

Miss Creed ignored this taunt. Of all the internecine wars that she and Captain Knowles conducted within the factory, that with Gittins was by far the most bitter.

'How fortunate we have been to escape the blitz,' Captain Knowles made a feeble attempt to change the conversation as a rumble of gun-fire echoed in the distance.

'We'll be lucky if we escape it much longer,' Morgan assented. 'I think I'd better get back to the factory, just in case.' He glanced at Ruth. 'And you'd better come with me,' he suggested. 'If they should happen to drop anything you may be needed.'

He led her off.

'Do you really think we'll get a raid?' Ruth asked as she picked her way along the muddy path.

'How should I know?' Morgan put out a hand to help her over a puddle. His overcoat was pulled up about his ears, his hat drawn low over his face. 'But this party has gone on long enough. Besides, I want to talk to you.'

'Oh!'

He steered her towards the centre of the road where the mud was firmer.

'Now,' he asked, tucking an arm under hers, 'tell me: what's the matter?'

'Nothing,' she peered up at him, unable to see his face. 'I – I don't even know what you mean.'

'You don't, eh?'

'No,' she released her arm, 'I don't.'

'Right,' now he was smiling, a Cheshire cat grin. 'I'll start all over again. How long have you been in this factory? Three months?'

'Four.'

'And you still hate it.'

'I – ' she hesitated, face downcast, 'I didn't say that I hated it.'

'But you do.' It was a statement, not a question.

'I don't know why you should say that.'

'Listen.' Suddenly he stopped dead, turning to face her, speaking with extraordinary earnestness. 'I don't know anything about you, but I rather like you: and I think you're being silly. You've been here long enough to know that we're doing one of the most important jobs in the whole of this war... perhaps not the most important, but one that comes pretty high up... and you – you've been wandering round for three or four months like a child at a party waiting for someone to come and fetch it home – ' he broke off. 'Haven't you?' he asked after a moment in a more ordinary tone.

She nodded, trying to force back tears.

'Why?' He was standing very close to her now.

From behind a tree a voice shouted: 'Mr Morgan!'

They looked up to see Dr MacIver's chauffeur approaching. 'The Superintendent came about ten minutes ago, he told them, 'and Mr Gittins arrived just now. They said they were going to meet you.'

'Oh,' Morgan's face was expressionless, 'did they leave any message?'

'The Superintendent said if you missed him would Mr Gunn please go along to his house. Mr Gittins didn't say nothing.'

As they settled into Dr MacIver's car Morgan leaned forward to make sure that the glass partition behind the driver's seat was firmly closed. Then he laughed.

'What's funny?' Ruth asked.

'Oh, just the Superintendent superintending... What were we talking about?'

'About me,' she replied, trying to conceal her embarrassment.

'Oh, yes.' He was slumped back against the cushions and seemed to have lost interest. 'I want you to tell me all about yourself sometime. Will you do that?'

She flushed in the darkness. 'Yes,' she murmured. 'I'd like to.' And then she noticed that his eyes were closed, as if he were already asleep. He looked heavy, clumsy, almost, she thought, loutish; but his hands, resting on his knees, were sensitive as well as strong, and his face in repose had an astonishing serenity. When the car, after ten minutes or so, turned on to the main road he sat up suddenly and tapped on the glass. 'Put me down at the factory,' he told the chauffeur, and then glanced at Ruth. 'Not asleep?'

'No.' She found herself smiling. 'But you were.'

'Was I?' His manner was remote, abstracted. 'I've got rather a lot on my mind just now… but we'll – ' The car stopped and he did not finish the sentence. 'Good night!' For a moment he took her hand, and then he was gone.

NINE

WHEN MA VENNING took Kitty Baldwin home to inhabit one of her spare rooms, she suggested that Rose Widgery should move into the other. But Rose, who was neither happy nor comfortable in her billet in Grape Street, refused to move; and, though she cried herself to sleep every time she went to bed, she stuck to her resolution.

Grape Street was like nearly every other street in the older part of Dustborough. The narrow black houses differed from one another only in the stage of dilapidation they had reached. Some still had lace curtains at the two windows that faced the street, paint of a recognisable colour at the front door, and steps that were whitened every morning. Number 78 was not one of these. Mrs Arklow, Rose's landlady, was too busily occupied in dealing with the problems created by her husband and six children to be able to take more than an occasional interest in the face that she and her house presented to the world. She was perhaps not more than averagely incompetent, but the natural tendency to blame what she vaguely called Life, rather than herself, for her misfortunes had, with the years, developed to a point at which she was almost incapable of accepting any responsibility for anything.

Thus it came about that Rose, before she had been in the house more than a few hours, found herself putting the younger children to bed, getting Mr Arklow's supper, and cutting sandwiches for him to take to work the next day. Mr Arklow worked at Blimpton, too, but since he was employed on the maintenance staff and his hours were longer than those worked by the factory operatives, Rose did not usually travel at the same time as he did.

Her life outside the factory was, however, almost entirely taken up with looking after the Arklow family. On Saturday afternoons Kitty Baldwin and Griselda Green, who had eventually moved to the Vennings' house, would try to persuade her to go to the cinema with them or, if the weather were fine, to take a walk into the country. Usually she said she hadn't time, and sometimes she would pretend, without actually saying so, that she was going out with someone else. In fact, she spent her leisure in cleaning, washing, mending and cooking, and Mrs Arklow soon got into the habit of leaving all the more difficult and tiring jobs for her to do. Rose was quick and neat, for her aunt, who had brought her up, had sent her into domestic service when she left school, and she had received a good training. Nevertheless, she knew that it was impossible ever to get the dirty little house, with its only water-tap in the back yard, and with all its rooms perpetually crowded with children, into any sort of order; and she would have given up after the first week had she not found it impossible to tolerate the state of affairs that she found when she first arrived. She stayed on, and as she came to realise how badly the Arklows needed not only her help but also the twenty-five shillings that she paid each week for her board and lodging, she began to be afraid that she would have to stay with them until the war was over.

Nobody at Blimpton knew how hard she was working, and only Griselda saw how much she had changed in her first month at the factory. Several out of the party of girls who had visited Morgan had, a few days later, been shifted on to other work. Norah had been sent for by the foreman, and had been told, to her own intense bewilderment, that she had been selected to go to the training school for assistant forewomen. She was sure that there had been a mistake, and that the labour officers had somehow or other confused her with Griselda; but the foreman only laughed at her, and told her to thank her stars that she was to have six weeks' proper training and, if she passed her examinations, a job with real money at the end of it. Kitty Baldwin and Doris Chandler remained with Ma, but Griselda and Rose were transferred to the South-East Group, where they were employed in filling shells.

The job was easy to learn, and not particularly tiring to perform. Often there were long intervals in which the workers were held up, either because some of their number were absent or because people in another part of the factory had fallen behind with their part of the job. In these pauses the girls sat around and gossiped and told stories, or stole off in ones and twos to look for their boyfriends or to get a quiet cup of tea in the canteen. Sometimes they worked hard, and when things were going well they would sing for an hour or two at a time. On the night-shift, particularly, the over-looker would often start up a song, and girls who had not slept properly during the day would rouse themselves and join in. But as a rule the work proceeded at a slow, monotonous pace, a pace made necessary, so Rose and Griselda were told, by the need to avoid any risk of accident.

It was difficult to believe that the work was dangerous. Rose and Griselda soon became accustomed to handling TNT, to breaking up the dry biscuit, or to helping to pour the thick, treacly liquid into the empty shells. Both jobs, though simple enough, were messy, and Rose, after cleaning up the house in Grape Street, often felt that she could not stand the shop in which she worked, with its odd smell and dusty atmosphere. After a fortnight the white magazine uniform began to look crumpled and dirty, and the front of the trousers bore a nasty smear where the man she had been working beside had spilt some of the melted TNT when he was chatting to her, instead of looking at what he was doing. Mrs Baker, the over-looker, promised to speak to the assistant forewoman about getting both girls a spare set of overalls; but the other girls in the shop laughed unkindly behind Mrs Baker's back, and said people were lucky if they got a clean set once in six months. Griselda looked up the book of rules that had been issued to them on the day they were taken on at the factory, and found a regulation which stated that all Danger Building clothing must be washed at least once every six months, and more often if cleanliness required it. Mrs Baker was discouraging. She pointed out, quite truly, that those workers who had been in the factory long enough to have had their uniforms washed found, when their clothes were returned to them, that they had shrunk so much that it was almost impossible to wear them with any degree of comfort.

In any case, most people were unwilling to complain. This was not because they were afraid of their superiors or anxious not to cause unnecessary trouble, but because it was too much bother. They grumbled good-naturedly about the work and about the long journeys, for many of them came from villages on the other side of Dustborough and spent four hours each day in getting to work and in getting home again; they grumbled about the food in the canteens, about the lack of soap and towels in the ablution rooms, and about the pilfering that went on in the shifting-house. Sometimes, when they had spent half a shift developing some particular grievance, somebody would say that something ought to be done about it; but they never did anything. When things seemed to them, as they occasionally did, to be almost unbearable they would all, by a sort of tacit agreement, stay away from work the next day. Those who were married often took a day or two off to do the family wash or to catch up with their arrears of housework; the younger girls stayed away whenever they had something better to do than to come to work, which was often; and many, both men and women, entirely gave up trying to get to work during the snowy weather.

Rose, however, could not afford to stay away. She had come to Blimpton because she had been told that high wages were to be earned in munitions factories, and her aunt needed all the help that Rose could give. She had promised to send home ten shillings each week, and had secretly hoped that she would after a short time be able to send very much more. But since there was no piece-work at the factory and since, too, the Arklows were always borrowing small sums which they forgot to repay, and for which Rose did not like to ask, she found that she simply could not afford to take a day off.

All the same, she used to tell herself, if it hadn't been for Griselda she would have had to give up. Rose suspected that the older girl belonged to what the people at home in Devonshire called the gentry, but Griselda never talked about her family or her past life, and Rose was too gentle and incurious to ask questions. There was no intimacy between them, but they used to look forward to meeting every day on the bus, and they generally went to the canteen together, though Griselda, who was sometimes very gay and amusing, soon began to get to know many of the other workers on the Group; but she was never so caught up by other people as to forget Rose altogether, and always after the mid-shift break she would ask what Rose had had to eat. Rose would answer evasively at first, and then would, as often as not, admit that she had had nothing but a cup of tea.

'But you must eat,' Griselda would tell her repeatedly.

'I know,' Rose would agree, 'but I'm not hungry. Really I'm not.'

Then after a few weeks, Griselda began to suspect that Rose

was ill. Rose insisted that she would be all right as soon as she became used to the work, and the other girls in the shop would assure Griselda that there was nothing to worry about. Most of them suffered from minor ailments of one kind or another, and complaints about digestive troubles were made fairly frequently by at least half the girls in the shop.

'It's the work,' Mrs Baker explained to Griselda on one occasion when Rose was looking more than usually pale, 'it's just how it gets you. Must be something in the TNT makes people feel funny.'

'That's right,' Mrs Ford, one of the older workers, agreed, 'it never hurt me. Touch wood. But some people can't stick it at all. I suppose it all depends on your stomach – '

A small crowd began to gather.

'Do you remember that girl over in 39?' somebody asked.

'Do I not!' another exclaimed. 'You mean the one that had – ?' Whispered reminiscences ran like shudders across the room.

Nellie Dimmock, a quiet sallow girl who usually said very little, drifted up to Rose.

'Don't let them scare you,' she warned her in a low voice. 'It's nothing to get all worked up about. Why, look at me!'

Rose looked at her, puzzled by her tone.

'Don't you see,' the girl lowered her voice still further, 'I've got blue round my mouth the last few days – '

'Why!' Rose looked again and saw the faint blue tinge of the skin. 'What is it?' she asked, suddenly frightened, 'why don't you go down to the surgery?'

Nellie smiled, a bitter unhappy smile. 'That's nothing,' she said, 'my dad's had it. A lot of people on this side get it. You get over it all right if you're careful.'

'But you ought to go to the doctor,' Rose persisted.

'You bet!' Nellie led her off to a corner. 'If the doctor found me with this on my face I'd be taken off contact before I had time to turn round. And lose my danger money!' she began to move back towards the centre of the room. 'I wouldn't mind if I could afford it,' she admitted, 'but if I didn't get my danger money I'd never have a penny to call my own.'

As she finished speaking a worker from a neighbouring shop rushed in. 'Mrs Baker!' she called, 'I was to tell you that the doctor's on her rounds.'

'Where?' Mrs Baker began to rub her hands nervously on her uniform.

'Just come through the shifting-house. She'll be along any moment now.' The messenger hurried out to carry the warning to neighbouring shops.

Nellie seized Rose by the wrist. 'Come on!' she urged her, 'you don't want to get taken off contact, do you?'

Rose, not quite understanding what was happening, but sensing that several shillings a week of her pay were somehow in danger, allowed herself to be led into hiding.

A few minutes later Ruth Aaron came into the shop, accompanied by one of the assistant labour officers.

Usually Ruth disliked these routine visits to the Danger Buildings. The foremen and over-lookers treated her with a respect in which she always seemed to detect a touch of patronage. The operatives, and especially the younger girls, generally looked as if they were going to burst into laughter as soon as she was out of earshot. She felt that they regarded her as a foreigner, as a person who had no right to interfere with their habits, to reprimand them for allowing their hands to become stained with explosive or for failing to observe the rules laid down for their protection. She was so wrapped in her own fears that she could not guess that to many of these men and women there was something almost terrifying in the frigid air of authority with which she tried to arm herself against her own nervousness.

But today Ruth was almost happy. In the morning, coming down early to breakfast, she had found Dan Morgan alone in the dining room.

'Come and join me,' he had commanded her, looking up from his newspaper.

She had hesitated, afraid to break the rules of precedence which determined the seating arrangements of the residents of Mowbray Lodge.

'Come on,' he had insisted, without getting up.

She had obeyed. This was the first time that she had seen Morgan alone since their visit to the hostel a week earlier; and now, as soon as her porridge had been put before her, Morgan had suggested that they should drive into Dustborough that evening, have dinner at the White Lion, and go to the cinema.

She had flushed with pleasure, too surprised to speak. Her social life at Blimpton had hitherto been confined to an occasional evening at the Gittins', and one rather formal dinner party given by Dr MacIver's sister.

'Don't blush,' Morgan had said, speaking almost roughly.

'I'm not blushing,' she had insisted.

'Very well, you're not blushing. I'll have my car outside at six-thirty.'

Then he had got up abruptly, and left her to finish her breakfast alone.

Now it was nearly five o'clock, and she knew that she would have to hurry if she was to finish the number of visits that Dr Gower had allotted to her, and get back and change into fresh clothes for the evening.

Mrs Baker had mustered the workers into a row, and they filed slowly past, each pausing long enough for Ruth to look at their hands, and to examine their faces for signs of poisoning. Though the hands of most of the workers were stained a deep yellow and their faces, too, had often a sallow tinge, Ruth found none with symptoms which suggested that dust from the explosive was having any serious effect on their health. But, when she had finished, she warned them briefly of the need for cleanliness in their work and in their personal habits. 'I'm sure,' she addressed them nervously, 'that you've been told that you must wash thoroughly before you go to the canteen, as well as before you leave the Group.'

The operatives gave a little murmur of compliance. They knew better than anyone that it took a long time to wash off the stains, and that those who washed most thoroughly usually got only the left-overs when they arrived in the canteen, and, if they stopped to wash again on leaving the shift, often missed the bus that took them on the first stage of their journey home. Nobody thought it worthwhile to mention these facts.

Mrs Baker stepped forward. 'Will that be all?' she asked.

'Yes,' Ruth turned to Miss Elliston, the labour officer, for confirmation, 'I think that's all. Are you sure I've seen everyone?'

Miss Elliston consulted a list. 'There should be fourteen,' she counted, 'and you've only seen ten,' she turned to Mrs Baker, 'are the others away today?'

Mrs Baker gulped and nodded.

'Very well,' Ruth turned to go, 'I'll see them next time.' She stood waiting irresolutely while Miss Elliston consulted with Mrs Baker about the names of the absentees.

And then Griselda spoke in a loud clear voice. 'There are only two people away,' she said. 'The other two were here a few minutes ago.'

'Then where are they?' Ruth asked.

'They just went out,' Mrs Baker looked round as if she expected them to return at any moment but managed, at the same time, to cast a malignant look towards Griselda, 'I mean,' her manner was apologetic, 'they have to go out sometimes, like. It just happened they went a few minutes ago.'

'Oh well,' Ruth shrugged her shoulders, 'I'll have to look at them next time I come round.'

By this time she was at the door; Griselda, who had been edging her way forward, was now only a yard or so away. 'Dr Aaron?' she said.

'Well?' Ruth spoke impatiently. She was in a hurry, and, besides, there was something in the girl's manner that woke in her a whole host of slumbering memories and of fears that she had, in the last few hours, forgotten.

'I think you ought to see those two girls,' Griselda spoke almost as if she were issuing an instruction.

'*You* think so!' Mrs Baker broke in. 'You leave this to me, young lady! I'll have you know I'm in charge of this shop.'

Griselda ignored the interruption. 'One of them is ill,' she continued, 'and I think it may be something serious.'

'Then why hasn't she been up to the surgery?' Ruth demanded;

she addressed Mrs Baker, 'Send her up to the nurse as soon as she comes back. I'll look at her before I leave the Group.'

'She'll refuse to go,' Griselda insisted flatly.

'Why?'

'Because she can't afford to be ill,' as Griselda looked at Ruth a sudden hostility seemed to rush up between them, 'and she's determined to keep on working… I think she's hiding.'

'Hiding?' Miss Elliston repeated.

'Of course she's not,' Mrs Baker lied uneasily. Miss Elliston had not been on the Group very long, but she had met people like Mrs Baker in other parts of the factory.

'Where is this girl hiding?' she demanded sharply.

'I never said they were hiding,' the over-looker was lost now, afraid either to affirm or deny. 'The two of them just went out for a minute, kind of. I wouldn't let my girls hide. They wouldn't dare.' Again she glowered at Griselda.

Freda Elliston looked at Ruth, waiting for her to give some lead. Ruth glanced at her watch. She knew that she would now have to stay until the two girls returned. She turned to Mrs Baker. 'Get them,' she commanded.

'I'll send someone down to the ablution room,' Mrs Baker offered.

'I think you'd better go yourself,' Freda Elliston told her, 'and be quick. Dr Aaron is in a hurry.'

Mrs Baker, looking deeply offended, bustled out. She knew that if this incident was reported to the foreman she would be reprimanded and would probably be reduced to the rank of an ordinary operative. The prospect filled her with a deep sense of injustice, for the practice of hiding sick workers from the medical officers was well established, and well known to almost everyone in the factory except the doctors themselves.

In a much shorter time than it took to walk to the ablution room Mrs Baker returned, with Rose on one side and Nellie Dimmock on the other. The two girls had been hiding in the nearest air raid shelter, and now they were shaking with cold and fright.

Ruth looked at Nellie Dimmock first. 'How long have you been like this?' she asked, noting the symptoms of poisoning.

The girl began to cry. 'It only came on yesterday,' she said.

'Well, it's lucky that we've caught you,' Ruth spoke with unusual briskness. 'We'll have you taken off contact immediately. And,' she looked at the girl, her face very stern, 'you must never go away and hide when you're feeling ill. If you'd let this go for another couple of days it might have cost you a month in hospital. Come and see me in the surgery tomorrow; and now Miss Elliston will tell you what to do about changing to another shop.' Ruth turned to Rose, and Rose, shame-faced, very pale, and embarrassed beyond words, held out her hands for the routine examination.

'Come here,' Ruth told her, pulled out a thermometer and proceeded to take the girl's temperature and pulse. Then she spoke to Miss Elliston in a low voice, and the labour officer hurried out, to return a minute or so later.

'Are they coming?' Ruth asked.

Freda Elliston nodded. A nurse came in with an armful of blankets.

'But I'm not ill,' Rose protested apprehensively as the nurse began to wrap the blankets around her. Her cap had fallen off, and her fair hair fell loose and soft around her face.

'Yes you are, dear,' the nurse spoke in the peculiar tone which is commonly reserved for dealing with the very sick.

'You're a very stupid girl,' Ruth told her crossly, 'you should have come to see me weeks ago. Now we'll have to take you over to Dr Gower's surgery to find out what's the matter with you.'

Rose, too weak to reply, allowed herself to be laid on a stretcher and carried out to an ambulance. Now, for the first time, she allowed herself to feel ill, to drift away from the world into a strange fog of warmth. Voices floated around her as if from an immense distance. 'I was all right until just now,' she kept telling them, but her own voice seemed to make no sound, and no one replied to her.

When the ambulance arrived at the central surgery Ruth found that Dr Gower was out, visiting one of the Groups. She spent nearly half an hour at the telephone, trying to trace him, and leaving messages at every place at which it was possible he might be found. Occasionally she peeped into the waiting room where Rose lay dozing. Ruth was not sure that her guess (for her decision to bring Rose to the surgery was based on guesswork rather than diagnosis) had been correct: Rose was certainly very ill, and her symptoms seemed to indicate severe poisoning; but Ruth was too inexperienced in dealing with the rarer industrial diseases, and perhaps also too afraid of Dr Gower, to be willing to take any major decision; so she waited anxiously, thinking of how little she knew, and trying to guess what her father, who was very experienced and very wise, would have done in similar circumstances. Now and then she glanced at the clock. A warm current of anticipation welled up beneath her fears as she thought of the coming evening, and her dark eyes grew luminous with excitement.

Gower returned at last, and seemed surprised to see her. He had been sent for by the Superintendent just as he was leaving his surgery earlier in the afternoon, and so had not received any of her messages. But in a few minutes he had examined Rose and, as soon as he had closed the door behind him, he confirmed Ruth's suspicions.

'I suppose you haven't seen a case like this before?' he asked.

'No,' Ruth rolled up her sleeves and began to wash her hands.

'Hm. Clever of you to recognise it.'

Ruth blushed at the commendation. She was unused to hearing praise of her work.

'I was only guessing,' she admitted.

'That's all you could do.' Gower removed his horn-rimmed spectacles and began to rub a patch of hair above his right ear. He had a remote, but at the same time determined, air, and seemed quite unconscious of his unusual good looks. To the girls in the factory his habitual sternness only added to the glamour of his appearance: tall, broad-shouldered, with a long, saturnine face like (Finch once remarked) that of an El Greco angel, with burning eyes that were full of contempt for every human weakness. Ruth was more afraid of him than she cared to admit even to herself.

'Where does this girl live?' he asked.

'In digs. Somewhere in Dustborough.' So much she had learned from Miss Elliston.

'Any good?'

'I've no idea.' Ruth dried her hands and glanced at herself in the mirror as she took off her linen coat. She felt it unreasonable that Gower always expected to be fully informed about the domestic circumstances of any worker who happened to fall ill.

'We'll have to take her into hospital,' he decided slowly.

Ruth looked at her watch. With luck there would be just time for her to accompany the ambulance to the cottage hospital and get back to Mowbray Lodge in time to meet Morgan.

'It's no use sending her to Dustborough,' Gower was explaining. 'They'd kill a case like this within a week. I'll ring up Coking and see if they can take her.' At Coking, Ruth knew, was one of the Ministry of Health's Emergency Hospitals, staffed by highly qualified men and women who would know how to deal with almost any problem; but Coking, Ruth also knew, was nearly twenty miles away.

Gower looked up from the telephone. 'Get on the other line and ask for an ambulance,' he instructed her. By the time she had ordered it Gower had finished talking. 'I hope this won't interfere with your plans for the evening?' he asked with polite formality.

She looked suddenly crestfallen as she flushed with disappointment. She pressed her lips together, determined to say nothing.

He got up. 'I'm sorry, but there's no one else I can send...'

'It doesn't matter.' She knew that she must telephone to Morgan, but as long as Gower was in the room she was unwilling to do so. The only other telephone in the surgery was in the waiting room, where a nurse was sitting with Rose.

'Can I send a message to anyone for you?' Gower asked, sensing her confusion.

'No, thanks.'

'Well, I'll just take a last look at the patient while you put your coat on,' he suggested, and went out.

Ruth at once picked up the receiver. For some time she could get no reply from the operator, for the Blimpton telephone, like so much of its other equipment, tended to be erratic, particularly in emergencies. When, at last, the operator happened to notice that Ruth was trying to make a call she put her through first to the manager of the South-East Group, and then to the chief electrician, and at last to Gittins.

'I'm trying to get to Mr Morgan,' Ruth told him.

'Ah! Dr Aaron,' Gittins greeted her, 'I hear you've got a case of toxic anaemia on South-East – '

Ruth gave a little gasp, unable to understand how the news, known only to herself and Gower, could possibly have got to Gittins.

'Yes,' she said, 'I'm trying to get Mr Morgan. Could you get me put through from your end?'

'But this isn't a matter for Mr Morgan,' Gittins assured her blandly. 'This is a question for the Superintendent and for me, as Principal Clerk – '

'It wasn't – ' Ruth began, 'I mean, I wanted to – ' but Gittins would not allow her to finish her sentence.

'Would you ask Dr Gower to come over as soon as he's free?' Gittins' voice persisted. 'This is the first case we've had, and we must act promptly. The consequences may be quite unforeseeable,' he rolled the word around his tongue. 'Quite unforeseeable,' he repeated.

Ruth dropped the receiver with a bang. Then she heard the ambulance draw up outside.

TEN

IT WAS GENERALLY conceded that Gunn's second visit to Blimpton was more successful, or at any rate more fruitful, than his first. The people who had been responsible for filling his fuze were disappointed that he seemed to have forgotten all about it, but, since they were fairly certain that it would be a failure and, indeed, guessed that it would probably destroy the barrel of any gun from which it was fired, they did not feel justified in nursing the slight sense of grievance which the incident had aroused. On the other hand, the Superintendent, Gittins and the Resident Engineer were surprised and gratified when a steady trickle of building workers began, during the week following Gunn's visit, to arrive at the hostel site. It was unfortunate that most of the newcomers were bricklayers, since the hostel's real need, now that it was approaching completion, was for plumbers, plasterers and painters; but, since two or three plumbers and at least one painter did eventually appear, nobody liked to point out that, broadly speaking, a mistake had been made.

But Captain Knowles and Miss Creed scored the largest triumph. Within three days of Gunn's visit they were notified by the Establishments Division of the Ministry that a Senior Assistant Labour Manager, male, was to be appointed to the factory, and would arrive as soon as the normal process of selection, medical examination, agreement as to salary and terms of contract, vetting by MI5, and all the other essential preliminaries could be carried out. It was intimated that a candidate capable of passing all these tests had already been found and might, if no hitch arose, be expected to arrive at Blimpton within a fortnight.

Neither of the people responsible for this appointment was really satisfied. Miss Creed had hoped that a woman would be sent, for it seemed to her that a man might, if he were really determined, succeed in inserting himself next to Captain Knowles as an additional source of authority in the factory. Knowles, too, was secretly rather annoyed: he had supported Miss Creed's plea for additional staff only because he believed in maintaining a common front on issues which were never likely to be dealt with, and he had not realised that Gunn would interest himself seriously in a demand such as Miss Creed had put forward. Knowles disliked having subordinates, because he seldom knew what to do with them, and the gratification of having a large staff seemed to him at times to be outweighed by the difficulty of keeping the members suitably employed.

It was therefore with some sense of foreboding that Knowles greeted his new assistant when he eventually arrived at the factory. George Parsons, though some years younger than Knowles, was old enough to have served for a few months in the Army towards the end of the last war, and this experience was perhaps the only thing that the two men had in common. As they shook hands Knowles peered at him over the top of his spectacles, as if trying to find the main clue to the character of his new subordinate. He saw a mild and friendly looking man, solidly built, slow of movement, fresh-complexioned, healthy and rather unnoticeable.

'Well, well,' Knowles began, and could not think of what to say next. He often spoke to the various members of his staff about the necessity of starting on what he called the right foot, but he himself was apt to have difficulty in deciding which the right foot was.

Parsons waited with an air of pleased expectancy, his brown eyes glowing with enthusiasm at the thought of the work which he was about to undertake. He had been employed for some years by a firm controlling a large group of chain stores and had, some years before the war, risen to be a district manager. This was a post which involved heavy responsibilities of a rather limited type, and Parsons had worked his way up to it slowly, steadily and inconspicuously. His employers had trusted him, but he had always seemed to them to lack the drive needed to rise to the top of a highly competitive business. At each promotion he had proved equal to his responsibilities, but he never gave the impression of being too good for the job he happened to be doing; he was good enough, but never outstanding. People said: 'Pity we haven't got more men like Parsons...' but even this was in a sense a tribute to his limitations rather than his qualities. When his employers suggested that he might be lent to the Ministry for the duration of the war he agreed at once, without so much as asking what he would be called upon to do. He thought that a war job would enlarge his experience.

Now, watching Knowles twirl the ends of his moustache, he waited for the process of enlargement to begin.

'Well, well,' Knowles said again, and began to shuffle the papers on his desk, sniffing as he did so. Whether the sniff was due to a perpetual cold or to the natural configuration of his long, thin nose nobody was ever able to determine. 'I hope you'll like it here,' he added after a pause.

This remark did not seem to call for any reply.

Knowles referred to the papers on his desk. 'I see you come from the XYZ Company,' he observed.

'Yes.'

'Ah,' the Labour Manager relaxed, as if he had come on to firm ground at last. 'Of course,' he went on, speaking now with friendly condescension, 'I'm an EELS man myself.'

There were people in the factory who were apt to refer to this phrase as Knowles' signature tune. But it was more than that. To have been, and still to be, an employee of Empire Exploiters Limited, the vast combine whose ramifications defied the researches even of the most curious, was the main source of Knowles' pride. He had, in fact, been taken over with the other assets and liabilities of his uncle's business some years ago when the great betel-nut monopoly was being formed, and since his uncle's factory was relatively unimportant he had been left there, first as assistant labour manager and then, as his superiors died one after the other, as Chief Employment Officer. At Blimpton he held his head up. He was not merely Captain Knowles, but Captain Knowles of EELS. He never failed to tell visitors, and now be began to tell Parsons, that he was not really an employee of the Government, but had been lent by his employers for the duration of the war; and, he added, he could not, of course, have undertaken this piece of war-work if the great combine had not agreed to make up the salary he earned as a temporary civil servant to that which he had received as an employee of big business. (He did, however, omit to mention that this act of patriotism cost his peace-time employers a mere £100 a year [which would otherwise have been collected by the Government in Excess Profits Tax], and that this was regarded as a bargain price to pay for the opportunity of putting a competent man into the job which Knowles had been holding on to so long and with such remarkable tenacity.)

The XYZ Company was a mushroom growth in comparison with EELS, and as Knowles recapitulated the main points of interest in his relationship with the company he began to feel that he would probably get on pretty well with Parsons after all. He began to tell him about the hostel.

'It'll soon be finished,' he said, 'thanks to Gunn. D'you know him, by the way?'

'No. Who is he?'

That relieved another anxiety.

'Oh, just one of the people from the Ministry. One of the big shots, I believe… anyway, it won't be our business to staff the place when it's finished. The Ministry'll have to do that for us. Of course I take an interest in it. Naturally. But they can't expect me to do anything about it. I've got far too much on my plate as it is.'

'I expect you are very busy,' Parsons assented.

'Busy! Everyone in the place is yelling at me to get labour. Everybody!' He pulled out a pile of papers from a drawer. 'Look at this! Finch is still asking for six bus drivers. He's been asking for them for months. A fortnight ago he put in a demand for two garage mechanics – '

'It shouldn't be difficult to get those. I mean with all these garages closing down all over the place.'

'That only shows how little you know. Don't you remember that Beaverbrook sent out a special call for them six or seven months ago? I understand that he took them all into the Ministry of Aircraft Production.'

'Oh, but – '

'Yes, I grant that there may be exceptions. I hope there are, and I hope that I may be able to get hold of a couple of men, but frankly,' his eyes turned towards a damp spot high on the wall, 'frankly, I don't think it's likely. I've already spent some time trying to make Finch understand what we're up against in trying to find skilled labour. He doesn't seem to understand the problem at all. Then,' he found another damp spot just above the chart showing his office organisation, 'the production people are just as bad. Take Morgan. He's been telling me for the last two months that he wants a dozen first-class maintenance fitters. Yesterday he sent me a note pushing the demand up to twenty. It's quite unreasonable!'

'I suppose he needs them?' Parsons asked, trying to relate these facts to what he had imagined were to be his duties at Blimpton. The expression of eagerness on his homely face was rapidly giving way to one of acute bewilderment.

'Thinks he does, I suppose. But what can I do? As it is, I spend practically half my time chivvying the Employment Exchange manager at Dustborough. I suppose he's doing his best; but the men aren't there, you know. They simply aren't there.'

'Can't the Ministry help?'

'Help!' Captain Knowles had a special way of laughing: a way that seemed to imply that anyone who thought his observations intended to be funny would be convicted of weak judgment and frivolous outlook. He took off his spectacles, and gave his new assistant a piercing stare.

'I mean – ' Parsons began, and then apparently decided that his meaning needed no elucidation for he said no more.

'Of course you're quite right, in a way,' Knowles continued. 'When people from the Ministry come down here they always tell us that they've come to see what they can do to help us. But,' he added, 'I ought to explain to you quite openly that that isn't what they come for. The main reason for sending people down here is to find out what we're doing, so that they can go back and send us minutes telling us to do something totally different.'

This was not an original remark. Knowles had overheard it being made at dinner one night, and, though he had disapproved of the originator, he had appropriated it at once, and by this time he had used it so often that it appeared to be his own. In fact he did the officials of the Ministry an injustice: they seldom found anything for which to reprimand him, for the sufficient reason that, as far as they were able to discover, he rarely did anything at all.

'The Ministry,' he went on, 'the Ministry, I ought to tell you, is not popular with those of us who have the responsibility of running things at the factory level. The people up there seem quite incapable of understanding our problems. They seem to think that we have nothing to do but fill up forms. I suppose I spend very nearly half my time filling the things up – well, that's one of the jobs I'm going to pass on to you now. I suppose you've filled up a good many forms in your time, one way and another?'

'Oh, yes.'

'Well, then, look at this.' Knowles opened a drawer and pulled out a double sheet of foolscap. The other took it. 'This is what they call the Labour Return. We have to send it in every week. If it doesn't reach the Ministry by the first post on Tuesday mornings we get a telephone call from the fellow who's supposed to deal with it.'

Parsons glanced down the form. 'I see,' he said, running a finger down the columns, 'this is a list of all labour requirements?'

'That's it. I don't know what they do with it when they get it. They say they pass it on to the Ministry of Labour, or something. But I must warn you that nothing ever comes of it, absolutely nothing.'

Parsons was still looking at the form, and now bewilderment gave way to anxiety. In the left-hand column he found a list of all the various grades of labour employed in the factory, and against each grade the number of workers required. 'I see that this is dated last Monday,' he observed.

'Yes,' Knowles agreed, 'we always keep a copy. In case of any queries, you know,' he looked up, and, seeing the other man still intent on the row of figures, remarked: 'It's quite straightforward, once you get the hang of it.'

'Yes,' Parsons put the form down, and then almost at once picked it up again. 'I can't find any demand there for motor mechanics,' he said.

'What!' Knowles snatched the form from him, put on his spectacles and began to examine the list. 'Heavens above!' he exclaimed, his face taking on an additional shade of purple. 'How on earth can that have happened?' He picked up the telephone and when, after a short interval, the operator did not reply, put it down and bellowed in the direction of the room next door: 'Miss Watts! Miss Watts!'

There was a light tap on the door, and a girl entered, carrying two cups of tea on a tray.

'I'm sorry it's late,' she said, 'but we had to send over to the Main Canteen for milk.'

Knowles glared at her. 'Didn't you hear me call for Miss Watts? Where is she?'

The girl put the two cups on the desk and picked up the tray.

'There aren't any biscuits,' she said.

'I don't want biscuits. I want Miss Watts. Where is she?'

'Oh, she's around somewhere. I'll tell her.'

'Get her at once. If she's not in the building go and find her. Only get her.'

The girl went out, and after a moment or so Miss Watts entered. She looked at Parsons with frank curiosity. He was younger than she had expected, and more determined. He was frowning now – she liked the way in which his crisp dark hair was cut short above the square, rather low forehead.

'Did you want me?' she asked.

'Did you copy these figures?' Knowles handed her the sheet, sniffing noisily as he did so.

'Yes.'

'Well, I'm afraid you've made a mistake.'

'Oh, I don't think so,' the girl looked from Knowles to Parsons, and then back again at Knowles. 'I checked it over before I sent it.'

'You left out the demand for garage mechanics. Look.'

She glanced down. 'But there's no demand here.'

'That's what I said,' Knowles thumped the desk with his fist. 'How many times must I tell you that you must copy the original absolutely exactly?'

'I did.'

'You couldn't have done. Look again.'

'But don't you understand,' the girl spoke with some exasperation, 'this *is* the original.'

'*This* is the original?'

'Yes. You told me when I first came here that we must always keep the original in the office. It's the copy I send to the Ministry.'

For a moment there was a deep silence. Parsons, who had risen when the girl entered, stood with his head bent, looking at the floor.

'Is there anything else?' Miss Watts asked.

'No,' Knowles avoided her glance, 'you can go.'

As soon as she had gone he pulled out a tobacco pouch and began to fill his pipe. 'It's damned awkward,' he remarked, 'damned awkward. I'll have to send them a teleprint.' He lit his pipe. 'Of course,' he added, 'it doesn't really make a ha'porth of difference. If we'd asked for these men three times a day for three months we still wouldn't have had 'em. Now,' he took a gulp of tea, and, with a motion of his free hand, seemed to wave the distasteful subject away, 'is there anything else you'd like to know before I settle you into your office?'

'I'm sure there's a great deal I ought to know,' Parsons said diffidently.

'Oh, you'll pick it up fast enough, once you get started. It's only a matter of getting a grasp of the general routine. You'll find your way about in no time.'

Parsons gave the other man a slow, speculative glance. 'I think,' he suggested, speaking almost shyly, 'that it would be useful if I could see something of the factory before I really settled myself in the office.'

'Why not?' Knowles glanced at his watch, 'I'd take you round myself, only I've got to rush off to a meeting in a few minutes. But I'll get young Bates – he's one of my junior assistants, you know. Then when you come back I'll take you over to meet the Superintendent.'

'That wasn't exactly what I meant,' Parsons reddened slightly. 'I was thinking that it would be very useful if I could spend a short time – a week or two, perhaps – working in the factory, so that I could get some idea of the workers' problems at first-hand.'

Knowles put down his pipe, and pushed his teacup away. 'What an extraordinary idea!' he exclaimed. 'Whatever made you think of wanting to do that?'

Parsons did not reply. The idea had been suggested to him by Dr Gower, whom he had met in the train on his journey from London: and it had not been the only suggestion that Gower had made.

'You can't possibly do a thing like that,' Knowles continued, 'it would give the workers an entirely wrong idea of your position. Why, if once you'd worked beside them, they'd never respect you again. After all, what we've got to maintain in this factory, above everything else, is discipline.'

'I understand. But – ' Parsons, not certain how to go on, paused as someone knocked at the door, opened it and entered.

It was Miss Creed. She knew that Parsons had arrived an hour ago, and was slightly offended that Knowles had not already brought him to her room. Her hat, which she seldom removed during working hours, was slightly askew over her faded blonde hair, but her expression was stern.

The necessary introductions were made, and then Knowles, with a swift and significant glance at his old ally, said, 'Mr Parsons seems to think that he would like to spend a week or two working in the factory – '

'Why, I think that's a perfectly splendid idea,' Miss Creed beamed, straightening her hat and ignoring the signs that Knowles was trying to make to her.

'He means, as an operative,' Knowles pointed out.

'Yes. I *quite* understand,' her smile was now turned directly on to Parsons, 'I'm sure the Superintendent could have no objection, especially as you've never worked in a factory before…' she sat down. 'That is so, isn't it?' she asked.

'Oh, yes,' Parsons stumbled.

'And that's such a disadvantage! Yes, you should certainly spend a few weeks on the Groups. And, of course, since you've come down here at such short notice, that will give us – Captain Knowles and myself – an opportunity to decide which part of our work you should take over.' She refused the cigarette which Knowles offered her, and took one from a small tortoiseshell case. 'I'm afraid you'll find it a little difficult, being responsible to two people,' she blew out a puff of smoke, 'but Captain Knowles and I work very closely together, and I'm sure you'll fit in as soon as you begin to know the ropes.'

Parsons muttered something unintelligible, to the effect that he hoped he would be useful; then, all at once, Knowles began ringing bells and telephoning, summoning such of the assistant labour officers as were in the office, to meet the man to whom many of them would now be directly responsible.

They drifted in slowly. Some came alone, others in small groups as if bound together by an invisible thread of fear. There were perhaps twenty of them in all. Some were quite young, and a few were far advanced in middle age; but most of them seemed neither old nor young: they were shadowy, indeterminate, their personalities obliterated by the presence of Captain Knowles and Miss Creed, and by their anxiety that this newcomer, this man of whom they had heard so much and yet knew so little, should not bring a further discord into their harassed lives.

They were members of Blimpton's middle class, priding themselves on their status, yet fearing to exercise any authority. They stood about awkwardly, waiting for their turn to be introduced, to shake hands, to be allowed to go back to their own offices, waiting for the moment when they could compare their impressions and decide what line to take.

'Now,' Miss Creed surveyed the crowded room, 'Mr Parsons would like to be shown over one of the Groups.'

Nobody came forward. Sebastian Bates edged a step or two nearer the door. Pamela Grant looked up and caught his eye, but when she smiled he stared over her head, pretending not to see her. Old Mr Willoughby whispered something to Freda Elliston, but Freda, though she had been about to go over to the East-West Group when she was summoned to Captain Knowles' office, was not willing to waste any time in escorting Parsons.

'Miss Braithwaite!' Miss Creed caught sight of Phoebe, who was standing against the wall, her hands in the pockets of her tweed jacket, her feet, in their sensible ugly flat-heeled shoes, planted far apart, as if she were holding on to her ground with some difficulty.

Phoebe's face brightened, and her eyes, behind the thick spectacles, began to gleam. As she stepped forward the others started, with little sighs of relief, to drift out of the room.

'Now, Miss Braithwaite,' Miss Creed had taken complete charge of the situation. Captain Knowles sorted out some papers from the tray on his desk and began to pack them into his despatch case. It occurred to him that if he were quick he might possibly be able to get away to his meeting without being obliged to take Miss Creed with him.

'Now, Miss Braithwaite,' Miss Creed repeated, 'I want you to show Mr Parsons everything you think he ought to see on East-West... I know I can trust you to use your judgment... after all, we want to make him feel thoroughly at home here, don't we?' she turned on her cold, uncomfortable smile, and then switched it off again, quickly.

Knowles was fastening the straps on his despatch case, as if preparing himself for a long journey. 'I'll expect you back at about – '

'Five o'clock, sharp,' Miss Creed interrupted.

'Yes, that'll do,' Knowles agreed glumly and turned to Phoebe Braithwaite. 'Better get a car to take you over,' he suggested. 'It's a filthy day for anyone seeing the place for the first time.' He was already at the door, but Miss Creed had been too quick for him. She gave Phoebe some brief and whispered instructions and then followed him out.

'Is there anything special you want to see?' Phoebe asked Parsons, looking at him with faint distaste. She could see at once that he was not what Miss Creed, in her softer and more intimate moments, called 'our kind of person'. Very few people at Blimpton were. But Parsons, with his slight cockney accent and the look of eagerness about his eyes, struck Phoebe as being quite remarkably peculiar.

'There's such a lot I have to learn,' he held her overcoat while she slipped into it. 'I think I'd just better put myself into your hands for the afternoon.'

Phoebe, slightly mollified, led the way out.

It was snowing again. The roads were slushy, and the yellow mud splashed against the sides of the car as Phoebe pointed out the landmarks. The car park near the main entrance was crowded with buses that had brought the afternoon-shift to the factory and that were now waiting to take workers coming off the morning-shift back to Dustborough and to fifteen or twenty other places scattered about the county. Men and women stood about in the snow waiting for their friends. Loudspeakers poured dance tunes into the cold and suffocating air. An old man slipped on a piece of ice and two girls rushed to pick him up.

Phoebe began to explain how the three shifts overlapped. 'You see,' she counted off the hours on the fingers of her woollen gloves, 'the morning-shift comes on at a quarter-to-seven...'

Parsons was staring out of the window, listening but watching, as he did so, the strange landscape of the factory, the scattered, impermanent-looking buildings, the mounds of earth thrown up against the sky, the little figures of men and women scurrying along the roads.

'And do you think you're going to like it here?' Phoebe asked as the car drew up at the entrance to the East-West Group.

'Well, yes,' Parsons felt in his pockets and handed his pipe, tobacco and matches to the gateman, 'yes, I think I am.'

ELEVEN

DAN MORGAN, OR Daniel Llewellyn Morgan as he sometimes preferred to call himself, probably worked harder than any other man or woman in Blimpton. He was usually in his office by 8.30 in the morning and seldom left it, except to visit some other part of the factory, before 7 at night. Sometimes he carried a pile of work back to Mowbray Lodge, but more often he spent the evening, and occasionally also a large part of the night, in going round the Groups, discussing technical questions with shop-managers, engineers, chemists and electricians, or in arguing over social problems with junior labour officers, foremen, trade union officials and casual groups of workers. All these people were his friends, and he would do anything for them, provided always that he was certain that he was getting everything out of them. His critics described him, with uneasy contempt, as a sentimental tough guy, and the judgment had in it an element of truth. He was that, and much more. He was a man in whom personal ambition, a passionate enthusiasm for the work to be done and a consuming interest in, and love for, the people doing it, were not yet perfectly fused. His mind drew, it sometimes seemed, no clear distinction between the things he did because of the strength of some momentary impulse (or, rather, to gain some immediate, complete and final satisfaction), and those which he did in order to reach some sharply-envisaged and distant end. He was in love, but faithlessly, with a constant succession of general ideas. Sometimes he seemed to accept the stale, clichéd generalisations which figured among the small-talk of his business acquaintances: 'When the revolution comes,' he would say, 'I'll be one of the first to be hung up on a lamp-post,' and then he would embark on a disquisition on the writings of Marx, Lenin or Jean Jacques Rousseau. His audiences were puzzled, not knowing what to take seriously, and he himself was, on these occasions, like a leader who had not yet found a sense of direction. But within the factory his leadership was acknowledged. For him, and for those working for him, the war had become a battle for ammunition, for shells, bombs, land-mines, grenades, and for the explosives with which to fill them.

This morning he had been in the factory since a little after seven, straightening out a difficulty which threatened to hold up the output of an important component. When, after three hours, a solution of the problem seemed to be in sight, he hurried back to his office. He opened the door and saw Ruth Aaron standing at the other end of the room, looking out of the window. She did not seem to hear him as he entered.

'Well?' he asked as he took off his overcoat, 'admiring the view?'

She turned, startled. 'It's terrible, isn't it?' she asked, trying to hide her confusion. Her dark hair was brushed severely away from her face and coiled into a bun at the nape of her neck. There were deep circles round her eyes and she looked as if she were afraid to smile.

'Terrible!' he threw back his head and laughed, showing his sharp, uneven white teeth. They gave him, Ruth thought, a devouring look. 'My dear girl, that's the finest view you'll ever see anywhere in the whole round world... do you ever think of what we're going to make of this factory?... But of course you don't...' he crossed the room and picked up the pile of letters that lay on his desk. 'Excuse me,' he apologised, scarcely noticing her as he began to read.

This was the first time that she had ever visited him in his office, and she began to wish that she had not come. She sat down on the edge of a chair, smoothing her skirt over her knees, and watching him covertly through lowered lashes. His usual look of faded sunburn had become this morning a rather grey sallowness. He seemed tired and preoccupied, but even now his air of vitality had not altogether deserted him.

'Well, young woman,' he dropped the letter on his desk and sat down, 'what have you got to say for yourself?'

'I came to apologise.'

'And what do you have to apologise for?' he was watching her but at the same time drawing towards him, with an unconscious gesture, another pile of papers.

'About the other night.'

'Hoh!' he pulled out a handkerchief and wiped his forehead.

'That was a dirty trick you played me. I nearly froze to death.'

'You didn't wait?'

'Of course I waited…'

'I'm terribly sorry.'

'It doesn't matter,' he smiled, his mocking, irresistible smile. 'But you mustn't do it again.'

'Oh, I won't!'

'Okay, you won't – but why did you?'

'Why,' she stood up, feeling herself dismissed, 'I was going round one of the Groups when I found some wretched girl – '

'I know that,' he interrupted, 'but why didn't you send me a message?'

'I tried to,' she looked absurdly, disproportionately distressed. 'I telephoned but I couldn't get through – '

'Never mind,' he shook his head, still smiling. 'Now sit down and tell me how it happened – '

'But I was just telling you – '

'No, not that,' he shook his head again. 'I want to know how that girl was allowed to get so ill when we've four doctors in the factory.'

Ruth took the cigarette he offered her. 'I should say it was the girl's own fault,' she said slowly. 'She'd only been here a few weeks, four or five at most – '

'Who passed her for contact work?'

'I'm not sure. It's difficult to remember.'

'But there must be a record.'

'Yes, of course,' Ruth assented, feeling suddenly guilty, remembering the sick girl's anxiety to be of no trouble to anyone. 'By the way,' she added, 'she was talking about you on the way to the hospital.'

'About me?'

'Yes. She said that you told her that if only the workers were patient things would come right in the end.'

Morgan frowned. 'I hope I haven't ever told anybody that.' He sat back, his ugly face looking extraordinarily alive as he tried to remember the journeys he had made around the factory and the people he had met during the past few weeks. 'What did you say her name was?' he asked.

'Widgery. Rose Widgery.'

He wrote it down.

'Right. Thanks.' He watched the door close behind her, and then remembered that he should have made an appointment to have dinner with her one night soon. The notion struck him that Ruth's grave and often melancholy air was perhaps due not to any private grief but to an innate dullness.

He got up and went to see the Superintendent.

The two men did not get on well, but each did his best, for reasons of his own, to maintain an appearance of amity. Brown generally succeeded in concealing the fact that he was rather afraid of Morgan; and Morgan, who could not understand why Brown, and not himself, had been appointed by the Ministry to be Superintendent of Blimpton, tried, not very consistently and not always successfully, to restrain the contempt he felt for his superior. Gittins, who usually contrived to be present when they met, found their disagreements peculiarly trying, since his desire to keep on the right side of the Superintendent, as the factory's highest source of authority, conflicted with the sense of loyalty which one established civil servant always feels for another of a higher grade: and Morgan, though he had spent some years in the outside world, had originally been a child of the Great Arsenal.

This morning the atmosphere was especially frigid. The factory had had an unusual number of visitors from the Ministry during the past week, and tempers were somewhat strained in consequence. The Works Department had sent a Representative down to arrange for the transfer of a number of building workers from the hostel site to the West Group, where most of the shops were still uncompleted. Architects had arrived to discuss the demolition of those parts of West which were ready for use, and the replanning of the whole Group for the filling of heavy calibre bombs. Colonel Jervis had spent two days in the factory helping Gittins to stave off a visit from an irate manufacturer of empty bombs who had been told, with no more truth than tact, that if he could not improve the quality of his product he would lose his contract. The Chief of the Inspection Department had announced that he could not carry out the duties of his department efficiently unless he was given at least a quarter of the new entrants to the factory every week. In the midst of all this Gunn had telephoned to Miss Hopkins to tell her that he was on his way to Blimpton, and then had simply failed to arrive; and Miss Hopkins, who had arranged a talent contest in the North-West Canteen for his especial edification, had spent a whole evening in Mrs Gittins' drawing room expounding her theories of popular entertainment to the extreme boredom of her host and hostess, neither of whom had the courage to tell her that they considered the workers at Blimpton totally undeserving of the enthusiasm which they seemed to arouse in her.

The three men settled down to prepare the agenda for the Superintendent's fortnightly meeting. To this meeting there came the managers of each of the Groups, the chief officials of the various servicing departments, and half a dozen of the factory's senior administrative officers. Almost everyone dreaded these occasions, which were devoted partly to inquests in the failures of the preceding fortnight, and partly to the explanation and elaboration of plans laid down by the Ministry.

'Have you seen the new programme?' Brown began as soon as Morgan entered the room.

'No.' Morgan sat down wearily. He felt as if he were beginning to have a cold in his head.

'Ah!' Brown's eyebrows began to writhe. 'Well, I'm afraid we're in for it this time. Just look at this.' He handed Morgan a bundle of papers, and then, as the latter glanced through them, went on: 'I've just had a call from the Chief Controller...'

'I suppose he says we've let him down badly?' Morgan asked, with a touch of sarcasm in his voice.

Gittins leaned forward. 'Nobody can say it's the fault of the factory,' he said softly, eyeing the two men with a look of anxiety, of doubt.

The Superintendent sat up very straight. He was growing stouter and his movements were heavy and ponderous. But his eyes, small as buttons in his red face, were quick and sharp. 'It's impossible to control what people say,' he observed, 'and as you've often remarked yourself, Gittins, passing the buck is precisely the occupation for which most civil servants are trained... Nothing personal, of course. But the CC seems to have been told that we're to blame for the drop in output in the last three weeks.'

'He does, does he?' Morgan asked.

'Yes. It looks as if some of the visitors we've had down here have been talking out of turn.'

'But they're largely right.' Morgan spoke as if there could be no argument on the point. He was still looking at the papers that the Superintendent had given him. His head was bent, but his squared shoulders gave an indication of belligerence.

'Oh, come!' Gittins pleaded, 'you know perfectly well – '

'That we're short of this, that and the other thing,' Morgan interrupted. Now he looked up. His light hair was ruffled, his yellow eyes bright and angry. 'Of course we are. And I'm not suggesting for a moment that we could have done a hundred per cent of our programme. But we did get the Ministry to cut it for us, you remember, and I've no doubt that we could have done most of it – eighty or ninety per cent, anyway – if we'd really set about it.'

Brown mustered his dignity. The trouble, he often told himself, was that it was impossible to tell when Morgan would start one of these attacks; and when he did there was almost nothing that could be done with him.

'Take the shell-filling programmes,' Morgan continued, 'we've done seventy-one per cent on the 3.7, and even that has only been managed by switching more than half the industrials from the 25-pounder – '

'But – ' Gittins tried to interrupt.

'And there,' Morgan continued, 'you have the issue in its most simple form. The Ministry, the War Office, possibly even the Prime Minister – though there's no need to look as high as that – everyone is crying out for more anti-aircraft shells, and we sit here and say we're not to blame!' He got up and began to stride across the room. 'How many people were killed in Bristol last night?' he paused rhetorically.

'Oh, they went to Bristol last night, did they?' the Superintendent asked in a conversational tone.

'No,' Gittins murmured, 'Liverpool.'

Morgan shook his head. 'I'm not talking about last night's raid,' he spoke more calmly, but his rich Welsh voice carried a deep undertone of rage, 'I'm trying to point out that if every anti-aircraft gun in this country stopped firing, if every city in this country was burned to ashes, there'd still be people in Blimpton ready to say that it wasn't our fault that we'd fallen behind with our part of the programme,' he had walked to the end of the room, and now he stopped dead. 'And I say it is our fault,' he declared, 'not entirely, but very largely. In the last week of January our absenteeism was twenty-three per cent. In the first week of February it went up to thirty-one per cent. Now it's somewhere around twenty-seven per cent. Why?'

'Why?' the Superintendent repeated. He seemed to be hypnotised. His eyes had retreated until they were no more than pin-points beneath the shaggy brows. His small mouth was pursed into a straight line.

'You must bear in mind,' Gittins managed to put in, 'that we've got a very poor grade of labour.'

Morgan threw out his hands in an eloquent, remotely foreign gesture. 'You know I don't subscribe to that theory,' he replied. 'People are what you make them. The finest people on earth can't travel twelve miles to work every day when there isn't any transport.' He sat down, his fury momentarily gone. 'And do you know,' he added, 'there are people in this factory who've been walking four miles each way through the snow every single day for a fortnight in order to try to get here? There's one old girl,' he smiled as his memory conjured up a picture of Ma Venning, whom he had met on the North-West Group some hours earlier, 'there's one old girl who bullied the manager of the Dustborough Co-op into lending a van every day for a week when the bus she came on broke its back axle. The girls in her shop haven't missed a single shift through all this spell of bad weather.'

The other two men began to look a little more at ease.

'That's a very fine story,' the Superintendent commented, 'I'll see that it gets to the Minister. Old Outrage would like a story like that – gives a magnificent touch of human interest...'

'I'll ask Dolphin to pass it on to the local press,' Gittins added quickly. 'What was the woman's name?'

Morgan frowned. 'It's not a very creditable story to us, is it?' he asked.

The others looked at one another, as if uncertain of his meaning.

'People ask awkward questions, you know,' Morgan went on, 'and they'll want to know why that bus – and several dozen other buses – broke down in the bad weather. Who is going to tell them that Finch's orders for spares were withdrawn without his knowledge? Is anyone going to see that Lord Outrage knows that we haven't enough men in the garages to keep the buses properly serviced? Is anyone going to tell him, or Sir John Lentil, or the Chief Controller, that it's only by the greatest good luck that we haven't a death from TNT poisoning on our hands or our consciences or whatever you call our organs of responsibility?' He pulled out his cigarette case, and struck a match on the back of it, watching it as it burned down. 'Let's get down to business,' he said, with another swift change of manner. Now when he turned to the Superintendent it was as a subordinate. 'Before we go over the programme,' he suggested, 'there are several points that I should be grateful if we could clear up…'

TWELVE

FOR THE FIRST time since he had arrived at Blimpton Otway Dolphin had something to do. In a sense this was rather a relief to him for though he was of a naturally lazy disposition, he enjoyed his leisure best at those moments when the prospect of work hung, like a shadow, a short distance in front of him. His duties as Public Relations Officer to a factory whose very existence was, quite literally, a State Secret, were necessarily somewhat complicated. Often he did not know what was expected of him, and on these occasions he did nothing. When he had been at Blimpton about two months the Director General of Propaganda at the Ministry sent him an assistant, who was thought to be in need of a period of taming in the provinces. The two of them spent half an hour each morning discussing the programme for the day, and, that done, settled down quietly, the assistant to write poetry, and Dolphin to plan campaigns for making Blimpton popular among the inhabitants of Dustshire.

Now, at last, it was necessary to put some of these plans into operation. The Superintendent had declared, at the end of his fortnightly meeting, that everything must be done to stop the spate of rumours that appeared in the local newspapers about the inefficiency, disorder and unmentionable goings-on in what was called, in print, 'a local establishment'.

So Dolphin, after consulting Gittins, Morgan, Dawson and half a dozen other people, drove into Dustborough on this dismal Saturday morning, to open his campaign. He called first on the manager of the local Employment Exchange.

'Must I see him?' Wood, the Exchange Manager, asked his assistant when Dolphin's card was brought in. 'Can't you deal with him yourself?'

'I think you'd better – he seems to be one of the high-ups,' his assistant apologised.

They were both inclined to be annoyed, for they treasured their Saturday, as the only day in the week in which someone from Blimpton did not drop in to see them.

They were still hesitating when Dolphin entered. He had dressed specially for the occasion, and wore, with his one good suit, as much of the manner of a successful stockbroker as he felt he could carry. His thin hair was cut shorter than usual, and sleekly brushed. His plump, rather pale but lively face wore an expression of extreme and not quite easy formality.

For ten minutes they drank tea, smoked cigarettes and chatted about the weather.

'And now, what can I do for you?' Wood asked at last. He was a tired, efficient man. A few greying hairs were brushed across the top of his bald head; but his eyes, behind gold-rimmed spectacles, were keen and young.

Dolphin explained the purpose of his visit. 'We know you're doing everything you can to get us the women we need,' he acknowledged blandly.

'Thanks.' Wood's voice was dry.

'But of course we need five times, ten times as many as you're sending,' Dolphin continued.

'I know that,' Wood picked up a pencil and began to beat a tattoo on his desk. 'It's not easy, but we're doing what we can at this end. Blimpton isn't exactly popular with the local people – '

Dolphin laughed. 'And I know that,' he said, 'but the girls don't have such a bad time, really.'

'Don't they?' Wood put down his pencil. 'Of course, I haven't been over to see the place for three or four months... But we hear things. And people see the girls here, in the town, walking round with the rash on their faces... Yesterday the father of one of them came to kick up a row with us, said he was going to write to my Minister. We'd directed the girl to Blimpton, and now she's got into trouble, as they say; and the father says it's our fault – Oh, yes, we know all about Blimpton.'

'Ah! – '

'I know,' Wood looked at Dolphin, noting the wide eyes and the long, malicious mouth, 'I know the other side, too,' he continued, 'I've been a civil servant all my life, and there isn't much you can tell me about officialdom. I realise that you've got your difficulties.' He stopped for a moment, while his tongue explored an aching tooth.

'What are you going to do?' he asked. 'Square the press?'

'Well, I hadn't thought of it in those terms... I'm meeting the editor of the *Dustborough Echo* at the White Lion for lunch. I was hoping that you might be able to join us...'

'No, thanks,' Wood spoke a little less acidly, 'it wouldn't do. Old Meakin is a decent chap, but he's got to keep on the right side of the local big-wigs, and I'm not precisely popular with them since I've begun to drag their girls away for your benefit.'

'Yes,' Dolphin assented reflectively, 'I can see that.'

'But why the White Lion, of all places?' Wood asked.

'It's the best pub in the town, isn't it?'

'The food's all right, I suppose; but I hope you realise that you're bearding the lion in his den, as they say?'

Dolphin raised his eyebrows questioningly.

'Don't you know that it's the headquarters of the Chamber of Trade and of the Dustborough Manufacturers' Federation?'

Dolphin still looked puzzled. 'I didn't know,' he admitted, 'and now you tell me, I'm afraid I must confess that I don't quite get your point.'

'No,' Wood sat up now, and as he spoke the look of weariness left him, though only for the moment. 'Those are the people who are really trying to make trouble for you,' he said, 'if you can fight them successfully you'll be all right. But it won't be easy.'

'I'm afraid I must be frightfully stupid,' Dolphin looked at the other man with his widest and most open smile, 'but I still don't quite follow.'

'No? Well, you see,' Wood spoke as if he were describing some simple natural phenomenon to a not very intelligent child, 'those people are employers of labour. You want the labour. They have it.'

'Ah!'

'We've already taken quite a crowd of people from them, but they know, and we know, that it's only just beginning. We haven't got a lot of power over them, but we've got some, and to a certain extent we use it. We directed three toolmakers from Gurneys to go to Blimpton a fortnight ago, and old Gurney is creating hell's delight over losing them. Besides, a lot of the girls aren't waiting to be pushed. In spite of all that's to be said against Blimpton – and you'll admit that there's plenty – a girl who goes there at least gets a week's pay for a week's work. Your wages are pretty nearly half as high again – and sometimes nearly double – the amount a girl can earn at Gurneys' or Brights' or Smithson's, or anywhere else about here for that matter. All those boys are busier now than they've been for twenty years – and I know what I'm talking about: I came here in 1919 – and they'll stop at nothing to prevent their people from signing up at Blimpton. If the factory was heaven itself, and the Archangel Gabriel was Superintendent, you'd still hear rumours in Dustborough about the terrible immorality that went on there...'

Dolphin laughed. 'And as it is – ' there was no need to finish the sentence.

Wood got up. 'If there's anything else I can tell you,' he said, 'come and see me again.'

'Thanks.'

Wood opened the door, and the two men shook hands. Then, as Dolphin turned into the corridor, the other called him back. 'There's just one more thing,' he spoke in a low voice, 'I heard quite by chance that Gurneys are hoping to get a big contract from your Ministry. If they do, that'll ruin your chances of getting any more labour from them... I don't know whether there's anything that you can do about it?'

'What are they making?

'At the moment they're doing light engineering stuff, motor-car accessories and that sort of thing... if the people in your Ministry had any sense they'd close the place down. I haven't been able to find out what contract it is that they're hoping to get... but it's madness to hand out any work at all in this area when you need every girl you can get at Blimpton.'

Dolphin frowned. 'If you could find out what the contract is for,' he suggested, 'we'd at any rate know which Department is responsible. Otherwise it may take weeks before we get on to the right people. You know what my Ministry's like...'

Wood smiled with an air of tolerant superiority. The Ministry of Labour provided him not only with a livelihood but, in spite of his occasional tussles with his superiors, also with a religion. He was often heard to remark that he was heartily sorry for civil servants who happened to be working for other Departments, and particularly for those in what he called the Mushroom Ministries.

'I'll make some inquiries,' he agreed. 'If you could get moving at the same time – '

'Of course I will,' Dolphin promised, 'as soon as I get back to the factory.'

As he turned his car out of the side street in which the Employment Exchange was situated, and threaded his way towards the High Street, he felt more cheerful than he had done for a long time. Usually he disliked coming to Dustborough. The narrow streets, the little corner shops decorated with hideous enamelled advertisements for tea and cocoa and patent medicines, the pubs which seemed designed for the promotion of drunkenness rather than enjoyment, the great gothic Town Hall and the two railway stations, filled him with such depression that sometimes he almost – though never quite – wished that he had stayed behind in Italy and allowed himself to be interned for the duration of the war. For ten or twelve years – he was always a little vague about dates – Dolphin had lived in Spain, in Italy, and on the French Riviera, and had supplemented his small private income by writing gossip columns for the local newspapers on the comings and goings of English and American visitors. Occasionally he had written articles for one or other of the London weeklies, and he was always on the point of writing a novel which was to be in the manner of *South Wind*, only wittier. When he, reluctantly but prudently, returned to England in the summer of 1940, he was surprised to find that the Ministry of Information showed no eagerness to accept his services; and, after hanging about for a few months waiting for the people in Bloomsbury to change their minds, he had at last been thankful to accept an invitation to go to Blimpton. He was considerably surprised, after his first few weeks at the factory, to find that he was beginning to enjoy himself. His life, though idle, was frequently amusing, and as long as he could avoid spending much time in Dustborough he was fairly contented. But his job, such as it was, lay in the town rather than at the factory. Now, as he swerved to avoid an Army lorry, he reflected that there was perhaps more entertainment to be derived from life in Dustborough than he had so far realised.

Meakin was waiting for him when he arrived at the White Lion. He was a withered little man with pale eyes, protruding teeth and no chin. His manner was extremely, almost embarrassingly, humble. He had edited the *Dustborough Echo* for nearly thirty years, and, until recently, his life had been haunted by the fear that he would not have enough matter to fill up the next issue of the paper. Lately this fear had receded. News items came in from all sorts of people who had, in peacetime, been content to leave Meakin and his small staff to find things out for themselves. At the same time, advertising revenue began to increase in the most extraordinary way. As his paper supply became more restricted Meakin often had difficulty in finding room for the large display advertisements which the local tradespeople seemed so anxious to insert. Then one of his biggest advertisers suggested that Meakin should increase his charges. He did, but the volume of advertising continued to grow. Only recently he had found out why; and now he was worried, for he was an honest man and had, too, a suspicion that if he published many more of the stories that came to him about the state of affairs at Blimpton he might get into trouble with the authorities.

He sucked up his soup, waiting for Dolphin to give a lead; but the latter chattered on about all sorts of apparently irrelevant subjects until the cheese was put before them.

'Talking about the weather,' he said then, for, with great skill, he had made that reliable topic of conversation last, on and off, through the three preceding courses, 'I've been meaning to tell you a story about one of the grand old girls out at Blimpton.'

Meakin stirred his coffee, and took a sip of brandy. He showed no interest as Dolphin described the way in which Ma Venning had commandeered a van to carry workers to the factory during the bad weather.

'I understand that she's lived in Dustborough all her life,' Dolphin finished. 'She does you credit, don't you think?'

'Yes. Yes, I suppose she does.'

Dolphin glanced at his watch. 'I'm going to see her this afternoon. I wonder whether you'd care to come along and hear what she's got to say?'

'Oh!' Meakin gave a start and put down his coffee cup, 'I'm afraid I couldn't do that,' he said abruptly, and looked around the room as if searching for an excuse.

'No?' Dolphin tried to meet the wandering gaze, and failed.

'Matter of fact,' the editor swallowed the remainder of his brandy at one gulp, 'I like to get home on Saturday afternoons to do a bit in the garden – '

'Of course. Still,' Dolphin added, trying to keep the coaxing note out of his voice, 'I could run you back in my car afterwards, if that would help.'

'Yes. But – well – to be perfectly frank – ' the other seemed to derive some courage from the contemplation of his empty glass. ' – it might be just a trifle awkward if I were to run a story like that at the moment.'

'Really! Why?'

'Um – well, some of our advertisers might not care for that bit about the Co-op van – '

'But you needn't say where the van came from, surely?'

'No. No, I suppose not.' Meakin, aware that he had said too much, was looking thoroughly uncomfortable. He took off his spectacles and polished them with a silk handkerchief which he carried specially for the purpose. Dolphin had lighted a cigarette and was blowing smoke-rings with an air of unconcern which he suspected of being slightly overdone. 'I've arranged for a photographer to come down to meet me,' he said, offering the bait as casually as possible. 'It's the sort of human story that the London papers – ' he broke off as a waiter began to hover near. 'But if you like to use the story first…' he went on when he had paid the bill.

'I'm sure it's very good of you,' Meakin's hesitation seemed to grow increasingly agonising. He took off his spectacles once more and blinked around the now empty dining room. 'Perhaps I could think it over and see how – how I'm fixed for space. I'm sure you understand my difficulty…'

'My dear chap!' Dolphin jumped up. 'Now let's just peep into the lounge and see what's become of that photographer fellow. You might as well meet him, just in case…'

The lounge, however, was empty. Meakin seemed to be in a hurry to be gone, and yet unable to say goodbye.

'If I *should* be able to use that story,' he was beginning when a girl strolled into the room with a proprietory air. She was small and very slim, and her long blonde hair hung like a curtain over the collar of her suit of pale pink tweed.

'Why, Mr Meakin!' she exclaimed, waving back her hair, and releasing a flood of perfume. 'I'd no idea that you were around! Daddy and I were only saying just now that we didn't know where you'd got to…' She turned to give Dolphin a long curious look.

'I don't think we've had the pleasure of meeting before, have we?' he asked, returning her stare with an inviting, provocative smile. He knew that she must be the daughter of old Little, who ran the hotel. She was young, perhaps not much more than twenty, and it struck him that she was precisely the type of dumb blonde that he thoroughly understood.

Meakin introduced them nervously. He had hoped to get away without meeting 'Big' Little. Now, even if he went, it would be too late. The damage was already done. Dolphin had begun to talk about Blimpton.

'Why don't you ever come out to see us?' he was asking.

'That awful place!' Mavis Little gave him another, and longer, stare.

'Besides,' she added, 'nobody ever asked me!'

'Well, I'll ask you. Let me come over and fetch you one day next week…'

'Oh, I don't think I could!' Suddenly she giggled. 'From all I've heard about the place, if once you got me there you'd never let me get away again!'

'I didn't know we had that sort of reputation.'

'Didn't you?' she spoke flatly. 'You'd be surprised… but still I might come over one day, if you promise not to keep me.' She took a cigarette from her handbag and waited for Dolphin to give her a light.

'Oh, I'm not going to promise that.' He lit a match, cupping the flame in his hand. As it flared up he suddenly blew it out. He lit another, and as the flame touched the tip of her cigarette he leaned forward and looked into her eyes. The technique was one which he had often used, but now he was conscious of being a little out of practice. 'I'll come and fetch you on Tuesday,' he said, and then he smiled. 'Of course,' he added, 'when you join the factory we won't be able to send a car to fetch you every day.'

She threw her head back and laughed. 'That's all right,' she assured him, 'I'll drive myself to work.' She paused as her father came into the room, and for a moment there was an uncomfortable silence.

Meakin stepped forward.

'Why, hullo, Meakin!' 'Big' Little was a large red-faced man with a hearty manner. Everything about him seemed designed to announce his occupation: his appearance, his clothes, even the way in which he jingled the small change in his trouser pocket. A certain flatness in the colour of his narrow blue eyes and the thin, shrewd lines about his mouth tore across the impression that he made, and served to explain why the White Lion had grown from a modest pub to be the chief centre of hospitality in Dustborough.

'Daddy,' Mavis broke in as soon as her father had seated himself, 'Mr Dolphin wants me to go over to Blimpton and see the factory.'

'As a matter of fact,' Dolphin interrupted quickly, 'I was trying to persuade Miss Little to come and work with us.'

Mavis perched herself on the arm of her father's chair. 'Can you imagine me as a factory girl?' she asked, addressing herself to Meakin.

Meakin gave a start. 'I think that was only Mr Dolphin's joke,' he suggested.

'No. I was perfectly serious,' Dolphin was standing with his back to the fire, 'though of course I wasn't suggesting that Miss Little should become an operative. If you'll forgive my saying so,' he seemed to be addressing himself to no one in particular, 'and if there was any irony in his manner it was not perceptible, 'we've been very disturbed to find that there's a good deal of – ' he hesitated, 'a good deal of – shall I say hostility? – in Dustborough to the people who are working for us at Blimpton – '

'You can't wonder, can you?' Little asked. 'We didn't ask to have the factory put there – '

'Didn't you?' Dolphin asked quickly.

Little cast a sharp glance at Meakin. The latter sat twisting the bottom button of his overcoat and did not look up.

'I seem to remember,' Dolphin continued, glancing from one man to the other, 'I seem to remember that before the war started – in 1938 to be exact – ' a curious smile played about his mouth as he spoke, ' – there was a deputation from Dustshire to the Minister for Co-ordination of Defence.' He seemed to hesitate. 'Or was it to the Prime Minister? No doubt you will remember the details...'

Meakin had by this time succeeded in twisting the button off his coat. Now he looked up.

'What's this?' Little demanded of him, 'I thought – '

'I don't think this has anything to do with Meakin,' Dolphin interrupted, 'he didn't organise the deputation, did he? And,' he added, turning his smile full on, 'he hasn't been refreshing my memory, if that's what you're trying to suggest.'

'I'm not suggesting anything.'

'No... and I don't want to waste time digging up ancient history. But when you say that you didn't ask to have a munitions factory in Dustshire, I do feel, and I hope you'll forgive me,' his glance caught that of Mavis who had, throughout the conversation, been watching him with startled curiosity, 'I do feel that it's necessary to remember that Dustshire actually went to the trouble of sending an influential deputation to London – '

'There was a lot of unemployment here at that time,' Meakin ventured.

Little signalled to him to be silent, and then turned to Dolphin. 'I don't know how long you've lived in this county,' he said, 'but when you've been here a bit longer you'll understand that people in Dustshire aren't in the habit of taking things lying down. We asked for an aircraft shadow factory. We never expected to get one of these huge great ammunition dumps. It's too damned big altogether.'

'Of course it is,' Dolphin assented amiably. 'I couldn't agree with you more.'

'And now you're bringing in the dregs of the population from all over the country. The state of affairs in this town has become a crying disgrace... and from all I hear about what happens over at Blimpton the factory might just as well not be there. For all the work that gets done, I mean – '

'Why don't you come over and have a look at things for yourself?'

'Oh, I've been over once or twice. But you know what these visits are. You only see what the people up there want you to see – '

Mavis put a hand on her father's shoulder. 'You forget that Mr Dolphin comes from Blimpton,' she remarked.

'No. I didn't forget. But he'll admit that what I say is about right. If you go to Blimpton you see what you're meant to see, and you're damn lucky if you get a glimpse of the real state of things.'

'Well,' Dolphin sat down, sensing a thaw. 'There's another point of view about that. If you come over for an afternoon, naturally we show you the best things first... who wouldn't?'

Little nodded. Meakin, now more at ease, had begun to scribble something on an odd scrap of paper that he had found in his pocket.

'But if you'll come for a week,' Dolphin went on, 'I can promise that you'll get a pretty fair idea of the real state of affairs. Of course, you wouldn't be able to see the whole of the factory even in a week, but you'll see all that we've been able to get going so far.'

Little shook his head. 'You may be right, but I just haven't got the time to spend... Not just now, anyway.'

'Then why not let Miss Little come over? A man in your position ought to get an idea of what we really are doing; and if Miss Little spent a week or two in my office she'd soon know nearly everything there is to know about life at Blimpton.'

Mavis jumped up, and for a moment stood quite still, staring at Dolphin. 'What would I do in your office?' she asked.

THIRTEEN

AFTER SIX WEEKS in the Training School Norah passed her examinations and became an assistant forewoman. She did not, on the whole, enjoy the period of training, but she found the course less difficult than she had at first expected. The other trainees, both men and women, were better educated than she was, and at first she was often discouraged by their casual, off-hand manner, by their chatter about the importance of their peace time jobs and, above all, by the ease with which they put pen to paper. When they went into the canteen she would sit rather apart from them, and she preferred to spend her leisure with the girls she had begun to know during her first few days in the factory rather than with strangers who seemed to her to be snobbish, cold and stupid.

But, at the lectures and demonstrations which she attended she found that she had several advantages over her fellows. She learned quickly, and soon absorbed a surprising amount of the simple technical knowledge with which it was necessary for even the lower grades of supervisory staff to be familiar, but which most of the women found confusing and difficult.

'How did you guess?' one or other of them would ask when she had solved some problem or answered some question that had baffled all the other women in the class as well as a fair proportion of the men.

'I didn't guess,' she would retort with all the haughtiness she could command.

'But how did you know?' they would persist. 'How do you manage to remember?'

She would shrug her shoulders. 'My brothers are engineers,' she would say, 'and I used to hear them talking at home.' Then her dark eyes would flash as she added, 'Besides, I've worked in a factory myself; and if you're a worker you either get the hang of things or you get out.'

Afterwards she would describe these incidents to Kitty Baldwin or Griselda Green, and would remark, with a trace of self-consciousness, 'I think I gave her quite a turn – the stuck-up little snob!'

'But she was probably much more frightened of you than you were of her,' Griselda would remonstrate.

Then they would begin to argue.

On one of these occasions Griselda and Norah were making the most of their free Saturday afternoon by having an early tea at the Copper Teapot, the newest and cleanest of Dustborough's three tea-shops, which was, by some unwritten agreement, generally accepted as being out of bounds for factory operatives. They sat at a table by the window, watching the crowds of shoppers and idlers trudging by in the rain.

'You know,' Griselda remarked, as she finished pouring out the tea, 'I think it's time someone gave you a good shaking.'

'And why?' Norah turned the plate of cakes around, the better to inspect its contents.

'Because you're letting these little manicurists and sales ladies and greengrocers, or whatever they are, undermine your self-confidence. You know quite well that you're every bit as good as they are.'

Norah smiled; her expression mischievous. 'I know I am,' she admitted, 'and if I hadn't known it when I came here I'd know it now after all the lectures I've had from you – '

'And from Kitty.'

'Oh,' Norah took a bite of cake, 'Kitty never knows which side she's arguing on.'

'But why do you make such a fuss about all these silly little people?' Griselda persisted. Her grey eyes were extraordinarily clear as she watched the other girl with puzzled, friendly interest.

Norah pulled off her hat and shook out her dark curls. She seemed nervous and excited. Her manner, shifting rapidly between arrogance and humility, contrasted oddly with Griselda's calm, slightly exhausted air. Several people sitting at other tables turned to stare at them.

'I don't know,' Norah was looking out of the window, scanning the faces of the passers-by. Three girls got off a bus, paused dubiously outside the café and walked on, arms linked, elbowing people off the pavement. A group of soldiers stood in a doorway opposite, waiting for something to happen. 'I suppose,' she continued after a brief pause, 'it's the way they talk about their homes and their families and the holidays they used to have and the sort of cars their boyfriends used to drive – '

'All that's so trivial!'

'Is it?'

'You know it is.'

'Yes, I do really,' Norah's glance returned to Griselda. 'You never talk about what you used to do before you came here... '

'I?' Griselda pulled herself up with a jerk. Her grey eyes were remote, gazing at nothing. 'Why should I? I'm interested in the present, in Blimpton.'

'So am I,' Norah put down her cup and pushed her plate away. 'But I must say I do get terribly homesick sometimes.'

'I suppose we all do, now and then.'

'Camden Town,' Norah went on dreamily, 'you wouldn't think anyone could get homesick for Camden Town, would you?'

'Why not? Someone wrote a poem about it once.'

'Oh?'

Griselda repeated a verse or two from Flecker's ballad. When she came to the lines:

> 'Perhaps she cast herself away
>> Lest both of us should drown;
> Perhaps she feared to die as they
>> Who die in Camden Town.'

Norah, who had been staring moodily out of the window, turned again to her companion.

'That's all rubbish!' she exclaimed vigorously. 'It's not a bit like that! It's poor, of course, but... well, before the blitz it was sort of gay... I must say I wouldn't want to live there always, but I miss it terribly... I always used to walk up Park Street with the boys on Saturday nights and go to meetings in the park on Sunday mornings. They asked me to speak once – '

'What about?'

'Spain, I think it was. I didn't though... I don't know enough, that's my trouble... Did I tell you dad wrote that Tom's in the Middle East?'

Tom, Norah's eldest brother, was in the Tank Corps.

'No. You didn't tell me?'

There was a short silence.

'More tea?' Griselda asked.

'No, thanks… yes, I will. Griselda?'

'Yes?'

'How do you stick it, working as an operative, I mean?'

'Stick it?' Griselda smiled. 'I like it… didn't you know that?'

'Yes…' Norah assented doubtfully. 'But I can't make it out, quite. I mean, anyone can see that you don't belong to the working class – '

'Oh, don't start all that class stuff again!'

'Sorry, but – '

'Well?'

'You never seem to speak about your family,' Norah hesitated, as if uncertain whether to continue. 'I don't want to pry…'

'No,' Griselda leaned forward, elbows on the table, 'and I don't want to make any mystery about myself… I thought I'd told you – ' she looked around the room and then her glance returned to Norah ' – as a matter of fact, I haven't got much of a family. My mother died when I was a baby – '

'But your father?' Norah asked, her tone conveying a sympathy which she could not find the words to express. She was unable to imagine a time when her life would no longer revolve around her own family.

'My father!' Griselda laughed, suddenly, briefly. 'My father is more alive than anyone you ever met!'

'And what does he say?'

'Say?'

'I mean, about your working at Blimpton?'

'Oh!' Griselda shrugged her shoulders. A glint of anger darkened her eyes, but her high, broad forehead was serene, unfurrowed. 'He doesn't know…' she was staring out of the window as she spoke, and now she added: 'There's someone out there who seems to be trying to catch your eye.'

'Where?'

'I think he's coming in…'

Norah turned as a young man approached their table. 'Why, Mr Tyndale!'

'I hope – ' he looked at Griselda doubtfully, and then back to Norah. 'You said you wouldn't mind if I came along...' He had a face from which most of the natural eagerness had been erased, leaving a look of anxious, but adequate, intelligence.

'Of course!' Norah blushed. 'This is my friend, Miss Green. Actually she's an operative, so I suppose by all the rules we oughtn't to be having tea with her – '

The young man thrust a limp hand towards Griselda. 'Pleased to meet you.' As an ex-assistant manager of a branch office of an insurance company he was anxious not to appear snobbish. 'Nasty day, isn't it?' he added, and sat down. His hair was darkened by a probably recent, and certainly excessive, application of brilliantine. He wore gold-rimmed spectacles, and behind them his mild blue eyes had a strained look, as if from too much reading too little enjoyed.

Norah examined his appearance with critical approval. He had come out top, and she second, in the test at the end of the assistant foremen's course and this was, so far, the chief bond between them. He returned her gaze with shy admiration, and looked around for another conversational opening. But, as usual, words failed him.

Griselda turned to look at the clock and then began to gather her things together.

'No, don't go,' Norah urged her.

'I must. Kitty's waiting for me...'

'What's the hurry?'

'Do you like it at Blimpton?' Henry Tyndale asked abruptly.

'Yes,' Griselda's smile was for a moment very near to laughter. 'Don't you?'

He blushed deeply as if the question, thus reversed, had become improper. Griselda, with her smooth hair, rather off-hand manner and light, beautiful voice, was disconcertingly unlike any operative he had yet met in the factory.

'You don't have to like it,' Norah assured him. Her manner though friendly, was tinged with mockery. 'Lots of people simply hate it.'

'Everyone is so – '

'Well?' Griselda asked.

'I don't know quite how to put it,' he stirred his tea and some of it slopped over into the saucer. 'You see,' he floundered, 'it isn't just that it's dreary. I suppose they can't help that. But it's all so dead and alive…'

'Oh no, it isn't,' Norah contradicted energetically, 'you only say that because you never talk to the right sort of people – '

'But who are the right sort?'

'I'll tell you,' Norah began. 'First – '

Griselda made her excuses, and left them. As she stepped into the street she turned to look back. Norah and Henry Tyndale were deep in argument. They had already forgotten her.

When she reached Ma Venning's house she saw a car parked outside the gate. Kitty Baldwin stood at the front door, beckoning her to hurry. She wore a new blouse of pale-yellow satin, the colour of her hair.

'Come on!' she urged in a hoarse whisper. 'We kept them waiting in case you came back – '

Griselda stood perfectly still. 'Who?' she asked.

'Someone from the factory – and a photographer from London – '

'What – whatever for?'

'Silly!' Kitty tucked an arm under Griselda's elbow, but the latter remained firmly in the doorway, apparently immovable. 'They want to put our pictures into the papers – '

'I don't think I want my picture in the papers, thank you…' Griselda released her arm and stepped quickly past the other girl, into the narrow hall, and then up the stairs, into her bedroom.

Kitty followed her more slowly, and paused to tap on the bedroom door before entering.

'Whatever's the matter?' she demanded. Griselda had flung her coat on to the floor, and now began to unfasten her skirt with one hand while with the other she rummaged in a drawer, looking for the slacks she usually wore about the house.

'Nothing,' Griselda replied abruptly. Her face, above the dark sweater, was very pale.

'But you're all wet...'

'Yes, I had to walk. I must change before I come down.'

'Better hurry. The photographer has to catch the train – '

'Oh!' Griselda sat down on the edge of the bed and shook out her hair. 'But I told you – I don't want to have my photograph taken...'

'Why ever not?'

She shrugged her shoulders. 'I just don't want to. Besides,' she surveyed herself in the mirror, 'I'm as dank as a mermaid.'

Kitty flung her a towel. 'Go on. Hurry.'

'Right. But don't wait for me...'

Downstairs, Dolphin and the photographer were drinking tea in the kitchen. Ma Venning looked around her with pride. In the dingy afternoon light the bright fire seemed to be reflected everywhere, in the rows of copper pans that stood on a high shelf, in the polished woodwork, in the starched tablecloth, in the gay pieces of pottery that stood on the dresser. She lifted the kettle from the hob and went to refill it at the sink.

'Hold it!' the photographer commanded abruptly.

She obeyed, laughing at the sudden flash.

'That'll do,' the photographer began to pack.

Ma put down the kettle. 'But what about my girls?' she asked, 'I thought you were going to take us all together?'

The photographer glanced at Dolphin. Ma, her serene, farmer's-wife's face crowned with thick grey hair, was a picture. Girls, his look said, could be found anywhere.

'Another time, perhaps,' Dolphin suggested, turning his wide, inviting smile on Kitty as she re-entered the room. 'We're sure to find another opportunity soon...' And, shaking hands effusively, satisfied with his day's work, he led the photographer out.

'Oh! Gosh!' Kitty exclaimed as she began to clear the table. 'I do think that was *too* mean of our Griselda!'

'I'm sorry,' Griselda, coming into the room, dressed in slacks and a red jersey, looked suddenly radiant.

'Well, of all the – !' Kitty turned to survey her with open admiration. 'And if that photographer had seen you looking like that you'd have been a film star by tomorrow week! Wouldn't she, Ma?'

Ma put a hand on Griselda's shoulder, looking into her face. 'No, my dear,' she shook her head. 'I think Griselda's better off with us – and I believe she thinks so, too.'

Griselda gave the older woman a quick hug. 'There isn't much you don't know, is there?' she murmured, and ran to get herself another cup of tea.

FOURTEEN

IT WAS ON Sunday of the following week that Dan Morgan set out to keep the promise he had made to himself to visit Rose Widgery in hospital. At first he drove slowly, threading his way through the streaks of mist that lay in motionless patches across the fields and lanes. But as the car climbed out of the hollow in which Blimpton lay he saw that the afternoon was wonderfully fresh and clear. The pale sun cast a translucent glow over the fields and hedges, and the woods in the distance shone with a soft green light, as if the spring were just about to break over the trees. He stopped to open the sunshine roof and, as the fresh breeze drifted in, threw his hat into the back seat. Then, as he started up the engine and drove on he began to hum the most famous of all Welsh hymn tunes, Cwm Rhondda.

He was still thinking about the factory. He and Gittins had spent the morning in making telephone calls to London, in trying to find out which department in the Ministry had been responsible for giving a contract to Gurneys' in Dustborough. They had both calculated that the staff doing Sunday duty were more likely to give away this important information than would be those whose everyday job was to handle such queries. On Sundays everyone seemed to be doing someone else's work. But on this particular Sunday the head of the engineering contracts section happened to be at the Ministry himself, and he flatly refused to answer any questions whatever. Morgan, thinking back over the conversation, decided that he would have to go to London himself for a day or two to try to clear the matter up.

As he thought of what he would do in London he began to regret, as he had done a thousand times before, the foolish quarrel he had had with Russell in Cincinnati ten years ago. He could no longer remember very clearly what it was that they had quarrelled about; but there were always people in London ready to remind him that but for this quarrel he would now be making tanks instead of filling ammunition. Morgan prided himself on being a good engineer, and, perhaps more than anything else in the world, he wanted to make tanks. Now that Russell was chief engineer of Empire Exploiters Limited no one, it was clear, who had ever quarrelled with EELS would be allowed to get within sight of the mechanism of a tank.

His thoughts returned to Blimpton. It seemed to him that although there was nothing that was technically very difficult about the job that they were trying to do the factory would never get into running order. The first and greatest obstacle was the Superintendent.

'Or am I just jealous?' he asked himself aloud.

He smiled, and all at once began to sing the words of the tune that he had been humming:

'Guide me, O thou great Jehovah,
Pilgrim through this barren land...'

and as he sang he pictured to himself the small Welsh village in which he had lived as a child, the cottage on the hill-side crammed with his parents and brothers and sisters; the steep hill on the other side of the road where the boys from the village school played every evening until dusk; the way in which his father would come out of the house at supper-time to call them in, standing in the doorway and whistling, with two fingers in his mouth, the long sweet piercing signal that called the children home. He remembered, with extraordinary vividness, the endless days at the village school, the smell of ink and paper, mixed with the smoke that rushed down the chimneys on windy mornings, the sing-song voice of the schoolmaster drilling the class in arithmetic; and then, as he reached the last line of the hymn, he began to picture his mother sitting by the kitchen fire on a Sunday evening, singing to the children and telling them the legend of how the Welsh women in their red flannel petticoats came out of their chapels one Sunday morning and went out on to the cliffs to frighten away the invading armies of Napoleon who mistook the great sea of colour for the uniforms of all the regiments of Wellington.

He had left school at fourteen, determined that he was going to be a great man and do good in the world. He smiled wryly, as he reflected on the diminishing meaning of these once satisfying phrases. And then, as he remembered his early struggles, the hardships he had endured so easily, the fun he had had and the successes he had won, his smile deepened. He had started, reluctantly, at the pit-head, but after a few months his uncle, who was foreman at a small engineering works at Swansea, had offered to find him a job, not as a regular apprentice (that would have been too expensive), but as an odd-job boy to make tea and run errands and pick up what skill and knowledge he could in his free moments. He had been at first docile, then riotous; but after a month or two the excitement of leading a gang of town boys had palled, and he had begun to work, making himself useful, going to night-school, learning so thoroughly and quickly that his employer decided that it would be a good investment to send him to the university. At twenty he had graduated, and returned to the factory as assistant works manager. Even now he could not disentangle the motives that had sent him back to the village a few weeks later to become engaged to the shrewd, cool-eyed daughter of the colliery manager; he had done it partly to show that it could be done, to show everyone at the first possible moment that though he had started at the bottom he would always and inevitably reach the top of every tree that was within reach; partly, too, it was because he thought she would be useful… and partly it was because he loved her smooth English voice that was like water flowing over sand. She was ambitious, too, and clever enough to see that he had a future.

'Only it wasn't enough of a future,' he said to himself, remembering the sudden success and the bad times that followed. It was now six, or perhaps seven, years since she had left him. He had heard from someone that she had married again, but the details had been vague…

As the buildings of the hospital loomed up through the trees his mind jerked forward to the present. He wondered for a moment what Ruth Aaron would say, when he met her in Dustborough later on, if he suggested taking her to a service at the Baptist Chapel instead of to dinner at the White Lion. Suddenly he laughed.

The hospital was in an isolated position and the patients received few visitors. Nevertheless, when he asked for Rose Widgery he was told that she already had someone with her, and, as he stood about in the waiting room the doctor in charge of Rose's case came in to see him. The girl was recovering, but she was still very weak and visitors were only allowed to remain with her for a few minutes.

But when she saw him her face brightened.

He took her hand. 'Well, young lady?' he asked, 'when are you coming back to us?'

'Soon,' she said, 'as soon as I can. I promised you that I wouldn't leave... do you remember?' Her fluffy fair hair lay like a cloud around her face. Her blue eyes, as she looked at him, were eager, a little feverish.

'Yes. I remember. But I think we'll be able to manage without you for the next few weeks...' he chatted on until the nurse beckoned to him that it was time to go.

'You'll come again?' Rose asked as he got up.

'I will, indeed. And when you're up and about we're going to send you away for a real holiday before you come back to the factory.'

Rose's face clouded. 'I don't want to go home,' she whispered.

'Then you shan't go home. Next time I come we'll fix everything up. And when you get back to Blimpton we're going to give you a room in the new hostel... and we'll probably find you a new job, too.'

Slowly she released his hand. When he reached the door he turned to look at her. She lay quite still, watching him with a look of utter satisfaction.

As he turned the car out of the drive he saw that a girl was waiting at the bus halt and then, as he came alongside her recognised Griselda Green.

'Good day,' he greeted her as he stopped the car. 'Can I give you a lift?'

A moment passed before recognition dawned in her face, and then she smiled. 'Thanks. I was waiting for the bus.'

'So I noticed,' he opened the door for her to get in beside him. 'I think we've been visiting the same person.'

She turned to him, her big eyes wide with astonishment. 'You've been to see Rose – Miss Widgery?'

'What's so surprising about that?' he spoke almost harshly. 'She's one of my girls, isn't she?'

'Your girls!' Griselda watched his averted profile, seeing again the strong, yet sensitive, line of his mouth, the prominent, ugly nose, the creases of humour about his eyes. 'I didn't know that anyone at

Blimpton felt any responsibility for what happened to the workers.'

'Well, you live and learn.'

'So it seems... if it doesn't sound impertinent I'd like to thank you for visiting Rose. She's had rather a bad time.'

'I know... that's why I came. Do you come often?'

'Nearly every week. But then, she's a friend of mine. And besides, I haven't got as many other things to think about as you have.'

'Oh!' he grinned. 'You'd be surprised if you knew how much thinking I can squeeze into a day.' The sun, slanting through the open roof, emphasised the darkness of her hair against the pallor of the clear, smooth skin, and sharpened the fine line of jaw and throat. But it was the girl's grey eyes, wide apart, their expression changing quickly from amusement to sobriety, that people chiefly remembered. 'I've been thinking quite a lot about you, for one thing,' he went on.

'About me?'

'Why not?'

'But you don't know me. You've only seen me once before.'

'That's just the point. I've been trying to think out what a girl like you imagines that she's doing in a filling factory.'

'I don't understand what you mean.'

He grinned, not without malice. 'It's no use taking that line. You're not a working girl.'

'You've no right to say that. I work.'

'You do, eh?'

'When there's work to do!'

He laughed. 'Still harping on that?' he asked. 'How's that other girl doing – the one who led the deputation?'

'Norah McCall. She's been promoted...' She paused. 'You did that,' she went on after a moment. 'Didn't you?'

'Clever girl! When did you think that out?'

'Just this minute. I ought to have guessed before...'

'But you didn't?'

'That's what I said.' She began to fumble in her bag.

'Here,' he felt in his pockets and handed her a gold cigarette case. 'Give me one, too.'

He drew into the side of the road while a farm cart passed. For a minute or two they smoked in silence.

'What else have you been thinking?' he asked at last.

'Nothing,' she told him. 'Why?'

'You seem to have something on your mind.'

'No. Nothing whatever.' They looked at one another, with curiosity, and an interest faintly tinged with hostility.

He started the car again. 'You weren't by any chance wondering why that girl was picked out for training and you weren't?'

'No,' she said, 'no. Norah's a very capable girl.' She paused for a moment, watching his strong hands resting on the steering-wheel, and the thick, muscular body, so extraordinarily alive. 'If I may say so,' she went on, 'that was a pretty smart thing for you to do.'

'Say what you like. But why smart?'

'Oh!' she stubbed out her cigarette, 'I suppose it's an old trick really…'

'What's an old trick?'

'Why, promoting the agitators so that they won't do any harm,' her voice sounded contemptuous.

'Well,' he began angrily, 'of all the – ' he broke off, laughing suddenly, uncontrollably. Then anger won, and he sobered. 'How dare you accuse me of doing a thing like that?' he demanded.

She sat quite still, not attempting to answer, and then shook her head very slightly.

'How dare you?' he demanded again, rage and amusement still striving for mastery.

'I'm sorry,' her smile was charming. 'I didn't mean… but people do that often, don't they?'

'People!' he lit another cigarette and then handed one to her. 'Lord Outrage might, I suppose…'

'Lord Outrage?'

'He's our Minister. Didn't you know that?'

'Yes… yes, I suppose I did…'

'But I – ' he thumped his chest rhetorically, ' – I don't model myself on the thugs of big business.' He looked at her once more, at her shabby clothes and the incongruous, self-confident bearing of her head. 'You're not one of the comrades, are you?'

'Comrades?'

'Communists.'

'Not yet. Since I came to Blimpton I've discovered that I'm what is called politically uneducated... as you see for yourself... I'm sorry you thought I was being rude...'

'Okay,' he wiped it out with a gesture of his free hand. 'And next time we meet – if ever we do – don't forget that if there's any fighting to be done I'm on the side of the workers... So you don't want to know why I didn't arrange for you to go to the training school with Miss whatever-her-name is?'

'But why should you have arranged it? She was the leader. I was just one of the crowd.'

'You'd stick a mile out of any crowd.'

'Nonsense!' a hint of annoyance was perceptible in her voice.

He did not reply. The lane twisted up hill. The ploughed fields, still heavy with rain, had a black and desolate look. When they came to the beech woods the trees, arching overhead, seemed to darken the whole sky, and the day grew suddenly cold. But at the top of the hill the woods ended, and they saw the whole countryside spread out before them, a vast bowl of green and yellow light with Dustborough, far away below them, half hidden in the mist. Away on their left they could see the faint shimmer of the network of railway lines that connected Blimpton with the outside world, but the factory itself was invisible beneath the haze.

Again Dan stopped the car.

'Like the view?' he asked.

'Lovely.'

'Do you know the Welsh valleys?'

'No.'

'Ah! That's another kind of country altogether...'

He took another cigarette and gave one to her.

'Now, tell me,' he sat back, twisting himself round so that he could see her more easily, 'what are you doing in this factory?'

'I told you,' she blew out a puff of smoke, 'working. When there's work to do.' His yellow eyes were expressionless. 'What makes you so suspicious? Why shouldn't I work at Blimpton? Thousands of other women do.'

'You're different.'

'How?'

'I don't know,' he returned her stare, examining her with a sort of mockery. 'Your clothes are all right. But there's something about the way you wear them... my wife would have put her finger on it at once... And your face... it's wrong, too.'

'What's wrong with my face?'

'It's lovely – but it's not the sort of loveliness one sees in a factory... I was brought up to be very class-conscious, you know – well, of course you don't know, and it doesn't matter. But if I still used that kind of jargon I should say that you had the sort of face that belonged to the ruling class.'

'Oh!'

'And your voice! Your voice gives you away at once... '

'Does it?' her tone was immediately self-conscious. 'No one else seems to have found anything queer about me – '

'That means nothing. Probably no one else has ever looked at you properly. Most people at Blimpton can't see anything that doesn't arrive packed in boxes.'

'Yes, I've noticed that.'

'You have?'

'Mm,' she nodded.

'So you don't think much of us at Blimpton?'

'How can I generalise? I can speak only of what I see, and that isn't very much – but it isn't very good, either.'

A silence fell between them. In the fading light the factory seemed to have come closer, and each of them, glimpsing the other's problems, appeared to hesitate, reluctant to go further, yet unwilling to go back. Wrapped, as they were, in their own private and secret thoughts, they were united by an awareness, unspoken and still vague, of their common interest in the vast tangle that lay below them: the hundreds of buildings in which a thousand different jobs were waiting to be done: and the men and women who were to do them, adapting their lives, their habits, their interests to meet demands of which they were not told, to fulfil purposes which they could only imperfectly understand.

'Now,' Morgan said at last, 'I think you'd better tell me all about it.'

'Yes…'

He waited, and, when she did not continue, asked with surprising gentleness: 'What are you running away from?'

'Oh!' she exclaimed startled, her defences momentarily pierced.

'You don't have to tell me if you'd rather not.' His attention seemed to be fixed on some point far away towards the centre of the landscape.

In a few seconds she had recovered herself. 'I'm not running away,' she told him, 'I came to Blimpton because I wanted to learn something about the world…'

'Well, my dear,' he smiled down at her with a look of quick understanding, of something like tenderness, but his voice was still a little mocking, 'you've certainly come to the right place – and the right person. What would you like to know? My early history? Or Blimpton's?'

'Blimpton's.'

'Okay.' He began to describe the origins of the factory, the history of its construction, the difficulties that had been experienced in the first few months, and the problems that faced them now. All, or almost all, of what he said was known even among the most junior of the managerial staff, and to many of the skilled workers, but little of it ever reached the thousands of girls and women on whom the factory finally depended. Griselda listened, intent, absorbed, interrupting only to clear up a point that she did not understand or to ask the meaning of some unfamiliar technical term. The story was only half completed when they reached Dustborough.

'And now,' he looked at his watch, 'I've got a date for dinner… but perhaps we could go on with this another time if you'd like to hear some more?'

'I should love to.' She offered him her hand, and then was gone, striding down the High Street as if the town were hers.

FIFTEEN

WHEN RUTH AARON arrived at the White Lion she found Morgan already there, waiting for her.

'I hope I'm not late?' she asked, and was embarrassed to find herself blushing.

'No.' Morgan looked at her with critical, appraising eyes. This evening, with her hair brushed smoothly off her forehead, and coiled into a knot at the back, she looked more than ever like an Old Testament heroine. Her dark eyes, set slant-wise in the long oval face, glowed with an almost reddish tinge. 'I've had a busy day,' he added vaguely.

'Working?'

'Partly.'

She unfastened her grey lambskin coat. Beneath it she wore a dress of dark silk, embroidered with a bright pattern of flowers at the neck and wrists. Miss Hopkins, confirming an unspoken promise of intimacy by looking through Ruth's wardrobe, had described the dress as exotic. Yet wearing it, Ruth was conscious of appearing rather dim. Already she began to wish that she had not come. She had been looking forward to this evening with a passionate, unreasonable anxiety, but now, as she sipped a cocktail and waited for whatever Morgan might be going to say, she was overcome by a sense of failure, almost of doom. He made a joke, and she laughed, but too late, as if she were unwilling to find it funny. She knew, or thought she knew, that he had asked her to dinner only because there was no other young woman at Mowbray Lodge and few (or, rather, few who were qualified to meet the Assistant Superintendent socially) elsewhere at Blimpton. She expected him to find her disappointing, and because of this her desire to please promised to be painful to them both.

In fact, he did not seem to notice her very much. He chose the dinner with as much care as the menu and the waiter would allow, ordered wine, and chatted about a number of indifferent subjects: the weather, the progress of the war, rationing, the blitz. Then Ruth began to talk about Blimpton. Lately, ever since the evening of Gunn's visit to the hostel, she had been trying to take an interest in her work, to feel a sense of responsibility for that part of the life of the factory with which she was concerned, So far, she had not been successful. She was homesick, longing perpetually for the radiant warmth of her mother's incessant chatter and for her father's apparently casual, but persistent and encouraging, interest in whatever she might be doing. Never articulate about her own feelings, she wrote them stiff little letters, designed chiefly to conceal what she really felt: her sense of her own inadequacy as a doctor and as an individual, her horror of meeting new people, of being regarded as a confidante by strange women who, she thought, had little sense of decency and no reticence, her fear of Gower's disapproval and, now, her growing obsession with Morgan…

'By the way,' he interrupted her description of MacIver's last visit to the surgery, 'I went to see a patient of yours this afternoon.'

'Of mine?'

'Yes,' he began to tell her about Rose Widgery. She listened, preparing an excuse for not having done something which it had not, until now, occurred to her to do.

'How you find time…' she murmured, conscious of something critical, hard and faintly ironical in his glance. 'I wish you'd asked me to come,' she added. 'I haven't had a chance to get over to the hospital since she's been there.' Even as she said it the remark sounded unconvincing.

'Oh, well,' he seemed not to be listening, and now he broke off to stare around the crowded dining room, as if looking for someone whom he did not really expect to see. 'Oh, well,' he repeated, 'you must come another time.'

She clutched at that, not daring to ask when. 'But you,' she ventured again, 'you seem to have time for everything.'

The glint in his yellow eyes sharpened. 'Not quite everything… if we go now we'll have time to look in at the Gittins' party.'

'Just as you like,' she agreed, trying to conceal her disappointment, to compensate, by an exaggerated cheerfulness, for her failure to make the evening enjoyable.

Although many people at Blimpton disliked Gittins, there were few who were unwilling to accept his hospitality. Mrs Gittins, whose position in the social hierarchy of the Great Arsenal had been somewhat lower than her husband's status there seemed to warrant, took a keen pleasure in being the first lady of Blimpton. Her hospitality was as lavish as conditions would allow, and perhaps more generous than Gittins' circumstances warranted. It was also somewhat indiscriminate. Part of the pleasure of visiting the Gittins' lay in the fact that one seldom knew who else would be there.

This evening the party was smaller than usual. When Ruth and Dan Morgan arrived they found, beside Mr and Mrs Gittins, only Dr Gower, Parsons, the new labour officer, and Nicholls, the chief chemist; and of these, Gower seemed to be the centre of interest. As a rule he avoided social functions, not because people bored him, but because he seldom had time for general conversation and the pleasant emptiness of leisure. He was a man who subordinated everything to his passion for research and for the application of its results. His was not a remote and coldly scientific passion; but nor was it simply a humane interest in the welfare of the twenty-thousand men and women who would ultimately make up the working population of Blimpton; it was based, more than anything else, on a deep hatred of every kind of inefficiency. He accepted the necessity for war, and the need for-high explosives with which to wage it. He accepted, too, the effects of these explosives in devastated towns and factories, in men and women and children blown to pieces, or left alive with some essential part of themselves destroyed for ever. These were the results of a course of action which seemed to him inevitable, and he could feel no indignation at the personal tragedies which they involved. But he disapproved, loudly, persistently and energetically, of such of the consequences of war as were not inevitable. He waged a perpetual battle against not only dermatitis, TNT poisoning, influenza epidemics, but also against boredom, fatigue, and the deadly monotony of the death-creating jobs. He argued that people who spent their working hours in making the instruments of death had a special right to life, and to all the pleasures that life had to offer.

'The trouble,' he was saying when Ruth and Morgan came into the room, 'the real, fundamental trouble in this factory is that nearly everyone is bored – utterly, unspeakably bored – with their jobs, their lives, the people they work beside, everything.' He pushed himself further down into the armchair, and stretched out his long legs towards the fire. The flames, picking out the hollows in his cheeks, emphasising the long line of the jaw and the ardour of his deep-set eyes, made him look like a younger, better directed Don Quixote, or perhaps a Loyola, recognising right and refusing to be satisfied with compromise. 'It's a peculiarly English disease, but none the less unforgivable.' He looked across at Ruth. 'You're bored, aren't you?' he demanded.

'Sometimes,' she admitted, slightly offended at being thus singled out.

'And who isn't?'

'I, for one.' Morgan, standing up, leaning back with one elbow on the mantelpiece, and with a glass of beer in his hand, took up the challenge. 'Nicholls for another.' Nicholls sat helping Mrs Gittins to wind a skein of wool. He was a plump young man, fresh-faced, good tempered, inclined to be ironical about his own enthusiasms. 'And you yourself, Gower... you don't know the meaning of the word – '

'But the workers – '

'The same with the workers – as long as they have enough to do – '

'Which isn't always,' Parsons ventured. He was still inclined to be shy in the company of people who had been at Blimpton longer than himself.

'And isn't always our fault,' Gittins added quickly.

'Certainly.' Morgan put down his glass. 'But no one who has enough to do is ever bored – '

'I have enough to do,' Ruth interposed defensively, with a glance at Gower.

Morgan shook his head. 'Enough to do in your working hours, perhaps. But when you're not working – what do you think about? How do you occupy yourself? Sitting about in Mowbray Lodge – '

Gower looked up sharply. 'But isn't that precisely the point?' he demanded, and Ruth, surprised at this sudden rescue, began to smile. 'Most people at Blimpton work only eight hours or so a day. The rest of the time they're simply stranded – '

'Oh, no!' Parsons leaned forward, eager, almost indignant. 'The difficulty for most of them – especially the women – is that they have far too much to do. Don't forget that with the distances they have to travel they're away from home for ten, twelve hours each day, sometimes more. And in the time that's left they have to keep house, shop, look after their children – '

'But aren't they bored, just the same?' Gower persisted.

'Some. The younger people…'

'Exactly. They have no interests. They loathe the factory.'

'That's the odour of death,' Nicholls remarked lightly.

'Who loathes the factory?' Morgan's yellow eyes were sparkling with a fierceness which he did not often display.

Gower continued to fill his pipe. His long fingers were unnaturally white, like paper. 'People do, you know,' he said easily, and lit a match. 'And I've explained why. They're not interested, and they're not healthy. Or perhaps I should put it the other way round… I'm not speaking at the moment of our failure to organise an adequate health service – '

'Who's failure?' Morgan broke in.

'Ours. In the last resort, mine – or should I say MacIver's?' This was the first time that Gower had betrayed, by even so much as a change in his tone of voice, any resentment at MacIver's persistent lack of interest in the task for which he was, as Senior Medical Officer, primarily responsible. Mrs Gittins put down her ball of wool and went out, tactfully, to brew fresh coffee. She knew that she would hear all about it afterwards, anyway.

But the criticism, if criticism it was, turned out to be no more than a parenthesis. 'If people aren't healthy,' Gower continued, addressing himself chiefly to Morgan, 'we can't expect them to be happy – '

'NO!' Morgan took a step forward. His head was erect, his body taut. 'I don't deny that – but you're only skimming the surface… of course we have our special health problems. But if we were filling chocolates or making silk stockings our real, inescapable difficulties would be much the same. We have no sense of community. We don't even try to begin to live together like human beings. We do our own isolated little jobs, but we avoid the big issues. It's something much deeper than boredom. We don't attach enough importance to what we're doing – ' he looked around, fiery-eyed, challenging anyone to dare to disagree.

'You're right there,' Nicholls allowed the kitten to slip off his knee, and bent to give it a final pat before it ran out of the room. 'We don't bring our lives with us when we come here. We settle down, yes, but even when we're more or less dug in we don't start any new life. We exist in a permanent state of suspension, waiting for the war to be over. Our lives aren't even turned inwards.'

'Backwards?' Parsons suggested.

'I think that's absolutely true,' Ruth murmured.

Morgan turned on her. 'Of course you do! And why? Because although we're supposed to be fighting a war for democracy there's scarcely a handful of people anywhere in the factory – either among ourselves or among the workers – who really understands what it's all about. Democracy! How can you expect a long fancy word like that to mean anything to people who can scarcely even understand how their wages cards are made out? And if we start putting it into words that people really can grasp the meaning of – if we start talking about fighting for human brotherhood, love – if we try to say what we really mean or ought to mean we – we – we become embarrassed, tongue-tied, ashamed in case anyone should hear us. All the beliefs to which I was brought up – and most of you, for that matter – have become so uncomfortable that we daren't talk about them any more. We're emotionally dead – oh, I don't mean that we no longer marry or have our little hole-in-the-corner affairs – but the feelings that really draw people together and make the basis of a community are buried, hidden under this English sense of decency, of being ashamed to express any wish, any desire that isn't purely personal and narrow and selfish. We don't love each other at Blimpton. Until we do all this talk about health services is like digging a drain through a cemetery – '

He paused for a moment to take breath. They were, as he had

said, embarrassed, avoiding one another's glances, feeling the walls of the cosy room crack, about to fall, to destroy their comfort, their precarious security, leaving them exposed to a violence that none of them, meeting Morgan daily, knowing him (they thought) well, almost intimately, could have anticipated…

'Think,' he spoke now more slowly, 'think of the new towns that have sprung up since the last war. Fundamentally, they're all exactly like Blimpton. Welwyn Garden City for example – '

'The healthiest place in the country – ' Gower objected ' – or very nearly.'

'But it's not alive! That's what I'm trying to tell you. There's no real community. Oh, I know,' he waved another interruption aside, 'they've got folk dancing or handloom weaving or a concert club. I've been there. And I tell you, those things aren't real. They're as satisfying as a workhouse Christmas Party. People in middle-class garden cities don't know what it is to be alive. It's the same, or worse, in the town-planners' nightmares that have been built for the workers: Dagenham or Wythenshawe at Manchester. Ask anyone who has lived in one of those places. The people are just dropped there, like flowers bedded out in a public park. They have no roots. They look all right – but so do we… They eat and sleep and make love in their tidy little boxes – but you can't say that they live in them, because the fact is that they simply don't know what it is to be alive. And here at Blimpton – '

Gittins, who had been listening with an air of acute anxiety, opened the door to let the kitten in again. 'At least we're doing a pretty good job,' he observed.

'Are we? We're filling a certain amount of ammunition… but even technically we've a long way to go before we can be satisfied. And our other responsibilities – you all know just as well as I do that most of us refuse to recognise that they even exist… we've been given the dregs of a social brew that was already stale when I was a boy, and we're content to allow these people to muddle along, totally unaware of the world that they're living in now – '

'But surely,' Gittins interrupted, 'that isn't our job. It's up to the Unions, if they want to do political propaganda… well, good luck to them so long as they keep the Communists in order…'

'Oh!' Morgan shook his head, laughing momentarily. 'You're trying to side-track me, Gitty – '

Gower, who had been listening, motionless, said suddenly: 'It sounds to me like Fascism!'

'What does?'

'Leading the workers, giving them opinions.'

'Oh, God!' Morgan retreated again towards the fireplace. 'Can't you see that this isn't a matter of employers and employed? After all, everyone in this factory is in the same mess, and we're all employees, all workers… all on the same side of the fence?'

'But are we?' Gower insisted. 'If I come to you tomorrow morning and tell you that I want another sun-lamp or a hundred thousand towels or a new surgery, am I going to get your backing in putting the proposal up to the Ministry? When it comes to spending public money are you protecting the tax-payers' pocket or the workers' health?' And then, as Mrs Gittins began to pour out fresh coffee, Gower stood up, facing Morgan, and for a moment it seemed that war, the long-overdue war between the production side and the medical officers, was at last to break out. 'Do I get your backing, or don't I?' Gower repeated.

Ruth, confused by this outbreak, looked from one man to the other. But Morgan only shrugged his shoulders, impatient at what seemed to him to be no more than an evasion of the issue. 'You get your soap regularly now, don't you?'

Nicholls smiled pleasantly. 'Isn't it odd,' he asked the company at large, 'that even when we do start to talk about the New Jerusalem we finish up with nothing more interesting than a piece of soap.'

'Well,' Gower spoke acidly, 'you won't reach the New Jerusalem without it. And towels…'

Morgan looked at his watch and beckoned to Ruth. 'I've got to go over and look at the night-shift. Can I give you a lift?'

The party began to break up. It had not been a success. Outside, the wind was rising. The night was very dark, without stars.

'And what do you think of all this?' Morgan asked as he started up the engine.

'I don't know,' Ruth replied and she pulled on her gloves and drew her coat more tightly around her. 'I haven't thought very much about the world, I'm afraid.'

'But about Blimpton?'

'It frightens me. I see what you mean – at least I think I do. But it's all so vast and – and I find it so extraordinarily difficult to make contact.'

'With?'

'Anyone.' Looking ahead into the darkness she added, more boldly than she would until a few minutes ago have imagined possible: 'Think how I bored you this evening!'

At that he gave a great guffaw of laughter. 'Bored me!' he grew serious. 'As a matter of fact I had something on my mind. I met someone today...'

'Yes?'

'Nothing... you could be quite useful in this factory if you could only let yourself go, be a little more friendly... people want to like you... take a few days off – go home for a weekend, and when you come back you'll see – '

'What?

'What you can do.' He drew up in front of the stone portico and, leaning across her to open the door, patted her lightly on the knees, 'And when you come back we'll talk. Really talk.'

'Yes,' she smiled in the darkness, suddenly confident with a certainty that would not last beyond the door of her room. 'You've certainly given me something to think about,' she added, and the triteness of the phrase echoed after her as she went into the house.

SIXTEEN

THE SUPERINTENDENT SAT hunched over his desk, reading a minute from the Chief Controller of Armaments in the Ministry of Weapon Production.

The telephone rang. The voice of a secretary announced that the Chief Controller was on the line.

Brown straightened his shoulders, jerked his tie into line with his shirt-front, and ran his free hand along his eyebrows, smoothing each hair into position. It was as if the great man was about to enter the room in person.

'Hello,' Brown cooed into the telephone, 'yes... yes... I received it by this morning's post... our plans are already going forward.'

The voice from the London end of the wire cackled on.

'Of course,' Brown repeated, his voice smooth and subordinate, 'I see no difficulty at all... none whatever... No... I assure you... Yes, I'll let you know at once if anything looks like going wrong... Yes... No, quite unnecessary for anyone to come down... yes, of course... Oh, absolutely... yes... thank you... goodbye.'

He put down the receiver. Then he rearranged the furniture of his desk, moving the pin-tray from the left to the right, bringing the 20-millimetre cartridge case a few inches forward, and pushing the 2-pounder shot to the other side of the ink-stand.

At last there was nothing left to do but to re-read the minute. He had already been through it six or seven times, but now he read it again, twice.

Next, he pushed the buzzer that connected him with Gittins. The latter came in almost at once.

'Gittins, look at this!' Brown handed him the minute. It was against moments such as this that the Principal Clerk daily prepared himself by arriving at the Administration Block at an hour of the morning at which most of his colleagues could safely be presumed to be occupied with their breakfasts. However, he made a fair show of surprise as he scanned the document.

'It won't be easy,' he commented as he put it down. The remark seemed to him, as soon as he had made it, to be an almost injudicious under-statement: for the Chief Controller had written to inform the Superintendent that, as a result of an air raid on the filling factory at Gasping it would be necessary for Blimpton to double its output of certain natures of ammunition during the next two months.

'Of course we can do it,' Brown looked less confident than he sounded. The factory was still behind with its original programme.

'This means doubling the planned output,' Gittins reminded him, 'and you know where we stand in relation to the plan.'

'Yes. I know. Let's get Morgan.'

A shadow passed over Gittins' face, and the furrows around his mouth deepened. His eyes, behind the gold-rimmed spectacles, were wary, alert.

Brown picked up the telephone.

'I don't think he's back yet,' Gittins spoke doubtfully.

'Back? What do you mean? Where's he gone to?' Brown pushed the bell on his desk to summon his secretary. 'Ring all the Groups and find out where Mr Morgan is,' he told her, 'and ask him to come over here as soon as possible. Tell him it's urgent.'

Gittins waited until Miss Gadd had closed the door behind her. Then he said: 'Morgan went up to London on Sunday. He said he'd be back this afternoon.'

'To London? What does he want to go running up to London for?' the Superintendent jumped up and began to pace across the room. His legs were so short that standing always seemed to place him at a disadvantage. 'He didn't tell me he was going – ' he sat down again. 'Why is it that nobody in this factory ever consults me before they go marching off in this – this truly extraordinary way?'

Gittins rubbed the bald patch on his head and said nothing. But something in the way in which he looked at the Superintendent, his glance more direct than usual, suggested that his loyalties, hitherto sharply divided, were beginning to find a new direction.

'What did Morgan go to London for?' Brown repeated.

'Some private business, I think... he said he'd look into the Ministry if he had time. He must have left you a note.'

Again the Superintendent rang for Miss Gadd.

'Did Mr Morgan leave a note for me?'

The secretary lifted her fluffy head and glanced at Gittins, who nodded. Then she went to the filing cabinet, drew out the note, laid it in front of the Superintendent and flounced out of the room.

Brown's expression made it plain that he had not seen it before.

'What's all this about the Ministry placing a contract in Dustborough?' he demanded, his eyebrows bristling with menace. A vein in his forehead began to throb as his face took on a deeper shade of red.

Gittins explained. When he had finished the Superintendent gave a long snort. 'We've no right to interfere with a question like that,' he declared. 'The people at the Ministry are surely capable of deciding for themselves where they want to place their contracts – '

'But – '

'And,' the Superintendent continued, 'I will not have Dolphin interfering in these matters of high policy. He's here to promote good relations with the local people. If we start poking our noses into this – ' he gave another snort, and his face began to grow purple ' – it'll only make a lot of bad blood, just when we're having as much trouble as we can manage from that particular quarter. Morgan should have consulted me before trying to stop a thoroughly reputable local firm from getting work which they are no doubt perfectly capable of carrying out... Who has Morgan arranged to see about this?'

'I don't know that he's arranged anything.'

'Oh. Well, we'd better have Dolphin in. No. You see him. We must get down to this new programme. Better get Dawson.'

Dawson came. The three men began to discuss how they were to meet the Ministry's new demands. First, the Superintendent pointed out, they would have to open up new sections of the factory. The group that was nearest to completion was at the far end of the site, nearly four miles away from the Administration Block. Dawson, after making six telephone calls, announced that the builders' men could be out of the shops within ten days.

'And then – ' Dawson hesitated.

'Then we have to appoint a shop-manager,' Gittins finished the sentence for him.

'I thought of transferring Jenkins from South-West,' the

Superintendent suggested unhopefully.

'Then who would go to South-West?' Gittins asked. He had already decided the next dozen moves in what was after all his favourite game. He knew just who would be promoted, who would be passed over or reduced in status, and who would merely be transferred from one Group to another. He was anxious not to appear to be in any hurry, but at the same time he knew that it was important that the changes should be decided, committed to paper and sent to the Chief Controller for approval before Morgan returned. When Morgan was present Gittins felt that it would be necessary to support him. But, until then, he had a chance to move independently, to pay off a number of old scores, to remove into obscurity several young men who had so many ideas about how to run the factory that they did nothing but make unnecessary work for those who, like himself, were certain that they had nothing more to learn.

But the Superintendent would not accept his suggestions. Even Dawson plucked up his courage and dared to disagree. Soon they were wrangling bitterly. The Superintendent lost his temper and began to shout. Gittins, relying less on his own vast knowledge of Civil Service Regulations than on the ignorance of the other two, plodded on calmly, gaining a handful of minor promotions for people who might one day come in useful. The major question, that of the appointment of a new shop-manager, got lost in the confusion.

'And now!' Brown thumped his fist on the table with a resounding bang. 'And now – '

Then the door burst open and Gunn rushed in.

'I knew I'd find you getting down to it,' he shook hands, motioned them to remain seated and drew up another chair, 'but I told the CC I'd come down and give you all I've got on this. You'll be all right, once we get going. Blimpton can do it, I told the Minister. Yeh, I told him. I said, you leave this to the boys on the spot, and I'll just run down there and do what I can to help them turn the heat on. High pressure organisation, that's what you need down here. And that's what you're going to get. Say,' he pulled off his overcoat and threw it towards a chair at the other end of the room, 'what's got you all so worried?'

The Superintendent drew his eyebrows together, threw back his shoulders and puffed out his chest. 'A factory like this,' he observed rather coldly, 'is a great responsibility.' He frowned magnificently and folded his hands across his chest. This Napoleonic gesture seemed, however, to be lost on his audience.

'As the personal representative of Lord Outrage – ' Gunn began afresh.

'Ah, yes,' the Superintendent allowed himself to relax, 'we're most grateful to you for coming to our assistance... We have our difficulties, you know, we have our difficulties...'

'You're telling me!' Gunn pulled out a notebook, 'I've heard a thing or two... Let's get right down to brass tacks, or whatever it is you call them in these parts. I want to put you on your feet, and I've got no time to waste.' He consulted the notebook. 'Hostel finished?' he asked.

'Um,' the Superintendent turned to Gittins, 'I think – '

'The warden will be settling in at the end of this week,' Gittins explained.

'Then you'll be able to put some girls in next Monday?'

'Well, I wouldn't say that,' the Superintendent saw that there was nothing more to be got out of Gittins. 'I wouldn't say we could get things moving as quickly as all that.'

'Why not?'

'For one thing,' Gittins told him, 'we still haven't got the girls... to put into the hostel, I mean.'

'Better get Knowles to come over,' Brown whispered to Gittins; but the Principal Clerk appeared not to hear. There were occasions, and this was one of them, when he found it necessary to demonstrate publicly that his duties were concerned with the general administration of the factory, and that he was not to be mistaken for the Superintendent's private secretary.

So the Superintendent had to make his own telephone call. When he returned to the conversation he found that Dawson was complaining about the supplies of empty components.

'Gaines,' he was saying, 'are the worst bottle-neck at the moment.

But we're having a lot of trouble about fuzes, too... they always seem to get lost in transit... two truckloads turned up at Worsing a month after we sent an SOS to the Ministry to find out where they'd got to...'

'I'll ask Finch to come over,' the Superintendent bobbed up again and, with a glance at Gunn, explained, 'he's our Factory Transportation Officer, you know. He's not on our establishment, unfortunately. For some reason he answers direct to the Ministry...'

'Fuzes,' Gunn repeated the word to himself in an undertone, and the puzzled expression which he habitually wore seemed to become intensified. As he frowned his low forehead contracted almost out of existence. 'Fuzes,' he repeated again, and then, all at once, light seemed to dawn and he asked, 'Say: didn't I bring some fuzes down here for you to fill?'

'Yes,' Dawson agreed, 'we filled them.'

'Any good?'

'It's hard to tell until they've been tested out. Fired, I mean.'

'Why haven't you fired them?'

'I understood that you wanted to be at the trials.'

'That's right. Can we try 'em after lunch?'

Dawson hesitated.

'Well, can we?' Gunn looked at his watch, 'shall we say 1.45?'

'I'll have to ask Captain Bunting. He's in charge of that side of things.'

'Okay. Ask him to come along.'

'Now?'

'Sure, let's get the whole bunch.'

Bit by bit the bunch arrived: Knowles, Finch, Bunting; the local representative of the Ministry's Inspection Department, the Manager of Services, the Security Officer; Nicholls, the senior chemist. Dr MacIver, who happened to be paying his weekly visit to the factory, drifted in quietly, and was soon followed by Gower and Ruth Aaron; the shop-managers from the North-East and South-West Groups arrived in the company of two shop-stewards and an assistant forewoman. The assistant forewoman had been arranging with the shop-manager of North-East for one of the operatives on the Group, who had been guilty of taking a metal lip-stick case into the Danger Area, to be given an official reprimand and, when the Superintendent telephoned, she had been so anxious to conclude her indictment that she did not notice, until she entered the room, that her argument had carried her to the office of the Superintendent himself. She sat down in the only empty chair and waited for someone to tell her that she might go back to her work.

But nobody noticed her. Everyone seemed to be talking at once, and nearly all of them appeared to be addressing Gunn, who remained perfectly still, the weight of his body thrown on to the back of his chair, his legs stretched out under the table so that he was lying rather than sitting. His eyes were half-closed, and he looked as if he might have been asleep.

In fact, he was even unusually wide awake. Although he was sitting with his back to the door he noticed when Dolphin slipped in and when Gower, after muttering some excuse to Dr MacIver, hurried out. The talk broke around his head like surf, splashing torrents of noise high into the air and then suddenly falling away into silence. Most of those who were talking seemed to be addressing the Superintendent, yet much of what they said was directed at Gunn. Finch, in particular, took the opportunity to condemn both the local and headquarters organisation of the Ministry in a fashion that he would not have thought worthwhile if he had not had at least some reason to believe that most of what he said would be repeated in London, possibly even to the Minister himself. The Superintendent declared, in a long and extremely involved speech, that while he was a man of his word and, moreover, a man accustomed to dealing with crises and unforeseen difficulties and with the surmounting of insurmountable obstacles, nevertheless if the Ministry did not, in future, honour its undertakings in a way in which it had not done in the past, he could not be responsible for the consequences.

Gunn lifted his eyelids. 'What undertakings?' he asked.

'Eight hundred women a week,' Brown replied shortly.

'We received only one hundred and twenty-three female entrants last week,' Knowles rushed to the Superintendent's aid.

'And how many girls left the factory?' Dolphin asked in a soft malicious tone.

Knowles did not answer, but the tip of his long nose quivered at the challenge.

'Two hundred and eleven, wasn't it?' Dolphin pursued him. 'So that the total number of employees was down by – '

Gittins motioned him to silence. This was one of the things that Gittins knew how to do well: the lift of his hand held the slightest, most delicate hint of a threat. 'We'll soon have this Essential Work Order,' he pointed out, 'and then they won't be able to leave – '

'What's that?' Gunn asked.

'The Essential Work Order,' someone repeated.

'Yeh. I heard that. But what is it?'

'The Ministry of Labour – ' Knowles began to explain.

'What, that chap Bevin?'

'Can't stand him,' the Superintendent declared boldly.

'It means that people won't be able to leave their jobs,' Knowles was heard to say, 'that is…' his voice droned on.

Gunn shook himself like a dog jumping out of a pond.

'Okay,' he said, 'I get it. I think I've got the whole set-up now.' He looked around the room. 'Where's that fellow – what's his name?'

'Morgan?' someone suggested.

'Yeh. Morgan.'

'I'm afraid he's away on leave just at the moment,' the Superintendent told him smoothly.

'What does he mean, going off on leave just when you have to double your output?'

The Superintendent dismissed the company. Reluctantly, one by one, they filed out of the room.

'He didn't know about this when he went off,' Gittins explained.

'Then why don't you send for him to come back? I like that chap. He's got something.'

'Yes,' Gittins agreed, 'everyone likes Morgan.'

'Though he's apt to take the law into his own hands, you know,' the Superintendent, having got rid of his audience, sat down and once more began to expand. 'We can't afford to have people doing that in an organisation of this size… of course, he's my deputy, and I wouldn't say a word against him.'

'You could do with him now.'

'Yes. I expect him back shortly.'

'When?'

There was a slight pause. The Superintendent glanced at Gittins.

'I really couldn't say,' Gittins lied with less than his usual aplomb. He suspected that the situation was about to become unmanageable.

'Listen,' Gunn changed the subject abruptly, 'I got an idea. How many girls work at the factory at Gasping?'

'Ten or twelve thousand,' Gittins hazarded.

'Then why don't we bring them down here? Just until they get that place cleaned up a bit after this blitzing. That'd fill your hostel for you.'

The Superintendent's eyebrows jerked wildly. This seemed to him to be quite the silliest idea that he had heard for some time.

'That's a very original suggestion,' he said after a slight pause, 'a very original suggestion indeed, if I may say so. But I doubt whether it is altogether practicable.'

'Why is that?'

'The difficulty is – ' chorus-like, the Superintendent and the Principal Clerk pulled out the well-worn phrase. One after the other they began to enumerate the difficulties. Only two of the Groups at Gasping had suffered any serious damage; of the two or three thousand women who would be temporarily redundant some would probably be needed in other parts of the factory. Some were married; others, no doubt, had local ties that would make it difficult, if not impossible, for them to work away from home. The Superintendent of Gasping would probably oppose the suggestion in case Blimpton should refuse to allow his girls to return to him when they were needed. Moreover, Gasping, though nearer to Blimpton than many places from which workers were being transferred, was not in a region which the Ministry of Labour had scheduled as being a supply area for Blimpton, and in these circumstances it would not be surprising if the Ministry of Labour refused to co-operate...

'See here,' Gunn jumped up, 'those ain't – aren't – ain't – difficulties. They don't amount to a row of beans. You need the girls

– don't you?'

'My dear fellow,' the Superintendent was abject, 'you know we do.'

'Well, then, that's all there is to it.' He got up. 'We'll fix that. You have the hostel ready and I'll get the girls. What's today?' he glanced at his diary. 'Wednesday. I'll go straight on to Gasping after lunch. I ought to be there in time for dinner. Then the girls'll have to have a few days to pack their bags and that sort of thing. Say we get the first batch here next Monday, how'd that do? Six hundred on Monday, and another six hundred on Monday week – '

'But – ' the Superintendent roused himself, 'I don't see how – '

'You just leave it to me. I'll handle the details – special trains and that kind of thing – '

'But the Ministry!' Gittins broke in.

'What Ministry?'

'Our Ministry. We'll have to get their approval. There's the Chief Controller's department to be consulted. Then the labour people – '

'Look here, didn't I say I'd handle all that? If you'll get someone to put in a call I'll speak to the Minister right now.'

The Superintendent rang for Miss Gadd.

'And now,' Gunn went on, 'if I'm going to sell this factory to the girls over at Gasping I'll want a line on the things you've got here that'll attract a girl – concerts, beauty parlours – '

'Beauty parlours!'

'Where they put this stuff on their faces before they go into the danger zone.'

'Oh,' Gittins spoke wearily, 'protective creams, you mean. They do that sort of thing at all the filling factories. It's the same everywhere…'

He slipped out of the room and returned with Dolphin; but the latter, though willing enough to ingratiate himself with Gunn, had little to suggest. He described the factory concerts, and Gunn insisted that Miss Hopkins should be sent for to have lunch with him. That settled, the visitor began to show signs of impatience.

'See here,' he said, 'if we're going to put this proposition across we must know what it is we're trying to sell. We've got to offer the girls something they haven't got at home – '

'Bathrooms?'

'How d'you mean, bathrooms?'

'In the hostel. Most of them don't have bathrooms in their own homes.'

'No, that's certainly something,' Gunn considered the point. 'But bathrooms ain't glamour,' he went on, 'you're not going to get girls travelling two hundred miles just to have a bath.'

'Personally,' the Superintendent interposed, 'I always believe in appealing to the patriotism of the working classes.'

'But patriotism,' Dolphin reminded him with a cynical smile, 'is not enough.'

Gunn looked at him sharply, as if struck with the originality of this remark. 'You're darn right,' he spoke more cordially, 'patriotism is not enough! I like that,' he scribbled the words into his notebook for future use. 'What we've got to have is patriotism plus glamour. Where's the glamour?'

The three officials were still trying to find the answer to this question when the door opened a few inches and Mavis Little put her head through the aperture. Dolphin looked up and signalled to her to go away just as the Superintendent commanded her to enter.

Gunn's narrow eyes opened to their fullest extent as he turned to look at her.

'Well! he exclaimed.

'Well?' the Superintendent asked in quite a different tone.

For an instant the girl stood in the doorway, and then, with a wave of her blonde curtain of hair, she advanced into the room.

'Mr Dolphin is wanted on the telephone,' she said, glancing from one man to another and finally fixing her gaze on Gunn.

'Who is it?' Dolphin asked, trying to conceal his exasperation, 'couldn't you take a message?'

'It's Mr Meakin.'

'All right. Tell him I'll ring him as soon as I'm free.'

Gunn continued to watch her as she turned to go out of the room. She wore a tight fitting pale green suit, elaborately curved, and a frilly open-work blouse. As soon as she had closed the door behind her he said: 'That's what we've been looking for. That's glamour.'

'Two-pence coloured,' Dolphin murmured. He had had some difficulty in persuading Gittins to allow him to take the girl on to his staff, and he was already convinced that the effort had not been worthwhile. He saw that he would have to find some other means of placating the factory's enemies in Dustborough, since Mavis seemed likely to prove almost as coldly critical as her father, the proprietor of the White Lion...

'All the same,' Gunn repeated, 'that girl's got glamour. She's worth any number of fancy posters.' He thought for a moment. 'Maybe I'll get her to come over to Gasping to have a talk with the girls later in the week. To tell 'em about the factory, you know the kind of thing.'

'But she doesn't know anything about the factory,' Dolphin pointed out, 'she's an office worker.'

Gunn brushed the remark aside. 'That's the trouble with you chaps,' his tone, though patronising was not unfriendly. 'Hidebound... still, I suppose you've got to be if you're going to stick it here. Now let's get hold of that nice little woman who runs your entertainments. Maybe she'll be able to give us a line...'

SEVENTEEN

FOR SOME REASON known only to himself Gunn insisted on having lunch alone with Miss Hopkins. Then he left for Gasping. His fuzes were put back into store to await his next visit. His telephone call to the Minister was cancelled. And Morgan, who had been inquiring for Gunn in almost every department of the Ministry of Weapon Production, returned to the factory just five minutes after he had left.

Morgan was worried. His visit to London had not been a success. His attempt to learn something about the contract that was being placed at Gurneys in Dustborough had had to be postponed while he discussed the details of Blimpton's new programme with various members of the Chief Controller's staff. Then he heard that the superintendent of the factory at Worsing was about to retire, and he spent some time in trying to discover what prospect he himself had of being offered the appointment, only to find that the job had already been filled. When, at last, he went to see the contracts branch he was assured that no contract had ever been placed in Dustborough. Still dissatisfied, he wandered from one part of the Ministry to another, making what purported to be purely social calls on old acquaintances, but trying all the time to find some clue which would lead him towards the information for which he was looking. Just as he was about to give up he found Colonel Jervis, who knew the whole story: and the story, quite shortly, was that the Superintendent of Blimpton had come up to London one day with old Gurney himself; that together they had taken the Director of Ancillary Articles out to lunch, and had so impressed him with the efficiency of Gurneys and with the need to provide work for the firm's skilled employees that he had promptly agreed to place his next contract with them. The details of the contract were now being worked out, and it was expected that the firm would begin to tool up for the new job within the next week or two.

On hearing this, Morgan's first impulse was to go and see the Director of Ancillary Articles; but when he telephoned to make an appointment he found that the Director was out, so he went, instead, to see the Director of Labour. The latter was, however, well protected by an efficient secretary who explained to Morgan that Mr Phipps, as a Director, could only discuss questions of policy with people on the same level as himself and that, if Morgan wished to pursue the matter further, he must do so through one of the directors in the Department of the Chief Controller of Armaments. This so enraged Morgan that he rushed out of the Ministry to catch the next train back to Dustborough before even beginning to think of what he would do next.

The long journey restored his balance and, after thinking carefully over all the questions involved, he decided to go straight to the Superintendent. But this proved less easy than he had expected. Gunn's visit had left most of the administrative staff at Blimpton in an extreme state of emotional stress. The sense of living on top of a volcano, which was always induced by contact with the most erratic of Lord Outrage's personal representatives, was heightened by the knowledge that a major eruption was due to take place within the next four or five days. Arrangements for the opening of the East-North-East Group and for the reception of six hundred new girls at the still only partly finished hostel kept everyone fully occupied for twelve or fourteen hours each day. The Superintendent seemed to be supervising most of the arrangements in person, and it was not until two days after his return from London that Morgan succeeded in finding him alone.

'Well?' Brown asked. The moment appeared to be embarrassing to both of them. Morgan advanced into the room, his arms flat against the side of his body, his round chin thrust forward, his face wearing an expression of restrained belligerence. The Superintendent, perhaps aware that this interview had been postponed for too long, seemed unwilling to take the initiative. 'How do you think things are going?' he asked at last.

Morgan shrugged his shoulders. 'If the girls turn up we ought to get somewhere near to programme requirements… but it's a big "if".'

'Why shouldn't they turn up?'

'I – ' he broke off to refuse the proffered chair, and moved a step or two nearer the Superintendent's desk. 'It's not so easy, he went on, 'to persuade six hundred girls to pack up and leave home at three days' notice...'

'No,' Brown sat back more comfortably. His pudgy hands made a move towards some object that lay a few inches in front of him, but he controlled himself, and only the slight motion of his eyebrows indicated that he was not really thinking about the subject of their conversation. 'Gittins was saying that only just now... and in the ordinary way I'd say he was right, but with that fellow Gunn – he's an extraordinary fellow, quite extraordinary. D'you know, I haven't had one word from him since he went off on Wednesday? By the way,' he looked up sharply, and his voice took on a biting edge of authority, 'why weren't you here when he came? What do you mean by running off in the middle of a week without so much as consulting me as to whether you can be spared, or – '. The change of manner was so sudden as to seem not altogether real.

'I went away for the weekend,' Morgan broke in. His hand, holding a lighted match, trembled slightly, betraying some doubt which he had hitherto refused to recognise. 'You weren't available. And I was kept longer than I had expected – '

'Kept?'

'In London.'

'And – ' now the Superintendent grasped the edge of the desk with both hands, lifting himself forward ' – what were you doing in London? And why couldn't you have let me know that you were detained – provided of course that you really were detained and not merely – merely gadding about shaking the hayseeds out of your hair? Oh, yes,' he shook his head, his features contracting into a look of acute disgust, 'I've heard about the way some of the people from this factory disport themselves when they have a few days' leave... don't imagine that because I say nothing I don't know... I have my sources of information, too. But I don't expect that sort of thing from you... a man in your position ought to set a better example to the younger, more irresponsible elements...'

'I haven't the slightest idea what you mean,' Morgan said slowly. A glint of what looked like anger but might even have been amusement appeared in his eyes. 'In any case – ' he brushed the subject aside, not waiting to finish the sentence. 'As a matter of fact,' he continued, 'I was kept in London on business. Our business.'

'What business?'

As soon as he had spoken the Superintendent seemed to realise that the question had been a mistake. But before he could correct himself Morgan replied, his voice taking on the singing, oversubtle Welsh tone that was most apparent in moments of difficulty or embarrassment. 'I think you know,' he said. 'It was impossible for me to see you before I left, and after what Dolphin told me it seemed important that someone should act quickly. We must get that contract of Gurneys cancelled – at all costs.' He threw out the final phrase with a certainty which was probably greater than he felt.

'What do you mean?' the Superintendent asked sharply.

'I think I ought to tell you – ' Morgan was standing very upright, his sallow, mobile face rigid, expressionless. 'I think I ought to tell you,' he repeated, 'that when I was in London I found that people are talking about how Gurneys came to get that contract. I decided that it was my duty to come and tell you what I know.'

'And what do you know?' Bracing himself to meet the challenge the Superintendent frowned impressively, his massive eyebrows advancing so far as to make the eyes themselves almost invisible. He paused, but Morgan remained obstinately silent.

The pause prolonged itself into awkwardness.

'I don't understand what you're getting at,' Brown continued at last. 'You've probably been listening to a lot of foolish gossip.' His tone betrayed an increasing exasperation. 'For God's sake sit down!' he fired suddenly.

Morgan took the visitors' chair. 'Probably,' he agreed. 'That's why I felt that I should come straight to you – as I have done. People in the Ministry are suggesting that you – '

'I? I – what?' This time the clutching fingers grasped the 20-millimetre cartridge case that lay on the desk. Feverishly, the Superintendent began to polish the shining brass with a corner of his handkerchief. 'Go on!' he persisted, as the other still seemed to hesitate. "What are they saying about me in the Ministry? That I happened to go up to town on the same train as old Gurney?'

'Sir,' Morgan was again standing, 'you must understand that I only repeat what I have been told, neither more nor less. It is – it must be – in the interests of us all that I should tell you this. The fact that you should have introduced Gurney to the Director of Ancillary Articles – '

'And why shouldn't I?' Brown jumped up and pushed his chair back.

'Certainly. Why not?' Morgan was mild now, conciliatory though not subordinate. It was as if his desire to fight, to enjoy a battle, had, since he came into the room, become slowly subordinated to what was, in spite of all lapses, his chief and permanent objective. 'The result,' he said, weighing each word, 'has been – or promises to be – unfortunate for us. If this contract goes through Gurneys will get labour that ought to come to us – '

'That's enough!' the Superintendent, who had been pacing the room, shouted from his vantage point beneath the far window. He stood quite still. 'Do you realise – ' his voice dropped to a hoarse, public-meeting tone, the tone he used in addressing meetings of the workers, ' – do you realise that you're accusing me – '

'Oh, no!' Morgan interrupted. 'Sir, I beg of you – '

'Well?'

'You must understand that I haven't come here simply to retail a rather unpleasant piece of gossip. Nor to make – accusations. You know how people talk… but what concerns me is not even the harm that such talk does – not only to yourself, but to the factory, to Gittins, to me, to all of us. My sole reason for telling you this story is to impress on you that in my opinion – for whatever that may be worth – it is essential for the sake of your – our reputation that, as I have already said, the contract should be cancelled.'

'But if it is,' Brown was subsiding, 'people will only think that there's some substance in this – this filth. Besides, the question does not concern us directly. Of course we may suffer a little – '

'And if Gurneys get that contract we *shall* suffer – apart altogether from the harm that gossip always does – '

'Mm.' By this time Brown had returned to his desk. 'Who told you this story?' he demanded.

Morgan shook his head. 'I heard it from various sources,' he replied evasively. 'You know how people talk...'

'About a perfectly innocent little lunch! Really, these civil servants... what does Gittins say?' He pushed the buzzer.

Gittins, arriving from the neighbouring room, achieved a look of mild surprise on being told the story. 'Very unfortunate for you, sir,' he commented when the Superintendent had finished.

'But you're not suggesting that people will take this seriously?' the Superintendent asked. He was himself again, aloof, slightly condescending. But his eyes, though no longer hidden, were blank, averted from the others' waiting glance.

Gittins shook his head. The area of baldness seemed to have extended itself considerably during the past few weeks. 'I'm sure I hope not,' he remarked. 'But after all my years in the service I think it would be better if – '

'If what?'

'If the contract didn't go forward.'

'Well,' Brown seemed to consider, 'I shall have to take your experience into account. Though I don't like to interfere with the Ministry's policy even if – ' he broke off, making a gesture of dismissal.

Outside in the corridor Gittins and Morgan looked at one another uncertainly. Morgan shrugged his shoulders. 'The dirty devil!' he murmured. 'I didn't handle it well – but I think I've stopped him.'

'Let's hope so.'

They turned, in opposite directions, each to his own room.

EIGHTEEN

AFTERWARDS, EVERYONE CLAIMED to have known from the beginning that Gunn would not succeed in uprooting six hundred women from Gasping and transplanting them to Blimpton. Nevertheless, the cynicism that was displayed proved inadequate to the occasion. Even Dolphin, who organised – and won – a sweepstake on the event guessed that sixty girls would arrive at the hostel within a fortnight. Girls did, it is true, arrive, but not from Gasping. The factory's weekly intake of labour remained at its usual low level, and the twenty-three girls who trickled in from Gasping during the fortnight following Gunn's visit made little impression on the total volume of work that it was possible to perform.

But the girls from Gasping, though few in number, had a considerable effect on the atmosphere of the factory. This was partly because almost everyone in Blimpton had heard, sometimes vaguely and generally inaccurately, odd stories about the plans that were being hatched in the Administration Block: and the workers were therefore curious to see the newcomers when they arrived; and, then, when they started work, the Gasping Girls, as they were called, proved to have very definite views about the superiority of the factory from which they had come compared with that in which they now found themselves. They complained about almost everything: about the long journey from Blimpton to Dustborough (for though they lived in the hostel they found that they had to go into town if they wanted to shop or to visit a cinema); about the food in the hostel, which they said was bad, and the food in the factory canteens, which everyone agreed was, if possible, worse. They grumbled at the overcrowding in the shifting-houses; and when one girl found, two days after her arrival, that her new rubber-soled shoes had been replaced by a pair that were almost worn out, she declared that she came from a factory where people were honest in their habits, and she refused to go out on to the clean-way until the shifting-house attendant provided her with a new pair. Then the newcomers began to agitate about the state of the ablution rooms and to demand clean towels every time they left the shift. They refused to use the protective creams and powders that were provided for those who worked in contact with explosives, and declared that their own beauty preparations were a better protection against dermatitis than anything that Blimpton, or any other filling factory for that matter, could provide. Finally, they had their own way of performing even the most simple operation; if a handle had to be turned to the left they explained that at Gasping they had always turned it to the right, and that the Gasping way was the correct and safe and, indeed, the only proper way of performing any filling operation.

The over-lookers complained to the foremen. The foremen complained to the shop-managers, and the shop-managers complained to the labour officers, to the Principal Clerk, to Morgan, and even to the Superintendent himself. The Gasping Girls, nobody doubted, were at least ten times as much trouble as they were worth. Yet it was impossible to send them back to their own factory, since to have done so would have been an affront to Gunn, if not indeed to Lord Outrage himself. Gunn telephoned to the Superintendent two or three times, and on each occasion he explained rather cryptically that he was so busy tearing up red tape in the Ministry that it was impossible for him to leave London. He did not refer to his failure (if failure it was) to organise a mass migration from Gasping, but each time he mentioned certain plans which were now being made, and which would, in the very near future, ensure that Blimpton received all the labour that could possibly be required.

'How's my little lot doing?' he would inquire each time before he rang off.

'Pretty well,' the Superintendent would reply, 'pretty well, considering the circumstances.'

Then, as he hung up, Brown would reconsider the circumstances. The more he considered, the more difficult the problem seemed to grow, and after a while he would pick the telephone up again and send for one or other of his staff to come and discuss it with him. At first he was unable to understand how such a small number of girls could exercise such an extraordinarily disturbing influence in a factory which already had a population of something over six thousand. It was Parsons who remarked that the trouble really started from the fact that the girls from Gasping were the only inhabitants of the hostel who were familiar with the routine of life in a filling factory.

'You see,' he explained one afternoon, about two weeks after the girls had arrived, 'the girls who are new to the hostel believe everything that the Gasping girls tell them – all the horrors, everything. You can't blame them if they begin to get a bit hysterical as soon as they get inside the factory.'

'I don't blame them,' Miss Creed, who had just walked in, did not wait for the Superintendent to reply. 'It's these other girls I blame. They've worked in a filling factory – they ought to have more sense of responsibility.'

'I wish you'd have a talk with them,' the Superintendent suggested, seizing the first straw.

'But I have talked to them!' Miss Creed sat down and pulled off her gloves. Her large white face was pale with indignation. 'I'm sorry to have to admit that as far as I can judge I made no impression on them whatsoever. As soon as I'd finished they started quoting their own labour officers at me, and from all that could gather…' she lifted her eyes towards the ceiling in a manner that was intended to indicate the sort of conclusions she had drawn about the labour officers at Gasping.

'Don't you think – ' Parsons began, looking first at Miss Creed and then at the Superintendent, 'I mean – well – the way it strikes me is – '

'Is what?' Miss Creed asked sharply. She had noticed, and already deplored, a tendency on the part of Parsons to express, in spite of his diffidence of manner, opinions which were strangely at variance with those of his superiors.

'I mean,' he began afresh, 'if I came from Gasping I should probably feel – and behave – very much like those girls. It's natural to be loyal to the place you happen to come from, after all… you know, the old school tie and all that…'

'Well, really!' Miss Creed exclaimed, and then found herself unable to continue. She stared hard at Parsons' shiny navy blue suit. It seemed to be too tight for him. Yet he was not getting fat; indeed, now he looked taut and muscular, and a look of resolution strengthened his pleasant but rather indeterminate features.

'The old school tie!' the Superintendent repeated. 'What an odd suggestion!'

'Very,' Miss Creed agreed dryly, and noted that Parsons could have done with a haircut.

'All the same,' Brown seemed to be pursuing his own thoughts, 'I suppose these girls do develop a sense of loyalty in time… though I can't say that I've noticed it myself.'

'Oh, but I have!' Parsons was suddenly eager. 'Some of the old hands here – people who've been in the factory seven or eight months – they talk as if the place belonged to them. I've noticed it, often. If we could get some of our own old-stagers to move into the hostel – '

'But the old-stagers, as you call them,' Miss Creed objected, 'have their own homes to go to. It would be ridiculous to expect them to move into a hostel simply to counteract the harm done by a dozen or so silly little mischief makers.'

Parsons turned to the Superintendent. 'It's worth trying,' the latter ruminated, 'if you can find the right type of girls… and I dare say that some of them who've been here a few months would be only too glad to get away from their lodgings… don't you think so, Miss Creed?'

'Oh, I should think most of them are happy enough where they are.' Miss Creed rose and began to put on her gloves. 'But, of course, if you'd like to get some of them into the hostel I'll get someone in the Labour Office to run around this afternoon and choose some girls.'

'They'd have to go as volunteers,' Parsons pointed out, 'I mean, we can't force them.' Miss Creed gave him a withering look. 'Oh, they'll volunteer all right,' she told him, 'I think we can trust Miss Braithwaite to see to that.'

Phoebe Braithwaite, however, did not find it easy to persuade girls who were living in lodgings in Dustborough to move into the hostel. Many of them had come to Blimpton because they had been promised accommodation which was described in the newspapers as being equivalent to that provided by a first-class hotel; they had arrived to find the hostel uncompleted and had been placed in lodgings which, however uncomfortable, provided them with some sort of a substitute for the intimacies of home life. Even those who had hoped eventually to move into the hostel assumed, when the opportunity came, that there must be, as they remarked to each other, a catch in it somewhere. Phoebe, as she trudged from shop to shop, trying to select girls whom Miss Creed would recognise as being of the right type, met everywhere with refusals. The few girls who were willing to move into The Beeches, as the hostel was called, seemed to her to be of exactly the wrong type. Among them was Doris Chandler, the cinema usherette from Oldham. Doris had come to Blimpton with the intention of living in the hostel, and nothing that had happened to her during the past three months had weakened her resolution. She had been shifted from job to job, doing whatever was required of her, but never quite understanding the purpose of the different operations that she was called upon to perform. She had made friends and lost them as she, or they, were moved around the factory; and sometimes she had found them again. She had changed her lodgings four or five times, and had suffered several periods of acute home sickness. But she had, in spite of everything, kept her two main ambitions steadily in view: first, to send home to her mother at least ten shillings every week; and, second, to live in a place where she would be able to have a bed of her own and a bath when she wanted one.

Yet now, when the girls in the shop in which she worked were being invited to move into the hostel, Doris found herself hesitating. She still remembered how, on her first day in the factory, Miss Braithwaite had separated her from her friend Winnie Poulton; and she had since learned that Winnie had, after less than a week in the factory, packed up her things and gone back home, too frightened to tell anyone that she was going. She knew, too, that Miss Braithwaite did not like girls who put themselves forward; so Doris waited to be asked.

She waited in vain. But as soon as Miss Braithwaite had left the shop the girls broke into an uproar.

'The Beeches!' one of them exclaimed, 'I know what I'd call it!'

'Twenty-five bob a week!' another remarked, 'and from all I've heard you have to pay extra for every cup of tea.'

'I wouldn't mind that,' a third observed rather more coolly, 'it's cheap enough for what you get. I mean, you can complain if it isn't what you like.'

'Complain!' several people repeated at once, 'what's the good of complaining?'

'I heard,' someone else told them, 'that the girls who've gone in are sleeping on bare boards...'

'Oh, no,' Doris chimed in, 'I know that's not true. Actually, it's lovely – '

'Well,' the first girl persisted, 'if it's so lovely why don't they take us over to have a look? Expecting us to take it all on trust... But you don't catch me that way. No thanks!'

Doris flushed angrily. 'I've heard it's lovely,' she insisted, 'honest, I have.'

'Then why didn't you say you'd go?' the other challenged.

'But she never asked me...'

The others burst into laughter.

'You come to Blimpton,' somebody said, 'and then you wait to be asked to go in that place! Can't you see they're just waiting for some poor sucker to offer to go?'

'I'm not a poor sucker!' Doris flared angrily. 'But I do want to live decent – '

Someone took her on one side and whispered something.

'All right,' Doris agreed, plucked up her courage and ran out on to the clean-way to try to catch Miss Braithwaite when she came out of the shop next door.

A fine misty rain was falling. The smooth surface of the clean-way was shining treacherously in the late afternoon light. Doris hurried as much as she dared – for running on the clean-ways was strictly forbidden – and then had to stand for five or ten minutes outside the shop where she guessed Miss Braithwaite to be.

As soon as the labour officer came out Doris rushed up to her. 'Please,' she demanded breathlessly, 'can I go in the hostel?'

Phoebe looked at her sternly. 'Who are you?' she asked. 'Where do you come from? What do you mean by standing out here in the rain?'

'I was in the shop just now!' Doris did not know how to go on. She saw at once that it was no good, that it would have been better not to have come.

'And why are you wearing your hair like that?' Phoebe continued in the same tone. 'Here, you'd better come and take shelter for a minute.' She led the way into the shop. 'Don't you know,' she went on, looking at Doris' long hair that fell untidily around her shoulders, at the cap perched perilously over one ear, 'don't you know that it's extremely dangerous not to tuck your hair under your cap? Don't you understand that you'll get your head covered in powder if you go about like that?'

Doris began to fumble with her cap. She knew the rules, but she knew that most people did not bother about keeping their heads covered, and she did not see why she should. It was worth an occasional ticking-off to try to look nice just in case – just in case anyone happened to come round.

'Why didn't you say that you wanted to go to the hostel when I came into your shop?' Phoebe demanded. The mist had clouded her spectacles, and she could not see very well. 'It's too late now,' she said firmly, realising in a flash that to tell Miss Creed that there were no volunteers would be difficult, but that to produce such a volunteer as Doris would be utterly impossible. 'You should have come forward when you had the chance.'

'But – '

'I've told you; it's too late now…'

She bustled off.

Doris turned in the other direction. She walked blindly, scarcely noticing where she was going.

'I'll go home,' she started to mutter to herself, 'I'll go home!'

Tears sprang into her eyes. She brushed them away angrily. She did not really want to go home, to go back to helping her mother with the housework and the shopping, to blacking the stove every morning and helping to get the kids off to school, to sharing a bed with Lily and Isabel, to being scolded by her mother or father or both of them together if she came in from work half an hour later than usual. She did not want to go back to the dingy cinema, to trotting round every afternoon and evening pointing out the empty seats by the light of an electric torch, trying to prevent people in the ninepennies from stealing into the shilling seats as soon as her back was turned. She was quite sure that she did not want to go back to all this, and yet, as she remembered the friendly kitchen at home with its smell of drying clothes and fish and chips, with everyone sitting round the table talking and laughing and shouting and with the noise of the wireless going on behind it all, she began once more to feel lost and lonely and afraid. She walked on, stepping aside now and then as the truckers passed her, pushing their dangerous loads.

One of them called out, 'Watcher, Garbo!' as he caught sight of her.

'Hello, Sid,' she greeted him wanly.

He stopped. 'Something up?' he asked. He was a thin and perky young man whose face and hands were stained faintly yellow. The round cap, like a convict's, was pulled low over his forehead.

'Nothing much,' Doris stood still for a moment, a yard or so away from him. 'And don't call me Garbo,' she added, pushing back her hair.

'I thought you liked the name – it suits you with that hair.'

'Oh, shut up about my hair!'

'All right, old girl, there's no need to get narky even if you have had a tick-off from the blue-band.'

'It wasn't the blue-band,' Doris began, stopped, and then began to move on.

'I say,' he called her back, 'what are you doing Saturday night?' his eyes searched her face. She was not pretty, but there was something in her appearance, in the jaunty way in which she usually carried herself, in the wavering dreaminess of her eyes, that made people look at her a second time, that made them wonder whether she was not perhaps a little more of a personality than they had at first realised; and then she would do her Garbo act, or her Deanna Durbin act, and they would see that she was after all just another little factory girl trying to look like her favourite film star.

'What are you doing Saturday night?' Sid Peachey asked again.

'I dunno. Why?'

'Like to come to the flicks, Garbo?'

'I dunno,' she said doubtfully, 'I dunno as I could. And don't call me Garbo, Mr – '

'Sid to you,' he reminded her, laughing a little. 'Meet you outside the Palladium. Six o'clock sharp. Don't forget.'

'But – '

'I'll be there,' he told her, 'don't you worry… Well, so long, Garbo.'

She walked on towards the ablution room, feeling, just for an instant, slightly more cheerful. She guessed that Sid Peachey was the kind of young man whom her mother would not have allowed her to bring into the house at home, and she herself did not much like him. She told herself that she wouldn't be seen dead going to the pictures with him; but, all the same, she knew that she would go if nothing better turned up. She didn't like picking up soldiers on street corners in Dustborough, which was what a lot of the girls did; and there were so few young men at Blimpton that a girl had to think herself lucky to be invited out at all, even by someone like Sid.

The ablution room was empty. The two great circular washing troughs looked like fountains which would never play again. The green walls were dingy; the roller towels hanging against them had not been changed since the morning shift went off duty, and they hung limp and wet, stained with great splotches of brownish yellow. Doris crossed the room and peeped into the shifting-house. The attendant sat at her table over on the dirty-side, her head resting in her hands. She seemed to be dozing.

Doris sat down, pulled off her cap, and began to comb her hair. There was no mirror either in the shifting-house or in the ablution room, and the girl was afraid to start rummaging around for the bag where her out-door clothes were kept, in case the attendant should wake up and report her for idling during working hours. But as she shook her hair over her face she heard footsteps approaching. She jumped up, and then realised that it was too late to try to hide.

'Who's that?' a voice asked.

Doris threw back her hair and blinked. 'It's me,' she said nervously, and then, seeing the uniform of an assistant forewoman, added, 'I wasn't feeling well…'

'What is it?' Norah McCall asked. 'Why,' she exclaimed as the other girl's face emerged, 'we know each other, don't we?'

But Doris had receded into herself, and her face was empty.

'Don't you remember,' Norah asked, 'that first day we came here?'

'Goodness!' Doris looked at her afresh. 'You were the one!'

Suddenly they laughed, remembering how they had taken their courage in their hands and had gone to complain to the Superintendent himself: remembering Dan Morgan as he sat in his office telling them about the factory, making them promise that they would stick it out…

Their faces sobered.

'What's the matter?' Norah sat down beside the other girl. 'You know you're not supposed to come in here while you're on the shift.'

'Yes, I know.'

'Why didn't you go along to the surgery?'

'Oh, I'm all right,' Doris glanced again at Norah's uniform. 'I didn't know you were an A F W. I thought, when – you know, when you took us along to the Admin Block – I thought you were the same as everybody else.'

'So I am!' Norah laughed easily, 'I just happened to get promoted, that's all.'

Doris was still fidgeting with her hair. 'I hate it here,' she said, and burst into tears.

Then, as she wiped her eyes, she began slowly and timidly to explain.

'I can't stick it any longer,' she finished up, 'I can't!'

'But you promised!' Norah reproved her gently. 'Don't you remember, we all promised we'd stick it for six months, whatever happened…'

Once more the memory of that January evening rose up between them. They remembered again the long walk in the dark, the moment of breathless fear as they stood in the corridor of the Administration Block trying to find the right door: the sudden brightness as they went into Morgan's office and sensed his friendliness, his surprising eager strength.

'Was it because of my hair she wouldn't let me go in the hostel?' Doris asked abruptly.

'I don't know... But it is a bit silly to wear your hair like that when you're at work. It's risky, too. You might catch it in something, and besides – '

'You mean I might get the rash?'

Norah nodded.

'I could have it cut a bit,' Doris offered.

Norah looked at her carefully. 'You ought to tuck it up under your cap,' she suggested.

'But nobody else does... well, hardly anybody... you always did have yours done short, didn't you?'

Norah nodded.

'But what I can't make out is why did she pick on me?'

Norah stood up. 'Come on,' she said, 'I'll walk down as far as your shop with you... ready?'

'About the hostel,' Doris persisted, 'could you – ?'

'Could I what?'

'Well, if I did up my hair the way you say, could you speak to Miss Braithwaite and ask her if she'll let me go in there?'

'Of course I will,' Norah agreed, 'now come on – '

NINETEEN

MISS HOPKINS HAD decided that she ought to leave Mowbray Lodge. She did not really want to go. She enjoyed the sensation of being at the centre of things, of knowing that she was certain to hear at least two, and often three or four, different versions of any event of importance that might happen in the factory. She liked to meet the officials from the Ministry who occasionally spent a night in the house, and she was by no means averse from indulging in a little wire-pulling: indeed, she had been at the factory long enough to have become convinced that nothing but the intervention of some powerful external force would ever secure for her the theatre for which she so persistently longed. Then Gunn had invited her to lunch. When she had described her plan to him he had not condemned it on the grounds of cost, or the shortage of building materials and labour. Instead, he had put down his knife and fork, looked at her across the table, and asked: 'Where's the talent?'

She had answered quickly that there was plenty of talent in the factory; but the question had rankled; not because she doubted the truth of her answer, but because she was certain that she was right, and yet she did not know how she could prove it; and because (though this was a secret that she seldom acknowledged even to herself) above and beyond her plans to build a theatre for Blimpton lay the deepest ambition of her whole life, an ambition towards which the theatre would inevitably help her: to find, just once, a genius. She was never quite clear about the sort of genius that she hoped to find. Sometimes she toyed with the notion of discovering a Bernhardt or a Duse in a suburban play-reading club; at other times she would stroll through a department store, seeking for a new Garbo or Valentino among the shop-assistants, looking around her with the eagerness that other women expended on the choice of a hat or a pair of shoes. She was so patient that she had on two or three occasions devoted months of hard work to the training of boys and girls whom she had eventually to recognise were without even the talent necessary to earn themselves a living. But these disappointments, if they did little to strengthen her critical faculties, did nothing whatever to soften her resolution. When she had been asked to join the staff at Blimpton she had agreed at once, excited at the prospect of having a real war job, that would give her a chance to meet twenty or thirty thousand people...

Unfortunately, she did not meet them. She saw them all over the place, rushing in and out of the Main Gates, crowding into buses and trains, leaping on to bicycles, tearing into the canteens, sitting or standing at their work, queueing to clock-on, to clock-off, to see the doctors, to get their pay. But though she saw them, it seemed to her sometimes that she never saw anybody more than once, so rapidly did they come and go; and she was so busy that she scarcely ever had an opportunity of talking to anyone for more than a few minutes. Nearly all her time was taken up by the routine work of arranging for the visits of concert parties, and the few concerts that she had organised from among the workers themselves had been hurriedly arranged in the intervals of looking up timetables, meeting trains, finding cars to transport visitors about the factory, satisfying the Security Officer that the soprano from Bournemouth was not a spy and that the Irish comedian was a Protestant Ulsterman who was not in the habit of paying midnight calls on the German Legation in Dublin.

And then Gunn had challenged her to produce a concert that would really show what talent the factory possessed. He had made no promises, but as he left he remarked quite casually that if Miss Hopkins did succeed in getting a lively bunch of boys and girls together it might be possible to persuade the Minister himself to come down to Blimpton to see them perform. Several weeks passed. Miss Hopkins tried to organise her duties in a way that would give her time to get about among the workers, but the shop-managers could not understand why she wanted to wander around the Groups at odd hours of the day and night, and she was not prepared to give them her reasons. Besides, she soon found that it was nearly impossible to get to know the things that she wanted to know about the workers merely by watching them at their work. It was necessary, she saw, to get to know people individually, to make friends with the workers themselves and with the lower grades of supervisory staff who were in and out of the shops all the time; and this she decided to do.

Because she liked people in the mass, she thought it would be easy. It wasn't. There was, quite literally, no common ground upon which she and the people she wanted to know could meet; and it was for this reason that she began to try to make up her mind to leave Mowbray Lodge. All she wanted, she told herself, was a neat little place to which she could, now and then, invite people to tea. The few comfortable houses in Dustborough seemed already to be full or, if they were not, their owners showed a marked unwillingness to say so to anyone who came from Blimpton. Miss Hopkins, torn between her love of comfort and her sense of duty, began to grow desperate.

One afternoon, after spending several hours trudging about Dustborough in the rain, climbing up and down the steps of semi-detatched villas, she found, when she was so tired that she could go on no longer, that she had nearly two hours to wait for a bus that would take her back to the factory. She went into the White Lion.

The lounge was dim and silent, but as Miss Hopkins made her way to the fireplace she saw that a girl was sitting in one of the high-backed armchairs, her head bent almost as if she were asleep.

'Beastly day,' Miss Hopkins observed cheerfully as she threw off her raincoat, fluffed out her grey hair, and pushed a bell to summon the waitress.

'Beastly,' the girl agreed. 'Why, you're Miss Hopkins, aren't you?' Her voice was listless, her face, beneath the careful make-up, haggard with fatigue, but now she sat up, looking with wonder at the older woman's bird-like eagerness, which nothing ever seemed to destroy.

'Yes,' Miss Hopkins blinked, 'I know you awfully well by sight – '

'Pamela Grant.'

'We've met, haven't we?'

'Well, not exactly. I'm in the Labour Office. Until they throw me out.'

'Why should they throw you out?'

'I don't know why they *should*,' the cold, level glance did not waver, 'but they will. Miss Creed thinks I'm not the type.'

'Oh.'

'Would you say I'm not the type?'

'The type for what?' Miss Hopkins asked. The sudden warmth had begun to make her feel a little dizzy.

'The type that makes a good labour officer. Have I got what it takes?'

'How can I tell?' Suddenly Miss Hopkins saw that the girl was very near to hysteria. She was not sure what she should do, so she sat quite silent for a few moments, and then the waitress brought in a tray laid with tea for two.

'Have some of this,' Pamela Grant suggested, 'if you order tea now you won't get it before the bus goes.'

Miss Hopkins gave the tray another glance. 'You're expecting someone?' she asked.

'It doesn't matter. You have some of this,' Pamela motioned the waitress to go away, and when she had gone added, 'I ordered the second cup for Braithwaite, but I should think she must be having tea with the manager. If she's not, then when she comes down she'll just be unlucky…'

Miss Hopkins took the proffered cup. 'Who is Braithwaite?' she asked.

'Oh, don't tell me that you don't know Braithwaite. She's the head prefect. Down on the Groups they call her Teacher's Pet,' Pamela took a sip of tea and put down her cup. 'I oughtn't to talk to you like this, ought I?' she asked, speaking all at once in a more normal tone.

'I don't think it matters,' Miss Hopkins smiled her gentle, wistful smile. 'After all, I have met Miss Braithwaite… I was a bit confused at first by you calling her Braithwaite. But I know who you mean, exactly.'

The girl laughed, and with her laughter the tension suddenly eased.

'We've been billeting the intake,' Pamela explained. 'We had ninety-six today, and they arrived on eight different trains,' she glanced at her watch. 'There's another party due on the seven-twenty. The people down at the Labour Exchange are absolutely worn out already… As a matter of fact, so am I… Well, anyway, we've got the whole lot bedded down for the night. Though from what I saw of some of the billets, I should imagine that at least half the girls who came in today will be looking for new lodgings by tomorrow morning. If not sooner.'

'But why aren't the new people being put into the hostel?'

'Oh, don't you know? They've had a frightful lot of trouble up at the hostel with those girls from Gasping. Some of the girls who go to The Beeches don't stay at Blimpton for more than a week. The Warden says it's because the girls from Gasping tell them such frightful stories about the things that happen in the factory... only some people say that that's not the real reason why the girls don't stay...' Pamela paused, as if uncertain how to continue.

Miss Hopkins put down her teacup, and sat leaning forward, her eyes bright, her attitude expectant. 'What do you think is the reason?' she asked.

'Me?' Pamela shrugged her shoulders. 'I wouldn't know... Miss Creed wants to put in two or three of the assistant labour officers into the hostel to investigate.'

'That might be a good plan.'

'Oh, do you think so?' a gleam of interest lit the girl's face for a moment, and then died away. 'It seems to me that it's just another typical piece of snooping. I mean, why can't they let these poor wretched girls lead their own lives?'

'You have to remember,' Miss Hopkins spoke reflectively, almost as if she were talking to herself, 'most of the people who come to Blimpton from a distance haven't got much of their own lives left by the time they've left their homes and their jobs and their friends...'

'That's true for all of us, isn't it?'

'Of course it is. But for those of us who're on the staff it's much easier. We have our professions, and though we've had to leave our homes, we're doing work that isn't so very different from the things that we did in peacetime...'

'But that's simply not true!' Pamela jumped up. Tears shone in her eyes, but her voice, when she spoke again was harsh, without a quiver. 'This is the first job I've ever done in my life. Before the war I hadn't the slightest idea what it was like to work, to earn one's living, to get up in the morning and catch a bus, and... and...' she stopped and sat down heavily.

'And?' Miss Hopkins prompted her.

The girl leaned back, her glance averted, looking into the fire. 'I've never talked to anyone like this before,' she said at last. 'I suppose it's because I'm so frightfully tired…'

Miss Hopkins seemed to be employed in counting the threads in the cover of her chair. 'We can none of us go on bottling things up for ever, you know,' she observed placidly.

'No… but there's no one in the whole place I can talk to… of course there are several other girls in the Labour Office who're in the same position in a way, except that they've got the slumming mentality, and I haven't… I'm just an utter and absolute flop… If there's any mistake that can be made, then you can trust me to make it… I oughtn't to have gone in for this sort of thing,' she continued. 'I wasn't really keen on doing war work, but Mummy thought I ought to do something… She said that I'd never in a thousand years begin to get on with factory girls. But the queer thing is that I do. I mean, we like the same things, clothes, dancing, films, amateur dramatics – '

'Amateur dramatics!'

At Miss Hopkins' tone the girl's eyes widened a trifle. 'That's part of your job, isn't it?' she asked.

The other nodded.

'As a matter of fact,' Pamela admitted, 'I used to think I was terribly good…'

'You like acting?'

'Yes…'

'Well, then,' Miss Hopkins frowned, her whole face puckering as if in an acute effort at concentration. 'Well, then,' she repeated, and as she spoke she looked, in spite of the deep creases around her eyes and mouth, suddenly young and excited, 'perhaps you could help me with some of the things I'm trying to do… that is, if you can spare the time?'

'What sort of things?' the girl asked.

Miss Hopkins explained. Gradually Pamela seemed to become interested. Miss Hopkins pulled a slip of paper from her handbag and began to make notes, for making notes always gave her a feeling of certainty; and as she wrote she went on talking. Soon the two were completely absorbed. They did not hear Phoebe Braithwaite when she entered the room, and when she spoke they greeted her with surprise, as if they had forgotten the occasion of their meeting.

'We've been talking about having a factory concert,' Pamela volunteered. Her tone was unusually conciliatory.

'Oh, yes?' Phoebe's face was flushed. Her eyes seemed to be focused on something out of sight. She wore a dingy leather coat, and beneath it a tweed suit, sad-coloured and rather shapeless. The sobriety of her appearance was contradicted by the jerky, secretive gaiety of her manner.

'I'm sorry I was so long,' she murmured and turned to Miss Hopkins, 'I went to ask Mr Little about getting digs for the new shop-manager on North-East, and, of course, I had to stay for a cup of tea, and then he went on talking about one thing and another…' the blurred, unfocused look returned to her eyes as the words tailed off.

Miss Hopkins rose and began to put on her mackintosh. 'It was lucky for me,' she observed pleasantly. 'We've had a most interesting chat. And just as you came in Miss Grant was arranging to get some of the forewomen – and men – to tea at her digs on Saturday so that we can get them to act as talent-scouts – you know – finding people who can sing and act and that sort of thing.'

'But why – ' Phoebe seemed to gather herself together. She straightened her shoulders, thrust her hands into her pockets, and spoke in a tone of acid indifference: 'Really,' she said. 'Isn't it,' and though she addressed herself to Miss Hopkins she did not look at her as she spoke, 'well, isn't it rather peculiar for Miss Grant to ask these people to her diggings?'

'Miss Hopkins can't very well ask them to Mowbray Lodge,' Pamela reminded her.

'And you see,' Miss Hopkins at moments of tension found it difficult not to become gushing, 'it's so tremendously important to begin in the right atmosphere. We all talk more freely after a cup of tea.'

'Yes,' Phoebe agreed slowly, 'that wasn't what I was thinking of.

I don't want to interfere in any way.'

'I'm sure you don't,' Miss Hopkins smiled uneasily, wishing that she did not always begin to collapse at the first sign of opposition.

'I mean,' Phoebe went on, 'if Miss Grant will forgive me for saying so, she is one of the more junior members of the staff. I was thinking it might be better if someone with a little more... a little more status in the factory – '

Pamela shot a quick sideways glance at Miss Hopkins. 'If Miss Braithwaite would allow you to ask these people to her place,' she suggested, 'I'm sure that would be a very much better arrangement.'

She leaned forward, her elbows on her knees, and a lock of hair fell forward as she did so, concealing her face.

'I'd be delighted,' Phoebe agreed at once.

TWENTY

RUTH WAITED UNTIL she heard footsteps crunching on the gravel; then she began to back the car out of the garage.

Looking into the driving mirror, she could see Morgan approaching. Now that the moment had come she was even more nervous than she had expected.

'Hullo!' He greeted her without any particular pleasure as she drew up beside him. 'Off for a pleasant Sunday afternoon?'

'Not exactly.' She took her hands off the steering wheel, and sat with her eyes cast down, terrified lest he should see in her glance, in any of her movements, how carefully she had planned this meeting. Although they lived in the same house and met nearly every day they had not been alone together since the evening, four or five weeks ago, when he had driven her back from a party at the Gittins' home. 'I thought I'd go over to Coking,' she said, 'to see that Widgery girl.'

'Oh!' At his tone she looked up. He was frowning, his eyes narrowed. 'That's where I'm going,' he added.

It was happening exactly as she had planned. Exactly. And yet she could see from his manner that there was something for which she had not calculated. He was withdrawn, reluctant. She stammered out the phrases that she had so carefully prepared. 'Can I give you a lift?' she asked, 'it seems silly to use two cars – and two lots of petrol... doesn't it?' She could hear the sound of her own voice, hollow and meaningless. She saw, or thought she saw, that he was not interested in her, that he would have preferred to make the journey alone.

Suddenly he smiled. 'You're sure you're only thinking of saving petrol?' he asked.

'Quite sure!' She found herself replying easily, and laughing a little as she spoke. She told herself that it was going to be all right after all.

'Then shall we waste yours or mine?'

'Oh, now I've got my car out let's waste mine.'

'Right.' He got in beside her. 'Do you often go to see this poor kid?' he asked as she drove off.

'No, I've only been once before.'

'Oh!'

She could feel him looking at her, but she drove on steadily, refusing to turn and meet his gaze. She knew exactly what he looked like: she kept always in her mind the image of that changing, ugly face. She knew exactly how the wrinkles around his eyes began to crease a fraction of a second before he smiled, and the way in which he pressed his lips together in moments of anger, holding back the torrents of his rage until he was quite certain of what he had to say. Now she knew that his yellow eyes, if she turned to look at them, would be curious, friendly, and yet still full of mockery.

'Do you go often?' she asked.

'Where?'

'To Coking.'

'No. Not as often as I'd like. We've got several of our people there now, you know. There's a foreman from North-West who fractured his skull – '

'Yes, I know.'

'You know?'

'After all,' shyness was creeping back into her voice, 'it's my job to know.'

'Of course… it's difficult to remember that you're a doctor.'

She flushed. 'I'm afraid I'm not a very good one.'

He threw back his head, ready to laugh. 'You say that too often… How was the weekend?'

'Which?'

'The one I told you to take. Did you take it?'

'Yes.'

'Enjoy yourself?'

'Not particularly.' In fact, the weekend in Manchester had been a failure. Her father had seemed overworked, preoccupied, and had been less patient than usual in listening to Ruth's account of the difficulties of life at Blimpton. Her mother, who had arranged several parties for the occasion, had been puzzled and disappointed at the girl's obvious unwillingness to meet any of her old friends or, meeting them, to take any pleasure in their company. Thinking back over her own conduct, Ruth began to drive more quickly, and then had to swerve to avoid a lorry that was coming head-on towards them down the narrow lane. 'Sorry,' she apologised abruptly.

'You're a silly girl. And a damn bad driver.'

'I know.'

'And you're scared to death of everyone you meet – aren't you?'

She laughed, a trifle shakily. 'I think you've told me that before.'

'It's still true, isn't it?'

She could feel tears pricking behind her eyes, but her profile maintained the tranquillity of a figure engraved on a coin.

'Isn't it?' he repeated.

'I suppose so,' she admitted. 'Partly true, anyway.'

'And now,' he smiled down at her, and the warmth in his voice, always difficult to resist, was suddenly comforting, 'suppose we change places, and while I drive you can tell me...'

Sitting in the passenger's seat, watching his solid bulk squeezed behind the wheel of the small car, she asked: 'What do you want to know?'

'All about you.'

'But – ' the beginning of a smile lifted the sulky line of her mouth ' – where do I start?'

'Right at the beginning. Where were you born?'

'In Manchester. I've lived there always.' Starting like that, she found it strangely easy to talk; and presently she found herself telling him things that she had never spoken of to anyone: of the close-knit unity of her family, so tightly bound together by their love for each other and their tradition of service to the community that when one of her brothers was killed it was taken for granted, without so much as five minutes' discussion, that she should give up her own ambition to study music in order to become a doctor: of her own unspoken deep resentment at a decision that she had neither the will nor the courage to combat: of her growing sense of failure in the months since she had come to Blimpton.

'But you're all right,' Morgan threw the words at her with a sort of rough kindness, 'you're doing the job.'

'Am I?' she asked. 'I don't think so...' Once more she began to think, as she had done so often in the last few weeks, of the Sunday evening argument at the Gittins' house. 'I don't understand this idea of yours,' she said abruptly.

'Which?'

'About making Blimpton a community. Bringing people together... I'm still a stranger.'

'And whose fault is that?'

She was surprised, stung into indignation. 'Are you suggesting that it's mine?'

'Isn't it?' he looked down at her, and his smile, touched with mockery, encouraged her to agree.

'What ought I to do?' she asked.

'You must decide that for yourself.' He slowed down as they approached the entrance to the hospital. 'I'll go and have a chat with MacDonald,' he said, 'while you see the girl. Then I'll take a peep at her when you've done.'

'Just as you like.'

The matron, her feathers rustling, led Ruth into the ward where Rose Widgery was sitting up in bed, clasping a magazine and a box of chocolates in her lap and looking eagerly from Griselda Green, who sat on one side, to Kitty Baldwin on the other. The three girls seemed to be absorbed in conversation, and it was not until Ruth had been standing at the foot of the bed for a moment or two that they looked up.

'Why, Doctor!' Rose exclaimed. Her fair hair, soft and short, was like a halo around her head. Her eyes shone with excitement.

'And how are you?' Ruth asked, wishing that she, too, had remembered to bring the girl a present, unable, or perhaps unwilling, to realise that her own arrival could mean so much.

'I'm better!' Rose answered eagerly, and then, overcome by shyness, could say no more.

'And happy?' Ruth went on, looking, as she spoke, not at the patient but at the two girls sitting on either side of the bed. They seemed to her extraordinary, both in themselves and in their contrast with each other. She found it impossible to place them, though the first, big, blonde and untidy, she guessed probably came from the factory. The other, in spite of her rather shabby clothes, had such a remarkable air of distinction, of being at home in the world and free, that Ruth, looking into the clear grey eyes, was confused, shaken by an envy which, meaningless but overwhelming, attacked her like a spasm of acute, almost unbearable, pain. 'Haven't we met somewhere before?' she asked, trying to muster her confidence but wishing, at the same time, to evade the penetrating curiosity of a glance which, revealing nothing, seemed to see so much.

'Not socially,' Griselda replied. The snub, uttered in a light cool voice, pierced like a dart. Ruth, fidgeting with the corners of her handkerchief, could not imagine that no hurt had been intended.

'But we've met?'

Griselda nodded. 'Oh, yes. In the factory...'

Then, at last, Ruth remembered. She flushed darkly, picturing again the wintry afternoon when Griselda, with a casualness possible only to those accustomed by habit to command, had stepped forward to insist that Rose Widgery and some other, now forgotten, girl, should be brought out of hiding to face the routine medical inspection. 'You must have thought me a frightful nuisance,' Griselda added, smiling with what seemed to the other to be an appalling graciousness. 'You know,' she went on, 'there are still girls who run away when they hear that you and Dr Gower are on your rounds.'

'Really?'

'I should just think they do!' Kitty rushed in. 'They're scared stiff of being taken off contact.' She shook her head in imitation of Ma Venning's manner of expressing a mild disapproval. 'But still,' she continued, 'you can't wonder, can you, that people don't want to lose their danger money?'

'No...'

Griselda got up as Rose, confused by a situation which she sensed but could not understand, tried to say something, and failed.

'Don't let me drive you away,' Ruth begged, as she sought for an excuse to cut short her own visit.

'But I think we've been here long enough,' Griselda said, smiling again. 'And, besides, Rose will want to talk to you.' She turned to Kitty, who obediently gathered up the litter that seemed to spread around her wherever she went: her handbag, a picture postcard from

Margate, a hat with red and white goose-quill feathers, a bright green umbrella, an orange-coloured silk scarf – for Kitty, greeting the spring, had come out of mourning two weeks ago with an explosive enthusiasm.

Rose watched them go, and after that lay back, her head against the pillows. Her small child-like face was puckered with anxiety, her blue eyes clouded. 'I expect I've been an awful lot of trouble,' she murmured, seeking, as always, in herself an explanation for whatever had gone wrong.

'You mustn't say that,' Ruth protested. Through the window on the other side of the room she could see the two girls who had just left, strolling down the drive, staring around at the empty flowerbeds, laughing at... what?

'When I come back – ' Rose began, conquering her shyness.

'You want to come back to Blimpton?'

'Of course I do!' a spasm of doubt crossed the girl's face. 'They won't stop me, will they?'

'No, indeed?'

'You're sure?'

Ruth nodded. 'But why do you want to come back?' she asked, startled by the eagerness of the question. 'Do you like working at Blimpton?'

'Oh!' Rose shook out her curls. 'I love it. I mean, I've got friends... and I don't want to go home.' One of her hands clutched. the white coverlet. Oh, I don't want you to think it isn't all right at home, only – '

'Yes?' Ruth pressed her gently, catching a first fugitive glimpse of a life that she had not until this moment even tried to imagine.

'Only, you see, I was in service, down Exeter way; and – well, nothing much ever happened... it wasn't like Blimpton, not such good money, and... well, there's always something *happening* at the factory, isn't there?'

More than that she could not explain, but Ruth, asking questions, piecing together the fragmentary sentences, began to be interested. The image of the two girls who had been here when she arrived was obliterated, and by the time that Morgan came in to fetch her she had learned most of what there was to know about the history of Rose's short and hitherto rather empty life.

'Well,' Morgan asked as they got into the car, 'enjoy yourself?'

'Very much.' She was still smiling at the recollection of a story that Rose had told her: a rather pointless little story about pigs. She began to repeat it. And then, turning out of the drive into the main road, she saw Griselda and Kitty waiting at the bus stop. Morgan put his head out of the window and waved to them.

'Ought I to give them a lift?' Ruth asked, and slowed the car.

'No. They said they'd rather take the bus.'

She looked at him curiously. 'I didn't know that they were friends of yours,' she said, puzzled.

'Hoh!' it was half a laugh, a laugh cut short in the middle. 'There are a lot of things you don't know about me, young woman!'

'I'm sure there must be,' she agreed frigidly.

Morgan took out his cigarette case and fumbled in his pocket for matches. 'And what do you think of her?' he asked as he watched a smoke-ring coil up and disappear.

'She's a nice little thing, isn't she? Not very bright, but – '

She broke off, wounded by a cackle of incredulous laughter.

'*Not* very bright?' he repeated.

'Of course,' she went on, trying to see his point of view, to make allowances, 'she was probably tired out before I arrived – '

'Oh!' he interrupted, 'I didn't mean the Widgery girl. She's just a nice little thing, as you say. But the girl you met when you went in – the girl we passed just now – Miss Green – what did you think of her?'

Perhaps his voice betrayed more interest than he realised, or perhaps it was only her surprise that he should have known about the meeting in the hospital ward that caused her to answer guardedly and after a moment's consideration. 'I didn't like her much,' she admitted unwillingly.

'You didn't, eh?'

'Not much,' she slowed down as they came to the crossroads. 'Which way?'

'Left. We'll go and see whether MacIver's at home for tea… that is if you don't mind?'

'No, I'd like to.'

'Good. Now tell me, what's wrong with the Green girl?'

Again she hesitated. 'Perhaps I'm prejudiced.'

'Why should you be?'

'Bad conscience. As a matter of fact, if it hadn't been for her we shouldn't have caught the Widgery girl until it was too late.'

'Too late?'

'To save her life – it was touch-and-go when they got her here, you know.' Briefly, jerkily, she told the story.

He was interested, asking questions, pressing to know why nothing had yet been done to make it impossible for workers to evade the routine medical examination. 'We must talk to MacIver about that,' he finished, scribbling a word or two in his pocket diary. 'But I don't understand' – he returned to the first question – 'why that should prejudice you against Miss Green. She's a most unusual young woman – '

'But – ' she smiled now, frank, disarming, '– one usually does have a grudge against a person to whom one owes something, doesn't one?'

'Maybe.'

'And besides – '

'Well?'

Again she hesitated, on the point of a further confession. But, twisting around, trying to keep her attention on the road and at the same time to understand what was happening in the mind of the man who sat beside her, she saw that his face was closed, his attention turned inwards, preoccupied with some thought that she was not to be allowed to share. He did not speak again until, a quarter of an hour later, she turned in past the lodge that led up to the house of Dr MacIver's sister.

MacIver, bored with the people who were staying in the house for the weekend, welcomed them with enthusiasm. The penalty, he whispered to Morgan, of living with his sister was that it was sometimes necessary to entertain her friends as well as his own: and they did not, he declared, mix well. In fact, they did not mix at all.

It had been a mistake, he realised now, to ask Sir John Lentill, the Permanent Secretary of the Ministry of Weapon Production, to join a party which consisted of one retired general, a field-marshal's widow and the two sisters of a long forgotten Minister of War. Conversation, at first gossipy and reminiscent, had, by Sunday afternoon, become acrimonious and at tea-time looked like ceasing altogether. The general and the old ladies, clutching at rumours of disaster which Lentill refused either to affirm or deny, reflected sadly upon the decay that had overtaken the higher ranks of the civil service, and made disparaging remarks about the organisation of the Ministry of Munitions in the last war and the Ministries of Weapon Production, Supply and Aircraft Production in this.

The arrival of Ruth and Morgan produced a brief relaxation in the tension. The party, sipping tea, divided itself into two, the women hovering around Ruth, hoping for some unspeakable revelation about factory life. Lentill, after asking Morgan one or two formal questions about Blimpton, suddenly announced that he must, after all, get back to London that night. This was the first occasion, in all the many weekends that he had spent in Dustshire, on which he had been obliged to meet anyone from Blimpton. (MacIver, the perfect host, found it easy, indeed natural, to avoid mentioning the, factory.) Lentill suspected, rightly, that the Assistant Superintendent's arrival had not been altogether accidental, and that Morgan wanted to use the occasion to further some interest which would, in the usual course of events, have been considered too trivial to be brought to the attention of the Permanent Secretary. The latter, determined that this should not happen, for some minutes kept the conversation firmly fixed to the subject of trains. When it was finally established that he could not, by any means whatever, get back to London that night he found himself at a loss. And Morgan, who had come in order to draw the attention of the Permanent Secretary to the necessity of cancelling the Ministry's contract with Gurneys in Dustborough had, he realised now, given too little thought to the problem of how to bring the conversation around to the subject that he wanted to discuss. The trouble, he reflected, was that there was no conversation to bring round. Even the old ladies, questioning Ruth, were beginning to flag, deflated by the girl's monosyllabic evasions.

'I believe,' MacIver smiled across at Ruth, 'that we've been getting quite a good type of girl into the factory recently.'

Ruth agreed eagerly. She was exhausted by her companions' avid speculations on the reasons for the increase in the number of illegitimate births.

'Quite a good type!' Morgan repeated. 'We've some very fine workers...' Earlier in the day, when he had planned this visit, he had guessed that he would find Griselda Green at the hospital, and he had left Mowbray Lodge with the half-formed intention of spending the rest of the day with her, and, in particular, of bringing her to meet MacIver and his friends. Now, more than ever, he wished that he had not allowed the meeting with Ruth in the garage to spoil his plans. 'But,' he went on, turning to Lentill, 'we haven't nearly enough yet, as you know – '

Lentill nodded, accepting the inevitable. Morgan, choosing his words carefully, afraid to say too little yet anxious not to appear to know too much, spoke chiefly of his own and Gittins' concern at finding that labour which should have been sent to Blimpton was about to be used elsewhere.

'But do you really have such difficulties in getting girls?' one of the women interrupted. 'If conditions are so much better – '

'Yes?' Lentill asked.

'Well...' the field-marshal's widow looked around and fixed her attention on Morgan. 'If the Churchill girls can go into the Services why can't Outrage put his girl into one of your Ministry's factories? Oh, yes,' she lifted a small imperious hand, 'I know that one more or less can't make much difference – but think of the example!'

'But surely,' one of her companions leaned forward, 'you don't expect people like – ' she stopped, turning to Lentill with a deprecatory smile. 'I mean,' she continued, 'that whatever one may say of Lord Outrage he hasn't the – what shall I say? – the Blenheim tradition of service – '

Morgan got up. 'I didn't know that Lord Outrage had a daughter,' he replied as he prepared to leave.

'Didn't she marry – ' one of the women began to ask. The end of the sentence was lost as Ruth and Morgan retreated towards the door.

'And now,' Morgan turned to Ruth as soon as they were alone, 'I suppose you're going to say that you wish I hadn't persuaded you to come?' He looked angry and dejected.

'No. It was quite interesting.'

'But those dreadful old women!'

'Oh!' Ruth took the cigarette that he offered. 'I don't think they meant any harm. And that was quite a good idea about Lord Outrage's daughter – '

'You think it was?'

'Yes.' She was no longer quite so certain. 'I was thinking: couldn't you talk to Mr Gunn about it?'

'Perhaps.' Morgan, brooding over what he was certain was his own failure to impress the Permanent Secretary, relapsed into silence.

TWENTY-ONE

SEVERAL OF PHOEBE Braithwaite's guests began to giggle as soon as the garden gate closed behind them, but they did not speak until they reached the end of the road. They walked quickly, looking neither to the right nor the left, and a passer-by, watching them, might have imagined that they were afraid of being followed or overheard. But when they reached the street corner they gathered into a little knot and everyone began to talk at once.

'I wonder what's behind it all?' Beryl Oakley, a sharp-faced young woman with greedy eyes demanded of no one in particular.

'Did you see those awful photographs?' another girl asked, tossing her head and smiling.

A husky young foreman met her glance. 'Well, it's the last time they keep me away from the sports' club on a Saturday afternoon,' he announced loudly.

'But you can be sure there's something funny in it when the Braithwaite woman starts shelling out invites – ' another was saying.

'Miss Hopkins is all right, though – '

'Yes, but what do they want to start organising a concert for at this time of the year?' another asked. 'I mean, if they'd done it in the winter there might have been some point – '

Henry Tyndale drew Norah McCall aside. 'Let's get away from here,' he whispered.

'Just a second.' She looked round the small circle, waiting until there was a moment's silence.

Old Mr Preedy from the South-East Group beckoned her to him. 'Don't let's have any funny business,' he was saying.

'That's right,' Norah broke in, 'if you didn't think it was a good idea – ' she glanced around, challenging anyone to disagree with her, ' – if you're not going to help with this you should have said so when you had the chance. Miss Hopkins asked us to say if we thought we couldn't do it. Didn't she?'

They looked at her in silence.

'We had a chance to say no – '

'I'd like to see anyone saying "no" to Braithwaite – ' one of the older women interrupted.

'The point is,' the husky young man rushed to Norah's support, 'we promised to help to get some people together for the old girl. We can't go back on it now. If the people on the Groups don't want to do it, it'll fall through quickly enough.'

Norah turned to him. 'It won't fall through,' she said, 'not if we go about it the right way – '

'After all,' Mr Preedy smiled with sudden benevolence, 'people have to have a bit of fun sometimes.'

With that, at least, they all agreed.

Norah and Henry walked off towards the centre of the town. 'I don't know what's the matter with everyone,' the girl remarked as soon as they were out of earshot.

'Don't you?' as he looked at her his face was dreamy, almost ecstatic. Sometimes it seemed to him that he could not remember the time when he had not been in love with Norah. He had grown up to an existence that was so uneventful, but so placid, so smoothly rounded that he accepted his own slight sense of boredom as easily as he took for granted the shabby comfort of his parents' house and the secure monotony of his job in the office of the insurance company. The outbreak of war had at first scarcely disturbed the routine of life in the little town; but when at last his friend Tom Walton was accepted for flying duties in the RAF, Henry had tried to join, too. He was rejected because of his defective eyesight, and the humiliation made him feel, for the first time that he could remember, thoroughly miserable. He did not know how to set about looking for a war job. He filled up dozens of application forms and wrote scores of letters, without receiving a single reply. Months passed, and he had become almost desperate when he was asked to present himself at Blimpton. At first he had been confused by the vast size of the factory, and by the intricacy of the organisation with which he was expected to become familiar; but he liked the sense of independence that came from living in lodgings, and as he came to understand his duties his confidence grew.

Although he lived at Pyfold and Norah at Dustborough, and although they worked in different parts of the factory, he usually contrived to meet her for at least a few minutes every day. On Sundays they would go for long tramps in the country, sometimes with a large party, sometimes just the two of them together. On these occasions they often came very near to quarrelling, for Norah would start to tease Henry about what she called his petty bourgeois origin, and then, in some chance way, the teasing would grow serious and a prickly hedge would spring up between them. Henry would become terrified as Norah mocked the comforts which she had never enjoyed, and accused him, and people of his kind, of being the backbone of what she liked to call English snobbery and stupidity; and then his fears would become almost unbearable, and he would grow speechless with anxiety as he tried to picture Norah meeting his mother, shocking his home town with her ridicule and contempt, and with her Irish-Cockney accent. But he was determined to marry her all the same, if he could ever collect sufficient courage to ask her.

This evening when he spoke Norah seemed not even to hear him.

'What would you like to do?' he asked again, after a slight pause.

'I've got to go back to my digs,' she explained. 'Mrs Johns has got her husband back on leave, and I said I'd be in to keep an eye on the kids so that they could get an evening out.'

'Oh.'

'You can come along if you like,' Norah offered, 'they won't mind.'

'I don't think I ought to,' he answered hesitantly.

'Please yourself.'

'It isn't that I don't want to come – '

'Well, then, come.'

Again he seemed to hesitate.

'What's wrong?' she asked.

'Nothing. Only I want to talk to you. We can't talk if you've got a houseful of children to look after.'

'Oh, they'll be in bed,' Norah reminded him easily. 'But anyway we can talk tomorrow.'

'That's just it,' he did not look at her, but walked on with his head bent, his face shadowed by the brim of his hat. 'I meant to tell you, tomorrow is all washed out. I had a card from Tom – I've told you about Tom, haven't?'

She laughed. 'Haven't you just!'

'Well, Tom says he can break his journey here tomorrow – he's been home on leave, and if he picks up the night train here he'll be back in camp first thing Monday morning.'

'So that cuts out our hike,' she agreed readily. Her tone was unresentful, matter of fact.

'Yes, but it isn't that... can I come back and explain? I mean – '

Norah shook her head. 'Look, Henry,' something in her voice caused him to lift his glance to hers, 'I don't mind a bit whether you come or not. Only for goodness' sake make up your mind one way or the other, and then we can talk about something sensible.'

'All right. I'll come.'

Norah's landlady had already put the children to bed and was herself waiting to go out when they arrived. She saw them seated on the best chairs in the little front parlour, and then left them. As soon as she had gone Norah jumped up. 'Let's go in the kitchen,' she suggested, 'there's a fire in there... unless you're too grand to sit in the kitchen?'

'Don't!' his smile was agonised.

'Well, you are being a bit high and mighty,' she led the way out.

'I'm not. As a matter of fact, I want to tell you a lot of things.'

'What things?' the girl's tone was uninviting. She began to stoke the fire in the kitchen range. Her face was flushed and her dark hair was crisp and shining.

'I wanted to ask a great favour of you.'

'Ask away.'

'It's about Tom.'

'What about Tom?'

'Well, you see I've got to do a special job tomorrow, and I don't suppose I'll be able to get away until about four, and I was wondering if... if... if you could possibly meet the train for me and look after him until I can get along?'

She stared at him for a moment, and then all at once began to laugh. She laughed and laughed, her eyes glittering with amusement as she watched his puzzled anxious face.

'I don't see what's so funny,' he said, as she stopped. 'Perhaps I shouldn't have asked you...'

'It's just so damn funny, asking me to meet one of your grand friends!'

'I always told you I wanted you to meet Tom,' his voice changed, and he went on with a new note of determination. 'I think it's about time you stopped making fun of the sort of people I come from,' he told her. 'It isn't their fault if they've been trained to be bank-clerks or shopkeepers instead of – '

'Engine-drivers and factory hands?'

'Whatever you like. You're awfully clever in some ways, Norah – '

'Clever?'

'Of course you are. But you exaggerate the differences between people. You think that people who own their own houses live in quite a different world from people who don't.'

'So they do!'

'Not really. Some people get on in the world, and others don't. That's about all there is to it.'

'No,' Norah disagreed soberly, 'there's much more to it than that... but I don't mind meeting Tom whatever-his-name-is if you've got to go to Blimpton.'

'Thanks. Actually I don't have to go to Blimpton...'

'Then why are you going?'

'I mean,' he watched her doubtfully, 'it isn't Blimpton I have to go to.'

He waited, but she made no comment. She had pulled down several pairs of stockings that had been hanging to dry on the line under the window, and now sat running them through with her fingers, estimating the amount of darning that she would have to do. She looked extraordinarily strong and handsome, and the finicky job seemed ridiculous, almost impossible. Presently she excused herself and went upstairs to get her work-box. When she came down Henry was standing with his back to her, staring out of the window.

'Norah,' he came back into the centre of the room, 'you know I said I wanted to tell you something?'

'Yes?' she put the work-box on the table and sat down. Some of the eagerness had left her face; she looked wary, ready to pounce.

'I don't know why it should be so hard to tell you...'

'No? Well, you don't have to tell me, whatever it is.'

'But I want you to know.'

She put down the pile of stockings and jumped up again. 'Shall we have some supper first?' she suggested.

'No. I want to tell you this...'

She stood still, waiting.

'I was sent for this morning,' he said at last.

'Sent for?'

'By Mr Gittins. You know, the Principal Clerk... he says they're going to start a new course for training people as shop-managers, and I've been recommended – '

'You have? Why, that's marvellous!' The familiar enthusiasm rushed back into her voice as she smiled up at him.

'You're really pleased?'

'Of course I am. It's fine. And you deserve it, too – '

'It means doing all sorts of exams before I get any promotion. But still – '

'Listen!' Norah interrupted. Upstairs a child was crying. 'I must go,' she said, and ran out of the room. Ten minutes later she returned. 'It's Vera,' she said, 'the little one. I don't know what's the matter with her, but I'll have to stay with her until she goes to sleep...'

'Perhaps I'd better go...' Henry followed her out into the little hall and put on his coat, while they made whispered arrangements for their meeting on the following day.

It was not difficult to identify Tom Walton as he stepped off the train. Even if he had not been the only passenger in Air Force blue to get off at Dustborough, Norah would have known him at once from Henry's description: the easy, swinging way in which he walked, square shouldered and narrow-hipped; the blue eyes lively and curious, and then, as he looked round and saw that Henry was not there, the sudden frown of impatience that clouded his face were all exactly as Henry had given her to expect. Standing just behind the ticket collector, Norah braced herself against the inexplicable shyness that assailed her as she watched him.

She waited until he had given up his ticket, and then let him pass her. She followed him through the booking-office and out on to the pavement.

'Excuse me,' she said at last.

He stopped dead, and looked down at her, half-angry, half-quizzical.

As quickly as she could, she explained herself, apologised for Henry's absence, and then waited for him to say something.

'And what do we do until half-past four?' he looked out at the dismal expanse of empty streets. 'How do we amuse each other?' He looked as if he were about to break into uncontrollable laughter. And then it seemed that he could contain himself no longer, for he said: 'I didn't know that Henry had a girlfriend. I'm delighted to meet you.'

Norah found herself blushing. 'I'm not his girlfriend,' she explained firmly. 'Not in that way, anyhow.'

'Sorry. But you're a girl, and you're his friend: only it doesn't add up to anything. Is that right?'

'Yes. That's right.'

Their eyes met and they began to laugh.

'And now,' he said again, 'we still have to think of some way of amusing ourselves for the next two hours. If it hadn't started to rain we might have gone for a walk in the country – if there's any country to walk in around here…'

'We could have gone back to my digs,' Norah explained, 'only my landlady's already got a houseful, and now one of the children is down with 'flu…'

'Shall we go to the cinema?' the young man still seemed to be laughing. 'Or don't you have any cinemas on Sundays?'

'We don't have anything on Sundays, unless – ' she paused, as if uncertain whether to continue.

'Unless what?' he pressed her.

'Unless you'd like to go to a meeting.'

'What sort of a meeting? Salvation Army?'

'You might call it that. It's in aid of the people who fought in the International Brigade. You know, in the Spanish War... I don't suppose you'd be interested...'

'Why not?' he looked at her afresh. 'Are you?'

'Why, of course!'

'Well, then, let's go.'

Before they reached the High Street they knew almost all that they needed to know about each other. In twenty minutes they had discussed the Spanish Civil War, Blimpton, Henry, the Royal Air Force, the deadliness of life in the country and the poverty-stricken gaiety of Camden Town.

'But I never knew that Henry's home town was like that,' Norah commented as they turned out of the High Street towards the hall where the meeting was to be held, 'I thought it was all sort of stuck-up, and snobbish and – '

'Inhibited?'

She laughed. 'I expect that's what I mean.'

'So it is. But so is all of England.' His face was glowing, exhilarated. 'You seem to have the right ideas about a lot of things,' he said, watching her with amusement and delight.

She was looking straight ahead. 'Goodness!' she exclaimed, 'there's Henry!'

They were almost in front of the hall, and there was Henry coming towards them, his hat pulled forward, his spectacles hiding his eyes.

'Hi!' Tom called.

Henry, about to enter the hall, started, turned round and came down the steps to meet them.

'What are you doing here?' he demanded nervously when he had shaken hands with Tom.

'The same as you,' Norah told him, 'going to the meeting – '

'Well, I know what's got you interested in politics,' Tom grinned, with a glance at Norah's radiant face.

'And to think I didn't even suggest that you should try to come along!' Norah reproached herself. 'Well, never mind, you're here, and that's the important thing. But why didn't you come up to the station?'

Henry reddened. 'I couldn't get away,' he murmured in a tone that was scarcely above a whisper.

Tom put a hand on his shoulder. 'Anyway,' he said, 'now you have got away after all, we don't want to go to this meeting, do we?' he turned to Norah. 'Or do we?'

'I'd like to go,' she replied.

'No!' Henry breathed the word with such intensity that it was almost as if he had shouted it. 'Don't go!' he looked up for an instant to give Norah a quick, pleading glance, and she saw that he had turned very pale. 'You mustn't go to that meeting. Please!'

Tom stood between them, and though his expression was puzzled his voice, when he spoke, still betrayed some lurking amusement. 'But you were going yourself? Why shouldn't Miss McCall and I come along with you?'

'Because – ' Henry bit his lip. 'I can't tell you just here – '

'Why not?' Norah demanded. A few people had passed them, straggling into the hall; a few more, perhaps half a dozen, were coming down the road.

'Oh, let's go!' Tom urged them impatiently.

They walked in silence as far as the corner of the street, and there Henry stopped. 'I must go back,' he said.

'And leave us?' Tom asked.

Norah stood with her feet a little apart, her hands in her pockets. 'Now,' she turned on Henry, her dark eyes blazing, 'what's all this about?'

'I... I...' he stammered, 'I can't tell you...'

'Oh, yes, you can!'

'Well, if you must know, it's a Communist meeting...'

'Is it?' Tom looked from one to the other.

'It isn't,' Norah contradicted, 'but even if it was, I don't see the harm – ' suddenly she stopped; her eyes widened with incredulity.

'So that was the important job you had to do!'

Henry did not meet the challenge. 'You don't know what you're talking about,' he said weakly.

'And you can't even deny it! I never heard of such a dirty trick in the whole of my life! Spying on what the workers do in their spare time... and who's paying you for this I'd like to know?... Or...' her voice was harsh with fury, 'or is that the price you have to pay to get promotion?'

'Norah! Please!'

'Don't you ever dare to speak to me again! Goodbye,' she turned to Tom, 'I don't suppose you want to run the risk of coming to this meeting to be spied on when you're in uniform?'

'Oh, I don't give a damn,' the young man shrugged his shoulders, 'but I'd like to understand what all this is about – '

'Perhaps Henry would like to tell you!'

'But, Norah,' Henry insisted, 'you don't seem to realise – '

'I don't want to hear another word!' she turned away and hurried off in the direction of the hall.

Inside, the meeting had not yet started. Fifty or sixty people were scattered on benches that were intended to accommodate two or three hundred. Norah glanced about her, trying to see whether anyone she knew was present, and then noticed Ma Venning sitting with three or four other women, who were quietly chatting among themselves.

Ma turned and smiled as Norah approached. 'I thought you might be coming,' she greeted her. 'It's not much of a crowd, is it?'

'Not much.' Norah, as she sat down, was shaking all over. The speakers came on to the platform, and the chairman, a mild-featured little man of about fifty, whom Norah recognised as a shop-steward from Blimpton, began, rather nervously, to address the audience. The girl clasped her hands in her lap and tried to listen; but, try as she would, she found her attention wandering each time the creaky swing-doors at the back of the hall opened. She did not turn round, and after a time she found that she was able to gather the sense of most of what was being said, and at the same time to scrutinise the people sitting near her. As far as she could judge, there were not more than two or three workers from Blimpton present, and these were not people she knew well. Presently the chairman sat down, and a young man, with a scar on his face and with an empty sleeve tucked into his right-hand coat pocket, took his place. He spoke haltingly, as if he found it difficult to communicate the intensity of his feelings but, as he began to describe the siege of Madrid and the first battles fought by the International Brigade, his audience warmed to him and when he paused his clumsy phrases were punctuated with cheers. Norah, leaning forward, intent on what he was saying, did not turn when she felt someone slip into the seat beside her, and it was not until the speaker sat down that she saw that her neighbour was Tom Walton.

'Not bad,' he murmured appraisingly: he might have been criticising a film show or a cricket match.

'It was grand!' Norah agreed fervently. Now that Tom had taken his cap off she saw him clearly for the first time, noting, without realising as she did so the humorous yet somehow arrogant face, the way in which his bright hair grew in a peak over his forehead, the spray of freckles across his nose.

The last speaker had risen, and was giving an extremely complicated account of the internal organisation of the British Foreign Office, of the State Department in Washington and of the origin and chief characteristics of what he called imperialist wars. Ma Venning and her friends began to fidget. Someone a few rows in front turned and motioned them to be silent. The argument from the platform grew more and more involved, until at last it was time to take a collection and to allow the audience to go home.

'Now, where's Henry?' Norah asked fiercely as the audience shuffled to their feet and began to sing the Internationale.

Tom shrugged his shoulders. 'I don't know,' he whispered back.

'Where are you meeting him?' Norah persisted.

'I'm not meeting him.'

'Oh!' they were standing in the gangway. Several people behind waited for them to move.

'I thought you and I might go and get a cup of tea somewhere...'

'I don't know...'

And then Ma Venning broke in on the silence that had fallen between them, and took them home to tea with her as inevitably as if that had been her intention in coming to the meeting.

The small house was full. Old Jim, deprived by the rain of his afternoon in the garden, was busy repainting the bathroom. Young Jim, at the end of his week's leave, was putting a final polish on his army boots while Kitty pressed the creases back into the trousers of his battle-dress. Griselda, wearing slacks and a dark jersey, was lying on the sofa, pretending to do the crossword puzzle in the Sunday paper.

Ma turned her lovely smile on Tom. 'I told you that you'd have to take us as you found us,' she said.

He moved a pile of Kitty's freshly ironed blouses from one of the chairs and sat down. 'I'm glad I found you,' he replied. He was already at home.

Only Norah was not at ease. The talk flowed around her, lively, gossipy, inconsequential, drifting now and then into little eddies of seriousness, and then flowing back to the main stream of chit-chat, stories about the factory, reminiscences of the days before the war, daydreams about the future. Norah, who was usually so gay and strong, who always had an opinion about everything, had receded into herself, scarcely noticing what was happening.

After a time Kitty came and sat beside her. 'What's wrong?' she asked.

'Nothing,' Norah frowned, 'I was just thinking.'

'What about?'

They sat in a circle, looking at her, waiting for her to give them the key to something.

'About Blimpton,' she said; and in that instant she knew that she would never tell them.

Ma's glance turned to the two young men: Jim, her son, in the Royal Artillery, and Tom, the stranger who was learning to be a fighter pilot. 'It does make you feel awful sometimes,' she agreed.

'What does?' the father asked.

'The factory. All these bombs and shells. Thinking all the time that we're just working to kill people.'

'Well, that's what the war's for, isn't it?' young Jim broke in.

'I know. But – '

'After all,' the young man persisted, 'they've killed enough of our chaps. And not only chaps, either, by this time. Don't forget, Ma, you wanted the war all right.'

'I didn't *want* it.'

'But you always said we had to have it.'

'Yes,' she paused for a moment, 'and I haven't changed my mind. I don't hold with all that talk we heard this afternoon about this being an imperialist war. It's not that... I don't know. It's all wrong, somehow. I don't mind the war – '

'What is it, then?'

'It's all so – '

'Cold-blooded?' Griselda suggested

'Yes. That's it. When you see the trucks being loaded up – '

'It makes you feel sort of proud – ' Kitty, who had been listening intently, suddenly interrupted. 'Giving it back to 'em... Do you know how many grenades they filled over in the shop where I was sent last week? Well, I can't remember exactly how many, but anyway it was a record.'

'Yes, that's grand,' Ma assented. She seemed to be wrestling with some difficult idea. 'I'm all for Blimpton,' she said, 'I love it. I wouldn't go anywhere else, not for any money. But sometimes you start thinking of all the people who're going to be killed next week or next month with the stuff the girls in your shop have been filling. What I mean is,' she looked around, scanning their faces as if trying to communicate something for which she had no words, 'what I mean is, sometimes you stop thinking about the war and the Nazis and the boys out in Crete and all that, and you just think of people being killed. Just ordinary people.'

Kitty got up and put the cat out. Then she came back.

'That's what we're there for, isn't it?' she asked.

'Of course it is,' Norah seemed to return to life, 'But I think I can see what it is that Ma's trying to say.'

'Well, I can't!' Kitty gave young Jim a sudden fierce stare, 'I can't understand it at all!'

Tom looked at his watch. 'I'll have to be going if I'm going to catch my train,' he turned to Norah, 'could you walk along to the station with me?'

'Surely.'

An hour later she returned. Her face was flushed, her eyes were very bright.

'Just in time for supper,' Ma greeted her.

'No, I must get home. But there was something I wanted to say – '

They waited.

'You know things are pretty bad in the hostel?'

Griselda stared. 'Of course,' she nodded, 'everybody knows that.'

'Well, I think one of you ought to go and live there.'

Kitty picked up the sock she was knitting. The needles clicked into the silence.

'We like them here,' Jim Venning said at last, 'don't we, Ma?'

'Like them!' Ma's smile cast a comfortable beam over the room. 'I don't know whatever I'd do without them. Besides, the hostel wasn't put up for girls who've got a good home to come back to.'

'It's no good asking me,' Kitty said flatly, 'I won't go.'

Griselda got up and began to lay the table for supper.

'They could come back later,' Norah continued, 'when things get a bit better. But we've got to get some of the right sort of people into that place, otherwise it'll muck-up the whole factory. Do you know that there are girls who've been there a month and who haven't done more than a week's work on the Groups all told?'

Griselda put down the breadknife. 'There's nothing you wouldn't ask people to do, is there?'

Norah met her glance. 'I hope not. Not if I thought it was right.'

TWENTY-TWO

'I'M SORRY, PARSONS,' Gittins, ensconced in the revolving chair, surveyed his office with a contented, but still critical, eye. He noticed that a path was beginning to be worn in the carpet between the door that led into the corridor and the visitor's chair beside his desk, and that the chart showing the incidence of dermatitis in the factory had not been brought up to date during the past week. 'I'm sorry, Parsons,' he repeated. 'I know how difficult things can be for those of us with family responsibilities, and if we had a house to spare anywhere on the site, believe me, you should have it – '

'I thought – ' Parsons leaned forward. His mild brown eyes were moist with anxiety. But the habit of obedience, of compliance with the wishes of his superiors, was so deeply ingrained that now, in spite of his determination to protest, he could not quite bring himself to finish the sentence.

'Yes,' Gittins continued, 'I believe you mentioned something in your note about the houses in Maytree Avenue. Surely Knowles must have told you that they were all allocated some months ago – a considerable time before you joined us, in fact?'

Parsons took a deep breath and thrust out his chin. Though trained to subordination, he was not naturally timid, and now he was almost desperate. 'But there's that row of cottages along the back – ' he urged. He had been trying, ever since his arrival at Blimpton, to find a house to which he could bring his wife and two young children; for some months they had been staying in London with a distant and none too hospitable cousin.

'Oh! that row of cottages!' Gittins raised his eyebrows in a fair imitation of the Superintendent. 'Out of the question, I'm afraid...'

'I understood,' Parsons was still diffident, but now that he had taken the plunge he found it easier to go on, 'that they'd been empty for some time.'

'So they have, some of them. But you see,' the older man explained with an air that was clearly intended to be tolerant, 'they're not classified as staff quarters. I'm sure I don't know what the Ministry would say if I allowed you to go into one of them.'

'But they are part of the – er – estate… ?'

'Part of the Ministry's property? Naturally.'

'Then – '

'No, I'm afraid it's not as simple as one might expect. As you know, these things seldom are,' he glanced up at the clock. Then he rose and moved around to the front of his desk. 'You must come and have supper – just a quiet little meal, you know – with the wife and me one day next week, so that we can talk over some of these procedural points. Meanwhile…'

Meanwhile, as he ushered Parsons to the door he explained that since the empty cottages were intended to house the families of skilled workers who were to be brought to the factory from other parts of the country there could be no question of allowing them to be used for other purposes until the electricians, fitters and toolmakers needed by the factory were recruited, and that in any case anyone who allowed a member of the senior staff to move into accommodation of a lower grade than that to which they were entitled would be guilty of gross impropriety. His manner was so smooth, so untouched by the other's agitation that it was impossible to judge whether he was deriving any satisfaction from his own rigid interpretation of headquarters' regulations. The half-smile neither deepened nor wavered.

'And, by the way,' he concluded as Parsons stepped out into the corridor, 'Dawson was telling me this morning that if you and Knowles can't find those maintenance fitters we've been asking for, we're going to get another bad hold-up on production before the end of the month.'

Just for an instant Parsons lost his worried look. 'I'm hoping to get that question cleared up this afternoon,' he replied confidently, and left.

He had ordered a car to take him to the South Group, but, because he had spent ten minutes longer in Gittins' office than he had intended, the driver had grown tired of waiting and had gone into Dustborough to collect the Superintendent's laundry. Parsons stood in the roadway, trying to decide what he should do. The sun was shining, and the air was filled with the soft freshness of spring. The flowerbeds on either side of the main gates were full of late daffodils, and behind them the cherry trees that had been planted a year or so ago were blossoming for the first time. He began to think of Peter and Joanna, his two children. He pictured them in the stuffy, over-furnished flat in London, playing quietly among the bric-a-brac, and sleeping uneasily on makeshift beds that his wife's cousin would have put up in the dining room. He thought of his wife, grown querulous with anxiety as she moved from one temporary home to another. He knew that she would not be happy at Blimpton, but he believed that she would be less unhappy there than in London, where the last severe air raid had shattered her conviction that whatever might happen to other people no harm could ever come to anything that was hers. Now, he knew from her letters, she was beginning to be fretful. She was, he guessed, nagging the children, and then consoling them with promises of country pleasures, a garden to play in, a dog, rabbits, goats, perhaps even a pony.

As these thoughts raced through his mind Parsons felt a sudden impulse to walk out of the gate, and to spend the rest of the day tramping around the countryside, looking for some friendly farm where he could settle his family for the summer. Then he began to remember the many things that he had to do that afternoon, and when one of the shop-managers came past on a motor-bicycle he hailed him and got a lift on the pillion to the entrance of the South Group.

The men's shifting-house was empty, but as he took off his shoes Parsons thought he heard a noise coming from the direction of the ablution room. He stepped over the barrier to the clean-side, and hastily unfastened the locker in which he kept a pair of the rubber-soled shoes without which no one was allowed to enter the Danger Area. He entered the ablution room just in time to see three or four men leave it by the further door. Something in their bearing made him suspicious, and he was about to follow them when he noticed a boy who was standing against the big circular washing-trough, his hands pressed against his head, his body contorted as if in pain.

'Something wrong?' Parsons asked.

For answer the boy, who was about seventeen or eighteen, leaned forward and vomited on to the floor. Then he wiped his mouth on the back of his hand and pulled himself up.

'Sick,' he said, 'bloody sick.'

'Hm.' Parsons came a little closer. The pervasive odours of the factory and the smell of stale bodies and unwashed clothes that always hung about in the ablution rooms were now driven away by the stench of the vomit. 'You're drunk,' he said, the kindliness seeping out of his voice.

'Drunk,' the boy agreed, 'bloody drunk.'

Then he vomited again.

When the boy had recovered a little Parsons led him back into the shifting-house, and helped him to lie down on one of the narrow benches that ran under the rows of pegs where the men's clothes were hung. The attendant who should have been tidying up the odds and ends of personal possessions left about by workers on the afternoon shift was nowhere to be seen. Parsons went to the telephone to ask someone in the shop-manager's office to locate Sebastian Bates, the assistant labour officer who was on duty on South that afternoon. Then he returned to the boy, who was by this time sufficiently recovered to realise that he had been caught by a person in authority.

'Will I be sacked?' he asked. Drunkenness, as everyone at Blimpton knew, was one of the most serious misdemeanours that could be committed in an ammunition-filling factory.

'Probably,' Parsons stood looking down on the boy. He was a fresh-faced youngster with a thatch of straw-coloured hair and a yokel's air of honest stupidity. 'What happened?'

The boy seemed to reflect for a moment or so. 'Mr Evans got married Sunday,' he explained laboriously.

'But today is Wednesday.'

''S right.'

The Labour Officer, who liked all dumb creatures, could see that it was possible to be sorry for the boy, but he had no time to waste.

'Who is Mr Evans?' he spoke curtly, wishing that Bates would arrive to deal with the tedious situation.

'Oh, Mr Evans!' the boy sat up, 'he's the bus driver. An' today when we stopped off at the Rose an' Crown it was on him, see? He said to me, he said – '

'Where's the Rose and Crown?'

'Just past Dimwater. Where the main road comes in.'

'Does the bus always stop there?'

'Not always. Not Fridays, never.'

Friday, of course, was pay-day, and people travelled to the factory with empty pockets.

'But other days?'

The boy was growing suspicious. 'I couldn't rightly say,' he lied awkwardly.

'You'd better tell me all about it.'

'Will I be sacked?'

'I don't know. Other people will have to decide that. But you'd better begin by telling the truth.'

'Yes...'

When Sebastian Bates arrived Parsons led him aside. 'Take this kid along to the Labour Office,' he said, 'and get him to tell you the whole story. Make some notes – the name of the bus driver, the people who usually travel on the bus, all the details. Then send the kid home – borrow a car if the Transportation Office can't let you have one – and tell him not to come back until we send for him – '

Bates opened his mouth in astonishment. He was not accustomed to receive precise instructions from his superiors.

' – then ring Finch and ask if he can see me at about five o'clock. I want to get this cleared up before the shift goes off – and it'll take some doing.'

He went out, wondering how many other bus drivers were in the habit of taking the workers pub-crawling on their way to the factory. The Superintendent, he knew, would make a great fuss when the story reached him and would issue an instruction that the practice must be stopped at once; but Parsons foresaw that it would be difficult to evolve any method of ensuring that the practice really was stopped, especially since the penalty of instant dismissal was one that was likely to injure the management more than it could injure those who might be dismissed...

He had walked only a few yards down the clean-way when

he met Dr Gower, who was returning from a routine visit to the detonator shops.

'Can you give me ten minutes?' the doctor asked.

'Now?'

'If you can.'

They stepped aside to allow a man bearing a tray of fulminate of mercury to pass. A hundred yards away two girls who were strolling towards the canteen saw the man approach, gave a loud shriek, ran down a side path, and stood pressing their bodies flat against the outside wall of the nearest shop.

'Silly thing to do,' Parsons commented as he watched them.

'Mm. Though it's dangerous stuff. In more senses than one.'

'Yes. They've been lucky down here so far.'

'Lucky?'

'I mean,' Parsons explained, 'they've had this section open a month – '

'And haven't had a blow yet?' Gower led the way towards the female ablution room. 'Do you realise,' he asked rhetorically, 'that if there were an explosion down here that blew the roof off three or four shops the damage it would do – the real, irreparable harm – would be almost trifling in comparison with the effect that dermatitis is having on this Group now?'

'Oh, come!' Parsons' admiration for Gower had, almost since their first meeting, been tempered by the conviction that the doctor was a fantastic person, imperfectly scaled down to the proportions of ordinary men. 'It can't be as bad as that,' he protested.

Gower pushed open the door of the ablution room and led the way in. 'I'm not exaggerating,' he spoke over his shoulder. 'You know how many girls there are on this Group now?'

'There should be four hundred and thirty-nine,' Parsons rolled the figures off competently. 'The afternoon shift this week – the blue shift – should be about a hundred and eighty.'

'And do you know how many have clocked-on this afternoon?' Gower's tall figure cast a long shadow on the dirty concrete floor. He removed his spectacles and looked about him, blinking slightly at the sudden dimness.

'No. I've only just come over.'

'Well, it may or may not surprise you to know that there are only seventy-three girls in the shops – '

'Seventy-three!'

'And a dozen of them probably won't last until the end of the week, though there's no sign of infection on them now.' The two men looked at one another. Gower, ardent, impetuous, frequently at loggerheads with his colleagues, gave the impression of knowing exactly what he wanted; but, now that the moment had come to seek the other's co-operation, he seemed, standing there, with his haughty good looks emphasised by the dinginess of his surroundings, so inflamed by rage at what he saw as to be, for the moment, incapable of speech. And Parsons, trained to be a loyal employee, disciplined, solid, reliable, and brought up to suppress his impulse to criticism, was still shying away from the heat of the other's indignation.

'That's what I meant,' Gower went on at last, 'by saying that an explosion wouldn't do as much harm as these filthy skin infections... oh, yes, everybody knows that dermatitis isn't a serious complaint. But what good do you think it does to have your female – and, my God, how female they are! – your sexless social workers from the Labour Office running round the shops telling these little back-street lovelies that dermatitis has never killed anybody yet and never will? These kids aren't afraid of getting killed – death just doesn't enter into their calculations. It can't. They're handling death all day long, but they don't feel it. It doesn't touch their imagination, except, perhaps, just for an instant now and then... But to see the rash starting on the face of the girl on the next bench, to know that you may be the next one – ah, that's where panic really begins to get a hold – ' he stopped for a moment to make a wide gesture towards the empty, dismal room. The two rows of wash-basins that ran down the centre were grimy and stained. The sodium sulphite soap was like newly washed blood, and blood-coloured smears streaked the roller-towel that hung behind the door. On a shelf at the far end of the room stood a jar or two of protective cream, and beside them was a cardboard container from which a dead white powder had been spilt on to the floor beneath. A waste-pipe had choked, and a trickle of water ran under one row of basins, picking up in its stream wisps of hair-combings, an old lipstick case, a discarded powder-puff.

Parsons frowned as he remembered the girls in the chain-stores in London, in Bristol, in the towns around Manchester, the girls he had known and looked after all his working life. Some of them, he speculated, would probably find their way to Blimpton before the war was over. Some, perhaps, had already arrived. 'They aren't all beauties,' he observed stolidly.

'No. But even the plain and homely souls don't want to lose such looks as they've got. They don't run away as the others do – '

'But no one can run away now,' Parsons interposed. 'You remember we were scheduled under the Essential Work Order a fortnight ago.'

'And what does that mean?'

'Why, no one can leave the factory without permission – '

'Yes, I know that. But what does it mean in terms of the labour force that you've got on production?'

'It's too early to tell.'

'Perhaps. But I'll make a guess. The people who want to leave won't come to you for their cards and go through the proper rigmarole, but they'll leave just the same. They'll simply stay away from work and say that they're sick – if they take the trouble to say anything at all – as long as they've any money left to pay the rent. Some of them will be genuinely ill – and the others will be simply fed-up or panic-stricken or merely bored... and it's all so unnecessary,' he finished abruptly. He crossed the room, took down the roller towel, and flung it into the bin that stood behind the door.

'What do you want me to do?' Parsons asked. A slight reluctance still appeared in his tone, but the words, and the way in which he braced his shoulders as he spoke, made it plain that he was ready to accept the other's leadership.

'Everything,' an ironical smile played around Gower's mouth as he watched the other man. 'I don't know what you can do, but I want all that, and then a bit more. In a general way I want more co-operation from the Labour Office staff – '

'But – '

'Yes, I know the procedure. MacIver should talk to Knowles, and then Knowles should tell you to have a chat with me and vice versa. I've arranged all that. I promise you that MacIver'll pay a state visit to Knowles not later than next Monday. Meanwhile, you and I will have to get down to it if this Group isn't to go out of production within the next fortnight. We'll clean-up down here first, and then when things are running more or less decently we'll deal with the other parts of the factory.'

Parsons glanced around. The shifting-house attendant could be heard pottering about on the other side of the door. 'Where do we start?' He was alert now, as if recognising this as the opportunity for which he had been waiting.

'First, we're going to arrange that every girl has her own towels – two towels for each shift, one for her to use before the mid-shift break, and the other to give her a real clean-up before she goes home.'

'I thought Gittins said it couldn't be managed?'

'Things get about, don't they?' Gower smiled wryly, 'but this time I think we may bring it off: first, because the production people are beginning to get the wind-up, and I've got Morgan to support me – you know how important this Group is to the programme? – and, secondly, because I'm suggesting that we merely want to experiment with cleanliness, that we've lost our whole-hogging belief in the virtues of soap and water.'

'I see…'

'Next. What sort of Labour Officers have you got over here?'

'Now? There's young Bates. He's a good boy.'

'And the woman?'

Parsons thought for a moment. 'I believe Miss Creed sent over a girl called Grant for this week…'

'Any good?'

'I don't know. She's a pretty little thing. Strikes one as rather brainless.'

'Could I talk to her – now?'

'Of course. I'll send her over to the surgery.'

'No. I'd rather see her here – ' once more his arm seemed to sweep around the room, ' – this is where her job starts... And I'm counting on you to see that she does it.'

At last Parsons was free. He had a hasty conference with the shop-manager, a worried young man whose time seemed to be almost wholly occupied with answering the telephone. In the intervals he talked about his troubles, the shortage of components, the way in which the manager of Services had let him down, the running fight that he was conducting with the inspection department, and various other things with which Parsons was not competent to deal. It was only when Parsons got up to leave that Hicks was able to bring himself to discuss the item on the Whitley Council agenda that the labour officer had come to see him about, and to answer a question or two about the reliability of the gate-man and the precautions taken to prevent the entry on to the Group of contraband and drunks.

'You terrify me,' he commented with blank sincerity when Parsons recounted the episode in the men's shifting-house. 'What are you going to do?'

As shortly as he could Parsons told him, and then left.

He returned to the Labour Office to find a tumult of disorder. In the big hall Miss Creed was receiving a party of some fifteen or twenty girls who had arrived unexpectedly from Scotland half an hour earlier. In the inner room, where most of the junior labour officers had their desks, everybody seemed to be doing everybody else's job, with the result that nothing whatever was in fact being done. He hurried down the corridor to his own office. His in-tray was overflowing with the pile of papers, letters, files, minutes, office circulars that had arrived during the last two hours. He began to go through them while he waited for the telephone call that he was expecting from the Ministry.

Presently Finch came in. He threw himself down in the only other chair that the room contained, and propped his long legs up against the radiator.

'Well,' he asked, 'how goes? Don't let me interrupt you.' He pulled out his pipe and began to fill it.

'Do you mind if I just finish this one?' Parsons glanced up from the reply he was scribbling to a minute from the Chief Engineer.

'Not a bit. Glad to have a few minutes' peace,' and then, when Parsons had closed the file and moved it to the out-tray, he added, 'you look all in. What's up?'

Parsons had a crooked, attractive smile, but now he seemed to produce it with difficulty. 'I'm a bit overwhelmed,' he admitted.

'Family all right?'

'Only so-so.' An elaborately framed photograph of the two children looked down at them from the top of the filing cabinet. They were dark and squarely built, like their father: but his essential sturdiness was missing. Their eyes were waif-like, as if they had lost something and already knew it.

'You ought to get them down here.' Finch spoke with dispassionate sympathy. He enjoyed being alone and found it difficult to understand the emotional ties that bound so many of his colleagues.

'I know. But I can't get a house.'

'Why not?'

'Gittins can't give me one.'

'Can't! You mean he won't.'

'He says they're all allocated.'

'Allocated, my face! Did he tell you who they've been allocated to?'

Instead of replying, Parsons began to look through the papers on his desk, searching for the note that Sebastian Bates should have left for him.

'Did he?' Finch persisted.

'No.'

'I thought not. Well, I'll tell you. I've been here since the beginning, and I know.' The young man stood up and, since the room was too small to allow of any movement, leaned against the high window-sill, smiling down, aloof, ironical. 'Gittins didn't want those houses to go up. To give the devil his due, he was dead keen to get the Ministry to put up some cottages for the workers – but houses for the senior staff – not on your life! He fought like mad to prevent the scheme from being approved – and why? So that Mrs G could take her rightful place in the world – so that she could queen it over the whole of Blimpton, instead of being just one of the wives – ' his face broke into a grin.

'I don't believe you,' Parsons said quietly.

'Ask anyone... Of course he had to give in in the end. You can stop the Ministry from doing most things, but when it comes to spending money – well... Anyway, there are the houses, empty. And I can tell you that every single one of them is allocated to someone who doesn't want it, either to men who haven't got wives and families or else to those who wish they hadn't and who intend to go on keeping their dear little encumbrances at a comfortable distance – MacIver, Nicholls, Gower... Oh, Lord!' he sat down. 'I'm turning into a worse gossip than the PC himself... But if I were you I'd put up a fight... what was it that you wanted to talk about?'

He listened carefully as Parsons described his meeting with the boy in South shifting-house. This was not the first incident of its kind that he had come across, but it was the first for some months to be brought officially to his notice.

'Is that all?' he asked when Parsons had finished.

'It's bad enough, isn't it? I'll have to report it to the Superintendent.'

'Of course. As a matter of fact, I often take a trip out to one of the villages in the evening so as to come in on one of the buses that's bringing the night-shift on... and it's a bit tricky when you get men and girls travelling on the same bus – ' he stopped as the telephone began to ring.

'Excuse me,' Parsons picked up the receiver, 'this must be the Ministry.' As he listened to the voice at the other end of the wire his face brightened. 'Yes,' he said, 'yes... of course, it's not all we need, but at least it gives us a start... quite... thank you very much indeed... Goodbye.' He replaced the receiver, and, when he turned to Finch once more, the confidence had returned to his manner. 'You see,' he explained, 'things do get done in the end. The Labour people up at the Ministry have wangled some fitters out of one of the EELS factories for us – not as many as we'd like, of course, but still – '

' "I'm an EELS man myself",' Finch's imitation of Knowles was so devastatingly exact that the other could not forbear to laugh. 'Which factory are they coming from?' the Transportation Officer asked.

Parsons consulted the pad on which he had been scribbling.

'Brokenby. That's Knowles' factory, isn't it? He'll be delighted.'

'You bet!' the mockery was barely audible.

'But about these buses – '

'Ah, the buses!' Finch sat up very erect. 'I'll do what I can, but I can't be everywhere at once... I showed you the scheme I got out to try to persuade the Superintendent to let me organise a service of bus wardens?'

'Bus wardens? No.'

'Didn't I? It was a good scheme.' He began to expound it.

During the winter, when travelling conditions were at their worst, he had proposed that a worker should be selected from each bus-load to be responsible for ensuring that the drivers stopped at the fixed stopping-places and nowhere else, and that the quieter passengers were protected as far as possible from the humours of their more rampageous companions. The wardens, as he called them, were to be chosen by the employees themselves, and were to be rewarded by receiving free travel. It was on this last point that Finch had failed to get the scheme approved. Gittins had, quite accurately, pointed out to the Superintendent that travel was already heavily subsidised, since no worker, from whatever distance he came, paid more than three shillings a week in fares; and he had proceeded to argue that the Ministry, daring as it could be when its officials began to think in millions, would begin to quail before the Select Committee on National Expenditure if any official were so rash as to allow one worker in every thirty or forty to travel to Blimpton for nothing.

'I might ask the old man to reconsider it,' Finch concluded on a tentative note. 'I'll tell you what: you put in your report about this affair on South, and I'll have a word with some of the chaps on the Whitley Council and get them to – ' he broke off as Knowles came into the room.

'Well?' the Senior Labour Manager looked around the room, which was now crowded almost to bursting point, as if he expected to find someone else there. 'What a day!' he exclaimed, and it was now clear that he was searching for something on which to sit down. 'What a day! Those wretched Ministry of Labour people – '

Finch excused himself and went out. But now that there was

a vacant chair Knowles showed no inclination to make use of it. He had spent the afternoon at a meeting at the Dustborough Employment Exchange, and, having been heavily defeated in every argument in which he had become involved, he now proceeded to reinstate himself in his own eyes by describing, with more virulence than accuracy, the outstanding characteristics of the Employment Exchange Manager, the Regional Welfare Officer, the Town Clerk, and the head of the local WVS.

'And now,' he asked when, after twenty minutes or so, his self-respect was somewhat restored, 'have you got anything for me?'

Parsons picked up the list on which he had, earlier in the day, set down the various jobs to be done. 'You'll be glad to know that the Ministry has found us some maintenance fitters at last,' he began.

'Have they?' Knowles sniffed, essaying a smile of cold superiority. 'I think we'll believe that one when we see the bodies.'

'Crabtree spoke to me himself. He said quite definitely that the men would arrive next Monday, and he asked us to be certain that there wouldn't be any hitch in the billeting arrangements – '

'Where are they coming from?'

'From one of the EELS factories.'

'Ah!' the process of restoration was miraculously completed. Knowles caressed his moustache and readjusted his spectacles. 'Then they'll be first-class men – none of these wretched dilutees has ever been allowed to set foot in any EELS factory – it's remarkable how they manage... but, then, they've got a real first-class organisation... of course, that's why they've been able to spare so many of the senior staff... I must say it's very decent of Russell to let us have these men just now. Where did you say they're coming from?'

Once more Parsons studied his scrap of paper. 'From Brokenby.'

In the silence all the noises of the factory seemed to tear into the room. Through the window came the pitter-patter of machine gun bursts on the proof-range, and through the flimsy walls the clatter of typewriters echoed against footfalls, stifled laughter, the sound of a kettle about to boil over.

'But it's impossible!' Knowles, looking for something to thump, found the top of the metal filing cabinet and winced to find it so much harder than the blotter he kept on his own desk for this particular purpose. 'Are you sure he said Brokenby?'

'Yes…' Parsons, as he watched his superior, grew more and more bewildered. He remembered Finch's face, the look of mockery and the half-spoken phrase that he had pretended not to hear. 'He said we'd get a letter confirming it tomorrow.'

'But it's preposterous! Perfectly preposterous!' Knowles took a turn around the empty chair, and then sat down heavily, his long nose quivering. 'I was at Brokenby myself,' he said suddenly.

'Yes. I thought – '

'Well?'

The other hesitated.

'Well?' Knowles repeated, his tone growing shrill.

'I thought… I thought it would be rather – well, rather an advantage to have some of your own men…'

'Yes.' With an effort Knowles began once more to recover himself. He stood up, and threw the raincoat that he had been carrying on to the chair. 'If it were merely a matter of the men's personal qualities,' he continued, 'I couldn't wish for anything better. There isn't a finer body of men – taking them, you understand me, as men – anywhere in this country. Loyal, hard-working, devoted to the interests of the firm. In all the years I spent there I never had the slightest trouble with the men. Never!' he fastened his gaze on Parsons, trying to see whether he was having an effect, whether he had erased the impression of that first panic-stricken moment. The younger man sat rock-like, acquiescent, expressionless. 'But all the same,' Knowles went on, 'they wouldn't be the slightest use here at Blimpton. I'm sorry to have to admit it, because I wouldn't say a word against my men – and, after all they are still my men – but it's no use shirking the facts. And the fact is that they're just not… not… what's the word I'm looking for?'

Parsons shook his head slightly.

'Adaptable. That's it. They're just not adaptable. They're too old. It would take them months – months, I tell you, months – to pick up the work. The production people would never stand it. Never! Badly as we need skilled men, I'm afraid these would be useless, oh, absolutely hopeless...' he glanced up at the clock. 'If you put through a priority call you ought to be able to catch Crabtree before he leaves the Ministry. There's no need to go into the details. Simply tell him – tell him that these men aren't suitable – '

Still perfect in his subordination, Parsons picked up the receiver and booked the call. But when the operator had replied he looked up and asked, 'Don't you think it would be better, sir, if you spoke to Crabtree yourself? I mean, he's rather high up in the Ministry, and – '

'Oh!' Knowles frowned momentarily. 'No. I don't see why you shouldn't talk to him. After all, you spoke to him earlier in the afternoon... And besides, if he remembers that I'm an EELS man he might think there was something personal in it... I'm sure you appreciate that... No, I'll leave you to handle it.' He sniffed once more and hurried out of the room.

TWENTY-THREE

THE SUPERINTENDENT GLANCED around the table. 'Well, gentlemen,' he said, 'I don't want to hurry you.' But his tone conveyed that he had already had enough. 'Is there anything else on Item Seven?'

A shop-steward from South-West uttered a preliminary sound, halfway between a hiccough and a groan.

'Eight,' the Superintendent said quickly.

Of all his duties at Blimpton, taking the chair at the meetings of the Whitley Council was the one he disliked most. It seemed to him absurd and, indeed, almost monstrous that he, and so many members of his senior staff, should be obliged to spend some hours each month in discussing with the trade unions questions which ought, he often argued with Gittins, to be dealt with by executive decisions from the top instead of by consultation, argument and counter-argument. But this was one of the few opinions on which he could never bring Gittins even to appear to agree with him. The Principal Clerk's loyalty to the established practice of the civil service was unshakable, and, besides, he enjoyed threading his way through the intricacies of a difficult piece of negotiation and coming back to his starting point with his objectives gained, his concessions won...

Brown sat back in the leather-padded chair, looking at the drawing he had been scrawling on his blotter. Gittins sat on his right, Knowles on his left. After them, on either side, stretched the two rows of tired, familiar faces: the representatives of the management, neat, bored and cautious, and opposite them the workers' representatives, cautious, too, but with a different kind of caution, afraid to count on support which might be withdrawn at the last moment, watching always for some invisible noose that Gittins or Knowles or the Superintendent might have prepared for them.

Today the meeting seemed interminable. The men were suspicious, restive. Things had begun badly, with an attempt on the part of Davies, the AEU branch secretary, to discuss the reason for the shortage of certain small tools. The Superintendent, on a nod from Gittins, had ruled the discussion out of order, on the grounds that the Council had no authority to deal with production problems. He had then pointed out, looking to Gittins for approval as he did so, that it was the business of the management to deal with production, and that while suggestions from the workers, if they were made in the right spirit, might be tolerated, it must be perfectly clear that the men and women in the factory were not employed in order to think about their work, but solely to get on with it.

At that someone had protested that if the workers came to the factory and found that they had nothing to do they had, to say the least, every right to know why. A young man who was attending the meeting for the first time had broken into an impassioned speech on the demoralising effect that idleness was apt to have on people who had never really known what it was to work, and had then attempted to move a resolution to be sent to the Minister condemning, in three short sentences, the planning and organisation of every department in the factory. His older colleagues had restrained him with some difficulty, making it obvious that though they disliked his methods they did not altogether disapprove of his sentiments. Then Morgan had intervened with some face-saving generalisation, and the meeting had settled down to its regular routine: agreeing about the grading of several new jobs that had been introduced into the factory since the last meeting; arguing about the wages to be paid to men who had been transferred against their will to work that was less congenial and less well paid than that to which they were accustomed; probing the complaints that were made about the canteens, about the shortcomings of the wages department, about the shortage of towels and the pilfering that went on in the shifting-houses.

Now they were talking about transport. The Superintendent pulled himself together with a jerk, and cast a suspicious glance down the table to where Finch was sitting. The Transportation Officer was saying just enough, not committing himself. Brown nodded approvingly as he listened. The train service from Hurling was to be altered so as to enable the workers who came from the villages beyond to make a connection with the regular bus service without having to wait in the village, as they did now, for three quarters of an hour on their way both to and from work. However, the shortage of buses and, more particularly the shortage of drivers, made it essential that as many workers as possible should travel to the factory by train instead of by bus, and the Public Relations Department was proposing to launch a campaign among the Operatives...

Dolphin chimed in with the details. Once more the Superintendent could sit back and relax. He began to finger his eyebrows, telling himself comfortably that he had known all along that there would be no nonsense about this foolish scheme for appointing bus wardens. He would, he had already decided, give the meeting a little talk about the need for sobriety and ask those present to use their influence...

But the talk was not as successful as he had expected. When he had finished it and was about to pass on to the next item old Fred Norton spoke loudly from the bottom of the table. 'It won't do, sir,' he said, 'it's no b — it's no use telling folks they've got to behave emselves. Somebody's got to see as they do. There's all sorts in this factory. These girls you're bringing in now, they're all sorts, good 'uns and bad 'uns. And if the driver or some of the boys starts a bit of nonsense – well, one thing leads to another, as the saying goes...'

A murmur of approval ran down the side of the table.

Miss Creed pursed her lips together. 'My girls,' she began. 'My girls – '

'Excuse me, madam,' the old man spoke with deep respect, 'but they're not your girls, not when they get outside the gates... and it's bad enough with some of these local girls getting into trouble... there was a case in the papers last week, I expect you saw, a girl from Dustborough who was working here until she was eight months gone, if you'll excuse my saying so with a lady present – '

'And the father working up in the packing department at this moment – ' someone interjected ' – and a married man, too.'

'What are you proposing?' the Superintendent asked hurriedly.

'I was thinking, if we could have somebody on every bus – '

'The Labour Department,' Knowles looked up from his notes, 'has quite as much as it can manage already.'

'If you people care to organise something among yourselves,' the Superintendent tried to catch Gittins' eye, and failed, 'there would be no objection whatsoever. Not the slightest.'

'But it needs organising,' Bob Roberts, the leader of the employees' side, pointed out. 'I'm sure Mr Finch would agree with me about that.'

Finch nodded without looking up. His narrow, youthful face wore a concentrated, rather theatrical frown. His long arms hung over the back of his chair. He was so loosely built that in moments of stress, such as this, he looked as if he were just about to fall apart.

'Besides,' Roberts went on, 'you can't expect a man – or a woman for that matter – to take on such a big responsibility if it's not official. They'd have to have some standing. I don't say that they should actually be paid – '

'There could be no question of that,' Gittins interrupted him.

'No? Well, I don't know how these things are managed in other factories, but you'd have to give something to a man in return for asking him to catch the same bus day in, day out, and getting him to report if there was any trouble.' He looked round, gathering the feeling of his colleagues. 'We could find the people to do it all right, if Mr Finch's department could see to the organisation. After all, it's in the interests of the factory.'

'That it is,' Fred Norton agreed heavily. 'There was that bit of bother they had down on South last week – '

Gittins whispered something to the Superintendent. The latter nodded. 'I think,' he rapped the table, calling the meeting to order, 'I think that since this suggestion was not put down on the agenda it is hardly fair – ' he paused to glare at Finch's averted head, ' – hardly reasonable, I repeat, to expect us to come to a decision at this meeting.' Then, looking up, he saw that the shadow of a smile passed over Gittins' face. Suddenly Brown's gratitude for the Principal Clerk's constant, unobtrusive guidance wavered, slipped and disappeared. He realised now that if he was ever to exert his authority in the factory, to make his own decisions, he must begin at once, and with this issue. Finch, he decided, should be allowed to fight it out, perhaps even to have his way in the end. The young man would, of course, have to be reprimanded for putting the workers up to state his case for him, but, after that, if he could get the scheme past Gittins he should be allowed to do so; if the thing went through

and were a success it might, and the Superintendent, too, began to smile, come to the ears of the Minister that... 'But,' he went on, 'if the meeting will leave this question over for further consideration...'
There was no promise, no more than the hint of a concession, but Gittins, scribbling a note, put down his pencil and rubbed the bald patch on his head...

They reached the last item.

'The appointment,' the Superintendent read from the agenda, 'of a representative in the place of Mr Edward Screwby, deceased.' He made a short, but he hoped adequate, statement about the virtues of the late Mr Screwby whom he could, he found, only imperfectly remember. 'And now – ' he turned expectantly to Roberts.

'Well, sir,' the other leaned forward, 'I had a word with you about it the other day, as you know. But since then we've been talking the matter over in the unions and, well, after looking things over carefully, we've been thinking that what with all the women there are in this factory, many more women than men as we all know, we think it's time we had a lady representative – '

'Hear! Hear!' two or three people applauded.

' – we've had to decide a bit quickly, and I haven't had a chance of talking it over with the lady herself, but subject to her agreeing – and knowing her as I do, I've no doubt she will – I have great pleasure, on behalf of the parties concerned, of putting forward the name of Mrs Venning.' He sat back, his hands folded across the bulge in his waistcoat. His round, smooth yet elderly face expressed a mild satisfaction as another murmur of approval ran around the table.

'Then I am sure we shall all be glad to welcome – ' the Superintendent was beginning when Gittins slipped a piece of paper in front of him. On it was printed one word: 'NO.' ' – to welcome our first lady representative,' he stumbled, trying to find a formula that would cover him against whatever might happen later. Experience had taught him the danger of ignoring the Principal Clerk's advice, and his newly formed determination to get his own way weakened slightly at this new evidence of Gittins' superior knowledge. 'I must point out,' he went on, tearing the scrap of paper into small shreds as he spoke, 'that this is a somewhat – somewhat irregular mode of procedure. It is customary, as we all know, to – er – consult the interested parties before bringing the name to the meeting; and I think – I am sure – ' he recovered himself sufficiently to give Gittins a hard and menacing stare, ' – that in the circumstances it would be – er – more constitutional to hold the matter over until the next meeting.'

'Well, Mr Chairman,' Bob Roberts was beginning to fold his papers, 'as I said just now, I've no doubt that Mrs Venning will agree. But if you prefer to hold the matter over until she's given her consent in Writing in the usual way, well, it's a pity, but there's no great harm done.'

'Quite. And that,' the Superintendent looked around the room as if daring anyone to interrupt, 'that concludes the business of the meeting.'

'Young Finch is getting too clever by half,' Gittins remarked as soon as the door of the Superintendent's room was safely closed.

'Oh, Finch is all right,' Morgan said easily. 'Finch is a man of ideas... I'd like to see us give him his head over this one.'

The Superintendent was lighting a cigar. Presently his face emerged from behind a cloud of smoke. 'I don't see why we shouldn't,' he observed cautiously.

Gittins, perhaps astonished by this gesture of defiance, retreated a step or two from his favourite position at the side of the Superintendent's desk. He had a shambling way of walking, and, with his round shoulders hunched forward and his suit looser and shinier than ever, he looked, as he perhaps intended, almost extravagantly humble. His eyes, shrewd and lively below the narrow, wrinkled forehead, were cast down as he spoke. 'Well, sir,' he began, and his voice was as mild and inoffensive as his appearance, 'if you're prepared to face the repercussions...'

He paused, but the magic formula, rolling so easily off the tongue, for once failed to produce its effect. The Superintendent, instead of asking what the repercussions would be, demanded a written report on Finch's scheme. 'And now,' he put down his cigar, 'what's wrong with that woman – Mrs Venning, didn't they call her?'

'Ma!' Morgan chuckled. 'She's a grand old girl. We ought to have had her on the Whitley Council months ago – '

'Indeed?' the Superintendent's massive eyebrows were lifted high in astonishment at this evidence of what he hoped might be an indication of disagreement between Gittins and Morgan.

'I'm afraid she wouldn't do on the Council,' Gittins began tentatively.

'Why not?' Morgan asked.

'Because she's a Communist.'

'A Communist!' the Superintendent repeated. 'Are you sure?'

'Absolutely.'

Morgan jumped up. 'So what?' he asked quickly, a hint of anger appearing in his voice.

They looked at him, each waiting for the other to reply. His hands were thrust into his pockets, his head thrown back. 'Even if she were a Communist,' he challenged them, 'you couldn't keep her off for that reason. If the unions want her, that's their affair, and we've no right – and no power – to challenge them. Besides – '

'We might produce some other reason, Gittins broke in, turning to the Superintendent for support. 'But I've got proof – '

'What sort of proof?' Morgan's eyes were bright with rage.

'She was seen at a meeting – a communist meeting – in Dustborough the other Sunday – '

'Do you mean to say – ' Morgan turned the full force of his anger on his old ally, ' – do you mean to say that you had her watched?' He paused again, challenging the older man to meet his glance, but Gittins, filling his pipe, refused to look up. 'Surely – '

'I wasn't concerned with Mrs Venning in particular,' Gittins replied at last, 'but I like to know what people in the factory are up to…'

'So you send people around to spy on meetings?' Morgan was striding up and down the room, his anger mounting at every step. 'Of all the mean, dirty, contemptible – '

'Morgan!' the Superintendent broke in, calling him to order.

'Sir?'

'Hadn't you better consider what you are saying?'

But Morgan, consumed by his own rage, refused to be checked.

'Mrs Venning is a decent, respectable, God-fearing woman – one of the best influences that we've got in this factory. I'm proud to count her among my friends... but that isn't the point. Whatever her beliefs or her political opinions, she's entitled to as much freedom to do what she likes outside the factory as you or I or as the Minister himself. And if ever I hear again of anyone snooping – snooping into the private lives of the workers I'll walk straight out of here and go and tell old Outrage, and the Prime Minister, too, if I can get anywhere near him. If we who're making the weapons to fight for – '

He broke off as the telephone rang. As the Superintendent leaned forward to pick up the receiver Gittins crossed the room and whispered to Morgan: 'Wait!'

'Why should I wait?'

'I'll explain afterwards. I found this out only by accident... '

Morgan, perhaps anxious to believe that this was true, shook his head.

'You know,' Gittins glanced up to assure himself that the Superintendent was still occupied with the telephone, 'I'd have told you if... if I'd been making any inquiries. I found this out quite by accident.'

'Then why didn't you say so?'

Gittins' smile was deprecatory but friendly. 'Why didn't you give me a chance?'

The receiver clicked back into position. 'Well?' the Superintendent asked.

Morgan was still frowning. 'I think we've agreed that Mrs Venning's name should be allowed to go forward,' he said rather coldly. 'That is, of course, subject to your approval...'

But outside in the corridor he turned on Gittins. 'You old scoundrel!' his manner was almost friendly. 'What have you been up to?'

The Principal Clerk shook his head. 'Nothing. I heard some gossip. You don't really imagine that I've had people watched?'

'I don't know... I simply don't know.' He stopped, his hand on the knob of the door leading into his room. 'But if ever you do such a thing again – ' the door opened, and, leaving the sentence unfinished, he went inside.

TWENTY-FOUR

THE SPRING EVENINGS were clear and sharp, like winter. When the night-shift workers entered the factory, at a quarter to ten, a thin rim of dusk still hung around the sky, but when the afternoon-shift left, half an hour later, it was dark. Torches flashed on and off down the clean-ways. The shifting-houses were crowded. Men and women coming off contact work did not bother to wash carefully. 'I'll clean this off when I get home,' they promised one another as they rinsed their stained hands. They jostled and shouted, flinging off their uniforms, hastily fastening the belts and buttons, the hooks and zippers of their own clothes, and then rushed out to reclaim their contraband at the entrance to the Danger Areas and to scramble for the buses that would take them to the Main Gates of the factory. Outside the gates the rush was intensified. Everybody wanted to catch the first bus; everybody, it seemed, was afraid of being left behind. Voices rose and fell, monosyllabic, tired; in the dark they seemed to come from nowhere; they were like the voices of England, all gathered together in one place: lively cockney voices, breaking into shrillness; the slow cold tones of the midlands, flat and unaccented; the singing voices of Wales, and the chipped, rough accents of Lancashire; soft, blurred country voices from twenty counties mingled into the chatter, the laughter, the sudden brief screams of townspeople lost in the darkness, homeless, fierce in their desire for rest and warmth and comfort.

One night Griselda Green, slipping into the last vacant place in the bus, found herself sitting next to Doris Chandler.

'Hello!' she said.

'Goodness!' Doris turned to her in the gloom. 'I haven't seen you for ever such a long time! Fancy you remembering me!'

'Oh, I remember people. Don't you?'

'Well,' Doris frowned, 'sometimes I do. But then sometimes I don't. And I've done my hair different since last time I saw you.'

'So you have,' Griselda looked at the small head shadowed against the window pane, the hair scraped up at the back, curls piled on top in a disorderly froth. 'Where are you working now?' she asked idly.

'In South. One of the det. shops.'

'Why, so am I... I haven't seen you down there.'

'No,' Doris put a hand up to adjust a hairpin, 'they only shifted me over there last Monday.'

'Like it?'

'Oh, it's all right, I suppose.'

It was all right. The shops were small, with benches running down each side, and a double bench down the middle. Each girl stood behind her glass screen, and on the other side of the screen within reach, but protected, lay the little heap of powder, the metal caps, the machine, no larger than a sewing machine but painted red, red for danger...

Doris leaned back against the worn upholstery. 'Had the rash yet?' she asked.

'No.'

'Lucky!'

'It isn't luck, you know. It's largely a matter of taking care.'

'That's what the doctor said to me when I got it. But I don't know as I believe her... she's a funny one, isn't she?'

'Who is?'

'The doctor. Dr Aaron. She's not like a proper doctor. Too young, if you ask me,' she was quoting, parrot-like, from a conversation she had heard in the canteen earlier in the day. Her attention seemed to wander. In the seats behind people were chatting, laughing, exchanging gossip, grumbling mildly about one thing and another. They talked about shopping difficulties, the price of canteen meals, the goings-on of the woman next door whose husband was called up only a month ago.

Suddenly Doris leaned forward. 'Do you think my hair looks all right?' she asked.

'Yes...' Griselda peered at her in the gloom.

'Are you sure?'

'Mm. It suits you.'

'Oh, but that's not what I meant,' Doris had lowered her voice to a whisper, hoarse and mysterious. At the back of the bus a group of young men had begun to sing:

'Roll out the barrel,
    Let's have a barrel of – '

'What I mean,' she went on, 'is, do you think they'll let me go in the hostel with my hair done up like this?'

Griselda smiled. 'I didn't know there were any rules in the hostel about the way people have to do their hair,' she replied.

'Oh, it isn't them up at the hostel. They wouldn't say nothing, I don't suppose. It's that Labour woman, Miss Braithwaite. She come round to ask who'd like to go in the hostel – '

'Yes, I know,' Griselda agreed gently.

'You heard she wouldn't let me go?'

'Yes, I heard.'

'Who told you that?'

Norah. For Norah had, until recently, been so absorbed in her job as to be able to talk of very little else. Her homesickness had been forgotten, and her sense of inferiority had, because of her growing awareness of her own competence, begun to disappear. Her natural gaiety of manner had become stronger, and less defiant. And then, quite suddenly, it had deserted her altogether. She had, since the Sunday evening when she and Ma Venning had brough the young airman, Tom Walton, home to tea, been moody and silent. She still spent much of her free time at the Venning house, and sometimes, as she watched Ma prepare a meal or helped Kitty and Griselda to wash up afterwards, she would begin to say something and then break off sharply, put on her coat, and leave. Ma was too busy and had, besides, too much natural delicacy to try to drag from the girl any unwilling confidences; and Kitty, who had once or twice ventured to ask what was the matter, had felt snubbed by Norah's refusal to unburden herself. Only with Griselda, who gave little and demanded nothing, did Norah feel completely at ease; but not even to Griselda could she speak yet...

'Do you think they'll let me go in the hostel now?' Doris began afresh.

'I don't know. I don't see why they shouldn't.'

'Honest?'

Griselda hesitated and Doris, watching, bit her lip. 'I'll die if they do!' she declared. Tears of rage sprang into her eyes, and she wiped them away with the corner of a dirty handkerchief, forgetting the Hollywood trick that she had watched so often: the trick of letting one tear roll down each cheek and then dabbing it off gently so as not to spoil her make-up. She was no longer a film star but a little girl from Oldham, longing for a bed of her own and the right to have a bath when she wanted one. 'If they don't let me go, I'll – I'll – '

A voice from somewhere behind shouted, 'Look! If that ain't young Garbo! Hi, Garbo!'

She turned around. 'Why, hello, Sid...' And then she got up and squeezed her way towards the back seats. Presently her voice could be heard high and shrill in the chorus of the next song:

'There ain't no sense
In sittin' on the fence
All by yourself in the moonlight...'

Griselda, left alone, put her handbag on the empty space beside her and stretched out her legs. Her head was thrown back, and the pale light deepened the shadows beneath her cheeks and emphasised the long curves of neck and jaw. She nodded and closed her eyes. Her mouth, in repose, lost its humour and revealed an unexpected, rather uneasy severity aimed, one might have guessed, against herself. She seemed to doze, but when at last the bus drew up in the Market Square at Dustborough she jumped out with lively, springing steps and turned rapidly down one of the side streets. Others, tumbling out after her, stopped to bid each other good night, or straggled homewards, arguing whether to stop for a quick one before closing time.

But presently, as she climbed the hill that led to the housing estate, Griselda heard footsteps behind her hurrying, until at last someone caught up with her, and a young man's voice said: 'Excuse me!'

'Yes?' He wore a square-cut raincoat belted in tightly at the waist, and his soft felt hat was pulled low over his eyes, but in the moonlight his face was clearly visible and it took the girl only a second to recognise it as belonging to Norah's friend, Henry Tyndale.

'I was following you.' He spoke breathlessly, waiting to be snubbed.

'So I noticed,' she agreed pleasantly, but a pucker of irritation appeared between her eyes.

'Then – ' he did not look at her but his face, downcast, was anxious, pleading, ' – could I speak to you?'

'That's what you're doing, isn't it?'

'Yes. But – '

They had been standing still. Now she took half a step forward. 'I'm on my way home. You can come along if you want to talk. What's it about? Miss McCall?'

He gulped. 'Did she speak to you?'

She shook her head. 'I don't think I know what you mean.'

'She didn't tell you?'

Abruptly, she stopped. 'Listen,' she said, 'if you want to ask me something, ask! If you want to send a message to Norah – '

'She won't have anything to do with me anymore.' He looked so woebegone, so utterly hopeless, that it should not have been possible for him to look ridiculous also.

'I thought – I mean – ' he floundered on. 'What I did – '

'And what did you do?' Her tone had become acid with contempt, or so, at least, the young man seemed to imagine.

'I – ' he began once more, trying to take confidence from the fact that he was an assistant foreman and she, after all, only a semi-skilled operative. 'I – ' he could not go on any longer. She was, he decided, too haughty. And besides... 'Good night,' he said, and rushed away.

Ma Venning, who had to get up early to be on the morning-shift, was on her way to bed when Griselda got in. The kettle was boiling on the hob, and supper was laid on one half of the kitchen table: bread, cheese, and the remains of yesterday's spam.

'You all right, dear?' Ma called down.

'Mm. Tired.'

'I'll come down and make your cocoa – '

'No need,' Griselda called back as she hung up her coat behind the door.

But Ma came, just the same. She was still fully dressed, but her thick grey hair hung in a pigtail down her back. 'I was hoping you'd be back soon,' she remarked, smiling a little to herself as she spoke.

'Norah was round this evening.' She made the cocoa, and put in an extra spoonful of sugar. 'She seemed ever so much better.'

'She did?'

'Yes. Quite like her old self. It seems that – well – ' the corners of her mouth turned up. 'Do you remember that RAF boy who dropped in one Sunday – the one I met with Norah?'

Griselda, munching bread, nodded. 'So that's it, is it?'

'He seemed a nice boy, didn't he?'

'Mm. When's he coming?'

Ma laughed. 'That's the funny thing. Norah said she saw him last Sunday – he just dropped in on her at her lodgings... You do think he's a nice boy, don't you?' For Ma, seldom uncertain about anything, had grown into the habit of asking Griselda's opinion about all sorts of questions, seeking not so much confirmation of her own sure judgment as the clue to something that puzzled her about the girl herself. Griselda talked little about her life before she came to Blimpton and Ma, unwilling to ask questions, imagined some tragedy, some strange misfortune whose scars it was, she felt, her business to try to heal. If anyone had asked her why she felt this, Ma would have found it difficult to reply, for Griselda was usually the gayest member of the household, and her occasional moods of depression rarely obtruded into the activities of others. 'Another thing,' Ma went on, 'she was saying again that she thought you ought to go into the hostel to help with some of those rough girls they're getting. Of course, I said we couldn't spare you...'

Griselda put down her cup. Her face was serious, her eyes very big in the pale face. 'But you think I ought to go?'

'You'd be a big help in that place.'

'Would I?'

'Of course you would – you've got a way with people. I don't know what it is... but as long as you feel you'd rather stay here...'

TWENTY-FIVE

DAN MORGAN WAS a yard or so behind Ruth as she came out of her bedroom on the upper landing.

'Hi!' he called.

The day's weariness slipped off her as she turned to greet him.

'Coming dancing?' he asked.

'Tonight?'

'You know they've a dance at the hostel?'

'Oh!' It was clear that she had not at first understood. Her voice fell as she added: 'They didn't ask me.'

'Never mind.' He put out a hand, guiding her towards the stairs. 'I expect they forgot... but I'm asking you. Won't that do?'

'If you're sure it's all right...'

'Of course it is. Leave it to me...'

At dinner it was obvious that nearly everyone was going to the dance. Miss Marshall, the warden of the hostel, had asked few of the senior staff to attend, because she was anxious that the first important social function held in the hostel should not be clouded by the presence of a large proportion of Blimpton's ruling class. But most of the residents of Mowbray Lodge were prepared to overlook this omission for the sake of an evening in a relatively novel environment. Even Miss Creed, dressed in flowered silk and decorated with amethysts, declared that she regarded it as a matter of duty to see that the girls who lived in the hostel were properly entertained.

'I'll be interested to learn something about Miss Creed's notion of propriety,' Dolphin whispered to Ruth when he had finished gulping down his coffee, '...just to see whether I can ever hope to come up to her standards...'

'Oh, I'm sure you never will!' Ruth laughed unexpectedly; and then, as Dolphin went on chatting, she began to look round the room, waiting for Morgan to signal to her that it was time to go. But Morgan, when he crossed the room, was deep in conversation with Nicholls. The two men approached Dolphin.

'What have you done with Gunn?' Morgan asked, for Gunn had

arrived at Blimpton late in the afternoon and, after a short talk with the Superintendent, had sent for Dolphin.

Dolphin shrugged his shoulders. 'As far as I know,' he replied, trying to conceal his chagrin, 'he's walking round the factory – '

'*Walking* round the factory!' someone interjected.

' – with that glamour girl I keep in my office,' Dolphin continued, ignoring the interruption. 'You know – the daughter of old Little from Dustborough.'

'I didn't know that girl was still here,' Dawson remarked with a trace of disapproval.

'Well, she is. And as far as I know Gunn is with her.'

'Does he know about the dance?' Morgan asked.

'Yes. He said he'd look in… I might chase around and find out where he's got to.'

'I wish you would,' Morgan agreed. And so, leaving Dolphin to telephone to all the Groups, they set off.

They arrived just as the Superintendent was getting out of his car, and as Miss Marshall led them in a hush fell on the bright and noisy hall. The orchestra, prompted by a signal from one of the house-matrons, stopped in the middle of a bar. The dancers pulled themselves to attention, Miss Marshall lifted her hand, and then the orchestra struck up the National Anthem.

The visitors stood in an embarrassed row, not knowing what to do.

'Is it all over?' Ruth whispered to Dan.

'No,' he told her, 'this seems to be for us.'

'But why?'

He shrugged his shoulders.

'In the absence of Royalty,' Finch, who was standing near, remarked acidly, 'they're trying to do honour to the next best thing – the majesty of the temporary civil service – isn't that so, Parsons?'

'Sorry,' Parsons came a step or two nearer, 'I'm afraid I wasn't listening.' His usually cheerful manner had, during the past few weeks, become dulled. Lines of worry were creased around his eyes, and his square, alert figure had developed the heavy look of middle age.

Finch led him aside. 'Has Gitty changed his mind about giving you a house?' he asked.

'No.' Parsons had, in fact, almost given up hope of being able to bring his wife and children to Blimpton. Most of the houses on the factory estate were still empty, but Gittins had made it clear that the rules governing their occupation could not be relaxed; and on the past two or three Sundays the assistant labour manager had been too fully occupied with making up arrears of work in his office to be able to spend any time at all in looking for lodgings in the neighbouring villages.

'Why don't you tackle the old man this evening?' Finch persisted.

'It's hardly the time to talk shop...' Parsons objected doubtfully. He had received no letter from his wife since the heavy raid on London during the previous weekend, and, though he told himself that if anything had happened to her he would have heard of it by this time, he was more alarmed than he was prepared to admit.

'Have you asked Morgan about it?' Finch went on, and, seeing the other's hesitation, began to move towards the corner where Dan and Ruth stood listening, or pretending to listen, to Miss Creed's strictures on what she described as the unnecessary luxury of the furnishings of the hostel.

The dancers, though still rather awkwardly conscious of their visitors, were once more beginning to enjoy themselves. Miss Marshall had, she thought daringly, invited a small party of soldiers from a neighbouring camp, and a few of the hostel residents were escorted by young men who worked in the factory, but for the most part the girls danced together, shouting and whistling to each other across the vast empty spaces of the hall, or turning in sedate circles, watching the young men through lowered lashes.

'Nothing is too good for these girls,' Morgan was taking up the challenge as Finch and Parsons approached, and then, smiling down at Ruth, he added in quite a different tone, 'if you'll forgive me, I think I ought to do my duty to some of the wallflowers.'

Ruth watched him as he crossed the room, and then for a moment she lost sight of him as Finch asked her to dance.

Griselda, chatting with two girls who had arrived from Aberdeen only that morning, did not see Morgan until he stood in front of her.

'Come!' he said.

A cloud of astonishment rose over the room as they began to dance; and then it broke, sending cascades of exclamations, of questions, eddying into the air around them. 'Who is he?' the girls who were new to the factory whispered as they watched. 'Who is she?' the Superintendent turned to Gittins, only to find that the Principal Clerk was himself asking the same question. 'Fancy the Assistant Superintendent dancing!' the girls from Gasping exclaimed in chorus. 'Do you think he'll ask me?' they murmured as they fluffed out their curls and smoothed their dresses more tightly over their hips. 'Stunning looking girl,' Finch observed to Ruth as he trod on her toes.

Neither Dan Morgan nor Griselda seemed to be aware that the whole room had become their audience. They danced in silence, smiling with delight. And, looking at them again, people saw that it was neither the girl's beauty nor the man's air of strength and controlled power that made them so remarkable.

'Don't they look happy?' Miss Marshall, as they passed, murmured to Miss Creed.

Miss Creed gave a start of incredulity as if happiness were a factor beyond her calculation. 'Yes,' she agreed grudgingly, 'I suppose they do.'

Parsons, chatting with Miss Hopkins, remarked that the pair looked like old friends.

'No,' the Entertainments Officer shook her fluffy grey curls, 'I wouldn't say that. They look too – ' she searched for the word, 'ecstatic.'

Parsons, slightly embarrassed, turned away.

The orchestra stopped and Dan took a pace back. 'It's nice to see you,' he said, and his smile, in spite of the faint look of mockery, stressed the under-statement. 'Where have you been all this time?'

'Here.' Griselda shook back her smooth hair. 'I live here.'

'Why?'

For a moment she did not reply. Standing there in the centre of the room, waiting for the orchestra, surrounded by gossipy, noisy couples, they looked at one another with a curiosity so intense that no question could satisfy it. They were smiling. His mouth opened a little, showing the sharp, devouring teeth, but he did not speak. He looked amused, quizzical, and at the same time delighted. And she, returning his glance, her eyes very bright beneath the broad, white forehead, seemed about to break into laughter.

Then they began to dance again, and as they danced she told him how Ma Venning and Norah had persuaded her that she ought to move into the hostel until the commotion created by the Gasping girls had settled down.

Morgan, listening, became once more serious, critical, impersonal. 'Ma's a wonderful woman,' he commented when the story was finished.

'Do you know her?'

'Of course. Everybody knows Ma... I wonder what made her think you'd have a good influence?'

'Why shouldn't I?'

'Why not, indeed?'

'You needn't laugh.'

'I'm not laughing. I want to find out what sort of a person you have to be to exercise a good influence in this – ' he glanced around the hall, ' – in this reluctant nunnery.'

'What a perfect phrase!'

'Ah! I've got a good line in fine phrases. You'll discover that when you get to know me better... But tell me, what do you do to set an example?'

'Oh,' she hesitated, 'I don't do very much really. I get up at the proper time, and I don't go to the cinema when I'm supposed to be working. I try not to complain more than twice a day about the food – '

'It's bad, is it?'

Her grey eyes widened. 'Didn't you know that?'

'I'd heard rumours.'

'Rumours!'

'You must remember, we at the factory haven't any control over the hostel. Miss Marshall is responsible to the Ministry – '

'Oh, I don't think she's altogether to blame.'

'You don't?'

'No. She does what she can. It's the organisation that's faulty.'

'You'd better tell me about this.'

They had already stopped dancing, and now he led her out. The corridor was crowded with girls hurrying to catch the bus that would get them to the factory in time for the night-shift.

'You see,' Griselda commented, 'they couldn't even arrange to have the dance on a Saturday night when everyone would have been able to come.' As they went from room to room, looking for some empty chairs, she explained that many girls who were on the afternoon and night-shifts had decided to stay away from work that day so that they could attend the dance. Then, as Dan followed her into the empty writing room, she began to tell him about the grievances of those who lived in the hostel: the food was poor, and the service in the canteen so slow that girls working on the morning-shift often had to go to the factory without breakfast. Miss Marshall and her assistants did the best they could, but it was impossible to recruit as maids and waitresses girls who could go into the factory and earn much higher wages than those paid to the domestic staff. Maids had to be taken from the dormitory blocks to help in the kitchen, and so beds were left unmade, stained and dirty towels lay on the floors of the bathrooms; girls bought food in Dustborough or had parcels sent from home, and picnics in the cubicles had already produced a plague of mice in one building. The electric hair-drier that had been due to arrive before the first batch of girls moved into the hostel was still on its way. The cinema projector was in working order, but no films had yet been sent...

'How do you know all this?' Morgan interrupted.

'Everybody knows. People talk... Someone has got to do something...'

'So you get hold of me on the first free evening I've had for weeks – '

'You know that isn't what happened.' She leaned forward to take a light from him and as their eyes met they began to laugh.

'Okay, you win.' He stood up, leaning against the empty fireplace. He looked, in spite of his rather sallow colouring and solid, almost heavy, build, astonishingly alive. It could be seen now that his features, which few could ever clearly remember, clothed a personality which no one, having encountered it, would ever completely forget. Yet he seemed to be withholding himself, using laughter as a shield.

'You'll do something?' she asked. She was impersonal now, and completely serious.

'About the hostel? I'll do what I can.'

'Thanks.' She got up.

'No. Don't go.' He put out a hand and, guiding her to the sofa, sat down beside her. 'Tell me,' he asked, 'why are you so interested in what goes on in this factory?'

Her eyes were shadowed as she watched the glowing end of the cigarette. 'It's my war, too.' She sat very erect, and her face, above the dark dress, was pale and remote. The air of gaiety which she had worn since the moment when he had first seen her at the opposite side of the hall had gone, and she seemed to be absorbed in her own thoughts. After a minute or two she turned to Morgan again. 'Isn't it?' she asked.

'It's everybody's war – and everybody's factory... but don't you ever think about anything else?'

'Yes. Often.'

'Such as – ?'

'Oh,' the smile that curved around her long mouth was oddly, perhaps unintentionally, provocative, 'the sort of things that women do think about... nothing very out of the ordinary, I'm afraid.'

'No?' He leaned a little towards her, waiting.

Someone opened the door, looked in, said 'Sorry', and went out again before either of them could turn round.

'We'd better go back to the hall.' Once more Griselda got up.

'Yes, it's not very private in here, is it?' He grinned, mocking himself. 'But I do want to talk to you...'

'What about?'

'Not about anything. I just want to talk to you – and I still want to find out what you're doing at Blimpton.' He got out his pocket diary and flicked over the pages. 'I've got to go over to Ratchford on Sunday, and I could take a passenger... that is, if you'd like to come?'

'Yes, I'd like to do that.'

'Right. Pick me up in my office at about twelve, and we'll get some lunch on the way.'

'Lovely.' She took a step towards the door. 'And about the hostel problems?'

'Well!' again he grinned, 'if you're not the most – '

'What?'

'The most business-like, the most persistent, the most impersonal female I ever met!... I'll tell you what,' his hand was already on the door, 'we'll do something right away.'

'What?'

'I'll introduce you to Gunn and you can talk to him about it.'

'Who?' she leaned over to a table and stamped out her cigarette, pressing it into the ash-tray with slow deliberation, watching until the last flicker of smoke had died.

'Gunn. The Minister's personal representative... you don't mean to say that you've never heard of him?'

'No,' her grey eyes looked straight into his. 'Why should I have heard of him?'

'Oh, he's always running round, chasing something... I thought you might have seen him about the place.'

'No, not that I know of... what... what does he look like?'

'Villainous looking chap, with hair standing right up on end. Not your type at all, I should say.' He opened the door. 'Come on – we don't want to miss him.'

She stood quite still, framed by the lintel of the door. The corridor was lighted by a single dark blue bulb, so that it was impossible to see her face.

Morgan put out a hand, touching her lightly on the arm. 'You're not shy?' he asked, and his voice revealed, in its striving towards intimacy, an unexpected gentleness.

'No,' her tone, cool, light, impersonal, acted as a rebuff. 'But if he's not my type there's not much point in my talking to him, is there?'

'Oh!'

'That isn't what I meant!' she corrected herself quickly. 'You'd put the case so much better – '

'I doubt it. Besides, he's a queer bird. If the Superintendent or I ask him to do something he'll probably forget about it. But if I bring a girl along – practically any sort of girl – he'll put a call through to the Minister right away – and you'll be getting caviar for breakfast tomorrow.'

'In time to catch the bus for the morning-shift?'

'Mm. Dropped by a Wellington, I shouldn't wonder... Now will you come?'

She allowed him to lead her along the corridor, but just before they reached the hall she stopped, opened her bag, and fumbled inside it.

'Lost something?' the man asked.

'My lipstick. It must have slipped out when we were in that room.'

'I'll get it for you.'

'No. I think I'd better go. I ought to do something to my face before I meet Mr – ' she looked up at him ' – Sten, was it?'

He laughed. 'Gunn... Now don't be too long – '

'I won't.' Quickly she turned away and disappeared into the gloom.

TWENTY-SIX

THE DRIVER PULLED up at the Half-way House.

'Time for a quick one,' he said.

'I'll have to report you for this,' Joe Dakers, the bus warden, protested feebly.

'Aw, we're on time, ain't we? And we shan't stop more'n five minutes.'

People were already scrambling out.

'I'll report you,' Joe stood up and shouted, 'every man jack of you!'

'Good old Joe!' someone called back, 'and don't forget the girls!'

'Come on, Garbo!' Sid Peachey beckoned.

Doris Chandler hesitated, but at last she, too, began to climb down.

The pub was warm and frowsty. Above the chatter the voice of a BBC announcer could be heard reading the nine o'clock news.

'There!' Sid put a glass of port in front of Doris and lifted his own mug of beer. 'When you've had that you won't feel so bad about not going to the dance.'

Doris sipped the port delicately. 'I'm all right,' she insisted, 'really I am.'

'What's the matter with our Doris?' Charlie Eastman, who worked on the bomb-filling Group, shouted across the room. 'Now what you need is a nice drop of something warm.'

'Oh, I'm all right,' Doris repeated. Her eyes were smudged with dark circles. 'I don't give a damn,' she declared; watching Charlie place the second glass in front of her.

Back on the bus, with Sid's arm around her, she began to feel better. But by the time they reached the factory she had once more begun to think about the dance that was going on at the hostel...

In the detonator shop at the far end of South Group two or three girls who lived at The Beeches had already arrived.

'Wish I'd stayed on,' Gladys Hicks grumbled.

'That's right,' Eileen Scott agreed, 'we could've still been dancing, instead of sticking around here waiting for something to do.'

'It's awful, all this waiting,' somebody sighed.

Doris sat down on one of the high stools, leaning back against the empty workbench. She looked lost and utterly hopeless, and she had begun to feel a little dizzy. She had been so certain that Miss Braithwaite would arrange for her to go into the hostel that even now she could scarcely believe that yesterday's refusal had been final.

'Still thinking about that labour woman?' Pearl Kaplanski asked her.

'It's so mean,' Doris said, 'the way she spoke to me – '

'Oh, you don't want to take any notice of that,' Pearl comforted her, 'she doesn't like you, and that's all there is to it.'

'But what have I *done*?' Doris' manner was increasingly woe-begone.

'I dunno, I don't suppose you've done anything special – '

'That's just it,' another girl chimed in. 'It ain't what you do,' she began to chant.

The chorus was taken up by those standing near, until in a few moments everyone in the room was singing:

'It ain't what you do,
  It's the way that you do it –
  That's what gets results!'

They had forgotten Doris. And then, at last, the night's work began to arrive from the stores, and the girls settled down in front of their machines.

Doris looked through the glass shield at the little heap of powder lying, harmless as dust, on the other side of her machine. Then she pressed the lever. It did not move.

'Mrs Coombes!' she called to the over-looker.

'Oh, what's the matter now?' Mrs Coombes asked crossly. She was a haggard young woman who struggled perpetually to adjust her domestic life to suit the hours worked by the factory. This evening she was more irritable than usual, chiefly because she had been kept awake all day by the noise made by her neighbours' children who had been having a holiday from school.

She glanced at the machine. 'It looks all right to me,' she said, and then something in Doris' manner caught her attention. 'You've been drinking!' she accused her.

Doris reddened. 'I only had a port,' she said.

'Then what's up with you? Here, try again.' She looked to make sure that the tiny metal disc was in position, and then waited while Doris tried to press the lever. Nothing happened.

'There!' Doris, vindicated, began to feel more cheerful. 'You see!'

'No, you're not doing it right,' the over-looker insisted.

Several other girls were standing about, listening.

'It's silly to take risks,' Gladys Hicks muttered, 'you never know what'll happen – ' She broke off as Norah McCall came in, brisk and fresh in the uniform of an Assistant Forewoman.

'What's wrong?' Norah asked.

'Nothing much,' Mrs Coombes replied unwillingly. 'This girl says her machine's gone wrong, but what I say is – ' breathlessly, almost unintentionally, she began to accuse Doris of drunkenness, of coming to work without having slept, of idling on the clean-ways with the truckers when she should have been working...

'Now wait a minute,' Norah interrupted her, and began herself to examine the machine. She did not understand the mechanism very clearly, but she knew her job. She turned to the over-looker, her face stern. 'You know what the instructions are,' she said, 'when in doubt, send for the fitter. You'd better get him to come over right away.'

Reluctant and ashamed, Mrs Coombes went to the telephone.

Doris seized the moment. 'It's not true what she said about me,' she whispered.

Norah patted the letter from Tom Walton that lay in an inside pocket. It had been addressed to her at the factory, and she had only been able to glance at it hurriedly before coming on duty. Now she was waiting for the moment when she could read it properly. 'But you did have a drink?' she asked.

Mrs Coombes rushed back. 'They don't know when he'll be able to come,' she explained. 'He's on a job down at the other end of the Group, and he's got to go somewhere else before he can come over here.' She led Norah to the door. 'I must get my output,' she pleaded when they were out of earshot. 'I had half my girls away yesterday, and now they're all here I've got to make it up. You know what Mr

Simmons is if he doesn't get his output...'

Norah tried to soothe her, promising to arrange that a fitter should be sent as soon as one was free, and exacting, in return, an undertaking that the machine should not be touched until the fitter had examined it. Then she hurried off to the foreman's office, wondering when the additional fitters, whose arrival had been expected for so long, would eventually reach Blimpton.

Meanwhile Doris was huddled in a corner, moping. After a time she looked up to make sure that Mrs Coombes was at the other end of the shop. Then she pulled out the lipstick that was hidden in the top of her stocking and began to daub at her mouth. It was at this moment that one of the Danger Building Visitors, whose duty was to ensure that the safety precautions were strictly observed, opened the door.

'What's that you're doing?' he pounced on her at once.

She stood up, trembling. The lipstick case slipped out of her hand and rolled along the floor.

'Pick that thing up,' he said, 'and give it to me.' His voice was stern. 'You know you're not allowed to bring stuff on to the clean-side.'

She dropped the metal case into his outstretched hand and looked up at him defiantly. 'I'm not the only one,' she said.

'I'll find that out for myself.'

It was true: here, as in every other part of the factory, girls and women smuggled in all sorts of prohibited articles, combs, pocket mirrors, odds and ends of jewellery. By the time the visitor had finished with the shop the names of nine out of the twenty workers present had been noted. Each would, later in the night, be sent for by the foreman to receive an official reprimand. Mrs Coombes' weariness turned to a hard, cold hatred. She knew that she would have to bear a large share of the blame, and that as a result she would probably be reduced to the rank of an ordinary operative.

She began to scold the girl who stood nearest.

''S not my fault,' Gladys Hicks said, 'the book says we can bring in rings.'

'Only wedding rings,' Lily Johnson reminded her with a malicious nod. 'I never wore my engagement ring. Never.'

'You never had one!' someone behind her retorted.

She turned quickly. 'Who said that?'

'Now come on,' Mrs Coombes ordered them. 'You've plenty of time to fight when there's nothing else to do.' She glanced at Doris. 'You, too,' she added.

'I'm waiting for the fitter,' Doris replied stonily.

'And I suppose you think you can wait all night for someone to come and tell you that there's nothing the matter with that machine?'

'There is something the matter with it!'

'So you can go snifting down the clean-way with your boyfriend? Is that the idea?' Mrs Coombes demanded shrilly. Her head was aching. She no longer felt sleepy, but she knew that in a minute or so she was going to scream.

'All right!' Doris took a step forward. Her eyes were bright with defiant rage. 'I'll show you!'

She crossed over to the bench and stood in front of her machine.

'You'd better wait,' Pearl Kaplanski warned her, 'you know Miss McCall said you was to wait.'

'Wait!' Doris echoed, 'they think I'm fooling, do they? Well, I'll show them!' She lifted her hand, grasped the lever and pressed it down with all the strength in her body.

The explosion lifted the roof a fraction of a second after the lights went out.

TWENTY-SEVEN

WHEN MORGAN RE-ENTERED the hall Gunn was already holding court. Mavis Little, pale but triumphant, stood beside him, and around them were grouped most of the senior staff of the factory in various attitudes of hopeful expectancy. The Chief of the Inspection Department, who looked forward to receiving an OBE, was being quietly jostled into the background by the Factory Storage Officer, who was impatiently waiting to be promoted to the headquarters' staff; and he, in turn, was being out-manoeuvred and out-talked by Knowles and Miss Creed who were badly in need of something but were not quite sure what. Miss Hopkins, whose plans were now so far advanced that she was ready to fix a date for her concert, was wedged tightly between Dolphin and the Superintendent, unable to utter a word.

'Ah, here you are,' Gunn beckoned to the Assistant Superintendent, 'I want to talk to you.' His gaze travelled around the semi-circle of faces. 'And you,' he said to one after another, 'and you. And you.'

'I think I'll be getting along,' Mavis suggested. She stood with eyes downcast, a lock of blonde hair falling over her face.

'Tired?' Gunn asked.

'A bit,' she admitted, her lashes fluttering as she looked up to meet the hostile, puzzled, superior stares of the Superintendent's entourage.

'I won't be long. If you dance this one with one of the boys here, I'll drive you back... Here, Dolphin, can't you see that this young lady wants to dance?'

With as good a grace as he could muster Dolphin led her away.

'Well, boys,' Gunn was saying, 'I got to talk to you.'

'Shall we go over to my office?' the Superintendent asked. His tone, without conveying any positive reproach, indicated that the big hall, with the orchestra playing at the other end, was scarcely a suitable place in which to conduct business.

'No, this'll do. I've got to get back to the Ministry before the morning, and I've no time to waste... That girl's father – is he one of the big shots around here?'

Nobody seemed prepared to answer.

'Is he? Or isn't he?'

'Um,' the Superintendent pursed his lips, 'I suppose one might say that in Dustborough he is a man of some – er – er – influence. A small town big shot, as they say on the other side, if you take my meaning…'

'Yes. I get it. I'll talk to him,' Gunn paused to make an entry in his notebook. 'Well, boys,' he went on, 'I got an idea. Matter of fact, I got a coupla ideas.'

They waited, each concealing his anxiety in his own fashion.

'First, I had a snack in one of the canteens. The food's lousy.'

'That's not our affair,' Gittins hastened to explain, 'the Ministry put in the caterers. We do what we can with them, of course.'

'Of course,' Knowles agreed.

'Well, you must change the caterers, that's all.'

'It's the Ministry's business,' the Principal Clerk reiterated stubbornly, 'they let the contract – '

'And we get the complaints,' Morgan added. 'Here in the hostel, too – ' Once more he looked around the hall, making sure, for perhaps the tenth time in as many minutes, that Griselda had not slipped in unobserved.

Gunn, it appeared, knew a firm of caterers who might be persuaded to take on the contract…

'Next,' he consulted his notebook again, 'are you still short of labour?'

The question seemed to cause some embarrassment. During the past two weeks the section of the factory in which trench-mortar bombs were filled had been almost entirely idle as a result of the disappearance in transit of a consignment of tail-units, and the workers had been hastily transferred to the filling of 25-pounder shell. The shell filling shops were now ahead of their programme, and the reserve stocks would be exhausted within the next day or two…

'We still have our difficulties,' the Superintendent observed cautiously.

'Thought as much. I was just downright unlucky with that Gasping scheme. Matter of fact, the CC told me the other day that these girls I did get for you – fine bunch, weren't they? – they'll have to go back to Gasping pretty soon.' He did not observe the sudden intake of breath, the smiles, the sighs of relief. 'So I thought I must do something else to help you out. Matter of fact, I did quite a bit of thinking, and I got an idea. I'm going to get you up a recruiting campaign.'

'What's that?' the Superintendent asked sharply.

'A recruiting campaign. Of course what you want in this country is to call up the women the same way as you call up the men. Conscript 'em.'

'We'll never get that,' said Knowles. 'Never.'

'No, you're right there,' Gunn conceded, staring at the Labour Manager as if seeing him for the first time. 'But I'll organise you a campaign. A real slap-up affair. Marches, parades – a convoy of 4000-pound bombs – fifty of them driving right through the centre of the city, then set 'em up in a line outside the Cathedral – '

'Empty, I hope,' murmured Dolphin, who had by this time succeeded in losing Mavis.

'Impossible. They're on the Secret List,' Dawson pointed out stiffly.

'Which cathedral?' Gittins asked.

'Pinchester. Didn't I say that? I've as good as got the bishop in my pocket – going down to Pinchester to see him tomorrow morning.' He glanced at his watch. 'Time I got going. Now where's that little girl I have to drive home?'

As soon as he had gone the Superintendent asked: 'Well, what do you think?'

'It might work,' Morgan conceded doubtfully. 'If he can get the labour it doesn't matter to us how he does it.'

'But are there any girls in Pinchester?' Nicholls asked.

They looked at each other blankly.

'The daughters of minor canons…' Dolphin suggested.

'Ladies!' Miss Creed exclaimed. 'You can't ask ladies to work in a filling factory!'

'I don't see why not,' Nicholls retorted coldly, 'it's not as if the work called for any particular intelligence.'

'Really!' Miss Creed was about to reply when one of the hostel staff interrupted to announce that Parsons was wanted on the telephone.

'He's not here,' Knowles said, 'you'd better tell them to try Mowbray Lodge.'

The girl explained that the call had been transferred from the Lodge to the hostel. 'It's a trunk call,' she added nervously, 'from London.'

'From the Ministry?' Knowles asked.

'I don't know, sir.'

'Parsons said he was going to look in at the factory,' Finch volunteered, 'he must be on his way over there.'

'All right,' Knowles agreed, 'I'll take it – though why the Ministry should call up at this time of night – '

He returned a few minutes later. Watching him as he crossed the hall, they could see at once that something was wrong. He walked slowly, and when he reached the little group he stood in front of the Superintendent, his mouth working as if he were trying to speak, and with horror glaring in his eyes.

'His wife?' Finch asked.

Knowles nodded. 'Dead,' he said. Beads of sweat stood out on his forehead, and he wiped them away with the back of his hand. 'In that blitz last weekend... They found her yesterday – what was left. But it seems they only identified her this afternoon... pinned under the wreckage... Someone will have to go over to the factory and break it to him...'

'Poor old Parsons,' Dawson began, and then, as if conscious of his own inadequacy, turned away.

'And the children?' again it was Finch who spoke.

Knowles gave a start. 'Children!' he repeated. 'Were there children?'

They looked at one another with deepened consternation.

'Two,' Miss Creed said, remembering the photograph that was the only decoration, the only personal possession, in Parsons' stuffy and overcrowded office. 'A boy and a girl.'

'My God, yes.' Knowles sat down heavily. 'He didn't say anything about children.'

'Who was calling?' Morgan broke in.

'The police.'

'Call them back,' Morgan suggested. 'No,' he contradicted himself, 'I'll go over to the factory and put through a priority call. We might as well leave the poor devil in peace for the next half-hour – but I'll have him over to the Administration Block so that he can talk to them when the call comes through – '

'Yes, do that,' the Superintendent concurred, 'and, Finch, you'd better arrange a car for him to catch the mail train from the Junction. Midnight, isn't it?'

Finch nodded and hurried out.

'Which police station did they call from?' Morgan was questioning Knowles.

'I... I...' Knowles looked up, his face utterly blank. 'I don't know. I don't think they said.'

'Where did he live?'

'Not in London,' someone remembered, 'his wife was staying with people. Relatives.'

'Was it Hampstead?' Miss Creed wondered, 'or Highgate?'

'Earl's Court,' Miss Hopkins suggested.

'Oh!' Morgan looked round despairingly, 'Doesn't anybody *know*?'

No one answered.

Outside, the night was dark and sullen. The wind had risen and Morgan, as he turned on to the Blimpton road, could hear, above the engine of his car, the shiver of the beeches. He drove slowly and, as always when some especially difficult or painful duty lay in front of him, he began to think about the past. He recalled, at first dimly and then with a swift but wavering clarity, that autumn day, now nearly forty years ago, when he had stood beside his mother and with, it seemed to him as he looked back, all the mothers and children in the village, at the pit-head, waiting for news of the men who were buried below. He could hear once more his mother's soft cry as the message came that his father had been brought out alive, and feel her arms about him as she picked him up and ran off to make sure, to find someone in authority to tell her that it was true. He remembered, too, the long wild sobs of his aunt, as she sat in the best chair beside the fire, calling the name of the husband she would never see again. It seemed to him, looking back, piecing together the fragments of his earliest childhood, that his aunt's wedding to William Rhys must have taken place that very same winter... He began to wonder what sort of woman Parsons' wife had been, whether the two had loved each other or whether, after the first shock, after the conventional, protective weeks of mourning, Parsons would feel only relief, remorse and the uncertain freedom of belonging to himself again...

At the Main Gate a policeman stepped out to identify him, waving his torch across the darkness.

'It's all right,' Morgan called, 'it's only me.'

'You're wanted, sir,' the man spoke hurriedly, 'over on South – '

'Trouble?'

'Sounded like it, sir. Said they'd had a bit of a blow.'

'Thanks, Turner. Call them back and tell them I'm on the way.'

Now he hurried, forgetting Parsons, seeing only a faint yellow glow on the horizon, a glow that deepened into red a mile before he reached the South Gate, and then died down.

Ambulances were parked outside the gate, empty, waiting. Striding down the clean-way Morgan passed stretcher bearers, their burdens covered in blankets.

'Where is it?' he asked them.

'Thirty-five.'

Then the clouds lifted, and he saw it: a building some way ahead, half-collapsed, a corner of it smouldering in spite of the hoses played on it from every side. Another unit of the fire brigade was spraying the shops on either side, soaking the roofs and walls, fighting against the rising wind, the occasional flying sparks.

The shop-manager said, 'Thank God you've come,' and then turned away to direct the rescue party who were burrowing into the far side of the shop.

A torch shone on a man stepping out of a broken doorway. It was Parsons, carrying a girl who lay still, unresisting, perhaps dead, perhaps unconscious. He placed her on a stretcher. 'Gently,' he said, 'I think she's coming round.' Then he looked up and saw Morgan.

'That's five out,' he said.

'How many more?'

'No one knows – I've got someone checking the clock-cards now.'

'Leave that to me,' Morgan began. 'Listen,' he started again, 'you'll have to hurry if you're going to catch the mail train – '

'The mail train?' Parsons asked, and then understanding pierced him. 'Is it…' his voice fell away, 'Is it?'

'Your wife. They don't seem to know about the children.' Morgan spoke roughly, seized by fear of pity. 'You'd better hurry.'

'I can't go now,' Parsons said, 'not until they've got them all out…'

TWENTY-EIGHT

THE FUNERAL TOOK place in Dustborough on the following Sunday.

Harry Foster, a member of the factory fire brigade, had been killed by a steel girder which fell from the roof as he groped his way into the ruined building, trying to find Doris and Pearl Kaplanski. Afterwards it was realised that both girls had undoubtedly been killed by the first explosion.

The procession which followed the three coffins from the Parish Church to the New Cemetery was led by the Chief Controller, who had come from London to inquire into the causes of the accident. The mourners, who came next, were followed by the Superintendent and other senior officials, and behind them came a great procession of men and women: workers from the dirty-side and from the danger areas, from the shell-shops and bomb-shops, from the fuze assembly sections, from the magazines, the stores, the painting shops; from the tool-rooms, the canteens, the inspection departments; from the Administration Block and from outlying offices. They walked silently, so oblivious of those beside them and of the onlookers watching from the street corners and from behind the lace curtains of the houses along the route, that each seemed to be alone. And yet, as they travelled along the familiar streets of the centre of the town and then into the prosperous strangeness of the suburbs, the old shuffling wearily in down-at-heel shoes, the young curbing their strides to the solemnity of the occasion, they were bound together for the first time, bound by their common life and by the impulse that had brought them to this meeting. Perhaps none of them could have said what that impulse was. It was not grief, for few of them had known the dead workers; and it was not fear, for those who worked in the danger areas knew the risks that their work entailed, and this accident, though by far the most serious, was only one of a number that had happened in the factory. But now, filing through the gates into the cemetery, their pity for those who had lost their lives and for the little group of mourners, Doris' parents, Pearl Kaplanski's sister and Harry Foster's widow, was fused with some deeper and more obscure feeling, into their awareness of each other and of the factory as something more than a collection of buildings, a place where they worked when there was work to do and were paid whether there was work or not...

On the following morning Mrs Foster left her three young children with a neighbour and caught the bus that took the morning-shift to Blimpton. When she arrived she found that she had nearly two hours to wait before the Labour Office opened. She walked up and down in the bright sunshine watching, expressionless, the night-shift workers streaming home, and then the office staff drifting in in twos and threes, talking eagerly, beginning a new week.

'What do you want?' Phoebe Braithwaite asked, when she was at last shown in.

Mrs Foster removed her new black gloves and laid them carefully on the table. 'I came for a job,' she said. She was a small anxious-looking woman who, though still quite young, was already beginning to forget that she had once been pretty.

'Where's your green card?' Phoebe asked, her tone impatient. Later in the morning she would, if the intake proved up to expectations, have to deal with the reception of nearly two hundred new workers. Now she was concerned only to get this woman out of the way so that she could get some odd jobs done before the rush started.

Mrs Foster, it appeared, had come without a green card.

'We can't take you without one,' Phoebe told her, 'you'd better go back to the Labour Exchange and get one. Then you can come back tomorrow.'

'But I want to start work today,' Mrs Foster spoke flatly, as if she were trying to explain something that the other could not be expected to understand.

'Quite impossible. No one is allowed to come here without a green card.'

'But I – '

'Sorry,' Phoebe stood up, dismissing her, 'that's the rule.'

Mrs Foster picked up her gloves and turned to go. But when she reached the door she stood suddenly still. 'You're sure it'll be all right tomorrow?' she asked.

'I should think so,' Phoebe was already settling down to examine the papers on her desk.

'You see,' Mrs Foster came back into the room, 'I didn't want to say anything about it, but there's reasons why I want to come out to Blimpton – '

'Oh, I expect it'll be all right,' Phoebe interrupted her, 'but you must get your card first. That's all.'

Outside, in the big waiting hall, Mrs Foster hesitated. She knew that there would be no bus going into Dustborough until the morning-shift came off at a quarter-to-three. It was now only a little after nine, and she was already tired. She sat down on one of the long benches, wishing that she knew where to go to get a cup of tea. There was no one she could ask. The place seemed to be empty.

Half an hour later, when Pamela Grant came through on her way to the factory, Mrs Foster was still sitting there.

'I say, Miss – ' Mrs Foster half got up, and then slumped down, and fainted.

When she recovered she found the girl leaning over her, a glass in her hand.

'Drink this,' Pamela commanded her.

Mrs Foster swallowed a mouthful, and then sat up.

'I'm not ill,' she said, looking around the bare room. 'I fainted, didn't I?'

'Yes, but lots of people do,' Pamela told her easily, 'I expect you're hungry.'

'Well, I could do with a cup of tea,' Mrs Foster admitted unwillingly, and allowed herself to be led into one of the small offices a few yards down the corridor. Pamela left her there and returned a few minutes later with a cup of tea.

'You won't have to wait much longer,' the girl said. 'The big party will be along in about half an hour. And I've asked someone to get you a sandwich before the other people come – '

'Oh, but – ' Mrs Foster sat up in alarm, 'she said I couldn't start today because I haven't got my cards. I've not been out to work since I was married, and I didn't think about having to go to the Labour before I came. My husband never said the girls had to get cards to come here,' she wiped a handkerchief across her eyes. 'He liked it here,' she added after a moment.

'Why did he leave?'

'He – he was killed. I don't know if you heard?'

'No,' Pamela said, 'I don't think I did.' She had taken the little woman into Parsons' office, as being the one place where they were not likely to be interrupted, but now she was sure that someone would come in… and then, as she heard the footsteps outside pause and go on again, understanding dawned. 'You're Mrs Foster,' she murmured, 'I didn't realise…'

'Oh, it's all right, Miss,' Mrs Foster put down her teacup, 'only it was a bit sudden like, and I thought if I could get started here right away – ' and then, for the first time since they had brought the news to her five days ago, she began to cry.

Then the door opened, and Parsons came in.

'Well?' he asked. He was very pale, and the lines about his eyes had deepened.

Pamela said: 'I thought you wouldn't be back today… This is Mrs Foster. You know.'

'Yes,' he assented, 'Mrs Foster and I know each other.' But he did not explain that after the accident, and before going to London to find out what had become of his children, he had insisted on going to see her, on making sure that everything that could be done was done quickly, with the minimum of fuss.

'And now I've come to work,' Mrs Foster told him, as she dried her eyes.

'Do you have to?' he asked, thinking of the compensation to which she was entitled.

'It's not that,' she said. 'Mr Roberts came round and spoke about the money. But it's not the money,' now she stood up, facing him across the desk. A wisp of hair had fallen over one ear, and she tucked it impatiently under her hat. 'Somebody's got to do the work,' she said, 'and now Harry's gone I thought to myself, I thought, well, it's your turn now. So I come along this morning, only it seems I can't start, not without my cards.'

'Oh, I think we can fix that,' Parsons picked up the telephone, and the old, eager look flitted across his face as he began to speak. It had taken him two days to trace his children to the hospital to which they had been taken. Now that he knew that they were safe and would live he was once more ready to get on with the job.

TWENTY-NINE

THE CHIEF CONTROLLER was not satisfied. He returned to London, leaving behind him a legacy of discomfort and suspicion, and a long list of questions that were to be answered as soon as those who had been injured in the accident were well enough to talk.

A week or so later the Superintendent and Gittins visited the hospital, and next day they called a meeting of the senior staff.

'Gentlemen,' the Superintendent looked round the table to make sure that everyone was present, and then whispered to Gittins: 'Where's Parsons?'

'I didn't ask him,' Gittins explained in a low voice, 'we've got Knowles – and, after all, he's the man in charge.'

'Ah!' Brown nodded assent and then returned to his audience. 'Gentlemen,' he repeated, 'I am sure you will all be relieved – very relieved – to know that we have at last got to the bottom of this unfortunate business. I am satisfied that the very... very unfortunate occurrence of South was an accident in every sense of the word... It is now your duty to satisfy the workers... There are, I understand, rumours...'

'There are,' Finch agreed dryly. He eyed the Superintendent with distaste, noting the increasing tension of waistcoat buttons, the deepening purple of the veins across the checks.

'Most of these rumours,' the Superintendent was returning Finch's stare, 'have proved to be totally without foundation. It is not true, as has been suggested in some quarters, that one of the operatives had a petrol lighter concealed about her person... Contraband, though of a less... er... more personal nature – toilet articles, I understand – had been taken into the shop. Fortunately, these things were confiscated before the accident happened... I shall, however, have to ask Captain Knowles and Miss Creed to arrange for a stricter – much stricter – supervision of the shifting-houses – '

'We do everything possible,' Miss Creed broke in, 'the difficulty is – '

'And,' the Superintendent continued heavily, 'there is another, and much more serious, criticism that must be made.' His eyes receded behind the massive frown until they were small and dull as the blunted ends of pins. 'It appears that one of the victims had been, to put it frankly, drinking – '

Miss Creed nodded energetically.

'Which brings me to my main observation. I have come to the conclusion that the system of bus wardens, which Mr Finch persuaded the employees' side on the Whitley Council to press for against our better judgment, has not... has not proved a success.'

Finch leaned forward and was about to speak when Morgan, sitting next to him, laid a hand on his arm.

'The amount of expenditure involved,' the Superintendent consulted a note that lay on the table in front of him, 'can clearly no longer be justified. The service – such as it is – will be disbanded as from next Sunday.'

Knowles leaned forward, the tip of his long nose quivering with the effort to restrain his indignation. 'If the Labour Office had been consulted in the first place – ' he began.

'You were consulted,' Finch, his voice rising, could no longer be held back, 'I've discussed the scheme with you twenty times in the last three months.'

'To the best of my recollection,' Knowles turned to him, pursing his lips in bitter, but remote disapproval, 'neither I, nor any of my staff – ' he turned to Miss Creed for confirmation, ' – were consulted about the choice of wardens, as you call them, to take charge of the buses.'

'I thought it was understood that the workers themselves were to choose the wardens,' Nicholls reminded him.

'They were,' Morgan said, 'and on the whole they've chosen well.' He had not been told, either by the Superintendent or Gittins, of the decision that had just been announced, and he was not sure whether to come to Finch's support now, in public, or to wait until he could discuss the question with the Superintendent alone.

'And the workers'll have to be consulted before the scheme is dropped,' Finch added quickly. 'Just because one of the chaps couldn't keep his bus-load from pub-crawling – '

' – and gave us the worst smash-up we've ever had in this factory,'

Knowles put in sharply.

'You know quite well that poor old Joe Dakers had nothing whatever to do with the smash-up, as you call it,' Finch said, growing more and more angry. 'You, of all people – '

'Now, gentlemen,' the Superintendent pleaded. The meeting seemed to be running away from him. He did not much care whether the bus wardens continued to operate or not, and the decision to disband them had, in fact, been made by Gittins, whose horror of the Select Committee on National Expenditure had mounted to gigantic proportions as a result of a visit paid by the Committee to the filling factory at Hopham where one of the Principal Clerk's oldest friends had recently become superintendent. According to Gittins, the Committee had condemned the whole organisation of the factory, with the result that most of the senior staff were likely to be dismissed at any moment, and replaced by men whom the war had not yet infected with an unwholesome passion for innovation... But now, looking around the table, the Superintendent began to feel that he had once more allowed the Principal Clerk to mislead him. The meeting was entirely out of control. Everyone seemed to be talking at once, and for an instant Brown felt that he could deal with six hundred and fifteen Members of Parliament far more easily than with half a dozen of his own staff.

'Now, gentlemen,' he said again, thinking that since the Select Committee had been to Hopham they would scarcely bother to come to Blimpton, and resolving once more to ignore any further advice that Gittins might give him, 'don't let us have any misunderstanding. This has been a trying time for all of us. We have all of us been worried – quite understandably worried – by the events of the last week or two. But now the matter has been cleared up satisfactorily – '

Finch said: 'I don't think it's been cleared up at all. Ask Knowles.'

Knowles cleared his throat noisily. 'Really,' he turned once more to the Superintendent, 'I don't think this is the time – '

But before he could finish Finch jumped up, tall, thin, flaring with indignation, 'Sir,' he spoke jerkily, addressing himself to the Superintendent, 'I think you should know that a lot of people in the factory are very unhappy about this accident, and they'll need something more than a bedside manner to get them to settle down again. You said there were rumours. There are. I travel on the buses with the workers, and I hear what they talk about. A lot of them have a pretty definite idea about the people who were responsible for the explosion. They may be wrong, but I think you should know what they say.' He sat down as abruptly as he had risen.

'And what do they say?' the Superintendent asked.

Now everyone was looking at Finch, waiting. He sat suddenly still, but his hands, resting on the table, trembled a little. The pause lengthened.

'Well?' the Superintendent demanded.

'They blame the Labour Office. To be exact, they put it down to Captain Knowles and Miss Creed.'

'How dare you?' Knowles demanded.

'Really!' Miss Creed began, and then stopped, closing her mouth into a hard line of disbelief.

'You asked me!' Finch retorted. He picked up his pipe and began to scrape the bowl with his penknife. He looked extraordinarily young and, in spite of his aggressive tone, defenceless. 'That's what people are saying.'

'It's nonsense,' Knowles sat back more easily, 'utter nonsense.'

Gittins looked at Morgan. The Assistant Superintendent met his glance and shook his head slightly. He had been very busy during the last ten days and, working late and rising early, had heard little of the current gossip.

The Superintendent glanced up at the clock. 'I've got another meeting in five minutes,' he said. This was not true, but it seemed to him to be the only way of bringing the proceedings to an end. 'Finch, I think you'd better tell Captain Knowles just what these fantastic stories are. And, Knowles, I'm sure I can leave you to deal with them in your own way.' He picked up his papers and waddled out of the room.

THIRTY

NORAH SAID: 'But I told Captain Knowles everything that happened. I didn't leave anything out.'

'I'm sure you didn't,' the shop-manager agreed.

'Then must I go?'

'I'm afraid you must. The Principal Clerk sent for you personally. That's an order.'

Norah smiled as she turned to go. She liked the shop-manager; and, besides, she was happy.

Outside the South Gate she lingered a little, feeling the warmth of the afternoon sun and the soft freshness of the air, full of the smell of wildflowers. The main road through the factory site had at this point been cut through a stretch of rising ground, and on either side of the cutting the long grass was bright emerald, flecked with patches of yellow, red, purple.

'Time they did something to that grass,' the gate-man observed. 'Ain't been cut since the winter. Another week of this weather, and it'll be all dried up.'

Norah nodded. A lorry was coming down the road, and she stepped out to hail it.

'Where to?' the driver asked.

'Admin Block.'

'Hop in.' He was a young man, sunburned and confident. 'I'm only going as far as East, but you won't have far to walk from there.'

'Thanks.'

The young man looked at her curiously. 'On the carpet?' he asked.

'Not that I know of.'

'But you never can tell, eh?'

'No, that's right, you can't.' But as she spoke her happiness seemed to be bubbling over. Her eyes shone, and she found it difficult not to laugh. Even now, at this moment, when she was going to describe again the evening when Doris and the other two people had lost their lives, she found it hard to adjust her feelings, to remember once more the sudden shock and then the long agony of suspense. And then, thinking of Doris she grew serious once more.

'Were you in South when they had that blow?' the young man asked.

'Yes.' Suddenly she wanted to tell him, to tell everyone, how, two days after the explosion, Tom Walton had marched into her lodgings and had insisted on taking her home to his mother for a few days' rest, and how, when she had protested that she didn't need a rest, he had taken a taxi all the way to Blimpton and come back with a note from Dr Gower himself telling her that she should not return to the factory for at least a week. 'There you are,' Tom had said, 'doctor's orders!' And then, while she was still protesting that she had no proper clothes, he had bundled her into a train, himself beside her. Now they were going to be married. 'As soon as I get my wings,' Tom had insisted, 'and it won't be long now – '

'Bad, wasn't it?'

Norah returned to the present as the truck lurched round a corner. 'Pretty bad,' she admitted.

'Like most things in this goddam factory. D'you know what I've got in the back of here now?' the young man jerked his thumb towards the load behind him. 'Rejects. Don't ask me how many, because I don't know. And I'm picking up another batch over on East. Then back for more. Would you believe it? They take all the trouble to make the empties and send the stuff here, and then when it's filled – when it's filled, mind you – all they can do is to burn it. Burn it! You'd think they'd have learned how to fill ammo before starting a war, wouldn't you? I mean to say – '

'Some of this new stuff is a bit tricky,' Norah replied, frowning.

'All the same, they could've found out what was wrong a bit earlier on, couldn't they?'

'Sounds like it. But I wouldn't be too certain,' she glanced out. 'Isn't this where I get down?'

Gittins picked up the telephone. 'Bring another cup of tea,' he commanded, 'and some sweet biscuits. Now,' he turned to Norah with a paternal smile, 'just tell me all about it in your own words. Everything that happened that night.'

Norah told him, exactly as she had told Miss Creed.

'And what do you think about it yourself?' he asked when she had finished.

'Well,' she hesitated, not sure of his meaning. 'If you mean do I think it need never had happened, well, I can't be sure because we don't know what did happen after I went out of the shop.'

'But you can guess?'

She nodded.

'And?' Gittins prompted her. His voice was kind, and though his eyes were shrewd his manner made it plain that Norah's statement would not be used against her.

'Well,' she explained uneasily, 'you know how it is. People get terribly browned off what with hanging about for stores and one thing and another. And then the machine broke down... of course I told them to wait for the fitter – '

'You think they didn't?'

She hesitated. 'That girl – Doris Chandler – she was in a terribly bad way that night –'

'She'd been drinking, hadn't she?'

'Not to notice. It wasn't that.'

'Then what was it?'

Slowly she began to tell him of how Doris had wanted to go into the hostel, and of her disappointment at being refused admission. She was halfway through her story when the door opened and Morgan came into the room.

'Do you want me?' Gittins asked.

'No hurry,' Morgan glanced at the girl, 'come in when you've finished.' And then, as he turned to go, he recognised her and his face lighted with pleasure.

'And what are you doing here?' he greeted her, 'telling Mr Gittins how to run the factory?' He turned to Gittins, 'Miss McCall is an old friend of mine, though it's four or five months since we met, isn't it?'

'Five,' Norah agreed, blushing a little at the recollection of that first day.

'And how's the rest of that little bunch doing? Still sticking it out?'

Norah said: 'One of them left. And Doris Chandler – '

'Was she one of them? I didn't realise – '

Gittins had been listening to this interchange with a mystified air. 'Miss McCall was just clearing up one or two points with me,' he said now, with an air of innocence that seemed slightly overdone.

'Indeed,' Morgan frowned. 'Do you mind if I stay?' He sat down, sprawling back in the big chair.

'You see,' Norah finished, 'there are two things, really. The one about the fitter – well, there was only one fitter on the Group that night. We need at least two over there on every shift... if the foreman had been able to send one right away I don't think the accident would have happened. Of course that's only my idea... And then that about Doris not being allowed to go in the hostel – '

'What was that?' Morgan interrupted sharply.

She told him, repeating everything.

'And why wasn't she allowed to go?'

'I don't know. I couldn't make it out. She spoke to me about it, and I asked Miss Braithwaite. She said Doris wasn't tidy. Well, she wasn't, but a lot of girls in the hostel aren't, either, and some of them aren't clean... Anyway, I spoke to Miss Creed, but she said it was for Miss Braithwaite to decide... As a matter of fact, I got a proper ticking off for interfering...'

She got up to go. Morgan followed her out into the corridor.

'You know, there's nothing to be gained by worrying,' he told her.

'But I'm not worrying,' she protested, and then added, 'not much.' But every time she went to bed the memory of that night came between her and her dreams, and often when she tried to think of Tom she would find herself remembering Doris and thinking that if only she had talked to Miss Creed in the right way, tactfully...

'Listen,' he spoke with a sort of rough kindness. 'We know why this happened. We can't change the past, but we're going to make very sure about the future. You know that you can rely on me?'

'Oh, yes,' she said, 'I know. We all know that.'

His smile kindled at the warmth in her voice. 'You do? That's fine. And now, tell me, how are the others – the girls who came with you to see me – how are they doing?'

She looked at him in astonishment.

'Yes,' he nodded, 'I asked you that a few minutes ago, didn't I?

But you only told me about one or two of them. What happened to that dark girl – ' he seemed to hesitate. 'What was her name?'

'Miss Green?'

'Ah! Miss Green. Do you ever see her?'

'Often.'

'You do? Then give her my greetings when you meet – and – and tell her that I expect to see her sometime.'

Abruptly he turned and went into Gittins' office, banging the door behind him. 'What did you ask that girl here for?' he demanded. 'She didn't tell you anything fresh. We know as much as we'll ever know about what happened that night. No one will ever be able to tell us whether Doris Chandler was trying to commit suicide – '

Gittins, who had been fingering a letter that lay before him on the desk, looked up sharply. 'Perhaps that's just as well,' he agreed with more than his usual dryness.

'Perhaps... But it's pretty clear by this time that she – that none of them – need have died. I don't like that business about the hostel – '

'I don't, either – '

'I suppose that that's what Finch was getting at the other day?'

Gittins shrugged his shoulders. 'I think so,' he said, 'but I haven't inquired. Finch should have come to me before flaring up in public like that. And if he wanted to have a row he should at least have said what he meant, instead of losing control of himself when the Superintendent decided to drop the bus wardens – '

'You decided that.'

Gittins shook his head. 'You're wrong there. I admit that always thought the whole thing a waste of money – but the old man made the decision himself – '

'Then I'll have to see that he changes his mind,' Morgan spoke with a sort of threatening humour. 'And you'll have to back me.'

Gittins waved the distasteful subject aside. 'Anyway,' he went on, 'I thought it best to let Finch have it out with Knowles – '

'While you made your own inquiries in the meantime?' Morgan broke in with friendly malice. 'Oh, yes,' he went on, 'I guessed that was what you were up to as soon as I saw that you'd got that girl in here,' he paused to light a cigarette. 'But she's got hold of the right end of the stick, you know. Old Mother Creed deserves to be buried alive for keeping girls out of the hostel when the Ministry's fussing its head off because we can't get the place filled. And then there's the question of the fitters.' Now he got up and crossed the room, pausing for an instant to look out of the window.

'Yes, Gittins was saying, 'about the fitters?'

'Sorry,' Morgan closed the window and came back towards the centre of the room. 'I thought I saw someone I know.' He jabbed out his cigarette. 'We've been crying out for fitters for at least six months. I don't know how the Chief Controller thinks we're going to win this war when the Ministry can't even find us a dozen maintenance fitters to keep this factory running. It's ridiculous. It's insane. It ought to be funny to think of all those hundreds of people in the Ministry of Weapon Production and thousands – or is it tens of thousands? – in the Ministry of Labour who can't scare up a dozen reasonably skilled men. Oh, yes, I know we've had some skilled labour since we opened up here. And some women. But how many? Never more than a quarter of what we've asked for – of what they tell us we ought to ask for. Oh, yes, I know – ' he turned as Gittins opened his mouth to speak ' – I know that we've nearly doubled our labour force since January. But what's the strength now? Still under ten thousand! And the Chief Controller promised last October that we'd have twenty thousand workers in the factory before the end of June. Twenty thousand! Is it surprising that we can't get the stuff out fast enough? *They* plan the programme. They tell us what they expect us to do. Oh – ' he flung his arms wide in a gesture of mingled rage and despair ' – they give us no tools and then they sit back and ask why we can't finish the job. These people sitting pretty in their mahogany offices who think they're winning the war by sending us a teleprint every other day to remind us of what a howling mess we're making of everything – oh, I'd like to see how they'd manage down here, filling ammunition when there's nothing to fill, and nothing to fill it with and nobody to fill it... And now they can't even get the Ministry of Labour to give us enough skilled fitters to keep the handles turning – '

Gittins, who had been watching the other's mounting rage, picked up the slip of paper that lay in front of him. 'You're wrong,' he said, 'look at that.'

Morgan took it from him and read: 'SEND IMMEDIATE EXPLANATION WHY ARRANGEMENTS MADE BY LABOUR DEPARTMENT FOR TRANSFER OF FITTERS TO BLIMPTON CANCELLED BY FACTORY LABOUR OFFICE ON APRIL 29. MINISTRY OF LABOUR REFUSES TO CONSIDER FURTHER DEMANDS UNTIL FULL INFORMATION GIVEN.'

Morgan read it a second time, put it down, picked it up and read it again.

'I don't believe it,' he said at last. Gittins was sitting back, rubbing the bald patch at the back of his head. His face was expressionless, telling nothing. 'Do you?' Morgan asked again.

Gittins nodded. 'It's true,' he said, 'I put a call through to the Chief Controller's office as soon as this came in. They're not quite certain they've got the date right – Crabtree didn't minute it at the time – but they're clear enough about all the other details. There's no doubt at all.'

'But Knowles must be crazy! No one who wasn't stark, staring mad would turn down an offer like that...' he paused for a moment. 'Has he seen this?'

'Knowles? No. I thought the Superintendent ought to see it first, and he was out when it came in.'

'Out?'

'Being entertained to lunch by old Gurney,' Gittins explained. 'Now they've got that contract – '

'They're relying on the old man to see that they get a follow-on?' Morgan asked. 'Well, we'll put a spoke in that wheel, Gitty. As long as I'm in this place I'm going to make very sure that no more contracts are given to Gurneys – or any other firm in Dustborough for that matter – until we're up to full strength here. If Dolphin can't keep the local people quiet, then we'll find someone who can. Now let's talk to Knowles.'

'Isn't that a matter that the Superintendent should deal with himself?' Gittins suggested. 'He'll be back within the next hour or so.'

But when the Superintendent returned, drowsy and belching a little, he thrust the teleprint aside and said: 'What rubbish! Knowles wouldn't do a thing like that! Sit down, Gittins, sit down, man.' He pushed a cigar into the other's hand. 'Very good host, old Gurney. And they've some remarkable brandy at the White Lion. Can't think where Little gets it...' he rambled on, pausing now and then in a puzzled way to look at Gittins' disapproving face. 'The trouble with you civil servants,' he finished up, 'is that you take this sort of thing much too seriously – '

'But this is from the Chief Controller!'

'Oh – ' Brown brushed the remark aside, 'I don't suppose the CC knows anything about it... This is one of the little fishes trying to stir up the mud – and that's about the size of it. Still, if you really think we ought to take some notice of it I'll have a word with Knowles now.' He picked up the telephone. 'Get me Captain Knowles... Knowles?... There's some damned idiot up at the Ministry saying that you refused to take some fitters he offered you. Any truth in it?... I thought not, but someone is starting a song and dance about it... well, find out what did happen and come over and tell me... as soon as you can... Right.' He put down the receiver and turned to Gittins. 'There you are,' he said, 'I knew there was nothing in it. But if you like we can have another chat when I've seen Knowles. Now where's that girl got to with my tea?'

Gittins, harassed but speechless, returned to his room. It was not until he was locking his desk and preparing to go home that the Superintendent sent for him again.

'I'm afraid there's something in this story after all,' the Superintendent began, 'it's most unfortunate. Most. Though I'm glad to say that Knowles has no responsibility – no knowledge even – '

'But it's his department!'

'Of course it's his department. But, as he says himself, he can't know everything that goes on. It seems that this wretched fellow Parsons – '

'Parsons?'

'Hmm. I'm afraid there's no doubt that it was Parsons who

turned this offer down. Most unfortunate. I rang London, and it seems that Crabtree – the labour man, you know – remembers that it was Parsons who spoke to him that day. Knowles tells me that he isn't at all happy about Parsons. As Knowles says, he's not quite – well, to be perfectly frank, he's not quite one of us.'

'He's a hard worker.'

'Yes, I grant you that. Of course, he was new to the job… I don't know whether in the circumstances I should ask the CC to overlook it… No, I suppose I can't do that. I think you'd better have a word with him… See what he has to say for himself… Rather awkward it happening just now, when he's having all this personal trouble. His wife died, didn't she?'

'She was killed. In that last big blitz.'

'Poor fellow! Was he fond of her, do you know?… Well, you'll tell me what you think when you've seen him?'

That evening, as Mrs Gittins was clearing the supper things her husband asked her: 'Who's coming on Sunday?'

Mrs Gittins put down the coffee pot. 'Dr Aaron,' she said, 'and Mr Parsons.'

'You've asked him?'

'Yes. I thought it was time he began to get about a bit again,' she gave her husband a slow, penetrating look, and then picked up the tray and bustled out of the room.

Gittins opened the morning paper, remembered that he had read it at lunchtime, put it on one side and began to shuffle the pile of books that lay on top of the bureau. He picked out a detective story and took it into the sitting room next door. But after reading a page or two he put it down and went into the kitchen where his wife was washing up.

He took a teacloth down from the line and began to dry the dishes. 'I ought to get you a maid,' he said.

'Oh, I don't need one,' she spoke absently, continuing to scour a saucepan. 'There's not much to do here and you need all the girls you can get over in the factory. What was it that you were going to say to me just now about Mr Parsons?'

'Parsons? Was I saying something about Parsons?'

She put the saucepan up on the rack above the sink.

'I suppose you still think I ought to have given him a house?' Gittins' voice, after the long pause, sounded oddly defensive. Usually he discussed all his problems with his wife, but this was the first time since the news of Mrs Parsons' death that either of them had referred to his refusal to give the labour officer a house on the factory site.

Instead of replying, she said: 'He's got no one to look after those two children of his when they come out of hospital. Do you think we should ask them here for a few weeks?'

'Wouldn't that look…' the dish began to slide out of Gittins' hand. 'Wouldn't people say…?'

'What does it matter what people say? They'll say it just the same whatever you do.'

'They ought to realise that I couldn't have allowed Parsons into one of those houses. Somebody's got to stick to the regulations. But if you'd like to have his children down here for a bit there's no harm in asking him – if you haven't asked him already.'

'As a matter of fact,' she said, 'I saw him about it this afternoon and he seems very pleased…'

THIRTY-ONE

KNOWLES DID NOT tell anyone of his conversation with the Superintendent, and when, several days later, Gittins questioned Parsons about his refusal to accept the fitters whose transfer to Blimpton had been arranged by the Ministry, the labour officer explained, without any hesitation at all, that he had been acting under instructions.

Gittins, who found this statement difficult to believe, but even more difficult to disbelieve, asked one or two formal questions, and then went to see the Superintendent.

'Well,' Brown asked when Gittins had finished his recital, 'what do *you* think?'

Gittins seemed unwilling to express an opinion. 'There seems to be a conflict of evidence,' he observed cautiously.

The Superintendent snorted his assent, and sat back, silent. His eyes were half-closed, but his eyebrows were writhing vigorously, and it could be seen that he was making an unusually concentrated effort. 'I always found with the natives,' he said at last, 'that when there was a conflict of evidence the best thing to do was to confront the parties.'

'But this isn't West Africa,' Gittins objected.

'I'm not speaking of West Africa,' Brown retorted coldly. 'We'd better ask them to come along.'

'Would you like me to stay?'

The Superintendent hesitated, torn between the desire to exercise his authority undisturbed and the fear that he might need the support of the Principal Clerk before the interview was over. 'Yes,' he decided, 'you'd better stay.'

The interview did not, however, resolve the conflict. Parsons repeated the story that he had told to Gittins, explaining that when he had informed Knowles that arrangements had been made to transfer men from another factory the latter had insisted that the men would not be suitable, and had instructed him to telephone to the Ministry to cancel the arrangement. Knowles, on the other hand, declared that on the day in question he had been at a meeting in Dustborough and that he had no recollection of having had any conversation with Parsons on the disputed subject. 'I've looked up my Office diary for that date,' he finished conclusively, 'and there's nothing there.'

Parsons stood very square and solid. 'I'm sorry, sir,' he insisted, his face reddening, 'but I remember distinctly.'

'Did you make a note of it at the time?' Knowles asked.

'No, I didn't.'

'There you are! You must have heard me tell the juniors again and again that none of us can afford to trust our memories in a place like this – we've all got far too much to do – '

The Superintendent was watching the end of his cigar, postponing the moment when the ash would fall. 'I don't like it,' he muttered, 'I don't like it at all.' And suddenly, because he could not think of what to say next, he dismissed them.

As the door closed behind them he flicked the ash into the wastepaper basket. 'One of those men is lying,' he remarked. 'I can't tell which. Can you?'

Gittins said: 'Knowles is frightened.'

'But what's he got to be frightened of? He's at the top of his profession – such as it is. He's got a safe job here as long as the war lasts; then I suppose he can go back to EELS if he wants to.' The Superintendent paused. 'And why should he have said those men weren't suitable?' he continued after a moment or so. 'He's not a technical man, is he?'

'No... Of course Parsons has been having a rough time lately.'

'You mean he's a bit...?' The Superintendent touched his forehead.

'Good heavens, no!' Gittins sounded shocked. 'But it's possible – just possible – that his memory's been playing him false.'

'Well – ' the Superintendent pushed back his chair and stood up, 'we've got to get this straightened out somehow. The CC rang up this morning – did I tell you?'

Before he left the office that evening Gittins went into the Assistant Superintendent's room. Morgan had just returned from a meeting in London. He was tired, and, as he listened to Gittins' gossip, inclined to be impatient.

'One of them will have to go,' he commented. He had flung off his coat and sat with his shirtsleeves rolled up above the elbow, glancing through three days' accumulated correspondence as he talked. 'Whatever happens, the factory is going to be too small to hold both Parsons and Knowles when this business has been cleared up.' He scribbled a line or two of instructions to his secretary. 'Matter of fact,' he went on, 'I'd like to see Parsons as Senior Labour Manager.'

Gittins opened his mouth, but so great was his astonishment that no sound came.

'If he were running that side,' Morgan ruminated, 'we might stand some chance of reducing our absenteeism.'

'It's gone up lately,' Gittins reminded him.

'It hasn't really, you know. It looks that way because people who leave without getting their release are included in the absentee figures – with the result that not even you know how many workers we really have got in this factory... well, now they've pushed our programme up again they'll have to find us some labour from somewhere.'

He began to describe the meetings that he had attended in London. First, he had been sent for by Gunn, whose scheme for a labour-recruiting campaign in Pinchester had been cancelled as a result of the implacable, but to him inexplicable, hostility of the bishop. Gunn, refusing to accept total defeat, had then decided to transfer his activities to Pinton-on-Sea, where the ban on summer visitors had emptied the town of almost its entire population. At Pinton Gunn had arranged to hold a parade of such Army stores as he could persuade the War Office to lend him for the occasion, and since these consisted almost entirely of uniforms, blankets and sample rations, along with three bren carriers and a few belts of small arms ammunition, he had decided to add drama to the proceedings by arranging a concert in the abandoned Pier Pavilion. The concert was to be organised by some of his theatrical friends, but the chief feature was to be a playlet, illustrative of life at Blimpton, written by Dolphin, produced by Miss Hopkins and acted by workers from the factory. Morgan had been obliged to listen to three different versions of the history of this scheme, the first from Gunn himself, the second from the civil servant whose duty it was to ensure that Gunn's activities were not allowed to interfere with the general conduct of the war, and the third from Miss Hopkins, who had spent the last fortnight in travelling backwards and forwards between London and Pinton with Gunn, and who was now in an extreme state of hopeful exaltation. It seemed improbable, Morgan told Gittins, that Blimpton would receive any additional labour as a result of all this activity, but the scheme had the advantage of keeping Gunn away from the factory, and the temporary absence of the small number of workers who were to take part in the concert could have no noticeable effect on production.

Next, Morgan had attended a series of discussions on technical problems which were common to Blimpton and several other factories. He had been called to a meeting at which the Chief Controller had described the changes that were to be made in the production programme during the next month or so. After that he had tried to find the Director of Hand Tools in order to discover why Blimpton's demands had been ignored for more than two months, but when he had at last succeeded in locating the building in which the Director had his office he arrived there only to find that the directorship had been abolished and that the man he had called to see was now supervising the production of refrigerating apparatus.

'Oh!' he looked up at Gittins, and though his face was sallow with fatigue his eyes were alert and watchful. 'Sometimes I'm almost glad that I'll never get a headquarters job,' and, as the other smiled, he added, 'you don't believe me, do you?'

Gittins rose, as if to go. 'A man like you can't bury his ambitions for ever,' he remarked, and though his tone was objective his voice was warmer and more friendly than usual. 'You know that I think you're wasted here.'

'You do? Do you really think that?'

The Principal Clerk moved towards the door. 'Oh, come off it, Dan,' he said, pausing with his hand on the knob, 'you know what I think of you without my having to butter you up about it three times a day – well, I must be off. Come round and have a drink later on?'

Morgan shook his head. 'Can't tonight. I said I'd look into the hostel and have a chat with Miss Marshall.'

'Oh!' Gittins, his interest once more aroused, stepped back towards the centre of the room. 'Would you like me to come along, too? Is there something special going on up there?'

'Nothing special,' the other grinned, making no effort to conceal his amusement; and then his face became serious again. 'Miss Marshall feels a bit stranded at times, and – well, I thought she'd like to know what's going on in London… that's all.'

But when, later in the evening, Morgan arrived at the hostel, Miss Marshall was not expecting him. She was out, visiting the sickbay.

'If she'd known you were coming,' her assistant simpered, awed by the presence of the powerful, almost legendary figure of the Assistant Superintendent, 'if she'd known you were coming she wouldn't have dreamed of going out – but if you don't mind waiting for just a wee while, I'll run over and fetch her.'

Morgan said that he would go himself and would hope to meet Miss Marshall on her way back.

He left his car parked in front of the main entrance, and turned down the drive. The field through which the drive had been cut had been ploughed and rolled, planted with grass and shrubs, and now, in the warm evening light, it shimmered with a sparse and vivid green. In two or three years, if the war lasted so long and if the ground were not ploughed up again to grow potatoes, there would be a lawn, a recognisable garden. But tonight the bright colours, spread so finely over the naked earth, deepened the sense of transience. The dormitory huts, splayed out fan-wise, were raw and cold with camouflage. In some, girls who worked on the morning-shift were already going to bed, and their laughter drifted out on to the evening air, thin with fatigue; in others, girls who would presently be catching the night-shift bus to the factory were changing their clothes, humming the tunes that they heard in the Dustborough cinemas, exchanging scraps of gossip or reading aloud the letters that they had received from their husbands and boyfriends. Outside the gate, on the other side of the hawthorn hedge, a boy and girl who had been walking along together, arm in arm, stopped suddenly, looking into each other's eyes, feeling – what was it: relief, despair or some wordless disappointment? – now that it was almost time to part.

Morgan turned and retraced his steps. The entrance to the sickbay was a few yards ahead, on his left. A nurse stood in the doorway, her hair curling up in fronds of gold around the luminous whiteness of her cap. She led him inside. Miss Marshall, her visit finished, emerged from the sister's office and greeted him with surprise and pleasure.

'You should have let me know you were coming,' she chided him, motherly and gentle. 'Or at least you should have let someone fetch me... or would you like to go round the ward?'

'Yes,' he said, 'I would.'

The ward, which contained perhaps sixteen beds, was almost full. The patients, not quite ready to settle down for the night, looked up, stirring expectantly. One of them said: 'It's Mr Morgan.' But all of them, with the exception of one who had arrived at the factory only a day or two earlier, knew him.

Miss Marshall and the sister stood in the doorway, talking in low tones, but watching, waiting until he should call them. He paused beside each bed, sometimes saying only a word or two, sometimes sitting down to talk for a few minutes, to ask a question or to answer some unspoken anxiety. Several of the patients were suffering from minor injuries inflicted in the factory, others from sicknesses contracted during their work or even perhaps before they came to work at Blimpton. At the far end, almost isolated, were those whose bodies and faces were inflamed with dermatitis. These, wrapped round in fear and shame and indignation, could not believe, in spite of the reassurances of the doctor who attended them every day, that they would recover with unblemished skins.

'It's wicked,' one of them said, looking up at Morgan through the mass of bandages that swathed her face. 'What'll my husband say when I tell him, and him out in the Middle East since before I came here?'

'But need you tell him?' Morgan sat down on the edge of the bed, slipping his cool hand over hers, showing no repulsion at the sores that scarred her wrist. 'You'll be better in a week or two – '

'But I'll lose my looks!' she broke in angrily, snatching her hand away.

'Who told you that?' Morgan demanded, the gentleness going from his voice.

'Oh!' the girl wriggled, turning her bandaged head, making a vague indication towards the other end of the room, 'that's what they all say!'

'But, my dear, that's nonsense. They don't know.' Something in his tone softened her and she relaxed a little, leaning against the pillows, feeling the coolness of his hand. 'You'll be all right as long as you don't scratch – there'll be nothing to show in a week or two. You know Dr Gower, don't you?'

She nodded. 'But he never comes round here.' That was true. Girls who fell sick were the responsibility of their panel doctor, and Gower, though he pointed out that the local practitioners often knew little or nothing of the treatment of industrial diseases, could not establish the right, even if he could have spared the time, to treat workers who were absent from the factory as the result of illness.

'He's had it,' Morgan went on. 'He gave it to himself. On purpose.'

'No!'

'He did, I tell you. You see, he wanted to find out how to prevent other people from getting it – '

'Oh, I know all about washing!' the girl interrupted contemptuously. 'I washed all right. Even when there weren't no towels to wipe on, I always went in the ablutions when I come off work.'

'Where were you working?'

She told him. And then he explained to her, as simply as he could, that the substance in which she worked was a new explosive, very powerful, but incalculable in its effect on the health of the workers who handled it. 'If this were peacetime,' he said, 'we probably wouldn't try to use it until we knew more about the way it behaves when it's lying around, loose... but we need it. It's terrific stuff. I'll tell you a story...'

When he had finished she asked: 'Can I tell my husband when I write?'

He shook his head. 'I shouldn't – but perhaps he knows it already…'

'Gosh!'

As he went out into the corridor the sister said: 'It's so kind of you to take such an interest in the girls, Mr Morgan!'

'Kind!' he turned on her with contempt. 'Kind! he repeated, and strode out. He had reached the point at which the path turned into the main drive before he remembered Miss Marshall and turned to see her panting along beside him. 'I lose my temper so easily!' he smiled, a little apologetic. 'But when people speak of being kind to those girls – as if one could ever do enough for them – ' He looked at her again, seeing the drawn, patient face, the flagging, tormented energy. 'You feel that, don't you?' he asked. 'In spite of everything?'

'Yes,' she agreed, 'I do. Though they can be rather trying at times…'

He listened, sympathising, encouraging, advising her how to straighten out her difficulties, how to deal with Knowles and Miss Creed how to get some additional furniture out of the Ministry of Weapon Production and some staff from the Ministry of Labour, how to plan the time-tables of visiting concert parties and lecturers, and how to discourage unwanted visitors…

'But things are going better?' he asked, absently stirring a third lump of sugar into his coffee.

'Oh, yes!' Miss Marshall agreed, 'everything is better. Even the food.'

'Ah! I spoke to Gunn about that. Did he do anything?'

Miss Marshall smiled, wistful, reluctantly amused. 'Not very much. Though I think he did his best – we do get oatmeal now – and we had a present the other day from Mr Gunn himself – six dozen cases of stuffed olives.'

Morgan's eyes widened. 'Could you say that again?'

'It is queer, isn't it?'

'And now,' Miss Marshall hurried along, leaving that peculiar incident behind her, 'we've really got the Residents' Committee functioning. The girls elect the members themselves – one from each block.' She accepted the proffered cigarette, leaning forward for him to light it. 'Though there's one thing I'm not happy about,' she added, 'it's a little thing, really…'

'Yes?'

'I don't know whether you remember the night when we had our first dance?'

'Of course.' All at once his manner had changed. He was retreating into himself, guarded, waiting.

'There was a girl you danced with once or twice – a rather striking girl. I thought perhaps you might remember her?'

'Yes,' he assented, 'I do. Miss Green.'

Carefully, Miss Marshall put her cigarette out, stubbing it into the ashtray until nothing was left but a few brownish shreds.

'She hasn't been making trouble?' Morgan asked.

'Oh, no!… At least not exactly trouble. She's an extraordinarily nice girl in many ways, and very well educated, too, I should imagine… in fact,' Miss Marshall smiled deprecatingly, 'if you'll forgive me for being so old-fashioned, I would describe her as being practically a lady…'

'Then what's the trouble?' He drummed on the arm of the chair with his fingers, crossed his knees, uncrossed them, looked at his watch, took out another cigarette and lit it.

'One can't exactly call it trouble, I suppose. But, well, the fact is she was elected on to the Residents' Committee and they wanted to make her chairman – and she refused.'

'Did she, indeed?'

'And it's such a pity, because she would have been quite ideal. She's very popular, and if only she'd take the trouble she'd be a real leader – a most excellent influence…'

'But she won't?'

'No. And there's another thing, too – '

'Well?'

'There was a girl who had TNT poisoning – I believe you took an interest in the case yourself – a girl called Rose Widgery. She came here last week from a convalescent home and Miss Creed asked me to take special care of her – but – but the next day Miss Green insisted that she should go into lodgings in Dustborough – said she knew some people where the girl would be well looked after… as a matter of fact I haven't mentioned it to Miss Creed yet – I'm afraid she'll make rather a difficulty about it when she finds out…' she hesitated. 'I wondered whether…'

'Yes?'

'I hardly like to ask you when it's such a small thing – but I remembered that I'd seen you dancing with her…' she broke off in confusion.

'You want me to talk to Miss Green?'

Her relief was so intense as to seem positively unreal. 'Would you? Could you?'

'Of course. Now, if you like.'

She glanced up at the gilt clock that stood among the bric-a-brac on the mantelpiece. 'She's on the night-shift this week – but I'll see if I can get her.' She hurried out of the room.

She came back a few minutes later, flustered and breathless. 'She's coming,' she announced, 'in a few minutes. It's so very good of you.'

'It's nothing,' Morgan got up, seeing his reflection in the half-curtained window: the suit he had changed into before dinner, the touch of vanity in the tie that he had chosen in London that morning, and above it the face, the face that he saw every morning in the shaving mirror and looked at so seldom: now he saw it, square and almost ugly, with the yellow eyes set rather far apart beneath eyebrows a little darker than the hair; the hair itself had receded a little, but, brushed back as it was now, it gave an additional, a needed, height to the rounded forehead. He turned abruptly, crossing the room to examine the print of Van Gogh's sunflowers that hung over the mantelpiece.

When the door opened he did not at first turn round.

'Come in, my dear,' he heard Miss Marshall say, 'we shan't keep you very long, but Mr Morgan wanted to have a little chat with you.'

'Ah!' he said, greeting her at last.

The girl had taken a step or two into the room, and now she waited, a small smile playing about her mouth.

'Miss Green!' he held out a hand.

'Mr Morgan!' She was dressed in a suit of some deep blue

material, well cut but shabby. A cotton blouse, also blue, but flecked with white spots, showed at the neck and wrist, hinting at some lost, indefinable elegance. Her eyes, reflecting the light from the window, were clear and pale beneath the smooth dark hair as she lifted her gaze towards him.

Miss Marshall asked her to sit down. 'We shan't keep you very long,' the older woman repeated; she looked at Morgan. 'Perhaps you'd like me to leave you for a few minutes?'

'No. Don't go.'

The clock ticked loudly, embarrassing the silence.

Miss Marshall was fidgeting with the lace bow that lay flat and smooth against her bosom. 'About little Miss Widgery – ' she said at last.

'Oh, yes.' Griselda looked from one to the other, serious, confident. 'Rose wouldn't be happy here in the hostel,' she explained. 'It's too big, too impersonal, too much like the factory. After all these months in the hospital she needs – ' she paused, searching for the word.

'Love?' Morgan asked. The word echoed against the narrow walls, tearing back into the room with extraordinary violence. Miss Marshall winced, as if something indecent had been said.

Griselda's eyes were lowered; in the fading light her lashes threw shadows like dark smudges over her cheeks. 'Love is a big word,' she said. 'Rose needs warmth, the sense of belonging to someone. And in a place this size... of course, people are kind enough. Miss Marshall is kindness itself – ' she looked up, speaking with a graciousness that was almost terrifying, ' – but Rose needs something more than anyone here can possibly give.'

'A world of her own,' Morgan added.

'Yes, and Ma – ' she turned to him again, ' – you know Ma Venning?'

'Indeed I do!'

'And Ma does all the small things so well, too. Rose needs good food, and quiet – '

'But who is Ma Venning?' Miss Marshall asked, trying very hard to keep up.

He told her. 'Rose'll be all right there,' he finished. He glanced at the clock and stood up. 'If Miss Creed makes any difficulty,' he told Miss Marshall, 'let me know and I'll talk to her myself. Well, young woman,' he addressed Griselda, 'if you're going to clock-on before tomorrow morning it looks as if I'll have to give you a lift as far as the Main Gate – '

'Oh, dear,' Miss Marshall fluttered, gratified and puzzled, 'I didn't realise that it was so late. I'm afraid the bus must have gone already… but if you don't really mind giving Miss Green a lift – '

'And if Miss Green doesn't mind taking one – ' Dan added with cold amusement.

'I? I'll be truly grateful.' Griselda followed Miss Marshall out on to the steps.

As the car turned out of the drive on to the Blimpton road he felt in his pocket, pulled out his cigarette case and handed it to her. 'Want to smoke?' he asked.

'No, thank you.'

'Then give me one.'

She took one, put it into his hand and returned the case. He did not speak again until they were nearly halfway to the factory, and then he turned to her with a swift and piercing look. 'Explain yourself,' he commanded.

'What is there to explain?'

He slowed down, turning to watch her. 'You know damn well what I mean.'

'About that evening at the dance?'

'We can start with that, if you like.'

'I had a run in my stocking – '

'I thought you ran off to polish your face, or whatever it is you do to it?'

'But when I got to my cubicle – '

'You found you had to change your stockings, and by the time you'd done that and got back to the hall you were surprised that I'd already gone… You expect me to believe that?'

'I don't expect you to. I don't know you well enough to expect anything.'

'No, you don't, do you? But that's the story you're telling?'

'You can put it that way if you like.' Her tone was indifferent.

'And then I made a date with you that night for the following Sunday – '

'That was the day of the funeral.'

'But you got a message from me?'

'Yes,' she acknowledged, 'I did.'

'Asking you to ring me – '

'And I did.'

'You did?'

'Twice. Your secretary said you were away.'

'But you left no message?'

'What should I have said?'

'I don't know. But,' he looked down at her with a grin that showed more anger than amusement, 'you could have saved me the trouble I've had chasing you around this evening.'

She raised her eyebrows. 'Chasing *me* around!' she repeated. 'Why should you do that?'

'Because I want to talk to you.' He drew up inside the Main Gate to allow the constable on duty to examine Griselda's pass. 'Now,' he said when they were once more alone, 'we'll go to my office.'

He parked the car outside the Administration Block and walked beside her up the steps. 'You know my room,' he said, 'go along and I'll join you.'

The room was in darkness, and as she felt along the wall and found the switch the telephone rang. She went to the desk and picked up the receiver.

A voice said: 'Is Morgan there?'

'He'll be back in a moment,' she replied. 'Will you wait?'

'Yep. Who's speaking?'

She smiled faintly to herself. 'This is Mr Morgan's secretary.'

'What's your name?'

'My – what?'

'Your name? What do they call you when they want you?'

Morgan came in and took the receiver from her. 'Okay,' he said after a moment or two. 'I'll do that... Oh, that was my secretary. No, you wouldn't know her.' He put down the receiver. 'Gunn,' he explained to Griselda. 'He said he thought he recognised your voice.'

'How funny!'

'Very, isn't it?' He sat down behind the desk and motioned her to the chair beside him. 'And there's another funny thing that I'm going to ask you to explain.' He drummed the desk with the tip of a silver pencil. 'The last time we met when I talked to you about Gunn you called him Sten. Why was that?' He looked up suddenly, catching her look of surprise.

But she shrugged her shoulders in swift unconcern. 'I don't know – a slip of the tongue, I suppose…'

'So I imagined. But who told you about the Sten?'

'What about it?'

'Anything at all?'

'Oh?' she smiled now. 'Is it on the Secret List?'

He nodded, and his face was grim.

'I'm sorry,' she said, 'if you still think I'm a spy.' She looked intensely, extravagantly amused, but the joke, if one had in fact been intended, produced no response. 'People talk, you know,' she continued. 'And some of us who fill ammunition like to know about the guns.'

'And who tells you?'

'All sorts of people.'

'In this case?'

She hesitated. 'Come on!' he insisted.

She said that she could not remember, but thought that it had been a member of the factory Home Guard. There were, she insisted, hundreds if not thousands of workers who already knew about the Sten, its mechanism, its performance, even the prices at which it was manufactured. 'But I'm sorry,' she finished, 'if you think I've been guilty of careless talk.'

'Oh!' he paused to light a cigarette and then, as an after-thought, thrust one at her. 'We'll see that you don't get so much to talk about in future. Now,' he pushed back his chair, 'what's all this that Miss Marshall was telling me?'

She flushed, as if startled by the abrupt change in the angle of the attack. 'You mean about the committee?'

'Yes. Why won't you do it?'

'Because I prefer not to,' she retorted coldly, rejecting the memory of their last talk, refusing to be drawn into discussion and explanation. She stood up and moved a pace or two away.

'Sit down!' he commanded.

To her surprise, she obeyed.

'Now listen to me!' he watched her, his round eyes flashing. 'I told you that I was going to talk to you. I don't know what you think you're doing at Blimpton. I don't even know whether you care very much. But you're intelligent and energetic and I thought until just now that you had some sense of responsibility... Have you ever thought of what it means to tear people's lives up by the roots to bring them here to do a job that in a civilised world nobody – nobody would ever be asked to do? Have you thought of that?'

She stirred uneasily. 'What else would I think about?'

'I don't know. I don't understand you. But I want to tell you what we're up against... You know, people come down here and make speeches in the canteens, telling us that we're saving civilisation. And I suppose we are. But what does a girl like you know about the kind of civilisation that we're trying to save? What do you know about the meaning of civilisation to the people in the back alleys? Perhaps you've learned something since you came here.'

'I've tried to. It takes time...'

'Time! You have to be born in those places to understand – I know. I come from the Rhondda... But Wales is another country. We still had books and music and fine words even when our bellies were empty and the woman next door was dying in childbirth because her husband was out of work and couldn't pay the doctor. But I know what it's like to go to school hungry with the rain coming in through a great hole in my shoe, to sit at the back of fifty other hungry, smelly brats who can't learn because the teacher doesn't know how to teach... But you! You'll never know what it's like to live six or seven people in three rooms and have the sanitary inspector come and tell you that you're not overcrowded because the baby isn't yet a year old. You don't know – you can't know – what it means to stand in a line morning after morning, with nothing inside you but a piece of bread and a little thin tea, hoping that you'll get a job and being certain – certain, I tell you – that you never will unless a war comes along and gives you a chance... But all the same – ' he stood up and moved away from the desk towards the centre of the room ' – this life that people in clubs and board-rooms and public meetings call civilisation – this existence that we're saving and destroying at the same time – it's a beginning, it's a place to start from. We have a hell of a way to go, but at least we know it. And even here, at Blimpton, we're getting to understand – some of us – what it is that we're after. We're beginning to do the job. We've nothing to boast about yet. I know that. We slip up. We make mistakes. We fall down on the programme, we fill stuff that explodes too soon, and sometimes – did you know? – we fill stuff that won't explode at all. But we're learning, every day, all the time – those of us who can learn, and that isn't everybody... and we're building a new life, bringing people together, showing them new possibilities – little things, like the bathrooms up at the hostel, and big things – a factory run not for profit but because it's needed, owned not by big business but by the people – everybody – '

He had been striding up and down the room, but now he stopped, standing a yard or so away from her, staring into her intent pale face. Her lips were parted, her eyes very bright as she waited for him to go on.

'And you!' he stood leaning forward, his hands thrust into the pockets of his trousers, his head rising massively from the strong shoulders. 'You come here and tell me that you prefer not to take any responsibility, that you don't want to help us – '

'But I do!' she jumped up, facing him. 'That's why I went to live in the hostel. That,' she flared, matching his anger with her own, 'that's why I came to Blimpton – because I thought I could be useful. But I must judge for myself what I'm to do – '

'Must you?'

'Yes!' she stamped a foot, and the childish over-emphasis of the gesture caused him to look at her again. She seemed, with her head thrown back and her dark hair flying loose, suddenly vulnerable, no longer angry, but more serious than he had ever seen her. 'It's true,' she said, 'that I don't know what it's like to live in poverty – though I've learned a lot in the past few months. But – I'm nearer to the girls in this factory than you or Miss Marshall. I came here to be one of them – and I think I'm succeeding. I'm not going to lead them. I've no right – '

'But a duty?'

'No,' she shook her head, frowning. 'It's difficult to explain – '

'Try.' He sat down now, just beside her.

'I'm not very good at talking about abstract ideas,' she took the cigarette that he offered, 'but it seems to me that leadership in – in a place like this must come – though I know this isn't always possible – from the people themselves. I said that I've been accepted – and I think it's true. But you've told me yourself that I'm not a working girl, and as far as my background, my origin, is concerned, I suppose you're right... If I became chairman of Miss Marshall's committee people would soon begin to feel that I was somehow different... and that's no good... the girl who took the job on will do it better than I – though that isn't the point either... People see that she's typical. What she can do anyone else can try to do...'

'Ah!' he blew out a puff of smoke, watching her through narrowed eyes. 'So that's your theory of leadership in a democratic society?'

She smiled at last. 'I wouldn't have used those words. But I suppose that's what I mean. Yes.'

'Perhaps you're right,' he assented thoughtfully.

'I think so.'

He seemed to find that funny. 'You know,' once more he got up, 'you really are the most unexpected person...'

'Why do you say that?'

He pulled himself to his full height, looking down at her. 'Because you are. You're beautiful and amusing and gay – '

'Thanks!'

'Well, so you are. And you have ideas. Not very good ones, perhaps – '

'Thanks, again!'

'But at least they're your own.'

'I'm glad you think so.' Suddenly, for no reason, she laughed, and he with her. 'And now,' she asked, 'don't you think I ought to start my night's work?'

'Soon. But before I drive you over shall we give the factory a treat?'

'She followed him across the room, watching as he unwrapped gramophone records. 'I bought these in London this morning,' he explained. 'We can get Tim Horton to put them on the factory broadcast.' He glanced up at the clock. 'It's just about time for Music While You Work. What shall we give them?'

She turned over the discs, looking at the titles. 'Who's going to enjoy these?' she asked.

'Everyone. You'll see. What shall it be – *Eine Kleine Nacht Musik*?'

'That would be wonderful.'

Tim Horton came and collected the records. Dan turned a switch beside his desk, and they sat, watching one another covertly, waiting.

Softly, poured through a thousand loudspeakers, the music filled the factory. Men and women paused at their work, looked up, seeking one another, astonished, bewildered, yielding slowly to enchantment. Then, as the sounds grew and swelled around them, something strange began to happen. In the shops where the heavy bombs were filled the men, poised uncertainly between life and death, moved to a new rhythm. Girls filling shells were silent, feeling the approach of something that was outside their experience, yet recognisable, as if it were for this that they had been waiting. The inspectors in their red caps were silent, too, their glances suddenly turned inwards. A foreman, issuing instructions, broke off in the middle of a sentence and shook his head, bewildered, trying to reject this unimaginable onslaught. At the far end of the factory, where men and women sagged over the benches, wiping down the empty shells, giving them a preliminary cleaning, the flagging conversations died as the music rose over the room, and people looked at one another with astonishment, finding friends and lovers, knowing, for the first time, the sense of belonging to one another. Henry Tyndale, making entries into a card-index, jumped up and turned off the loudspeaker, only to hear faint echoes coming from the shops on either side of the foreman's office. And Phoebe Braithwaite, who had been inspecting one of the shifting-houses, rushed into a lavatory and burst into tears. Rose Widgery, her eyes starry, whispered, 'It's the most beautiful thing I ever heard,' and remembered a summer evening a year ago, in Devonshire.

The last sound died away. After perhaps a minute Dan rose and turned off the switch. Griselda stood, watching him.

'Well?' he asked.

'Lovely.'

He took a step towards her, and then drew back. His face, usually so expressive, was mask-like, the yellow eyes unreadable. She watched him expectantly, and as she met his gaze her lips parted, but did not smile.

'Now,' he spoke almost roughly, 'I think it's time that you began to earn your living. And I want to get some sleep. Come along!'

They drove in silence, but when he stopped at the entrance to the South Group he put a hand on her shoulder and, drawing her towards him, kissed her lightly on both cheeks. Then he leaned across her to open the door. 'Hurry!' he said, 'before I change my mind... Good night.'

THIRTY-TWO

ON THAT FINE Sunday morning when the German armies invaded the Soviet Union Finch rose early, waking the other inhabitants of Mowbray Lodge as he turned the knobs of the radio set in the drawing room, releasing violent chords of martial music, announcements and odd scraps of comment in strange languages. By the time Gower came down to breakfast Finch's excitement was so great that he could scarcely express himself in words, but later, as one by one the others drifted in, he began to be aware of the sense of authority conferred on him by his unique knowledge.

'You're sure?' someone asked. 'Sure you can't be mistaken?'

'Of course I'm not mistaken!' Finch retorted sharply. 'Just because you don't know whether to be glad or sorry that we've got another country to fight the war for us – !'

'Oh! Come!' they protested, horrified, crumbling their toast, counting out the pats of Sunday butter, busying themselves with the marmalade.

Dolphin, sharing a table with Ruth Aaron, remarked: 'That was a silly thing to say. Finch is going to get himself into trouble one of these days.'

'Oh, but I'm sure he didn't mean it,' Ruth answered with one of those rushes of indignation that Dolphin always seemed to tap in her.

'I didn't know that he was such a friend of yours.'

'He isn't particularly,' she swallowed a last gulp of coffee and jumped up.

Morgan glanced up as she passed his table. 'And what do you think?' he asked.

She paused, her gaze wandering out to the shining morning. 'It's good news, isn't it?'

'It is. It's great. Sit down a moment.'

But as she took the empty chair Gower folded his newspaper and crossed the room. 'Coming, Ruth?' he asked.

'Off for a picnic?' Morgan, looking from one to the other, spoke with a shade of irony in his voice.

'Work,' Gower explained.

Miss Creed turned to greet Ruth. 'You aren't letting that dreadful man drag you off to work on this lovely morning?' she asked.

'Surely you do enough on the other six days of the week?'

'Oh, she works,' Gower defended her impatiently.

'Six days of routine,' Morgan folded his napkin, 'and one of research. Isn't that right?'

Miss Creed sniffed and went on. 'No one can do good work for more than six days a week,' she remarked to Parsons as she met him in the hall. 'You find that, don't you?'

'Well...' he began; but before he could finish she had turned to go up the stairs. Parsons, who had for some time been aware that Miss Creed's indifference was turning to enmity, went out into the garden.

'And what's the research?' Morgan, in the dining room, was asking. 'Still dermatitis?'

Gower nodded.

'Making progress?'

'Not as fast as we should.'

Reluctantly, Ruth got up, moving self-consciously in the new dress that her mother had bought for her in Manchester.

'Yes, it's a lovely colour,' Morgan remarked, 'isn't it, Gower?'

Gower blinked behind his shell-rimmed spectacles. 'I hadn't noticed,' he said vaguely.

'That's the danger of being a gentleman,' the other man got up. 'I'll look in and see you later in the morning, if I may.'

'I wish you would.' Gower, staring blankly at the pattern of flower petals scattered over her dress, followed his assistant out of the room.

In the garden Finch was haranguing Parsons. 'You're a damn fool,' he said, 'as I've told you before. If you don't say something yourself I shall go to Morgan – '

'But what am I to say?' Parsons bent to pull out a dandelion. 'I've told them everything. I'm sick of the whole business.'

' – so you allow yourself to be disgraced – and even though no one has said anything about it for the last ten days you know perfectly well that you are in disgrace – just because you're too proud – '

'It isn't pride!'

'Well, if you like, too loyal – too bloody loyal to say that Knowles was as pleased as punch to get the promise of those fitters until he heard that they came from his old factory – that they were EELS men who'd be certain to blow the gaff on the old humbug before they'd been here a fortnight.'

'But – '

'I warned you, didn't I? As soon as you said they came from EELS – '

Morgan, emerging from the shrubbery, asked: 'Doesn't anyone here ever talk about anything but Empire Exploiters?'

Finch drew himself up sharply. 'I wish you'd listen to this,' he said.

'Well?'

'I don't think – ' Parsons began hesitantly.

'All right!' Finch broke in, 'I'll talk.'

Morgan listened, his face closed, expressionless. 'Why didn't you tell us this in the first place?' he asked Parsons as soon as Finch had concluded his story.

'I didn't think… I mean, of course Finch put the idea into my head… but I couldn't really believe – '

Finch turned on him. 'You're too damn decent for a place like this – '

Morgan put a hand on his shoulder. 'Finch,' he said, 'you'd better forget it – '

'But Parsons – '

'Leave it to me,' Morgan commanded, 'I think you've done enough talking for one day – though I wish I'd known this sooner.' He hurried off to the factory and sent a telegram. Then he walked across to the surgery. Ruth was sitting at a desk in the outer room, making entries into a card-index.

'Where's Gower?'

She pointed to a door, barely looking up as she did so. 'In there.'

But, instead of going in, he sat down on the vacant chair beside her.

'Still nursing your sorrows?' he asked. It was a long time since they had talked.

She finished writing on a card, replaced it in the drawer, and took out another.

'Or is that an inappropriate question?' his tone was light, teasing, but with an undercurrent of interest, of something that was not quite tenderness. It was this strange, impersonal warmth that she found so confusing, so nearly unmanageable.

'As the Assistant Superintendent of the factory,' she replied distantly, 'I suppose you can ask anything.'

'Now I've offended you.'

She put down her pen and pushed the card away from her.

'Perhaps I should have been more tactful,' he seemed surprised, distressed almost. 'I always say the wrong thing to you.'

'Perhaps I'm that sort of person.'

'The sort of person to whom everyone says the wrong thing?' He jumped up, and now, looking at him, she saw that the moment had ended. 'Oh, no,' he was so cool and business-like that she saw that for him she was no longer there. 'You shouldn't say things like that. It's… it's too depressing.'

Gower came in, white-coated, professional. 'I'm glad you could come,' he drew a sheaf of notes from an inner pocket. 'About these experiments we're trying to do…'

He explained, quickly, impatiently. Ruth, watching, broke in to elaborate a point here and there. Gower brought out a series of charts showing the groups and individual shops where the incidence of dermatitis had fallen, where it fluctuated, where there had been sudden outbreaks. 'Here,' he pointed to a big pile of papers, 'we could get it down to almost nothing if we had more co-operation from your people on the production side. On this job – ' he named it ' – we're making no headway at all. I've told the shop-manager down there repeatedly that for the girls – and the men – on that section it isn't enough to wash at the beginning and end of the shift. They need a ten minutes' break every two hours – '

'But,' Morgan objected, 'he can't give them the time. It's impossible. That section is one of our worst bottle-necks – '

It was not the first time that they had fought this battle, but they flung themselves into it blindly, pitting the health of the workers against the clamorous demands for more, and still more production. 'In the long run,' Gower argued, 'the interests of the workers and the interests of production are the same – '

'Ah!' Morgan broke in, 'But don't you see that we can't afford to consider the long run when we're being harried night and day, all the time? Nobody hates this necessity more than I do – '

'But that's just the point! It isn't a necessity – '

'Then prove it! Take an example! Show me what we can do – '

Gower started again, listing the things that needed to be done: the allocation of workers to their jobs in accordance with the recommendation of the medical officer who examined them on their arrival at the factory; the reorganisation of certain processes; the installation of dust-extraction plant in some of the shops; the regular laundering of uniforms; two clean towels each day for every worker who was in contact with explosives instead of two, and often only one, each week; a fixed allowance of time for washing; proper supervision in the ablution rooms...

'I thought Knowles had arranged that on some of the Groups?' Morgan asked. It was seldom that he had time to examine these problems in detail.

'Parsons started a scheme, but when it had been going a week or two the girl who was running it – what was her name?'

'Grant,' Ruth offered.

'Yes. She got caught up in one of Gunn's circuses, and Miss Hopkins has carried her off to Pinton to act in a play.'

'Can't you get somebody else?'

'We might,' Gower glanced at Ruth. 'When is this Grant girl coming back?'

'I don't know. She wasn't awfully good.' Ruth turned to Morgan. 'We need someone with ideas – someone who can make these rather tiresome precautions seem important. It isn't just a matter of discipline. It needs imagination, leadership...'

'Can't Miss Creed find you someone else?'

'She might,' Gower agreed, 'but – but it needs someone rather special, as Ruth says. The girls don't like the Labour Office crowd, you know.'

Morgan lit another cigarette. 'Perhaps I could find you someone,' he suggested. A smile crossed his face, and the lines of ironic amusement around his mouth deepened. 'I'll see what I can do…'

He went back to Mowbray Lodge, took his car out of the garage and drove along the Addle Hinton road. When he came within sight of the entrance of the hostel he drew up, got out of the car, looked at his watch, got into the car again, and sat back, waiting. It was still only a little after twelve and he had not asked Griselda to be there until half-past. He smoked one cigarette, then another. He found a back number of a technical journal tucked into one of the pockets, pulled it out and made a fair show of reading it. But every minute or so he looked up, staring out at the bright countryside. Three or four girls came out of the hostel gate, turned along the road and passed him, singing. An Army truck drove past, swerving to avoid a dog. He threw a cigarette end out of the window and watched the swirl of smoke rising from the centre of the road. Then, at last, looking into the driving mirror, he saw her reflection, small and sharp and unimaginably bright.

He got out and took a step or two towards her. She was striding down the road, her head held high, walking as no one else did, as if she owned the world and was enjoying the sense of possession. But as she came nearer he saw that her face was sober, the bright eyes clouded, the mouth tense. His own air of eagerness diminished a little as he put out a hand to greet her. 'Nice to see you,' he said, and opened the door for her to get in.

She looked at him, smiling a little, but with an emotion that he could not fathom. 'I can't come,' she said flatly.

'Then why are you here?' he sounded irritated, but then, looking into her eyes, he asked, 'Is there something wrong?'

She nodded. 'Norah. You remember Norah McCall?' Norah, who had been going to marry Tom Walton as soon as he got his wings, in perhaps two months' time, had received a telegram from him the night before to tell her that he was being given embarkation leave and was coming to fetch her, to take her home to his parents so that they could be married at once, by special licence. And then this morning, less than an hour ago, Norah had telephoned to Griselda from Dustborough to say that the other Tom, her brother, had been killed in the Middle East and that she must go home at once, by the noon train, to do what she could for her mother. 'And so,' Griselda finished, 'I said I would meet Tom at Dustborough and explain…'

'I see…' All this time they had been standing beside the car, close together, but avoiding each other's glances. 'At least I can drive you as far as Dustborough,' Dan suggested now. His face was blank, but the singing Welsh tone in his voice, usually unnoticeable, was rising and falling in such a way that anyone who knew him well would have guessed that he was under the strain of some intense emotion.

'Thanks.'

'You're very fond of your friend Norah, aren't you?' he asked presently.

'Yes. I suppose I am.' She was staring out of the window as she spoke. 'I've made a lot of friends since I came here…'

'So you should. And Norah – she's feeling pretty bad?'

'I should think so – yes.'

'Does she love this young man?'

'Of course,' she turned round to look at him. 'I think so,' she corrected herself. 'But how can one tell?'

'How, indeed?'

The pause lengthened. The road was empty, but Morgan, looking straight ahead, seemed to be giving all his attention to the car. The sunshine of the past few weeks had bleached his hair and what in winter looked like sallowness had become sunburn. He would never be handsome or even, in appearance, distinguished, but the rounded, blunt features had, besides strength, an unexpected sensitiveness more noticeable when, as now, he seemed to be absorbed in some private thoughts. Watching him, the girl gave an involuntary shiver.

'Not cold?' he asked.

'No…'

'What, then?'

'I suppose it's – it's because I'm not looking forward to what I

313

have to do…'

'Talking to this young man?'

'Yes… I've only met him once.'

'Would you like me to come with you? Would that make it easier? No,' he answered himself, 'I suppose it wouldn't… But we'll meet next Sunday, shall we?'

'If you'd like to?'

'Would you like to?'

She smiled. 'Of course.'

'Good.' They had reached the railway station, and for a moment or two they sat still, not looking at one another, the bright day shadowed by the great gothic facade, and by the sense of tragedy rushing past them, inescapable.

'Goodbye,' she said, not quite ready to go.

'Goodbye, Griselda.' It was the first time that he had used her name. 'I like you for doing this… may I say that?'

'It's nothing. I couldn't have refused, could I?'

'No, but I like you for doing it, all the same.'

He watched her as she went, until at last she was out of sight, lost beneath the grim and smoky arches.

THIRTY-THREE

THE VENNING HOUSEHOLD was hushed by the expectation of Norah's grief. Ma, deciding that Norah needed an environment more friendly than that provided by the lodgings in which she had been living since she first came to Blimpton, made plans for Rose to share Kitty's room so that Norah could move in. Kitty, writing to young Jim Venning, stopped when she had written his name and looked up at the family photograph on the mantelpiece, her eyes bright and hard at the memory of her own husband whom she had, during the last six months, been slowly learning to forget. Rose, who now worked in the tailor's shop, sewing cartridge bags, walked about the house on tiptoe, as if death were lurking behind a door, and was suddenly afraid for her new security. And old Jim, feeling the tide of war pass over him, conscious that he was destined to end his life among the cisterns and toilet rolls, the porcelain and white tiles of the gentlemen's lavatory at the back of the council chamber in the Town Hall, stifled his cough behind a handkerchief and hoped that Ma would not notice how much worse it had become during the last few weeks.

And then on Tuesday, as if to show that the war in the west was not yet finished, two German bombers flew over Blimpton during the early afternoon, dropping their load at scattered points around the factory. Perhaps because of the camouflage, or perhaps because of the scattered confusion of the site, the damage was much less than had first seemed probable to the watchers perched on the roofs. One bomb fell on a railway siding, tearing up the rails and narrowly missing a truck that had been loaded with incendiaries and was about to be moved to its destination. Another hit the gatehouse at the entrance to the West Group, wounding the gate-man and two of his cronies who were chatting with him at the entrance; others fell among the shops on North-East, and in one of these eighteen of the forty workers present were killed outright, and the remainder injured, most of them seriously.

There was no panic. In less than half an hour after the last bomb had fallen the afternoon-shift were back at work, and if people were shaken by their brief experience they did not, for the most part, show it. But Ma Venning, in charge of the shop next to that in which the greatest amount of damage had been done, was instructed to send her workers home, while she herself was called to help with those who were least seriously wounded. Among them was Mrs Foster, whose husband had been killed a few weeks earlier in trying to rescue Doris Chandler and her companions. Mrs Foster was not badly hurt, but several splinters of steel had lodged in her right arm and, when Dr Gower had removed these, he handed her over to Ma with the mild but impossible injunction: 'Take care of her and see that she doesn't do too much.'

Ma took her home in one of the half-dozen battered cars that Finch had been able to muster to meet this emergency, but as soon as she got inside her own house, and before even the neighbours could gather to find out what was happening, Mrs Foster fainted. Ma revived her, put her to bed, made tea in the disorderly, over-furnished kitchen, and then went to talk to the woman next door, who, Mrs Foster explained, was supposed to be looking after the children. But the neighbour, it seemed, had chosen this evening to go to the cinema and Mrs Foster's children, all of whom in Ma's opinion should already have been in bed, were playing in the yard, trying to build a house with oddments collected from the refuse-bin.

Ma didn't like the look of it at all. She collected the children, washed them and put them to bed. Then she went into the best bedroom to look at Mrs Foster, who was sleeping heavily, her face unnaturally flushed, and with faint lines of tear-stains running down her cheeks. Ma sat down on the only chair, wondering what to do next. Her first impulse was to collect the whole family together and take them home with her, but she realised, without even having to think, that this was impossible. On the other hand, it seemed equally plain that the little household could not be left. Finally, she went out into the street and gave a child a penny to go and fetch Kitty, who had been working on the morning-shift and would not yet have gone to bed. She and Kitty, Ma decided, would have to manage things between them until Mrs Foster was fit to go back to work again.

Meanwhile, Norah had come back from London. Griselda met

her at the railway station, picked up her baggage and explained, first of all, that Ma had suggested that Norah should go there to stay for a few weeks.

'And why should I want to do that?' Norah asked, standing still and watching the train as it went out. She was very pale in her new black coat, and her eyes were dark, ringed with sleeplessness.

'Ma thought you would like to go. Of course you must please yourself.'

'Would you go? Norah demanded. She was nervous, on edge, her voice tinged with bitterness.

'I don't know. I don't think so,' Griselda answered slowly. 'Ma's a darling, but sometimes – sometimes it's better to be alone.'

'Yes. Did you meet Tom?'

'Of course – '

'Tell me – '

They looked around for a place to talk, and finally went into the refreshment room. Four or five soldiers were clustered together at one end, chatting idly with the barmaid. Otherwise the huge room was empty. The vaulted ceiling arched down upon them, casting vague shadows over the bare tables. Griselda led Norah to a corner, watched while she sat down, and then went to the bar to order drinks.

When she returned Norah was hunched over the table, her chin resting on her hands.

'Was Tom very upset?' she asked.

'He was, rather. He wanted to catch the next train to London – '

'But don't you see,' Norah gulped down the gin-and-lime, 'Mum couldn't have stood it, specially with him having the same name… my brother Tom was her favourite, I told you…'

'Yes. Your Tom realised that, too.'

'He wrote, did I tell you? I had a letter this morning.'

'Yes?' Griselda spoke with a curiously remote sympathy, ready to listen, but asking nothing.

'He's coming over tomorrow. He says we must get married this week, just the same. But I *can't* – didn't you tell him that?'

'I told him. But – '

'He didn't understand?'

'Well,' Griselda looked down into the clear liquid at the bottom of her glass, 'it isn't very easy to understand, is it?'

'It would be if you knew Mum!' Norah pulled herself erect and a faint flush began to appear in her cheeks. 'She's so terribly upset about my brother. It would seem awful if I got married now, so soon after – '

'But when Tom is going abroad?'

'Yes. Only Mum doesn't see it like that – and, after all, he might not go for ages. They don't always, do they, even when they've had embarkation leave?' She put down her glass. 'But still,' she said hopelessly, 'I expect he will.'

'Couldn't you be married quietly?'

'Oh, you don't realise! For years Mum's set her mind on having a slap-up wedding for me. Even before I had any boyfriends – real boyfriends – when I was just a kid at Princess Road schools, when my eldest brother got married Mum used to say "Ah, but when Norah gets married we'll have a real wedding in the house!"… She used to make me a bit cross at times, I can tell you!' A reminiscent smile flitted, ghost-like, across her face. 'If it hadn't been for my brother being killed we'd have done it all the same,' she finished limply. 'Now, it would be too heartless. It would just break Mum up…'

Griselda picked up the glasses and went to the bar.

'It's wrong,' she said when she came back.

'Wrong?'

'For the young to sacrifice themselves to the old. You want to marry Tom, don't you?'

'Of course I want to!' some of the old eagerness returned to her face. 'Oh!' she frowned, trying to find words that would make the other girl understand her difficulty. No one, she knew, had ever had such a wonderful family, so united, so strong in each other. 'I can't go against Mum,' she said at last. 'I can't.'

'But Tom?'

'Ah, Tom!'

'Couldn't you be married now, and tell them afterwards?'

Norah thought that over and shook her head. 'You shouldn't

have got me another drink,' she took a small sip, 'I'll be tight.'

'No, you won't... well, if you really can't be married, why don't you go away with him for a week, or for however much time he has left?'

'Go – ! You mean – !' For a moment she did not understand, and then the colour flooded back into her face. She was astonished, incredulous, shocked, not at the idea but at the fact that anyone should dare to suggest it, to speak of it openly. 'I did think of that,' she confessed, 'in the train, coming back.'

'Then why not?'

Norah picked her black gloves off her lap and laid them down on, the table, smoothing out the fingers. 'Tom wouldn't do a thing like that,' she said finally.

'Wouldn't he?'

'No... It wouldn't be right.'

'If you really think that, then you mustn't do it. But – ' Griselda broke off, meeting the other's glance.

'You mean: he might be killed?'

'There's that, too.'

Norah pushed her drink away. 'I suppose people do...' she fell silent, looking down at the table, tracing a pattern in the scarred woodwork. After what seemed a long time she looked up and asked: 'But where could we go?'

Griselda smiled dreamily. 'I know a cottage at Watermist. That's about thirty miles away. There's an old lady... I used to go there when I was a child. I go there on Sundays now and then... I could fix it for you...' she described it: thatch, climbing roses, a river at the bottom of the garden widening out into a pool where one could swim.

Norah listened, asking no questions, saying nothing. She got up. 'I'll ask Tom.'

Next morning, she went out to the factory early, and when she met Tom at the station she had in her handbag the shop-manager's written permission to take a week's leave of absence.

THIRTY-FOUR

ON FRIDAY DAN Morgan sent Griselda a note. 'The Minister,' it said, 'is sending representatives of an allied government to visit Blimpton tomorrow, and I am to have the honour of escorting them around the factory on Sunday. They will be leaving Dustborough by the 5.30 train. I will pick you up outside the tobacconist's at the corner of Station Road and Hill Street at 5.35 unless I hear from you that you are unable to come.'

Griselda smiled as she scanned the bold and upright handwriting. Then she tore the note into tiny fragments and put them into the waste-paper basket.

Betty Sims, who occupied the other cubicle, called over the partition: 'That paper makes a hell of a noise.'

'Sorry. I didn't know you were trying to sleep.'

'I'm not. I'm just nosey.' Betty slipped out of bed and put her head round the end of the partition. Her hair was rolled tightly into curlers, adding a touch of oddity to her sharp yet humorous expression. 'What was it?' she inquired. 'A state secret, or a billet-doux from the boyfriend?'

Griselda slipped off her dress and prepared to go to bed. 'I'm not sure,' she replied.

Betty shook her head. 'I don't know,' she sighed, 'I don't know how you pick 'em up.'

'State secrets?'

'Boyfriends, silly!'

'I didn't say that it was a boyfriend.'

'No, you didn't say. That's why I had to get out and have a look at you – ' Betty disappeared behind the partition and threw herself on the bed. 'How some girls do it!' she exclaimed. 'And where do you find them? That's what beats me... why, I've been here three months and I haven't hardly seen a man – not what I'd call a man. I mean – '

'Oh! go to sleep!'

THIRTY- FIVE

DROPS OF RAIN began to fall as Griselda turned the corner into Station Road. Dan's car was already there.

'I hope I haven't kept you waiting?' she asked as she got in beside him.

'No. I've only just come.' The trite pattern of words seemed only to heighten the barrier between them. They did not look at one another, but sat stiff and self-conscious, watching a squad of the Home Guard march past, their rifles resting heavily on narrow shoulders. The rain pattered down on to the roof of the car and splashed luminous against the windscreen.

Morgan said: 'I hope you won't imagine that I'm in the habit of doing this sort of thing?' He made a vague gesture with his right hand.

She laughed, lightly, briefly, with inexplicable amusement.

'Now why should you find that funny?' he demanded, exasperated. He slewed round to look at her.

'I don't know. I – '

'Well,' he conceded, offering her his cigarette case, 'perhaps you're right. Perhaps I shouldn't have put it like that.' A lock of her hair fell forward as she leaned to take a light. 'And now, young woman,' he said, 'I'm going to give you an unusual experience.' He started the engine. 'Have you got a hat?'

'Yes.' When she had stepped into the car she had flung it behind her, aiming carelessly at the back seat. Now she turned to see that it had fallen on to the floor. The fine straw looked crumpled, derelict. She leaned over and picked it up, straightening the ribbon. 'What do I need a hat for? You're not taking me to church, are you?'

'Chapel.' He turned a corner, driving slowly through the deserted streets.

'But why?'

'Is it so very extraordinary? What did you think we were going to do?'

'Talk.'

'Hoh!' he looked down at her with his wide, mocking smile. 'And so we will, afterwards. But now we're going to hear a sermon – or at least I am. You can sit in the car and wait if you'd rather not come in.'

'No, I'll come. But – '

He laughed. 'I told you that I was a Welshman. And I do like a bloody good sermon, as one of my compatriots once said. There's a famous preacher at the Baptist Chapel in Market Street – I saw the notice as I came past this afternoon. Of course, if you'd really prefer to do something else – '

'Oh, I see! It's an aesthetic experience?'

'Partly. Not altogether. I had a very religious upbringing. It leaves one with a – what shall I say? – an appetite.'

The chapel was sallow with pitch-pine and imitation stone. The light, filtered through green glass windows, was chill, almost wintry. A pervasive smell of red baize, hymn-books and household soap combined with the voluntary, played by an organist who sat perched high in the gallery behind the pulpit, to produce an atmosphere not so much of melancholy as of cheerless, uneasily preserved respectability. The building, like the Town Hall, the two railway stations, the market and the parish church, seemed far too big for its purpose, and, indeed, it was obvious from the size of the congregation that listening to sermons was not a popular form of relaxation in Dustborough. As Griselda and Dan were ushered into a pew members of the scanty congregation who were already seated nudged each other and turned round to look at them.

The preacher mounted the pulpit and announced the opening hymn. Griselda, standing beside Dan, followed the words in the hymn-book and then, as if too conscious of the extraordinary strength and richness of the voice beside her, she also began to sing:

'Lift up your heart, lift up your voice:
Rejoice! Again I say, rejoice!'

Dan's head was thrown back, his eyes intent, as if on some inner vision. He looked as if he had forgotten her, the bleak surrounding walls, the congregation, everything but the purpose that had brought him here. When he sat down small drops of sweat shone on either side of his forehead and, as the minister began to pray, Dan pulled out a handkerchief and began to mop his face.

The service followed its appointed course: another hymn, a lesson taken from the Old Testament, more prayers, and then the sermon. The preacher, who until now had been dwarfed by the exaggerated proportions of his surroundings, whose face had been no more than a blur against the yellow woodwork of the gallery behind him, seemed all at once to grow in stature. For a moment he looked down upon the congregation. 'I have chosen,' he began, 'to speak to you this evening about immortality.' He lifted his eyes, focusing them, it seemed, on some distant point beyond the sight, or even the imagination, of those who sat beneath him, tired, shabby, eternally middle-aged, the shop-keepers and clerks, the housewives and charwomen, the factory hands and craftsmen who were the inheritors of this monument to Dustborough's lost, irrecoverable prosperity. He spoke at first in a soft, barely audible tone, and then the great voice swelled to the roof, rolling out tremendously, but as if in a strange language. The words, polysyllabic, unfamiliar, washed over the bald heads, the Sunday hats, the blank receptive faces, leaving, like a strong tide, an after-tow of exhaustion, but also of exhilaration. Dan watched, his face rapt, absorbing every change in intonation, every gesture. Once he looked at Griselda, and then quickly returned his attention to the preacher. Griselda herself sat perfectly still, her face so obviously attentive that she easily might not have been listening at all.

When it was over, and they were once more outside, Morgan asked: 'Well, what do you think?'

'I don't know,' she looked at him doubtfully. 'It didn't mean anything, did it?'

'Why do you say that?' He turned off down a by-road. The evening had cleared, and as they left Dustborough behind them the air turned warm and soft and the summer trees, still bright with rain, were brilliant, almost spring-like. Griselda looked about her and smiled faintly, her lips parted, savouring, it seemed, some pleasure too delicate for description. Morgan, watching her, was smiling, too.

'Tell me,' he insisted.

'Oh! About the sermon!' she paused. 'If you really want to know

– I thought it was poison.'

'Why?'

'It isn't,' she was watching his strong hands on the steering wheel as she spoke. They were covered with light golden hairs, and the fingers, long and well-shaped, were squared at the ends, the nails cut short. 'It isn't the belief in personal immortality that I find so – so repellent... it's the use that it's put to... There was a little man sitting up somewhere in front – '

'Yes?'

'I know him slightly. He's been working in one of the bomb shops in the Group next to mine. Then one day last week he was taken off process work and put on to cutting the grass.'

'The grass has to be cut.'

'Certainly. But why should little Jones – who has a wife and family to look after – have to have his wages cut by more than a pound a week because it's dangerous to allow the grass to grow too high and there's no one else to mow it?'

'What's that got to do with immortality?'

'Everything. If Jones weren't persuaded every Sunday that he'll get a better deal in the next life than he's had in this he'd take more interest in what concerns him here, pay his union dues, ginger up the Whitley Council to make sure that sort of thing didn't happen...'

Morgan grinned. 'I didn't know you were a lady politician!'

'I'm not. I'm still trying to find my way around.'

'Well, you're not doing so badly.'

'Oh, I've a lot to learn... but all these people who sit around waiting for the next world – they're never really alive in this...'

'Very few people are.' He drew up at the entrance to a roadhouse. 'Shall we eat?' He turned into the driveway. The place was shabby, unkempt. The grass needed cutting, and the sign that hung over the entrance was faded into illegibility. Through the open windows a dance tune was being shaken from a worn gramophone. 'I can't think why I brought you here,' Dan observed as he brought the car to a standstill. 'Someone told me that it was a place to come to... do you think you can bear it?'

She smiled with bright-eyed amusement. 'It looks good enough for a working girl.'

'You know,' he shook his head, 'I think we've had enough of that line of talk. If you're going to keep it up I shall begin to ask you some awkward questions.'

'What about?'

'About what you did before you came to Blimpton.'

'That isn't any secret.' She walked up the steps beside him. 'I didn't really do anything.'

'Hoh! Now we're getting down to it. So you were one of the idle rich?'

She laughed, but rather uncomfortably. 'That's putting it a bit high... I haven't had to earn my living before...'

'And now you have to?'

She nodded, her eyes lowered. They sat side by side on a bench upholstered in faded cretonnes, self-conscious, apparently surprised at finding themselves together. The five or six other couples scattered around the room broke off their conversations to look at them, found nothing remarkable, and went on talking. Morgan was scratching a pattern of lines on the check tablecloth. He looked preoccupied, his blunt features expressionless. Then, as the soup was put before them, he turned to Griselda and asked: 'How would you like to do a real job of work for a change?'

'Isn't that what I am doing?'

'Oh, you're using your hands – but I've had a sort of idea that you've got a mind, too.'

Again she laughed. 'I'd like my father to hear you say that!'

'Well, bring him along, and I'll tell him. Where is he?'

She stared around, and for a second her face was blank. 'I – I suppose he's in London.'

'What does he do?'

'Oh! Business... making money... you know the sort of thing...'

'What do you mean? The black market?'

This time her laughter was genuine. She threw back her head and her grey eyes darkened with amusement. 'Maybe,' she said. 'I wouldn't know.'

'He doesn't trust you, eh?' Dan mocked, but the joke turned

heavy.

'I don't think it's that... he has old-fashioned ideas about women... What's this about using my mind?'

'Your mind! Oh, yes,' he put down his spoon and pushed the plate away. 'I rather think I've got a job for you. Gower – do you know Dr Gower?'

'I've seen him about.'

'He's got an idea that he wants to start a campaign on health precautions – cutting down dermatitis, getting people to keep themselves clean, that sort of thing. And – he's looking for someone who knows what the problems are... how long have you been in the factory? Six months?'

She nodded, leaning forward, waiting.

'I suppose,' he met her glance with a grin that was both more and less than friendly, 'I don't need to ask whether you have any ideas?'

'Oh!' excitement, mounting in her, was still under control, but her face flushed with pleasure. 'I know what ought to be done!'

'Well?'

'I've – I've thought a lot about all this...' and then, at first hesitantly, but presently with growing confidence, she began to outline, as if from a scheme already matured, plans for brightening the ablution rooms, for providing protective creams and powders that would be so attractive that people would use them willingly instead of, as now, only when an outbreak of dermatitis led to a day or two of panicky indifference to appearances. 'I'll confess,' she gave him a quick sideways glance, 'that I don't use these creams and powders that we're told to put on. I asked a doctor to make me something that wouldn't smell of candle grease and look like whitewash – I suppose that it's basically much the same as the stuff you provide and if you made it in bulk it shouldn't cost very much more. And – ' she broke off, wavering under the intentness of his gaze. 'Am I being silly?'

'No. Go on.'

She went on to discuss the problem of the towel supply, the difficulty of getting uniforms properly laundered, the need for caps that not only kept the explosive powders out of the hair but that also did not spoil the effect of whatever the hairdresser had done to one's curls. 'Of course,' she finished, 'that's only a part of it. There's also the question of the planning of the shops – messy work, bad ventilation – '

'Right!' he stopped her. 'I think you'll do. That is, if Gower approves…' Once more he was making patterns on the tablecloth, and when he looked up his glance was impersonal, focused on some problem of which the subject of this conversation formed, it seemed, only a small part.

'You mean – ' she was eager, but restrained, 'you're going to give me a new job?'

'I mean' … his attention returned to her swiftly. He smiled, showing the sharp, devouring teeth, 'I mean that I'm going to ask Gower to see you, and if he thinks you'll do… well, then we'll see. I think you ought to be pretty good.'

'I'll try!'

'Of course you will. But don't try too hard – we've got enough people at Blimpton who're busy knocking down brick walls with teaspoons.'

'Perhaps I'll be able to find some more powerful implement.'

'Such as?'

She shook her head. 'I don't know. But if you want to get things done someone has to find the weapons.'

'And you think you can?'

'I – I don't know… I,' she turned towards him and, speaking with great seriousness, added, 'I'll never be able to thank you enough.'

'For what?'

'For giving me this opportunity.'

'Oh that!' there was an edge of roughness in his voice and he did not look at her as he spoke. 'This job oughtn't to mean anything to a girl with your background.'

She stirred her coffee, and the teaspoon clattered noisily into the saucer. The silence that followed was like the quiet after an explosion, charged with the sense of disintegration. 'What do you know about my background?' Griselda asked at last.

'Only what you've told me. I'm taking you – or handing you over to Gower – largely on trust.' Suddenly he grinned. 'If the worst comes to the worst, you won't be able to do much harm. And you know, I rather like you… come on, let's go. Or do you want to dance?'

'Just as you like.'

'No.' The scratched record jerked towards its end, and no one came to change it. The room was almost empty, and in a few moments they got up. Dusk was already in the sky as they went down the steps. Griselda walked a little ahead, almost, it seemed, as if she felt herself to be alone. And Morgan, following, watched her for a moment or so, seeing again the high poise of the head, the smiling curve that was all that was visible of her face, and the soft dark hair moving slightly in the breeze. Then he caught her up and put a hand on her shoulder. She turned, looking up at him with frank, unexpected delight. 'I've enjoyed myself,' she said.

'So have I.' He opened the door for her to get into the car. 'But we don't get much further, do we?'

She waited until he was seated beside her, and then asked: 'How?'

'How!' he repeated on the note of self-mockery that others always found so bewildering. 'Every time we meet I imagine that I'm going to get to know you…'

'Don't you?'

He shook his head. 'We're still strangers… still talking about the weather, only for us the weather is Blimpton – '

'The climate of our lives. It's important.'

'And so are we… By the way, what happened to your friend Norah?'

'Oh, Norah!' She began to tell him, elaborating the details of her meeting with Tom Walton, describing the young man's look of eagerness as he stepped off the train and the moment of blank disappointment when he realised that Norah was not there to meet him. Then she told him about Norah, her family, the background of the life in Camden Town, the dismay, so deep that sorrow would come only much later, at the news of the death in battle of Norah's brother. Dan listened, saying nothing, but showing, in the occasional glance that he turned towards Griselda, an interest, a warmth of sympathy and of understanding that she had not perhaps expected.

The tension between them relaxed. They grew closer to one another now. She, talking, seemed no longer to be considering the impression that she made; and he, absorbed in the story, appeared at last to be unaware of the need to protect himself against the onslaught of emotions which, once admitted, might become overwhelming in their violence.

'And what happened when Norah came back from London?' he asked presently. His voice was low, almost inaudible.

Perhaps she had not meant to tell him, but there was no trace of hesitation in her manner. When she finished there was a long pause.

'Are you shocked?' she turned to him at last.

'Shocked?' he sounded surprised. 'What would I be shocked at?'

She did not reply, but suddenly the memory of the hour or so that they had spent in the Baptist Chapel in Dustborough rose lik a barrier between them.

'Were they happy together, those two?' Dan asked.

'I… I think so.'

'I hope so… you're a strange girl…'

'Why? Shouldn't I have told you'

'I don't know. I didn't mean that.' They were passing the factory, and then he turned the car to the right, along the Addle Hinton road. 'You take such risks with people – '

The statement, unfinished, quivered between them in the summer air. She did not ask him to explain, and the silence lasted until he drew up at the gate of the hostel. In the dim light his face was stern, over-disciplined, but when he leaned towards her his eyes gleamed, oddly bright. He took her hand in his and then, almost at once, withdrew it. 'Now go!' he said.

'I will. And thank you – '

'No. Don't thank me.' He leaned across her to open the door. 'Now – go!'

THIRTY-SIX

ONE AFTERNOON, ABOUT a week later, Gunn arrived at the factory. He dashed up the steps of the Administration Block, thrust a piece of paper, which was later recognised as being a pound-note, into the astonished hand of the attendant whose duty it was to scrutinise visitors' passes, and tore along the corridor, projecting himself, with quite unusual violence, into the Superintendent's office.

'What the hell's the matter with you?' he demanded.

The Superintendent sat hunched over his desk, his face buried in his hands, groaning.

'Can't you see – ' he began, and then the sentence seeped in and he looked around. 'How dare – why, Mr Gunn, what an unexpected pleasure!' He pulled himself up, one hand resting on the table. 'Forgive me. It's just a touch of indigestion – '

'Here. Take this.' Gunn poured out a glass of water.

The Superintendent drank it, shuddering.

'Nothing like a glass of water,' Gunn observed cheerfully. 'Been eating something?'

'I'm afraid so. I ought to have realised at the time – ' He shuddered again as he remembered the oozy taste of processed cheese in the Lobster Mornay that his cook had given him for lunch. He knew that she was too good, too loving a cook to have produced that revolting concoction by accident. No, there could be no doubt, he told himself, no doubt at all that she had done it from spite, because she wanted to leave Blimpton and because he had threatened that he would not let her go. But this afternoon he was worried by much more than the after effects of his lunch and the fear that he would, in the end, be forced to give in, to live for the rest of the war on boiled mutton and macaroni puddings. Everything seemed to be going wrong. First, there had been the problem of cleaning up the damage done by the air raid, of reorganising the shops so as to lose the least possible production time. Then, when this had been done reasonably satisfactorily, the workers' side on the Whitley Council had protested that nothing had been done by the Labour Office to help those who had been injured, or to assist in the filing of claims for compensation by the relatives of those who had been killed. Miss Creed had insisted that she had too much for her staff to do without sending them running round the villages consoling bereaved parents ' – and, in any case,' she had said, 'ours is a Labour Office, not a Welfare Department.' And she had put her feet down with such force that Dolphin had had to be recalled from Pinton to do the job. After that, the trouble about Knowles had cropped up again. Morgan had discovered – though he would not say how – that Knowles had only refused to accept fitters after he had discovered that they were being sent from the factory in which he had spent most of his working life. It had then become necessary to inquire why Knowles had left, what crime he had committed, and whether he had, when joining the staff of the Ministry of Weapon Production, failed to disclose some material facts about his past. The inquiry took some time and revealed very little. As an employee of EELS Knowles had been fussy, unpopular among the workers and a source of irritation to his colleagues. But his failure had been unspectacular. He had mismanaged a number of minor trade disputes, he had been harsh where he should have been conciliatory, and conciliatory where he should have been firm. He had misjudged people, and had been responsible for some unsuitable promotions and some even more deeply resented dismissals. But that was about all. Then why, the Superintendent and Gittins had asked each other, why should he have been afraid of what ten or twelve men whom he had known in the past would do to his reputation at Blimpton? And Morgan, looking through the file of correspondence accumulated on the subject, had said: 'But, don't you see, this makes it all the worse? If he'd murdered the managing director, or forged a cheque for £10,000, or run off with the doorkeeper's wife – well, as a rule these things only happen once, and a man can outlive them. But the petty meannesses, these failings that are parts of one's nature and can't be uprooted, these are the things that one tries to run away from. You know,' he closed the file, 'if those girls hadn't died one would feel almost sorry for the man – '

The Superintendent had not been able to see the point of that, and nor, apparently, had Gittins. All three had, however, agreed that it would be better for Blimpton if Knowles were to be transferred to some other factory. Meanwhile, tension in the Labour Office had become acute. Knowles had refused to have any further dealings with Parsons except through a third party, and the third party, namely Miss Creed, torn between her long-standing loyalty to Knowles and the hope that if he were superseded she would be promoted to take his place, was alternately arrogant and ingratiating. She made the Superintendent feel thoroughly nervous. And, on top of all that, the trouble about the contract with Gurneys seemed to be cropping up again...

'Still feeling bad?' Gunn asked. 'Here, take another glass of water.'

The Superintendent picked up the glass, said he felt better, and put it down, looking at it with acute distaste. 'I thought you were still at Pinton?' he asked.

'So I am, more or less.' Gunn sat down. 'But I had one or two ideas and I thought I'd run over and have a chat.'

'And how's it going down there?'

'The recruiting campaign?' Gunn thrust his hands into his pocket and threw back his head. 'Between you and me, I don't think there's much in these recruiting campaigns. They've been overdone. If people want to come to a place like this, well, they'll come...'

'And how many are coming?'

Gunn consulted a scrap of paper: that is to say, he unfolded it, appeared to read it, turned it over, examined the other side, frowned, tried how it looked upside down, then replaced it in his pocket and took out another slip.

'There'll be about eighty,' he said.

'Oh, well – ' the Superintendent changed his mind. 'Every little helps,' he observed brightly.

'Yes. Fifty – no, forty-seven of them I picked up in an hotel,' Gunn added.

'Chambermaids, eh?'

'Not on your life! Old ladies. The sort you find in these seaside hotels. Quiet. Never done a day's work in their lives, most of them – '

'But – '

'And,' Gunn, ignoring the interruption, referred again to the scrap of paper he held in his hand, 'the oldest is seventy-five – no, seventy-three. Of course they're not all as old as that. There's one only fifty-nine. But most of them are around sixty-five – anyway, that's the average age as far as I can work it out.' He looked up and, seeing the Superintendent's expression, stopped sharply. 'What's wrong? Feeling ill again?' He jumped up and made for the carafe of water that stood on the conference table.

'No,' the Superintendent refused the proffered glass. 'I'm all right, but – they're a trifle on the old side, aren't they?'

'Old! Of course they're old! That's why I made such a set at them. That doctor chap – what's his name? Gower. Yes, Gower told me the last time I was up here that the old ones don't get this der – derma – '

'Dermatitis?'

'That's it. They don't catch it the way the young ones do. That's right, ain't it?'

The Superintendent nodded, his eyes averted.

'So when I walked into that hotel and saw all these old ladies sitting around doing their knitting or tatting or whatever it is that old ladies do, I said to myself, Ed, I said – now's your chance to show the boys! Well, I settled right in, and there you are! They'll be along next Monday week, the whole bunch.'

'But – ' the Superintendent groped, speechless. 'But – ' he began again, looking around wildly, wishing that Gittins would come, or Morgan, or Dawson, anyone who could help him before it was too late. But no door opened, no telephone rang. 'How will they manage on the night-shift?' he asked, seeking some obstacle, some plausible objection.

'Oh, you'll have to keep them on days.'

'We can't do that, my dear fellow. With three-shift working – '

'Well, you'll have to worry that out for yourselves. My job is to get 'em. It's up to you folks here to see that they're properly used. Next,' a slight motion of the thumb indicated that the subject was closed. 'Next: what about the fuzes I gave you to fill the first time I came down here?'

The Superintendent racked his memory. 'We filled them.' He sat back, wondering what he could say to Gower, thinking that Miss Creed and Miss Marshall would have to manage the old ladies between them as best they could. Or perhaps they could be told not to come...

'Yep. We were going to fire them. You remember?'

'Oh, the fuzes! I'll get Hitchens.' He picked up the telephone.

Gunn got up and looked at his watch. 'Fix it for about five o'clock,' he commanded rather than suggested. 'I want to go over the factory now to look at your fuze-filling. I'll meet you on the proof-range at six, sharp.'

'I'll get someone to take you over – '

'No need. I can find my way around by this time.'

'But I'm afraid it's the rule,' miraculously, the Superintendent recovered his sense of authority. 'No visitors are allowed around the factory unaccompanied.'

'Okay.'

Dawson took small pains to conceal his annoyance at having to break off his afternoon's work. He was engrossed in an attempt to understand a new system of record-keeping that had been invented by someone at headquarters and that he had, a month earlier, been instructed to adopt. To be interrupted at this moment, just when the first glimmer of understanding of the scheme had begun to dawn, was peculiarly exasperating, especially since the magic associated with Gunn's name had lost its potency. Gunn asked question after question, some apparently pointless, some ignorant, but others so shrewd and well-directed that Dawson, looking to the shop-manager for corroboration as he answered, was slowly filled with an awed bewilderment. Most of the answers Gunn jotted down in a little notebook, but some he wrote on odd scraps of paper, with which all his pockets seemed to be filled. He hurried through the shops, chatting now and then with the overlookers, but seldom pausing to talk to the girls and women whose work he was trying to understand. Once he asked a nervous looking woman: 'Do you like working here?' but when she hesitated over her reply he hurried on, not waiting to hear what she had to say. And once, entering a shop where some forty or fifty girls were at long benches, assembling the finished fuzes, he nodded in the direction of one who sat at the end of a row, her head bent, her attention concentrated on the job before her, and said: 'Funny. Do you see that girl over there?'

He pointed. There was nothing but the erect set of the shoulders, the slightly better fit of the ungainly uniform, to distinguish her, at that angle, from fifteen or twenty other girls in the same shop, and from several hundreds they had seen in the course of the afternoon.

'Yes?' Dawson asked. His feet were beginning to ache.

'Funny,' Gunn repeated, 'she reminds me of someone.'

'Would you like to speak to her?'

'No,' he shook his head. 'Must be a mistake.' He followed Dawson out, down the clean-way into the next shop. He seemed preoccupied, and once or twice repeated questions that he had already asked earlier. And he no longer made notes.

'And this job – ' Dawson began as they went into still another shop.

Gunn looked round wildly. 'I must have dropped my notebook,' he said abruptly.

'Oh, I'll get someone to look around for it and bring it along,' the shop-manager offered. 'Do you remember where you were when you last had it?'

Gunn pointed vaguely in the direction from which they had come. 'Think I'll go myself,' he muttered, 'there are things in that notebook...' he essayed a wink and hurried off.

'Remarkable fellow,' Dawson observed to the shop-manager as soon as Gunn was out of earshot. Then, wasting no time, he began to expound what he could remember of the new system of record-keeping.

Meanwhile Gunn, his hand in his pocket as if to ensure that the notebook should not in fact fall out, hurried down the clean-way, looking right and left, keeping careful count of the buildings as he passed them. He went into a shop, looked around, saw it was the wrong one, and went into the next. This was the one, he was sure of that, but she wasn't there.

The over-looker came forward. 'Can I help you, sir?'

'No. I lost my notebook somewhere around. Couldn't have been here.' He left her and hurried out, rushing so fast that as he took the double turn around the blast-proof door he banged into someone.

'I beg your pardon,' she was about to hurry on, not seeing him.

'Griselda!' he put out a hand, clutching her as she was about to escape out of the shadowy darkness of the porch into the shop from which he had come. 'I knew it was you! What the devil – '

'Oh, my God!' she looked round, making sure that there was no one within sight, within earshot.

'But what the hell – ' he peered at her, making doubly certain that there was no mistake. 'I thought you were in America – '

'Oh, shut up!' she whispered. 'Can't you see – '

'Oh, this is great! What a story, eh: What a –'

'Listen!' she looked at him, wide eyed with anger. 'You haven't seen me. If you tell anyone – *anyone* – that you saw me, I'll – I'll – '

'Okay. I won't tell anyone. But why? What's it all about?'

'Oh!' her arms were flat against her side, her elbows digging into her waist as if she were trying to press herself in.

'I must see you. Honest, Griselda – '

She thought, transparently. He could see the thoughts chasing each other across her face. 'Meet me tonight,' she said, still whispering. 'No. I'll run out in half an hour. Pick me up outside the Peartree at Addle Hinton at a quarter to five.' And then she slipped past him into the shop.

'Did you find it?' Dawson asked.

'Yeah, I found it. Well, I'll be getting along now. I've got an engagement.'

And, leaving Dawson to find his own means of transportation back to the Administration Block, he hurried off.

He had been pacing up and down in front of the Peartree for more than half an hour when Griselda stepped off the bus. She was hat-less, dressed in a light cotton frock and with a coat flung over her shoulders.

'Gosh!' he stared at her, wrinkling his forehead. 'I wouldn't have known you in that get up!'

'Wouldn't you?' she laughed suddenly, pleasantly. 'But you did, didn't you: We can't talk here,' she said, making towards the car.

'Where do you want to go?'

'Nowhere. Just drive – not too near the factory. I mustn't be long –

I said I'd be back in an hour.'

'For pity's sake – ' the car began to move, 'what's it all about? Gosh! I can hardly believe it's really you!' Driving easily, with one hand on the steering wheel, he looked at her again. 'You've changed, though. You look kind of – serious.'

'Oh, yes, I'm serious enough. Damn you,' she spoke with the contemptuous affection that had always been so characteristic of her attitude to her father's entourage, and to him in particular. 'Why did you have to walk through that door?'

'But what's all the mystery? Don't you realise that this is the greatest story since... When this gets out it'll knock the Russians off every front page from here to San Francisco... "Cabinet Minister's Daughter Filling Block-Busters – Beautiful Society Widow Hits Back"... How's that for a headline, hey? Or – '

'Ed! Stop it, can't you?'

'Hell! What's wrong? What've I said? You're not sore at me for running into you like that? These people up at the factory – it beats me entirely. They never said one word. Not one. That fat old mouse-trap of a Superintendent; Morgan – '

'They don't know.'

'The hell they don't!'

'But how should they? I'm only one of thousands.'

'How long've you been here?'

'Six months.'

'So you did go to America, hey?'

'Yes.' She looked around. The country lane was empty; there was not a house, not even a haystack in sight. 'You can stop here,' she said, and then, fixing her gaze on him added, with an extreme cold violence, 'if you tell anyone that you've seen me I'll... I'll... '

'Okay. You'll kill me.' He remembered the first time that she had made that threat, a day or two after her twelfth birthday when he had caught her leading into a cinema four or five coloured children whom she had picked up somehow, somewhere, unknown to her prim English governess. 'If you tell Miss Pawley,' she had threatened in a hoarse childish whisper, 'I'll kill you! I will!' And between that day and the time when she had grown up and travelled about the world and married the heir to an ancient peerage he had heard the phrase twenty or thirty times, perhaps oftener. Every time that he caught her doing something unexpected, something that she didn't want old Outrage to know about ' – But what's all the mystery?' he asked again. 'You talk as if you'd done a murder – '

'I'll tell you.' But there she stopped.

'Was it – ? ' For an instant he was restrained, held back by the knowledge, the never admitted certainty, that her marriage had been a failure, that she had been unable to feel any sorrow, anything but a sort of ashamed, impersonal regret when Jock, her husband, had been shot down into the Channel and, drowning, had been transmuted, in spite of his mediocrity, his stupidities, his narrow, good-tempered complacency, into a hero. After Jock's death she had buried herself for two months at Watermist, looked after by her old nannie and feeling, Gunn obscurely sensed, a growing sense of guilt at her own indifference. Then, one day, her father had gone down to see her, taken her back to London and, a week later, packed her off to America with Nancy Elcombe and Nancy's three children. 'Why!' he exclaimed with fresh astonishment, 'the old man had a letter from you last week, from that place in Texas – I went up to see him and he told me himself.'

'Yes. I send letters. It's rather roundabout – '

'Of all the – '

'Listen!' she broke in. 'You won't understand… or perhaps you will.' Once more she paused, staring out over the fields. 'I wanted to be something on my own; to see what I could do if I were just a person. The old man – you know as well as I do that he started from nothing… One can think what one likes of what he's made of his life, but whatever it is, he's done it himself. You, too. And little Wilkes, and Timmy Elcombe. But I've had no chance – '

'Hey!'

'I said you wouldn't understand. Let me go on. That's not all of it. When I came here it was because I wanted to run away – oh, not from Nancy, but from the kind of life I've always led… But it wasn't only that. I wanted to see if I could really do something by myself, start at the bottom and build up, instead of arriving everywhere with a first-class ticket labelled "Lord Outrage's daughter" or "Jock Heath-Green's widow". I came here because… because it's the most difficult kind of place. And it's so big that I didn't think I'd ever be found out… It didn't occur to me that you'd be coming down, muscling in – '

'Skip it.'

'And now,' her face clouded, 'after all these months of sticking it out, holding myself down, wanting to run off and tell the old man what his factories are really like – now, I'm going to have a job where I'll really be able to do something. And I'm getting it because of myself – ' Looking at him, her expression changed. A hint of laughter hovered in her eyes and flickered out. 'I think that's why?' she said, as if speaking to herself, 'I'm sure – almost. But if you tell anyone – anyone at all – '

'Have a heart! Think of the publicity!'

'I've thought of that,' she replied dryly.

'Don't you realise,' he almost shouted, 'that if this got into the papers every little office girl in London would start running to Blimpton? Why, it'd get them like – '

'No it wouldn't. And if it did they wouldn't stay. That sort of cheap glamour wouldn't outlast a day in the factory: and I know what I'm talking about. I've stuck it…'

'Ah, you're your father's daughter!' he acknowledged with enormous satisfaction. 'You'll let me tell him?'

'Not now. Later, when… But not now. If you tell anyone – '

'I won't,' he submitted suddenly, 'I swear it.'

'You do?'

'If you say so. But when you change your mind – '

'I'll let you know!'

THIRTY-SEVEN

GUNN RETURNED TO London, his fuzes still untried. They could not, in any case, have been fired since Hitchens, who, the Superintendent declared, was responsible for their safe-keeping, disclaimed all knowledge of them, and even Dawson, questioned later, could not remember in which of the magazines they had been stored. The Superintendent ordered a search to be made and went home to offer his cook another twenty pounds a year.

Early in the following week Miss Hopkins came back from Pinton. The small party of workers she had taken there with her had performed in the Pier Pavilion on five successive evenings. On the first occasion they had been preceded by the appearance of a galaxy of stars, most of them of small magnitude, who had attracted something like three hundred people to the concert hall. But after that admittedly not very successful first night the Blimpton people, as Dolphin remarked, not only had the stage to themselves but most of the auditorium as well. Miss Hopkins, stifling her disappointment, had done her best to keep up the spirits of the rest of her cast and had, she mistakenly thought, succeeded. They liked her too much to allow themselves to indulge in their disappointment when she was present, but as soon as she was out of earshot they would discuss, endlessly but fruitlessly, what they would say when they got back to the factory, whether they would pretend that they had enjoyed themselves and done something useful, or whether they would admit to fiasco. Secretly, they were all convinced that before they had done a full shift they would blurt it all out.

Only Pamela Grant, the young assistant labour officer, was admitted to a share in Miss Hopkins' disappointment, and even she did not know how great that disappointment was or how closely she herself was concerned in it. For Miss Hopkins, before the last performance of the little play was over, had been forced by her own innate honesty (aided, however, by some outside help) to recognise that Pamela was not only no genius, but that she would never be more than a moderately competent amateur. She had chosen Pamela to take the leading part, that of an operative in the danger area of the factory, chiefly because she hoped that the girl would interest the famous impresario whom Gunn had promised to bring from London one evening, but also because she believed that the part of a worker would be better played by a girl who could act than by one whose only qualification was first-hand experience of working in the shops. And Pamela was undoubtedly better than anyone else Miss Hopkins knew; but she was not good enough. The famous impresario said that it was quite an interesting little sketch and that he would like to drop in at Blimpton sometime and see the place for himself. When, however, Miss Hopkins asked whether he did not think that Pamela Grant had unusual talent he smiled and shrugged his shoulders and replied: 'Talent, perhaps; but not unusual…' Then he remarked on what a long time it was since he and Miss Hopkins had met, and suggested that if ever she were in London they might perhaps have lunch together one day.

On her way back to Blimpton Miss Hopkins had telephoned to the great man's office, only to be told that he was out of town. So she lunched instead with a friend from the Ministry who warned her, quite confidentially but on the best possible authority, that it would be better for everyone concerned if no more were heard about schemes for a factory theatre at Blimpton. The Pinton episode, the friend continued, had been looked on with some misgivings by the welfare branch of the Ministry, and those concerned in it were scarcely likely to have their next enterprise encouraged. Moreover, there were no longer any bricks, timber or steel to be had for projects of a – the friend hesitated to use the word, but thought it better to be frank – frivolous nature.

Back in her bedroom at Mowbray Lodge, Miss Hopkins brushed her hair and prepared to make the best of things. Although she had sometimes talked about her dreams, no one at Blimpton knew how much they had meant to her, and now there was no one to share her disappointment. She fastened a bunch of velvet pansies at her throat and was about to go down when there was a tap on the door and Ruth Aaron came in.

'Ruth, dear!' Miss Hopkins greeted her warmly. 'What a long time it is! Sit down a minute, and tell me what's been happening…

How are things?'

'Some better, some worse.' Ruth perched herself on the edge of the bed, examining the toes of her high-heeled slippers. 'I hear you didn't have such an awfully good time?' Her sympathy was inarticulate.

'Oh, it wasn't as bad as all that!' Miss Hopkins replied with a bracing smile. 'Who's been talking? Dolphin?'

'Of course. We all thought it was because he was so annoyed at being called back to help with the welfare side after the raid – '

'Was he annoyed?'

'Oh, you should have heard him!' Ruth laughed at the memory, her face brightening with unfamiliar amusement. 'You know,' she added, 'sometimes I quite like him – he's such a silly little man… why do you look so surprised?'

Miss Hopkins hesitated, decided not to say what was in her mind, and asked instead: 'And you? Are you busy?'

'Yes, I am rather. We had two hundred and fourteen new entrants to examine yesterday – '

'Oh, that's splendid, isn't it?'

'For the factory?'

'Yes. Mr Morgan must be delighted to see the figures going up like that, isn't he?'

'I really don't know,' Ruth stood up. 'Hadn't we better go downstairs? The gong went ages ago…'

The evening was not as bad as Miss Hopkins had feared. Most people were glad to see her, but most of them, too, were so wrapped up in their own troubles that they wanted only to talk and were not at all curious about her misadventures during the past few weeks. She felt, however, a tension in the atmosphere that she had not noticed before. Knowles retired immediately after dinner without even taking coffee, while Miss Creed sat in a corner, turning over the pages of the *Illustrated London News*, and covertly watching Gower and Parsons who were arguing together in a corner.

'Well,' Morgan asked, taking the empty corner of the sofa, 'do you find us going on much as usual?'

'Yes, I think so,' Miss Hopkins glanced around to where Ruth sat listening to, rather than talking with, Finch. 'Yes, it all seems much as usual.'

THIRTY-EIGHT

KNOWLES DECLINED TO attend the special meeting, called by the Regional Welfare Officer of the Ministry of Labour, which was to take place at the Dustborough Employment Exchange. Miss Creed did not want to go, either. She regarded the Regional Welfare Officer as an interfering busybody whose chief interest seemed to be to think up novel ideas for other people to put into practice, and who was continually urging hard-pressed employers and labour managers to do things which, Miss Creed thought, ought either to be done by the Ministry of Labour or not at all.

Knowles said: 'Very well, if you feel like that send Parsons.'

'Won't that appear to be giving him too much authority?'

Knowles thought that over. 'You can't have it all ways,' he pointed out, 'and someone will have to go.'

Miss Creed put off the decision until an hour or so before the meeting was due to take place. A car was already on its way to fetch her when she went in to see Parsons and told him that he must attend.

His face fell. 'Is there no one else who can go?' he asked.

Miss Creed pursed her mouth. 'Really, Mr Parsons!' she protested.

'It's rather awkward,' he explained, apparently unconscious of the anger that he had aroused. 'You see, my children are coming down on the afternoon train to spend a few weeks with Mrs Gittins – '

'Really,' now the word had quite a different inflexion as Miss Creed's tone became charged with sweetness, 'That's extremely good of Mrs Gittins, isn't it?'

'Extremely,' Parsons agreed warmly.

'Such a sweet little woman, Mrs Gittins,' Miss Creed continued, ' – in her own way, of course. So quiet, and yet always so hospitable… and she actually offered to have your children to stay with her?'

'Yes,' Parsons sheered away from something in Miss Creed's manner that he did not want to recognise. 'I was hoping to get off for an hour to go and meet them…'

'Oh, that is awkward, isn't it? Yes, that really is awkward,' Miss Creed sat down, queenly, gracious. 'I'm afraid it's quite impossible for me to go to this meeting – there's so much to do, you know,

so much to do. And now these old ladies Mr Gunn sent along...
And Captain Knowles... But perhaps I could arrange for one of my
young women to meet the train for you – '

'Oh, that would be splendid!' Parsons accepted with relief.

Phoebe Braithwaite, her sympathetic expression imperfectly
concealed behind the thick lenses of her spectacles, was delighted to
go. She thought it a pity that Parsons should have ordered a taxi to
take the children from Dustborough to Blimpton and suggested that
Finch would have been able to provide one of the factory cars if he
had been asked. But, observing that Parsons met this suggestion with
disfavour, she said no more and went off to get her hat, wondering a
little at his scruples. He gave her a lift to Dustborough in the car that
was taking him to the meeting and, as they parted she decided, to
her own rather pleasant confusion, that although he was not exactly
a gentleman there was really something rather fine about him, even
apart from the sadness of his position.

Parsons returned to Blimpton early in the evening and went
straight to Gittins' office. The Principal Clerk had already gone
home for the night, but as he came out of Gittins' room Parsons ran
into Morgan.

'And how are the kids?' Morgan asked.

'I haven't seen them yet. I've just got back from Dustborough.
Can I talk to you for a minute?'

'Surely. Come along in... And what's the trouble? Morgan asked
as soon as the door of his office had closed on them.

'I'm not sure.' The meeting, Parsons explained, had been as
amicable as could have been expected; arrangements had been made
for the time, now probably not far distant, when the hostel would be
full and the billeting of workers coming to Blimpton from a distance
would again have to be undertaken. After outlining the plans that
had been made and describing the other main points that had been
discussed, Parsons added, 'And then, as I was coming away – '

'Yes?'

'The manager of the Exchange – Wood – you know him?'

Morgan nodded.

' – got hold of me. He says that if something isn't done about

Gurneys – '

Morgan smiled. 'Something has been done. Their contract is running out and they won't get another. We'll be able to scoop up their labour by the end of the month, if not sooner.'

'But they've got another contract. A1 priority, Wood said.'

'The devil they have!'

'Old Gurney himself was round at the Exchange this morning, making all sorts of demands for additional labour – '

'Additional?'

'Yes. Wood said that it was not his affair to sort out our priorities for us; but he pointed out that with the housing situation in Dustborough the way it is, it's important that we should get as much labour as we can locally. And people who live in Dustborough won't come out to Blimpton as long as there's work in the town – and – and of course Wood can't easily direct them when Gurneys have the same priority – '

'I see…' Morgan began thoughtfully. Suddenly he stood up. 'Thanks,' he said, 'I'll do what I can.'

THIRTY-NINE

THE SUPERINTENDENT SAID: 'Oh, yes, old Gurney told me that he was expecting to land that contract. A good man, old Gurney.'

Gittins looked across at Morgan, but Morgan seemed to be occupied in studying the design of his socks and did not look up.

'It's awkward for us,' Gittins began tentatively, nonplussed by the unusual frankness of the Superintendent's manner, for Brown, in conversation with his subordinates, seldom admitted to any knowledge of anything.

'Awkward for the Ministry of Labour,' the Superintendent conceded, 'it's their job to find the labour – '

'But if they don't succeed,' Gittins went on, still speaking with apparent reluctance, 'we're going to suffer. With the housing situation in Dustborough – '

'Oh, housing!' the Superintendent scoffed. 'If the worst comes to the worst we can always get that fellow Gunn to push the Ministry into building us another hostel. There's a fine site between here and Puddingbury. I happened to notice it the other day as I was passing... By the way, speaking of Gunn, you'd better give Hitchens another reminder about those wretched fuzes – '

Afterwards, Morgan said: 'So he's running a little speculation in land on the side, is he?'

Gittins shook his head in a fatherly way and opened another bottle of beer. 'Don't let your imagination run away with you.' He got up and closed the door, making sure that his wife was still upstairs putting the Parsons children to bed. 'If the old man had really had anything to do with Gurney getting those contracts – '

'You think he wouldn't have talked the way he did?' Morgan put down his glass. 'And that's where I think you're wrong.'

He explained, in detail, why; and then went on to elaborate a plan, brushing aside objections until, by the time that Mrs Gittins came down to lay the table for supper, the Principal Clerk had agreed that there could be no harm in Morgan running up to London for a day or two to clear up a few routine matters with people at headquarters and to make, if opportunities arose, some discreet inquiries into the history of the Gurney contracts.

He went on the following afternoon and returned three days later. Sitting in the train, thinking about the meetings he had attended and the people he had seen, he could not decide whether he had succeeded in making any impression at all. He had lunched with Colonel Jervis, who now seldom visited Blimpton, and had taken the opportunity to express a few vague doubts about the labour position generally. But Jervis, if he understood what Morgan was talking about, showed no interest and began, before the soup plates were carried away, a dissertation on the habits of long-haired dachshunds that lasted until the coffee began to get cold: then he talked, for a change, about Miss Hopkins. After that, Morgan had spent some hours in visiting Phipps and Crabtree of the labour department, trying to impress on them the fact that if Gurneys were allowed to go on working they could only do so by using labour that was badly needed at Blimpton. Phipps was non-committal, and pointed out three or four times that as long as Gurneys were producing a high-priority store they had as much claim as Blimpton on whatever labour might become available. When Morgan suggested that the work that Gurneys were doing could be carried out equally satisfactorily in any of twenty or thirty different factories in other parts of the country where the shortage of labour was less acute, Phipps said, with that disarming modesty which had endeared him to so many engineers, that of course he was not a technical man and could not discuss a question of that sort. He then ran his fingers through his thick grey curls and, flashing the diamond that he wore on his little finger, handed Morgan over to Crabtree, who remarked that it was extremely unlikely that anything could be done, but that he might come down to Blimpton for a weekend sometime and look at things for himself. Meanwhile, he suggested that if Morgan wanted to pursue that matter further he might go and talk to Barker in the contracts branch…

Morgan turned over the pages of his diary, counting the names of all the people he had seen. Russell was not among them: Morgan's journeys around the Ministry had not taken him as high as that; but now, watching the summer countryside roll past, he wondered whether he should not have gathered up his courage and gone in to see his ex-colleague, ex-enemy, the man who (so it was said) was now responsible for most of the major decisions made in the Ministry. Morgan frowned, speculating on whether among the small fry he had seen there had been anyone who had been sufficiently impressed with the case that he had made to look into it further, and whether such a person, if such there were, would have enough energy and enough interest in Blimpton's problems to pursue his inquiry into the Gurney contracts until a result was achieved. On the whole, Morgan thought, it seemed unlikely that there had been anyone. And in his uncertainty he condemned himself, roundly, fiercely, but entirely uselessly, because he had not been to see Russell, and now the train was more than halfway to Blimpton and it was too late.

The train was crowded and very hot. The afternoon sun poured in through the window, shining on the faded hair, the elaborately made-up face of the woman who sat opposite. In the furthest corner of the compartment a red-faced major snored, while his wife, watching over the top of a magazine, made little noises of protest, of a protest that seemed to be mixed with despair. Morgan glanced at his watch, then out of the window. The train was not more than ten minutes late, but there were still three stations at which it would stop before reaching Dustborough. The woman opposite asked if anyone would mind if the blinds were drawn. Everyone rushed to pull them down. An elderly businessman, his hands clasped over his paunch, remarked, for the tenth time since leaving London, that this was the hottest day that there had been this year. The train stopped at a station, more people entered, wedging themselves into the corridor, holding on to their luggage as the engine again began to get up steam. Motes danced in the narrow slits of sunlight that entered through gaps in the blinds, dizzily bright. Morgan opened his briefcase, took out a pile of papers, read a page or two, made a few notes and closed the folder and put it away again. At last, just when the compartment seemed about to burst into flames, the train reached Dustborough.

He had left his car in a garage in the High Street. Now, as he walked towards the centre of the town, the day seemed to Morgan to have become hotter than ever. Feet sank into the asphalt paving, so that at every step one paused, waiting for the squelching noise of mud. The dreary streets were almost deserted. A few children played beneath the arches of the railway bridge, and here and there women stood in doorways grumbling uneasily at the weather, the news and at the shortage of tomatoes and canned salmon. As he turned into the High Street, Morgan suddenly caught sight of Ma Venning, coming out of a shop. Beneath the dark straw hat her face, though flushed from the heat, wore its usual look of calm, reassuring confidence.

She greeted him smiling, and would have passed on.

'How are you?' he asked. 'Busy?'

'Yes.' She nodded down at her shopping bag. 'I'm on the morning-shift this week, and it's always a bit difficult getting things in the afternoon. Still,' she shifted the weight from one arm to the other, 'it's lucky we can buy anything at all, I suppose.'

'Mm. Well,' he raised his hat in farewell, 'we'll meet at the Council next week – ' And then, when he had already left her, he turned. 'How far do you have to cart that stuff?' he asked abruptly.

'Oh!' she glanced up at the Town Hall clock and her blue eyes, reflecting the sun, were surprisingly clear and youthful. 'I may be able to get a bus.'

Beads of sweat stood out on his forehead, and he wiped them off with a handkerchief. 'If you wait until I get my car out,' he offered unsmilingly, 'I'll give you a lift.'

'Oh!' she looked at him doubtfully, seeing the lines of exhaustion about his eyes, sensing worries at which she could not guess. 'I can manage all right – '

'No. You wait here.'

In a few minutes he returned, helping her into the car, lifting her parcels into the back seat. 'Now,' he got in beside her, 'tell me where to go.'

'Straight on.' She sat, square and comfortable, her hands folded in her lap, looking ahead as if something, perhaps the tense line of his shoulders or the way in which his lips were pressed together concealing the curve of his mouth and emphasising the jutting line of the round chin, would, if she had been watching, shown her a side of his character which he would have not wished her, or indeed anyone, to see. Pity, which came to her so easily, was suddenly overwhelming.

'Is this where I turn?' he asked.

She nodded. 'I hope I'm not taking you too far out of your way?'

'Not a bit... Tell me, how's your little Miss Widgery getting on?'

'Rose? She's living with us now – '

'Yes, I know.'

'Goodness!' she saw that he was smiling. 'There isn't much you don't know, is there?'

'I wish that were true.' He drew into the side of the road. 'Is this it?'

'Yes. Thank you.' She got out, looked at him, hesitated. 'Could I – would you care to come in and have a cup of tea?'

'Why, that's very kind of you.' He grinned, and the rough-hewn face became once more familiar. 'I was wondering whether I dare fish for an invitation – '

She laughed, her friendly, infectious laugh. 'Really, Mr Morgan, you are a one!'

And then, remembering that she had not brought the front door key she led him round the back, into the kitchen. The radio set on the table against the far wall was playing dance music, and Rose, listening and cutting bread and margarine, did not glance round as the door clicked open. Her short fair curls stood out around her head. In her flowered cotton frock she looked child-like, perfectly serene.

'You're back early, Ma,' she said, and then looked up and, seeing Morgan, blushed scarlet with pleasure and dropped the breadknife on to the floor.

He bent to pick it up. 'Well,' he smiled, looking first at her, then at the neat, gay room, taking in every detail, looking as if he were memorising the pattern of the wallpaper, the shabby comfortable furniture, the coloured pottery on the dresser, wrinkling his eyes as if he had expected to see something that was not there after all. 'You're looking fine,' he said at last. 'How's work?'

'I'm in the tailor's shop.' Rose blushed again. She was very pretty. 'I like it.'

Ma ran upstairs to put a clean towel in the bathroom, and then came down to show him the way. He cleaned and tidied himself, feeling suddenly fresh and cool and empty. As he came down the stairs he heard voices in the kitchen, and Ma saying, 'Wasn't it lucky I managed to get a cake?'

And then he went in, and there was Griselda silhouetted against the doorway, her smooth dark head framed by the sky, her face shadowed by the cool dimness of the room.

He stood suddenly still, his arms flat against his sides, his hands closing and unclosing. 'You!' he exclaimed, and the syllable was charged with such extraordinary, breathless intensity that Ma, pouring boiling water into the teapot, glanced up swiftly, in time to see the look that passed between them, a look in which eagerness, delight and something like hostility were so strangely mixed that she was, for the moment, too confused for speech.

Griselda took a step forward, and the light from the window shone on her face. The black brows were arched with amusement, the grey eyes clear and shining. 'You weren't expecting to see me?' she asked. Her light voice held an undertone of laughter.

Dan walked round the table and took the hand that she offered. 'No. I didn't expect this – '

Too late, Ma said, 'This is Miss Green. She used to live with us.'

'Yes,' Griselda turned to Ma. 'Mr Morgan knows that. We've met each other before.'

'Oh!' Ma looked again from one to the other as they retreated towards formality. 'I didn't know. I mean…' She was puzzled, but anxious not to intrude. 'Come along and sit down.' She bustled around, pouring out tea, watching them eat, fussing over Rose, getting up to fetch a pot of last year's strawberry jam, cutting the cake into chunky wedges that nobody could eat. She kept up a ceaseless ow of chatter about the factory, about the weather, about little Mrs Foster and the other people who had been injured in the air raid. Soon the awkwardness passed and Dan, asking Rose about her work, ceased to be a stranger. Rose herself, who was more at home at the Vennings than she had ever been anywhere in her life, forgot her shyness and made them laugh as she described the details of her life in the tailor's shop, cutting paper, sewing cartridge bags, making containers to hold the explosives that she no longer saw.

She was enjoying her work and, though she did not tell Dan this, was at last able to send her aunt in Devonshire ten shillings every week out of her wages without having to wonder, when she bought the postal order, whether she would be able to manage until the following Friday.

At last Dan got up to go. 'Can I drive you back to the hostel?' he asked Griselda.

'Thanks.' She turned to Ma. 'Do you mind – '

Ma shook her head. 'You go. There's no sense in waiting here and having to queue up for a bus…' She led them to the front entrance and stood in the porch, watching them until the car turned the corner. Then she went back into the house. Rose, clearing away the tea things, was humming a little tune. 'Wasn't he lovely?' she asked. 'I mean, he was just like anybody else, wasn't he?'

Ma nodded. She was still smiling, but her eyes were anxious.

Alone together, Dan and Griselda were silent, relaxed, not quite at peace. The streets were fuller now, the pavements crowded with people on their way home from work. The sky had clouded, and a steamy blanket of mist was gathering over the town as Dan threaded a way between the traffic. It was not until they were passing the rows of new villas along the Blimpton road that he turned to look at Griselda sitting beside him.

'Well?' he asked.

She stirred, smiling up at him. 'It was a lovely thing to do,' she said.

'What was?'

'Coming back with Ma. She'll never forget it – never.'

'Do you think she knew why I came?'

Again she smiled. 'Why did you?'

'You should know!'

'I?'

'You. I was looking for you… and now I've found you. But,' he went on, 'I'm glad I found you there. It's good in that house, isn't it?'

'Yes. There's something about Ma – '

'And the whole set-up. You know, the English are such cold people. Cold and sodden. But there… there it's different. I don't know what it is, but one feels it at once... you feel it, don't you?'

'I suppose I do. I go there whenever I can.' She lifted a hand, pushing back a lock of hair. 'They make me feel that – ' she paused, seeking a word '– that I belong to them. And in a way I do. But you – '

'It's like the world I came from.' His eyes narrowed, and he smiled as if at some sudden memory. 'Did I ever tell you about the day my cousin Emrys got married?'

'No?'

He laughed. 'It's a good story. I was only a kid at the time – ' he broke off as they came to the crossroads. 'What shift are you on this week?' he asked abruptly.

'Mornings.'

'Good. That gives us a whole evening. Can you stand that roadhouse place again?'

'I should think so! But,' she smoothed the gingham dress over her knees, 'I don't look very – very civilised.'

'Hoh! Civilised! Who wants to look civilised?' Now, at last, they were out of the town, and the air was suddenly much cooler, fresh and full of summer. 'If you feel cold later on, I've got a coat that we can put around you.'

'Fine.' The rich smell of cow parsley filled the narrow lane. 'Now tell me about your cousin Emrys.'

He began to tell it, and she listened, absorbed, laughing now and then at some vivid touch of detail, stopping him once or twice to ask a question. And then they were at the roadhouse.

'How's the new job?' he asked when dinner had been ordered. 'When are you going to start?'

'Next week, I hope.' She told him that she had been interviewed by Dr Gower, and that Gower was recommending that she should be attached to the Medical Department as temporary hygiene officer. 'He wants me to begin at once,' she explained, 'but he said he couldn't take me on until the papers had gone through – I suppose the Principal Clerk has to approve, or something?'

'Something like that,' he agreed. 'Or maybe it'll have to go to the Ministry to be okayed.'

She put down her drink and took a deep puff at her cigarette.

'Why should the Ministry come into it?' she asked, staring past him out of the window as she spoke.

'Oh!' he grinned, his manner easy and confident. 'You know what these formalities are – ' Then, seeing how rigidly she sat, how wide were her eyes as they looked past him unseeing, he added, 'Don't worry – they won't turn you down.'

'Then – why all the fuss?'

'Oh!' he shrugged his shoulders. 'The red-tape worms are afraid we shall begin to imagine that we're running our own factory if we're allowed to buy a tin-tack or take on a charwoman without getting their permission first. You'll learn that for yourself within the next week or two.'

'Is it – ' she looked at him, wide-eyed, 'is it so bad?'

'Sometimes. Not always. I spent six hours in the Ministry today, and it's given me a pretty jaundiced view. But some of those boys are all right. There was a chap I was talking to this morning... but I don't want to bore you.'

'Go on. I like it.' She sat forward, eager, interested, and he began to tell her something about his journey to London, leaving the details vague, but describing some of the people he had met and the difficulties he had had in trying to make them understand his point of view. And then he went on to tell her about the quarrel he had had with Russell in Cincinnati, so long ago now that it seemed almost as if it had happened in another world. But as he talked, telling her things which he had never mentioned to anyone, incidents so trivial and yet so preposterous that for years it had been impossible to think of them without shame, the last of his weariness seemed to fall away. His face was alive with enthusiasm as he described, with extraordinary clarity of detail, the huge factory in which he had been employed, so varied, noisy and crowded: a factory so different from, and yet so much like, Blimpton, where the most intricate machine tools were produced with, it sometimes seemed, less difficulty and less effort than was needed at Blimpton to fill a truckload of 25-pounder shells.

'And why did you leave?' she asked at last.

'Because – well, after that quarrel with Russell it was impossible to stay.' He brought out his pocket-book and paid the bill. 'I don't know why I'm telling you all this,' he added as they made ready to go. 'I've never talked to anyone this way before. And now – ' he followed her down the steps, 'now that I've managed to get hold of you I...' he broke off, watching her as she got into the car.

'Well?'

He grinned with his habitual self-mockery. 'I treat you as if you were a public meeting – you!'

'But you wouldn't – you couldn't – tell so much to a public meeting...'

'And you think that's the only difference?'

She did not reply, and for some time they drove in silence, feeling the stillness of the empty lanes, and the sudden quietness that settled around them as the evening gathered. As the sky paled the colours of the fields and hedges sharpened, and the contours of the distant hills grew misty. Presently the moon would rise, but now the countryside, suspended between day and night, had a sharp and fleeting beauty. Dan, driving slowly, put out a hand and touched Griselda lightly on the arm. 'Happy?' he asked.

Her smile, as he turned towards him, was dream-like, remote. 'Very,' she assented softly.

'Like to get out and walk a bit?'

She nodded. 'I'd no idea that there was such lovely country around here.'

'Ah! There are a lot of things that I can show you.'

He drew into the side of the road, and they crossed a stile into a field of late hay, newly mown. The gate at the far end of the field led on to a patch of open heath. Behind it, where the chestnut woods had been thinned, the grass gave way to willow herb, the tall spiky flowers turning from purple to red in the evening light. Before them the land fell away, and below, in the distance, they could see a white mist rising over Blimpton, hiding the factory from sight.

'You see it?' he asked.

At first it seemed that she did not understand, and then, looking into his face, seeing the proud curve around his mouth and the brightness of his round yellow eyes, she asked: 'Where?'

He pointed. 'Do you remember that first day – ?'

'When we came bouncing into your room?' her laughter was uncertain, a little shaky. 'I've often wondered what you thought of us...'

'My dear,' he paused, facing her, meeting her upturned glance. His hands, clenching and unclenching at his sides, were lifted now, poised half-outstretched. 'My dear, I've been thinking about you ever since... I don't know why, and I've been trying not to... you know that. But today – today I realised that it's no use trying any more...'

The moon was high overhead as they made their way back through the fields towards the road. They walked side by side, quietly, their hands touching, their faces peaceful. Then, as they reached the last stile, Dan stopped, and she saw that he was smiling.

'Yes?' she asked.

He stood looking at her, his hands on her shoulders, holding her away from him. 'And now,' he asked, 'now what?'

'What...?'

'I mean,' he released her so abruptly that she almost fell, 'that the next thing we have to do is to get married – '

'Married!'

She sounded so astonished that he laughed. 'People do, you know,' he said easily. 'It's quite usual...' Then, seeing that she was not looking at him, and that her eyes, unfocused, were suddenly clouded, he asked: 'Is there any reason why we shouldn't?'

The abruptness of his tone was startling, out of key. She glanced up, and as she met his gaze she smiled. 'But you don't know anything about me?' she said. A spasm of doubt crossed her face. 'Do you?'

'I know all that I need to know.' He lifted his arms and again held her by the shoulders. 'And there's a lot that you still have to find out about me...'

'Is there?'

Again he laughed. 'Plenty. Too much – and some of it I hope you won't ever need to know...' He drew her towards him once more, and she lifted her face to his.

After that they did not speak again until the car stopped outside the entrance to the hostel. And then he said: 'Ring me tomorrow. At five o'clock... tomorrow we'll talk.'

Five minutes later she sat down on the grass outside the dormitory block and took off her shoes. Then she tried the door. The catch was unfastened and she slipped in quietly and hurried down the corridor in her stockinged feet. Her cubicle was number 47 and the hinges creaked. She did not turn on the light, but groped along the shelf beside the bed, trying to find her torch.

On the other side of the partition made by the wardrobe cupboards Betty Sims woke up. 'Gosh!' she yawned, 'is it morning already?'

'No. Go to sleep.'

'Had a good time?' Betty sat up, reaching out to switch on the light.

'Mm. I don't need a light. I'll unfasten the blackout.'

'Okay. Oh – there's a letter for you. I brought it along.'

'Thanks.' Griselda shook out her hair and slipped off her dress.

'Aren't you going to read it?'

'In the morning...'

Betty was fidgeting noisily. The thick blanket had fallen off the bed. 'I can't find my feet,' she grumbled sleepily. 'That letter looked important. I put it over the washbasin so you shouldn't miss it.' She turned over on to her left side, straightening out the sheet. 'You must have some posh boyfriends to write to you on that paper – '

'Which paper?'

The washbasin was between the two windows, in the small space where the partition ended and the two halves of the room joined. The envelope, made of thick blue paper, had been placed on the glass shelf, and propped up by a tube of toothpaste. Griselda picked it up, staring blankly at the cramped, laborious handwriting. At last she opened it.

'Dear Griselda,' Gunn had written, *'I told you they weren't as dumb as all that at Blimpton. They know. This morning I was in the Ministry, telephoning. I got a crossed line. Some guy was saying to some other guy, What price old Outrage's daughter working at Blimpton? So the other guy said, Is that*

so? So then I said who the hell are you? And this first guy, he said, who the hell do you think you are butting into a private conversation, for all you know I might be the Minister himself. So then I got mad, and I said seeing that I'm Lord Outrage's personal representative – and then he rang off. I got the operator, but she couldn't trace the call. There it is, though. They know, Brown, Morgan, the whole bunch. I won't tell the old man until you give me the okay. You can ring me at the Ministry when you get this.'

Griselda read it again, and then a third time. The paper fell out of her hand on to the floor. She picked it up, tore it into small pieces, and put the scraps into an ashtray and set them on fire. She sat on the edge of the bed, looking round the cubicle as if seeing it for the first time: the green paint, the half-shaded light, the stain on the floor where a former occupant had spilled a bottle of nail varnish, the patch on the wall where the plaster had flaked off leaving a white island, the shape of Celebes, in the yellow distemper. She looked at all these things for a long time, and then at last got up, pulled out her cupboard suitcase from under the bed, and began to pack.

Betty sat up again. 'What are you doing?' she asked.

'Packing. I have to go to London in the morning.'

'You're not leaving?'

'I don't know. I hope not.'

'But they won't let you leave!' Betty jumped out of bed and put her head round the partition. 'Did you have bad news?' she asked, sympathy and curiosity mingling in her voice.

'I don't know. I have to see someone and make sure.'

'Oh!' Betty crawled back into bed. After a moment she asked: 'Is he really awfully gone on you?'

'Who?'

'Your boyfriend. The one you went out with.'

Griselda, fastening her luggage, suddenly looked very pale. 'I don't know,' she said. 'That's what I have to find out.' But the words, spoken only to herself, were inaudible on the other side of the partition.

FORTY

NEXT MORNING MORGAN came down to breakfast early. The dining room was empty, but he could hear the maids clattering about in the kitchen next door. He sat down at his accustomed place, and it was then that he noticed that there were flowers on the tables. He got up and went towards the window. Outside, the lawn was newly mown, and the heap of sand that should have been shovelled into bags six or seven months ago had at last disappeared. There was a light patch in the corner under the cedar tree where it had been lying. In the flowerbed at the other side of the garden the seed pods had been picked from the lupins, and the dahlias, not yet ready to flower, had been tied to bamboo supports.

He turned as he heard someone enter the room. It was Dolphin, dressed in a light summer suit with a pale green shirt and a tie to match. His plump pale face had lost its usual look of moon-like aloofness and he seemed excited, almost agitated by his eagerness to be first with what was evidently the best piece of gossip to have come his way for some time.

'Well?' Morgan asked as he sat down once more. 'What's been happening?'

'Don't you know?'

'Would I be asking if I did?' Morgan grinned slightly. He was perhaps the only member of the senior staff who did not need to be buoyed up by a constant sense of his own omniscience, and this willingness to admit ignorance was, he sometimes suspected, the chief reason for his popularity in Mowbray Lodge. 'Well, what is it?' he asked again as Dolphin continued to goggle at his own reflection in the mirror over the sideboard.

'That's just it!' Dolphin exclaimed. 'I don't know. Nobody seems to know for certain, but I rather think…'

'Yes?'

'Well, perhaps a royal visit.' He broke over as a maid came into the room carrying bacon on a tray and two pots of tea. 'Otherwise,' he continued as she closed the door behind her, 'why shouldn't they have told us?'

Morgan took a deep draught of the hot tea. 'Oh, we'd have been told,' he said. He looked very alert, his round eyes bright with amusement.

'But would we? Now, when I was down at Pinton – '

The entrance of Miss Creed brought him to a stop. 'Good morning,' she greeted them, bowing slightly at Morgan as if to stress the distinction between the deference due to the Assistant Superintendent and the contempt which she felt for the Public Relations Officer. And then, on her way to the table which she shared with Knowles, she suddenly stopped. 'By the way, Mr Morgan,' her smile was hollow, ingratiating, and as she leaned forward her beads clicked against the back of a chair, 'I do hope that you got Mr Gittins' message?'

'Which message?'

'Oh!' her long, lipless mouth pursed in disapproval. 'He was ringing up the whole evening, asking for you to get in touch with him. We simply couldn't trace where you'd got to... and Dr Aaron was out too when he tried to get in touch with her – '

'Yes.' Dolphin broke in, 'I saw her when I happened to drop in at the White Lion. She seemed to be with Finch. At least – '

'The White Lion!' Miss Creed repeated. 'Isn't that where that girl Little – or whatever her name is – comes from? I wanted to ask you about her – '

'Yes,' Dolphin waited, thinking, as he had often thought recently, that it was high time that he got rid of Mavis Little; for Mavis, now that Gunn's interest in her had evaporated, spent most of her working day in one or other of the canteens in the company of shop-managers, assistant labour officers and such members of the administrative staff as had a taste for blondes. She gathered, Dolphin suspected, almost as much gossip about the factory as Gittins himself and, he was pretty sure, spent her evenings retailing it to her father and his friends in the private sitting room of the White Lion. Nevertheless, Dolphin resolved as he straightened his shoulders and waited for what was to come next, if Miss Creed wanted him to sack Mavis then there could be no doubt at all that the girl would have to stay...

Morgan pushed his plate away and got up hurriedly. It was still only a little after eight, but when he reached the factory Gittins was already there, waiting in the Assistant Superintendent's room. He, at least, looked as shabby, down at heel, lively and faintly worried as usual. 'Thank God you've come!' he exclaimed. 'Have you heard what's happened?' Then he looked at the other man. Morgan had picked up, from the table that ran along the wall, two rounds of armour-piercing shot, and held them, balanced in the long brass cartridge-cases, one in each hand. They were heavy, difficult to balance, but he waved them as if they were no more than hollowed pieces of wood. 'Whatever's happened to you?' Gittins asked, and the habitual look of anxiety on his face deepened.

'Oh, that's how I feel this morning!' Morgan grinned and replaced the missiles on the table. Happiness seemed to be bursting out of him. 'Who's coming? The Minister?'

Gittins nodded. 'But that's not all of it. They rang from the Private Office yesterday afternoon to tell us, and the Superintendent wasn't here to take the call – '

'Well?'

'And he hasn't turned up since.' Gittins sat down wearily and began to rub the bald patch at the back of his head. 'I can't think where the devil he's got to. And the Minister's due to arrive at eleven-thirty – '

'Well, if he will come down at such short notice he's only got himself to thank if he feels that he's not being treated with proper reverence – '

'Oh, be serious!'

'I am serious.' Morgan flung himself into a chair and lit a cigarette. 'What are we going to do with the old boy when he turns up? Give him the dirt?' He jumped up. 'What an opportunity! And why shouldn't we? Why shouldn't we tell him everything – everything – we think he ought to know? That business of Knowles refusing to take the fitters he was offered and then passing the buck to that poor devil Parsons – '

'Something has got moving on that,' Gittins interrupted. 'Yesterday. I'll tell you later. But now – '

'Yes! Now! Why shouldn't we tell the Minister about Brown's little racket – because it is a racket – with those tenth-rate thugs in Dustborough? Don't you think he ought to be told that the Superintendent of one of his own factories is touting for contracts for firms that ought to be closed down? Oughtn't he to know that Brown is getting a rake-off for keeping us short of labour? – because that's what it amounts to. I couldn't get anyone at the Ministry to listen to me – at least I don't think they were listening – so why shouldn't we take this chance? Can you see why not?'

Gittins had turned suddenly pale as he realised that Morgan, though speaking lightly, was not joking. 'You can't!' he protested. 'You just can't do a thing like that. We'd be disgraced – '

'But if the Minister found that we were right?'

'There's the Secretary to consider. And the traditions of the service – '

'Meaning that ministers come and go but permanent secretaries nurse their grudges for ever?'

Gittins moved a hand and his pipe fell noisily on to the floor. 'Could you,' he pleaded, 'could you just stop being frivolous?' Age, which he had for so long warded off, seemed now to creep upon him. The furrows in his face no longer expressed humour, but only a patient, dogged anxiety. 'We've a lot of things to fix up for this visit. I've made a tentative programme – '

The door opened to admit Miss Gadd, the Superintendent's secretary. 'Could you come along to Mr Brown's room at once?' she asked, and retreated.

The Superintendent was sitting behind his desk, turning over a pile of minutes. 'Why didn't you let me know about this visit?' he demanded. This morning his complexion had taken on a new shade of purple. His eyelids were puffy, and his small eyes were half hidden beneath the beetling brows.

Gittins said: 'We tried to get you. I tried everywhere. If I'd known you were going to be away yesterday – '

'Never mind that. Now what's the drill?' Wherever he had been he had, it was evident, returned to Blimpton several hours ago, and his own plans for the Minister's visit were far advanced. They consisted, as far as Morgan and Gittins could understand, chiefly of arrangements for a private luncheon party at the Superintendent's house and of plans to secure that Lord Outrage should see, and be seen by, as few people as possible. 'But in case he wants to go round some of the Groups – ' Brown turned to Morgan, 'you might take a run round and see how things are looking – '

The run round, hurried as it was, took nearly two hours. By the time Morgan returned to the Administration Block a message had been received from London to say that the Minister would not be coming after all, or at any rate not for the next few days.

'And that means,' Gittins ruminated comfortably, 'the next time someone suggests that he should come to Blimpton he'll think that he's already been... Thank God for that. But I wish I knew what Brown had been up to... I can't think where he hides himself...'

Morgan shook his head. 'Tell me about Knowles,' he suggested.

There was not very much to tell. Knowles had, it seemed, been instructed to report to the Ministry at the end of the week and Gittins' informant had hinted that the Chief Controller was at last aware that the lack of fitters in the Blimpton factory had been due to Knowles' refusal to accept men from EELS. 'I still believe,' Gittins repeated, 'that if the men had been here we shouldn't have had that explosion... and if you ask me, that'll be the last we shall see of Knowles...'

Then Knowles himself came in, to complain that Gower had disorganised the routine of the Labour Office staff by his insistence that the medical officers should be informed when workers stayed away on grounds of sickness. The Senior Labour Manager was more than usually incoherent, and the tip of his long nose quivered each time he reached the end of a sentence. 'But this is a matter for the Superintendent to settle,' Morgan reminded him once or twice.

'I know. But the difficulty is...'

As soon as he had gone it was time for lunch. In the afternoon there was a meeting of the maintenance staff to be attended. After that plans for the building of additional storage accommodation had to be discussed with Dawson and an architect from the Ministry. Then Finch had to be given a chance to explain why he was not responsible for the loss in transit of five truckloads of bombs. Next, Morgan had to help the Superintendent to sort out the various new programmes that had been issued during the past two or three weeks. At five he returned to his room, and when, at ten minutes past, Griselda had not telephoned, he began to be impatient. At 5.15 he had to attend a meeting with the Factory Security Officer and the head of the Inspection Department in the Superintendent's room. 'If anyone rings,' he told his secretary, 'have the calls transferred. All of them.' When, by 5.30, the Superintendent had answered the telephone six or seven times he observed, with a snort of irritation, that if Morgan's secretary was not capable of taking a telephone message she had better be transferred to fuze-filling. At six Morgan returned to his own room to scan, in vain, the list of messages that lay on his desk. At 6.30 he telephoned to the hostel and was told by the operator at the other end that messages could only be taken for residents in the event of the illness or death of a near relative. He gave his name angrily, and made a note that the regulation should be at once relaxed. Ten minutes later he told his secretary to ring Miss Marshall and inquire if Miss Green could be found. Half an hour after that a message from Miss Marshall's deputy arrived, which stated that Miss Green had left the hostel early that morning and that it was not certain when she would be returning.

And then Gittins came in again. 'Not gone home?' he asked.

'Obviously.' Morgan tilted back his chair, and stared vaguely around the room. His round head was silhouetted against the window frame, and his face was in shadow.

'What's the matter?' Gittins asked. His tone was affectionate. He liked his friends better when they were in trouble.

'Nothing. At least – '

'Yes?'

'Nothing. I hope nothing.' Morgan stood up. He looked now extremely exhausted.

Gittins took a step further into the room. 'Come back and have a bite with me and the missis,' he suggested. 'I want to talk to you about one or two things that have cropped up...'

FORTY-ONE

ON THAT SAME afternoon Ma Venning arrived home from the factory to find Griselda sitting in the kitchen.

'Why!' Ma exclaimed as she bent to put down the big bag of potatoes that she had been carrying. 'What a pleasant surprise! I didn't think of you coming round again today – and so soon after work, too!'

Griselda got up. She seemed to have some difficulty in standing, and her hands, clutching the back of the chair, were rigid, the muscles tense. She was very pale, and there were deep shadows under her eyes and around her mouth. 'I didn't go to the factory today,' she began tentatively. Her clear, light voice sounded as if it were about to break.

Ma hung up her hat behind the door. 'Sit down, love,' she commanded. 'Aren't you feeling well?'

'It's not that.' Griselda stared around at the dim familiar room. Her eyes were wary. 'Are you expecting anyone?' she asked.

'No, not that I know of.' Ma came closer and, putting a hand on the girl's shoulder, peered into her face. 'What is it?' she asked. 'How long've you been waiting?'

'All day. I was going up to London on the early train and then I felt – I felt I must see you first. I think – I think I've come to say goodbye.'

'Oh, no!' Ma shook her head good humouredly. Her thick grey hair was as smooth as when she had put it up that morning. Beneath it her rosy face was reassuring, unperturbed. 'I'll make a cup of tea,' she suggested, tackling the situation in the usual way.

But when the tea was made Griselda was still sitting with her hands in her lap, her head thrown back, emphasising the curve of her chin and the slender line of her neck. 'You're sure there's no one coming?' she asked again.

'Well, you know how it is,' Ma began to pour out the tea. 'I'm not expecting anyone. But then, we weren't expecting Mr Morgan yesterday, were we?'

'No... I wasn't thinking of anyone like that... Ma, I wish I'd told you all about myself before…'

'My dear, I've never wanted to know anything that you didn't want to tell. Of course, we always knew that you were – '

'What?'

'Well – not our class. I mean, you speak differently, and – and there were such a lot of little things you didn't know when you first came.'

'Yes.' The shadow of a smile hovered around the girl's mouth, and then was gone. 'You've taught me such a lot of the things one ought to know – '

The front door banged, and she broke off. A moment later Kitty bounced into the room. She wore a tight pink frock with a spray of artificial flowers at the neck. Her face was flushed and healthy, shining with excitement. 'Gosh!' she exclaimed, 'I've got to hurry!' She and young Jim Venning, who was home on leave, had arranged, she explained, to meet at the tea-shop opposite the cinema. Ma bustled her upstairs. 'And you'd better go out the front way,' she suggested. 'Griselda and I want to talk quietly for a bit…'

'Talk! Gosh, don't we all talk enough in the factory?' She rushed upstairs and in a moment or so they could hear her singing in her bedroom.

'You see,' Griselda began again, 'In a way I was in the same position as Kitty. But not quite. My husband was killed, but I pretended not to have been married because – because all that hadn't meant very much to me.' She shook her head, and her dark hair fell limp and soft over her forehead. 'I don't know why… I wasn't really alive before I came here… Oh, I had what the girls call a good time. My father's rich, and famous – ' this time a smile began in her eyes ' – but not your sort, Ma. He gave me everything that I wanted – everything that he thought I wanted or that he thought I ought to want. I didn't have a chance… a chance to learn to do things for myself, to find out what I'm made of… and then I came here. I thought it would be hell, and it wasn't. I've had a wonderful time – '

'Then – '

'No. Listen to me. I've worked. I've made friends. I've – ' She stopped and lit a cigarette. 'And then,' she went on, speaking rather more calmly, 'I was offered this new job, helping Dr Gower. I thought that I'd got that – and other things – on my merits. Because of what I am, not because of who I am… and last night I got a letter to tell me that they'd known all the time – the Superintendent, Mr Morgan, everyone – '

'Known what?'

'About my father. You see, he's the Minister – '

Ma said gently: 'I don't think I understand.'

'My father is the Minister of Weapon Production and that's why – ' suddenly she leaned forward and buried her face in her hands. Her body shook with sobs, but no tears came. Ma got up quietly and emptied the teapot. Then she came back. Her placid face was furrowed, and she seemed to be looking for a meaning that eluded her. 'It doesn't make any difference,' she said firmly. 'My father – of course he was only a miner – always voted Conservative. Always.'

Griselda lifted her face, contorted in a spasm of hysterical laughter. 'Oh, Ma!' she exclaimed, and then she sobered. 'Don't you see, she explained laboriously, 'that the point is not what his politics are, but the position he holds? Don't you realise that they have to promote me, because if they recognise my – my qualities – someone is going to recognise theirs and they'll all get promoted for being clever enough to recognise that I'm an important person, a big shot at one remove? I came to Blimpton to be myself and everything that I've got – everything – has been because I'm my father's daughter… people haven't wanted me for myself – '

'That isn't true!'

'It is… I can't tell you everything. But I know it is. And now I'm going home.'

FORTY-TWO

SHE WENT, and she did not come back.

'Where's that girl you were sending over to me?' Gower asked Morgan at lunch on Monday.

'*I* don't know,' Morgan replied stiffly. 'Why should I?'

'I thought – well, you found her.'

Morgan got up suddenly. 'And now I've lost her,' he said and hurried out of the room.

But Gower rushed after him. 'If she doesn't come,' he insisted, 'we'll have to get someone else – '

'Okay,' Morgan's face was blank. 'But give her a chance. She'll probably turn up.'

But when, after a week, nothing had been heard of her, Gower insisted that someone else should be appointed to help the medical officers to clean-up the West Group. Miss Creed, hearing of this, decided to appeal direct to the Superintendent. Now that it was known that Captain Knowles would not be returning to Blimpton but was, instead, to be transferred to a new factory in Scotland, people were already speculating about the choice of a successor. Miss Creed, certain of her own worthiness but not entirely convinced that the judgment of her superiors was to be relied upon, was determined to make her position secure. 'In my opinion – for what that may be worth – ' she began, 'the duty of supervising the cleanliness of the workers should rest with the Labour Department.'

'But I thought your people already had too much to do?' the Superintendent asked.

'But if I had more staff – ' Miss Creed's large pale face flushed as she wondered whether the abandonment of the plural pronoun had not perhaps been premature.

'Well, I'll think it over,' the Superintendent conceded, anxious not to precipitate another boundary dispute between the medical officers and the labour managers over the division of their duties. Then he allowed himself to forget the problem. But during the next three or four weeks a sudden leap in the curve of the dermatitis chart made it obvious that something would have to be done. Finally it was agreed that Phoebe Braithwaite should be lent to assist Dr Gower, and that she, in turn, should be helped by three assistant forewomen, one from each shift, who would ensure that the regulations prescribed by Gower were in fact carried out. Among those chosen was Norah; and Norah, who was extraordinarily happy because Tom Walton had not, after all, been sent abroad but had gone, instead, to Scotland to finish his training, seized the job as if she had been waiting for it since she first came to the factory. During the months in which she had worked as an assistant forewoman she had learned most of the basic facts about the nature of the industrial hazards to which workers were subjected and she had often discussed the measures that were needed to raise the general level of health in the factory. Now it seemed that the reforms for which so many people had been clamouring were at last going to be made, at any rate on the West Group; and Norah was certain that later, but not much later, these reforms would be extended to the whole of the factory. Gittins, Dawson, the head of the works department and the chief electrician had agreed that the ablution rooms should be redecorated. But when one morning workmen arrived with coils of electric wiring and buckets of chocolate-coloured paint, it was realised that no detailed scheme had been worked out, and that sanction had not been given for the expenditure involved.

Phoebe, with a colour-chart in one hand and a bundle of sample curtain materials in the other, rushed about, panic-stricken.

'What do you think?' she asked Norah, straightening out a crumpled fragment of cretonne as she spoke, 'blue daisies on a pink ground, or – '

Norah didn't know. 'Something cheerful,' she suggested vaguely, wishing that Griselda were there to advise. 'I'm not very hot on colour-schemes,' she confessed. 'Why shouldn't we ask the girls in the shops to vote?'

'Vote?' Phoebe asked, blinking in the strong sunlight. 'Vote on what?' She thought the whole business silly and rather beneath her dignity. If she had wanted to spend her life in choosing curtain materials, she reflected with disgust, she might just as well have stayed at home...

'On what sort of curtains they would like,' Norah explained. 'It would make them feel – well, sort of – ' she searched for the word ' – responsible.'

'Well, really!' Phoebe took off her spectacles and polished the lenses, 'what a very peculiar suggestion!' And then, looking again at Norah's eager face, and remembering, as she did so, that in any case the material could not be ordered until the Principal Clerk had given the necessary financial sanction, she added, 'perhaps we might…'

So a notice was posted in the Group Canteen, half a dozen samples were hung along the walls and arrangements were made to collect the votes. The men on the group were at first inclined to jeer, and some of the women remarked that the idea was childish, but then they began to wrangle about the respective merits of the different designs put up for their inspection, and suddenly the whole thing was an immense success. Paints and distempers were matched against the material chosen, Gittins' approval was conveyed, through Miss Creed, in writing, and, as the workmen stripped the walls, gouged out the old lighting-fitments, put up shelves and laid long strips of mirror above them, everybody, or almost everybody, began to take an interest. Phoebe relaxed a little and, basking in an approval wider than she had ever imagined possible, found herself consulting Norah about what should be done next.

'Towels,' Norah said.

'We've got them.' It was difficult to believe it, but they had.

Norah brightened. 'Then uniforms – '

But Miss Creed refused to consider the suggestion that a new cap should be designed and that the drab uniforms should be brightened by coloured cravats and belts and shoe-laces. 'It's preposterous!' she declared, 'perfectly preposterous!'

Phoebe hesitated. 'It was Dr Aaron's idea,' she said, nervous lest her loyalty to Miss Creed should seem to be in doubt. 'And Mr Parsons – '

'Oh, Mr Parsons!' A quiver of distaste appeared in Miss Creed's voice. Then, as she hustled Phoebe out of the room, she sat down to wonder once more what she was to do about Parsons. Her certainty that she would be appointed to take Knowles' place had, as days and then weeks passed, begun to wilt a little. Now she was growing impatient. It was, she knew, not impossible that the Ministry might decide to send some complete stranger to take charge, and it was against this contingency that she had tried to arm herself by entering into an alliance with Parsons. This alliance was, however, curiously lop-sided. Indeed, Parsons did not seem to have noticed its existence; nor, Miss Creed reflected, did he seem to understand that if a newcomer were made head of the department his own position, as well as hers, might be jeopardised. The trouble, she concluded, was that Parsons had not been a civil servant long enough to have earned the importance of having a proper status in the factory hierarchy. He worked hard, never complained that he had too much to do, and was polite and considerate in meeting Miss Creed's demands. But he was independent. Too independent, Miss Creed repeated to herself as she nibbled at a stale and soggy biscuit. Then, all at once, with the bitter taste of stale tea in her mouth, it flashed across her, in one of those moments of intuition that came to her so seldom, that perhaps it was Parsons and not herself who was to be made Senior Labour Manager.

Nevertheless, her astonishment when the announcement was made public and she found that she had guessed right, was unbounded, almost overwhelming. She was at first speechless, and then angry, and then, with no one near in whom she could confide her indignation, deeply, horribly humiliated. She would have liked to persuade herself that a mistake had been made: but of that there was no possibility at all, since before coming to a decision Phipps and Crabtree had paid a joint visit to the factory and had, everybody knew, congratulated the Superintendent on the excellence of the work being undertaken by Gower and Parsons. After that, Miss Creed realised, too late, she should have recognised that Parsons' appointment was inevitable... though in what way he had contributed to the astonishing reduction in the number of cases of dermatitis she entirely failed to understand.

She thought of resigning, and even went so far as to draft a letter to Knowles suggesting that if there were a vacancy in the Scottish factory she might be prepared to consider it; but for several weeks the letter remained in her desk, partly because she was uncertain of what Knowles' reply would be, and partly, too, because she began to hope that she might be able to manage Parsons after all...

FORTY-THREE

PARSONS CONFESSED HIMSELF to be somewhat overcome by the honour that had been paid him.

'Honour!' Morgan scoffed. 'Honour be damned! This isn't a decoration that you're getting. It's a job, and you know it. It'll be a hell of a sweat – but you know that, too… and you know, or you ought to know, what some of us expect of you – ' he broke off, staring out of the window, his face moody. 'Why don't you take a week's leave?' he asked, 'and give yourself time to plan things out – get fit for the winter – take the kids to the seaside…'

'Later, perhaps.' Parsons was standing in front of the fireplace, looking around the room. 'Isn't it time you had a holiday yourself?' he asked, thinking it odd that he should use his new sense of authority for the first time to say something that almost everyone had been trying, and failing, to express for nearly two months.

'A holiday! Why should I want a holiday?' Morgan asked. 'Do I look as if I need a holiday?' He grinned, half-angrily. 'Well,' he lit another cigarette, 'I did intend to get a few days off back in the summer… and then my girl ran out on me – ' He jumped up and began to pace around the room. 'Why the devil should I tell you that?' he demanded.

Parsons did not reply. Instead, he began to discuss his plans for reorganising the work of the Labour Department. He was slow, but confident and enthusiastic. His dark hair was beginning to turn grey, but his eyes were younger than they had been when he first came to the factory, and his square and solid bearing had a new suggestion of authority. 'Now that we're at last getting the labour we need,' he concluded, 'we can really expect to get some of our own internal problems settled – '

He broke off as Gittins came in. 'Busy?' the Principal Clerk asked. Parsons said: 'I must go,' and left them.

'Well?' Morgan asked. His voice expressed no interest.

Gittins, looking infinitely old and full of malicious wisdom, took out his tobacco pouch and began to fill his pipe, prolonging the moment. 'Gurneys,' he said at last.

'Yes?'

'Jervis popped in just now, on his way to Ratchford. He couldn't stay, but he said – ' Gittins paused once more, pushing down the tobacco into the bowl of his pipe.

'Out with it!'

'Well, of course this is highly confidential, and old Jervis had no right to tell me…' he looked around as if to make doubly sure that they were alone. 'It seems that there's a high-level inquiry going on in the Ministry about the activities of – ' he jerked his thumb in the direction of the Superintendent's room.

A gleam appeared in Morgan's yellow eyes. 'There is?'

'Mm. Somebody got on to something. And then someone remembered something that you'd said when you were up in town during the summer… it seems that the stuff that Gurney had been turning out didn't pass inspection… and someone wanted to know why they'd landed another contract… they haven't got to the bottom of it yet, but there seems no doubt that there's been some funny business… couple of chaps in the Directorate of Ancillary Articles have been suspended from duty – '

'Whew!'

'So at any moment now…' he got up. 'I thought you'd like to know,' he finished, and then moved towards the door. 'By the way,' he paused, 'Jervis mentioned another queer rumour that's going the rounds… Do you remember that girl Gower wanted to have over in his department – a girl called Green?'

Morgan met the other's glance, his face expressionless. 'Yes,' he agreed, 'I remember her.'

'Well,' Gittins shook his head, with smiling unbelief, 'someone told Jervis that she's the Minister's daughter – '

'The – !' Morgan put a hand to his head, rubbing his left temple. 'What minister?' he asked blankly.

'Our Minister. Old Outrage… I said I couldn't swallow that one – I mean – '

'*That* girl? You mean Griselda Green?'

'Mm. You met her, didn't you?'

'Oh, yes. I met her…'

'What was she like?'

'Like?' Morgan was wiping the sweat off his forehead with a handkerchief. 'I really couldn't tell you,' he said. 'But – oh, I don't know...'

'She didn't say anything to you?'

'To me? No – it can't be... Who started this story, anyway?' he asked. 'Where did Jervis get it from?'

Gittins advanced into the room again. 'From some fellow in Establishments,' he said. 'As a matter of fact it sounds quite authentic, only... it's just impossible, isn't it?'

'I don't know.' Morgan shook his head. 'I suppose... Yes. It could be true. Go on,' he said. 'Tell me.'

'Well, it seems that when we sent up the papers for her promotion this fellow – Jervis did say who he was, but it's no one we know – he sort of smelt something funny, and tried to check up a bit... The old man has a daughter, you know... Jervis says it all fits in – of course, nobody's talking, but, well – ' he rambled on, recounting what he could remember of Jervis' story. 'Why did she leave?' he asked.

'Leave? God knows!' Morgan was sitting back now, holding on to the arms of his desk-chair, clinging to his surface of composure.

'I wonder whether there's anything in it... I suppose I could find out?'

'I don't doubt it. I've often thought – ' suddenly Morgan was on his feet, his eyes bright with rage '– we ought to make an example of that girl – '

'How? What for?'

'For running away when she had a job to do. Report her to the Ministry of Labour. You've been saying for weeks that we ought to get a prosecution under the Essential Work Order. Much better get a girl like that sent to prison than some poor little woman who's staying at home to do the family wash – '

'Prosecute! Yes, but – well, supposing she really is the Minister's daughter?'

'So much the better. It'll serve her right – '

'They wouldn't do it!'

'Not if they knew who she was – but they needn't be told – '

'Anyway, she's probably no more the old man's daughter than I'm your grandmother,' Gittins pointed out rather uncertainly.

'Oh, yes, she is!'

Gittins gave the other man a slow, curious look. 'You seem very sure, all of a sudden,' he remarked.

'Yes… yes, I understand a lot of things now,' Morgan glanced up at the clock. 'Hell! I ought to have been over on South ten minutes ago…'

FORTY-FOUR

THE SUPERINTENDENT WAS summoned to the Ministry for an interview. If he knew why the Chief Controller had sent for him, he succeeded in keeping this knowledge to himself, and only an increasing irritation in his manner and a growing tendency to repeat, to whoever happened to come into his office, excerpts from the better-known anecdotes about his early life revealed that anything was the matter. He was still preoccupied by the problems presented by his cook, and, an hour before he left, confided in Gittins that he was afraid that he would have to let the woman go.

'I can't think what's happened to her,' he grumbled. 'Why, only last night...' but his description of the soupe a l'oignon that she had given him at dinner lacked, as he would himself have said, body. 'By the way,' he continued, 'that fellow Gunn rang up just now to say that he's on his way down here. I tried to put him off for a day or two, until I get back – but you know what he's like... No sense of proportion... Well, you and Morgan will be able to handle him, no doubt – '

'And you'll be returning on Thursday?'

'Or Friday morning at the latest.' He pushed the bell on his desk. 'Where's that wretched girl got to now?' he muttered. But Miss Gadd, perpetually indifferent to anyone's needs but her own, was sitting cosily in the canteen, trying to ward off the chill of autumn with a cup of hot cocoa.

'If you ask me,' she was saying to Mavis Little, 'the old squirt's got himself into a spot of trouble with the high-ups.'

'Is that so?' Mavis shook out her hair and surveyed the occupants of the next table from beneath her eyelashes. 'What sort of trouble? Girls?'

Miss Gadd giggled at the very idea. 'No. Money,' and then, remembering a telephone conversation between Mavis' father and the Superintendent which she had chanced to overhear a few days earlier, she decided to say no more.

After lunch Gittins remarked to Morgan: 'I'll bet you sixpence that he won't come back.'

'Nonsense!'

'Very well, it's nonsense,' Gittins shrugged his shoulders and smiled, a superior, exasperating smile. 'But don't say that I didn't warn you – '

The thought: Now there will be a vacancy for a Superintendent: flashed between them and remained unspoken.

'Well?' Morgan asked. 'Are you going to tell me?'

Gittins mustered the knowledge which had led him to this conclusion, and repeated rather less than half of what he knew. 'There's no doubt that you put them on to this,' he began, and went on to describe the complicated agreement that had existed for some months between the Superintendent, two or three people in the Ministry and the chief employers in Dustborough, with Little, sitting in the centre of the spider's web at the White Lion, taking a rake-off from everybody. The Principal Clerk did not divulge the sources of his knowledge, nor did he give more than a sketchy outline of the part that the Superintendent had played in helping to provide the local factories with work and in depriving Blimpton of labour: but the facts could scarcely be doubted.

Morgan, enraged, amused, disgusted, and still half-incredulous, asked: 'Do you think they'll hush it up?'

'Hush what up?' Gunn demanded, bursting into the room at this moment.

Morgan and Gittins looked at one another, their faces closed, guarded against this awkward intrusion.

'Well?' Gunn asked, flinging off his overcoat.

For once Gittins looked almost embarrassed, but Morgan, meeting Gunn's glance, said: 'Can't you guess?'

'Jeez!' Gunn leapt across the room and gave Morgan a resounding thump on the shoulder. 'You knew all along? That's what I told her. I said to her, right at the start, the moment I ran into her, I said, those boys aren't as dumb as you seem to think. I said, you may put it across the Superintendent, but if you think that Gittins and Morgan don't realise who you are – '

'Who?' Gittins asked, 'Who – what?' And then he caught up and said, speaking rather slowly, 'As a matter of fact we didn't know that we had Mrs Heath-Green in the factory. Not until after she'd left…'

'You didn't, eh?' he looked from one to the other.

'If we had known,' Morgan interjected violently, 'we'd have treated her differently – the unspeakable little bitch – '

'Why? What'd she do to you?'

'Me? Nothing!' Morgan stood up, his anger filling the room. 'But d'you know what we're going to do to her? No? Well, I'll tell you: and you can tell her or not as you please. She'll find out soon enough, anyway… We're going to have her prosecuted under the Essential Work Order, have her sent to prison and make an example of her – '

'Oh!' Gittins broke in, 'You know we can't do that!' He turned to Gunn, 'That was just a joke that we thought up when we found out how we'd been had – '

'Had!' Morgan repeated. 'That's not at all my idea of a joke. No, indeed!' He stared at Gittins, not seeing him. 'I tell you,' he said, 'I've talked this over with Parsons, and he's taken action – reported her to the National Service Officer, or whatever the rigmarole is.'

Gunn was open-mouthed, dumbfounded.

'But since she really is old Outrage's daughter – ' Gittins began.

'All the better. I checked up on that before I spoke to Parsons. We're going ahead with it. Definitely. We'll see,' his voice was rough, near to breaking, 'we'll really find out this time what people are after, whether there's one law for the rich – '

'Hell!' Gunn found himself at last. 'You can't do it! You can't! Think of the Old Man's position – '

'I've thought of that. There's nothing I haven't thought of. Nothing, I tell you!'

Gittins, with a leave-this-to-me sort of smile, suggested, 'Perhaps we can discuss this later on. If you want to see those fuzes fired before the light goes – '

'Which fuzes?' Gunn asked. 'Oh! Those! Forget 'em. I've got the dirt now about the guy that sold me those… No, what I really came down about was these new hostels. Now that Bevin's starting all this conscription of women we're going to give you twenty new hostels – '

'What for?' Morgan and Gittins asked with one voice.

'To put the girls in. A thousand in each.'

'And what are we going to do with twenty thousand additional workers?' Morgan demanded.

'Well, that's your job, isn't it?'

Gittins shook his head, and reflected that this was the maddest scheme yet, since the factory's labour requirements were only a fraction of the number that Gunn was proposing to provide accommodation for. 'The hostel we have is barely full, you know,' he observed cautiously. But Gunn, embarking on a new project, was not prepared to listen to any objection, to any criticism. 'After all,' he pointed out, 'if you don't need hostels now, they'll come in useful for holiday camps after the war...'

FORTY-FIVE

WHITE, THE MANAGER of the Dustborough Employment Exchange, explained to Parsons that the Ministry of Labour had decided that nothing was to be gained by taking proceedings against Griselda Green for leaving Blimpton without permission. 'It's a tricky case,' he pronounced thoughtfully, turning over the pile of correspondence in front of him. 'You admit yourself that her position was – well, shall we say rather exceptional? She had only another two – or was it three? – days to work as an operative before her promotion was to take effect. So the questions that the court would have to decide would be: first, had she or hadn't she already obtained her release? Secondly, since she had accepted the new appointment but had not actually taken up duty could she be deemed to be already employed? And, if so,' – he looked up, smiling wanly – 'well, there seems to be some doubt as to whether the Order applies to managerial grades, and, frankly, if we're going to have a test case on that point we'd like something rather more clear-cut to go on – '

Parsons was obliged to agree that this was unanswerable.

'You mustn't imagine,' White finished, 'that this has anything at all to do with the fact that the girl happens to be the daughter of a Minister of the Crown – '

'You knew that?'

'My dear fellow!' White shook his head. 'Of course we knew. But if she'd been plain Mrs Green from one of the backstreets here we still couldn't have done it... By the way,' he added as Parsons began to take his leave, 'I hear that you're losing your Superintendent?'

'Oh, yes,' Parsons moved towards the door, 'I did hear some rumour about it.' Quickly, he began to talk about something else; and then, as he went out into the street, he reflected, too late, that it had been foolish not to admit, since everybody in Dustborough would soon know, that the Superintendent had been suspended from duty and that he, with several of his friends among the Dustborough employers, would be very fortunate if they were not, during the next few months, charged with conspiracy to defraud His Majesty's Government...

He hurried back to the factory to take the chair at a meeting at which Gower was to lecture to members of the junior managerial staff on the lessons that had been learned from the three months' experience of the use of new and intensified methods for maintaining health on the West Group. But when he arrived he found that Gower had been called away unexpectedly and that the lecture was to be given instead by Ruth Aaron. Ruth shuffled through the notes that Gower had handed over to her before he went, and consoled herself with the reflection that he would probably be back in time to answer questions at the end. Then she got up to speak.

For nearly a minute she stood perfectly still, paralysed by the sight of the hundred or so young men and women who sat in front of her, notebooks on their knees, bored, unexpectant. She tried to remember the message from Gower with which she had intended to begin, but the words made a meaningless jingle in her head and she could not translate them into sounds.

'We've done something,' she began haltingly. 'In the last three months we've achieved things in this factory. Among ourselves, by ourselves... We started to try to clean up a few of the shops, to reduce sickness, to get better production. And we've done it. We've shown what can be done... and we've shown that the only way, the only possible way, to get things done is for people to do them for themselves... We started this from above, from decisions made in the Surgery and the Administration Block; but we've made a success of it only because the workers in the shops – the grade three and grade four people who'll never get promotion, the people for whom the job means nothing more than the weekly pay-packet – because these people have begun to learn the importance of what they're doing... Because they've become interested, alive – and critical... because they've learned that the right to criticise has to be matched up with the duties of responsibility – of thinking out, when things go wrong, what ought to be done instead – '

They looked at her in astonishment. Here and there a hint of mockery, of unbelief glinted from behind their closed, polite faces. But most of them were roused, eager, and yet perhaps at the same time a little dazed. The gulf that divided them from the workers in the shops narrowed, widened, and then narrowed again as she went on to describe the details of what had been done: the appointment, in each shop on the group concerned, of a small committee to deal with the problems of factory hygiene, of contraband, of casual absenteeism; the inter-shop competitions planned to see increased popular interest in raising the general standard of cleanliness; the recent demand from the workers themselves for the adoption of new methods to increase production...

Pamela Grant, sitting dreamily in the front row, with the great word democracy still ringing in the air around her, remembered how, earlier in the day, she had entered a shop to discover a violent quarrel taking place and, on inquiring the reason, had learned that a newcomer to the factory had been seen by one of her workmates to be making up her face. The shop had been divided into two warring factions, one arguing that since the girl was new to the danger area she could not be expected to realise the importance of obeying the contraband regulations; and the other insisting that no one could, or should, be forgiven for bringing a lipstick into the shop. Now Pamela, peeping into her handbag, decided that after the lecture she would suggest that a supply of plastic lipstick containers might be bought by the stores department for re-sale. Then she began to wonder to whom she should make the suggestion... not to Miss Creed, certainly. Perhaps, she reflected, Dr Aaron herself might be willing to do something about it. She looked up, and seeing Norah McCall at the other end of the row, reproached herself with the thought that there, at least, was someone who would have no hesitation in pressing her ideas on her superiors, however aloof or reluctant they might be. The best plan, she decided, would be to discuss the suggestion with Norah first.

But as soon as the lecture was over Norah slipped out of the hall. She was on the night-shift this week, and wanted to see the afternoon-shift foreman before he went off duty. She pulled her coat tightly around her, and stood for a moment in the hall, thinking that if she were lucky she might get a lift part of the way from someone travelling in the same direction.

A voice behind her said: 'Miss McCall! Norah!'

She turned to find herself face to face with Henry Tyndale.

'Oh!' she said, her face flushing. She had seen him often enough since that distant Sunday afternoon when she had first met Tom Walton; but, in spite of Tom's insistence that she should forget everything about that unhappy episode but the fact that they had met, she had never quite been able to bring herself to speak to Henry. But now that she and Tom had arranged to be married on his next leave her indignation against Henry's inexplicable and, so far as she knew, unrewarded treachery melted and she felt a pang of something approaching pity.

'Why,' she said, watching him as he came nearer, 'you're quite a stranger.'

'Yes.' He looked very thin, and his tweed jacket was slovenly, baggy elbowed. 'Dr Aaron was fine, wasn't she?' he asked.

'*You* thought so?'

'Yes. Didn't you?'

'Of course *I* thought so – '

They looked at one another, dismayed.

'How's Tom?' he asked after a moment.

'Oh, Tom – Tom's all right. I saw him last weekend – '

'Oh!'

'We – ' she began, changed her mind, and started afresh. 'He just stopped off on his way down – '

'Down?'

'Oh, didn't you know?' a cloud crossed her face and was gone. 'He's being transferred to operations. Fighters.'

'How – . I mean – '

Someone called: 'Coming, Norah?'

'Okay.' She held out a hand to Henry. 'Be seeing you... and then slipped out into the darkness to climb on to the pillion of the assistant shop-manager's motorcycle.

Getting off at the other end she shivered as she felt the frosty air suddenly still. She ran into the shifting-house, changed quickly, and then hurried down the clean-way to the foreman's office.

'Mr Angus is down at Number Thirty-One,' somebody told her, 'he said, could you see him down there?'

'Right.'

The night was bright, so full of stars that she did not need to switch on her torch as she went out again. There was still nearly an hour to go before the afternoon-shift came off duty, and the clean-way was empty, with not even a footfall breaking the stillness. But from within the shops on either side came a faint hum of conversation, of people moving about; mixed now and then with the sound of metal clattering on metal, and the dull thud of some vast machine. Further on, people were singing. From a shop on her left came the soft melancholy hum of the Londonderry Air, mingling with the neighbouring strains of some marching tune from the last war, put to words by one of the engineers, topical, pointed, full of mockery. Then, further on still, the older women, in a shop where the day's supply of empties had already run out, were talking loudly, arguing about – was it the meat ration, or the latest crime of the canteen manageress?

Number Thirty-One was a large shop, and, after the darkness outside, Norah blinked suddenly, blinded by the warmth and light.

The foreman said: 'I'm glad you could come. Here's the thing I want you to have a look at…' and began to go into technicalities.

Norah, following closely, did not hear someone come behind her into the shop, and it was only when the foreman took the orange-coloured envelope into his hand that she asked, her voice catching with excitement: 'Is that for me?'

He handed it to her. 'How did you know?'

'Oh?' she looked at him, her eyes dancing. 'I just felt it might come.. only I wasn't expecting it so soon.'

He smiled, fatherly, sharing her delight. 'Aren't you going to open it?'

'Yes!' she began to tear at the envelope and then looked up. 'I know what's in it… Could I telephone?'

'Sure. Run along to my office.'

She turned to go, but at the door she stopped. 'It's a trunk call,' she said.

'Never mind – so long as you don't make a habit of getting married… and better not make it priority.'

She wanted to run, to dance, to shout, to tell everybody. Out in the darkness she no longer saw the night or felt the cold; and, rushing into the foreman's office again, she could only say to the young man who stood lounging against the wall: 'I must telephone. Quickly.'

He pointed to the instrument. 'I'll be getting along,' he said. 'Tell Mr Angus I'll be back later.'

'Yes.' She picked up the receiver and asked for the number of Tom's parents: for they had agreed between themselves that when the time came she should tell them in case anything should happen at the factory at the last moment.

'Half an hour's delay,' the operator told her, 'will you wait?'

'Yes, I'll wait.' She replaced the receiver and sat back. Then she pulled the envelope out of the pocket of her uniform and unfolded the slip of paper. 'NO!' she exclaimed, almost shouting as the words swam before her. The telegram fell out of her hand, and she bent and picked it up, seeing again the first two words: 'Deeply grieved...'

FORTY-SIX

THAT YEAR WINTER fell on Dustshire early, bitter, devouring. The gales of autumn died away, and snow began to fall. The news, crackling through the loud-speakers in the canteens, was full of menace. Then Moscow was saved, and the shop-stewards, sensing, though not able to see, the fever chart of output which (now that Blimpton was without a Superintendent) was kept locked in Dan Morgan's desk, demanded that a Joint Production Committee should be set up. The demand, endorsed by Morgan, was forwarded to headquarters where, as far as anyone at the factory could discover, it remained for a long time unread.

The Japanese attacked Pearl Harbor, and Blimpton received a new type of bomb to fill; but, a little later, when the first production difficulties were still being overcome, the Chief Controller's assistant wrote to say that a mistake had been made, and that the new bombs were to be filled, as had originally been intended, at one of the EELS factories. Then a group of time-and-motion-study experts arrived unannounced to make a study of certain filling operations. Their arrival coincided with a sudden change in the weather, and, as they stood around in the shops, stop-watches in their hands, the workers stamped their damp shoes on the floors and their grumbles were interrupted by a chorus of sneezing. By the time the weather hardened again the figures of absenteeism had leaped up to an unimaginable height. In the hostel one of the boilers showed signs of cracking, and Miss Marshall, after vainly pleading with the chief engineer to send men to repair it, put on her hat and trudged over to the factory to see Morgan. He was, she found, away, attending a conference in London; and she, bitterly disappointed, and afraid that half the dormitory blocks would soon be uninhabitable if something were not done, blurted the whole story out to Finch when she met him in the corridor. Finch, overwhelmed by the difficulties of keeping the buses and lorries on the roads and the goods wagons running to time, said, 'That should be easy,' and passed her on to Dawson.

Men were found, repairs made, and the inhabitants of the hostel, once more snug in their centrally-heated cubicles, began, perhaps for the first time, to think themselves lucky as they listened to tales of the fuel shortage in Dustborough. Housewives stayed away from work in the hope of being able to catch the coal-man before he was sold out for the day. There came a day when Ma Venning, after running out to look at the contents of the shed at the bottom of the garden, said, 'We've still got a bit of coke, and they promised last week...' she looked from Kitty to Rose. 'I think I'll have to stay home tomorrow and go round to the Co-op and see if Mr Butler won't give us a hundredweight or two to carry on with – '

'I'll go, if you like,' Kitty offered. Now that she was almost engaged to young Jim she liked to be able to claim the right to do some of Ma's odd jobs. Besides, Mr Venning had been very ill lately, and Ma already had more on her hands than she could manage...

Ma shook her head. 'They'll take more notice of me,' she explained. 'All the same,' she got up and began to clear the supper things. 'I don't like stopping off work for a thing like that – '

'Couldn't we – ' Rose began, blushed and stopped.

'Couldn't we what?' Ma asked, smiling at the girl's confusion.

'Well, that Mr – Mr Lester from the Town Hall who came to see Mr Venning last night – he said – ' she paused, putting the tea-cosy in the drawer of the dresser. 'He's an awfully nice man, isn't he? I mean for a councillor – '

Kitty laughed suddenly. 'What's it got to do with being a councillor? What was it he said – ?'

'He said his brother – the one who works at Hobson's – might be able to get us a gas fire – '

'What do we want a gas fire for?' Ma asked with unexpected sharpness.

Kitty put down her knitting. 'It'd save a lot of work,' she pointed out, 'specially just now.' She glanced up at the clock, 'I thought Norah was coming round.'

'Oh!' Rose put down the teacloth and turned to face them. 'I forgot to tell you – I saw Norah on the bus this morning. She said she wasn't feeling well – '

Kitty met Ma's glance. 'Should I go round?'

'No, leave her be.' And to herself she added: 'She'll tell us when she's ready.'

But Norah, lying in bed, staring up, in the uncurtained darkness, to the ceiling, was not ready to tell anyone: and yet soon, she knew, they would find out, someone would notice, there would be a scandal. Grief and fear and joy wove themselves into an inextricable confusion as she pulled the blankets more tightly round her and tried to meet the panic that came closer every night. And there was no one, no one at all, whom she could tell. She began once more to think of all the people she knew, to wonder how she would tell them, or how and when they would find out. Her mother... a shudder ran through her as she thought of her parents, of how shocked, how incredulous they would be that such a thing could happen to a child of theirs; they had not known Tom, and it was impossible, she told herself, impossible that they would ever realise how natural, even how right, it had all been... And Tom's parents, who had braced themselves to meet whatever kind of girl Tom might choose, and who had accepted her, not willingly, but with a feeling, concealed yet never quite invisible, that it might have been worse – Tom's parents, she had determined from the moment when she had first guessed, must never, never know. Ma. Warmth crept round her as she thought of Ma; but even Ma, she was certain, would never feel quite the same when she discovered that one of her girls had... had... 'OH!' she exclaimed aloud, 'Oh, Tom!'

Then, after a few minutes, she began to think of the people in the factory, the shop-manager, the foremen, the people she worked with every day, and she faced again the horrible certainty that she would lose her job. If she had been an ordinary operative people would have said: 'What, another?' and Miss Creed would have arranged, with cold efficiency, for her to go to a Home when the time came, and afterwards, if Norah gave her consent, for the child to be adopted. But as an assistant forewoman... she could not, she decided, face the pity and contempt with which she would be met; and, recognising, for the hundredth time that she would have to leave Blimpton altogether, she began to think of where she would go, of what she would do, of how she was going to live. Her thoughts raced round in circles, taking her nowhere, and presently she began to doze.

Soon, dreaming uneasily of the cottage at Watermist where she had spent six days, almost a whole week, with Tom, she woke up, feeling numb and cold, her head throbbing.

'I'll write to Griselda,' she said, half aloud, 'I'll write to Griselda tomorrow.'

FORTY-SEVEN

NEXT DAY MORGAN, who had been called to London to see the Chief Controller, returned to the factory. He climbed wearily up the steps of the Administration Block and, nodding to the doorkeeper, went straight to his own room. Gittins was already there, waiting. The smile that had been hovering behind his eyes all day at last emerged. He took off his spectacles and held out a hand. 'Well,' he asked, 'may I be the first to congratulate you?'

Morgan ignored the proffered hand. He threw his hat on to a chair, but did not unfasten his overcoat. His round head was bowed in defeat, and his eyes were dull. 'The hell you may!' he exclaimed, and picked up the letters that lay on his desk. 'Don't tell me that you haven't heard?'

Gittins, who had been watching, his face puzzled, now caught some of the other's dismay. 'You don't mean to say that they've appointed someone else?' His voice was hushed with incredulity. He had been so certain that Morgan was to be made Superintendent that he had not even bothered to think up a pretext for putting a call through to London to make certain; and at this moment, he knew, his wife was in Dustborough, trying to coax out of the grocer a bottle of whisky with which to celebrate.

'No.' Morgan sat down heavily. 'They haven't appointed anyone else.'

'Then what – ?'

'I'm going to tell you.' Morgan felt in his pockets, pulled out a bunch of keys, unlocked the top right-hand drawer of his desk and brought out a box of cigarettes. 'Smoke?'

'No, thanks.'

Morgan lit a cigarette for himself, and as the first puff of smoke blew out into the room he said in a flat and icy voice: 'We've been sold.'

'So it seems.'

'No, I mean it. Literally. Sold the way you sell a piece of cheese, or... or... Oh, God!' he ran a hand over his forehead. 'Gitty, you must understand – that old devil Outrage has handed this whole place over to EELS, lock, stock and barrel – every mortal thing – ' he broke off, jumped up, and moved towards the window. Gittins was grasping the edge of the desk with his hands. His eyes sought for something that he did not see, some evidence that would show that Morgan, and not the world, had become suddenly insane. When he looked up the Assistant Superintendent was still standing with his back to the room, apparently intent on whatever was happening outside. Gittins stared anxiously around, and his eyes were blank with incomprehension.

'It's not possible,' he said at last, and threw himself down in the armchair.

'I'm not talking about what's possible,' Morgan's head was still averted, but his voice was clear and firm. 'I'm telling you what's happened.'

'But they can't – '

'And I'm telling you that they have – '

'I thought,' Gittins hesitated, finding the words with difficulty, 'I thought everyone knew that we were… were catching up with things at last. We've been doing so much better – '

'Certainly.' Morgan turned to face the room once more. 'So much better that I was told that if I cared to stay on – '

'Stay on!'

'I said, no. If I can't run this factory for the Government, I'll be damned if I'll run it in the sacred name of private enterprise. Private enterprise, indeed!' His tone became more normal, calm, but with a deep undertone of passion. He threw off his coat and sat down. 'What sort of private enterprise is EELS? You know as well as I do why they're doing this – '

'Why?'

'Because they are thinking about the future. Not the war. To hell with the war – they're not going to make a profit out of running this place as long as the war lasts – and they probably won't care if they make a loss. But afterwards – '

'What use is a place like Blimpton going to be after the war?'

'There! You see!' Morgan thumped his fist on the table. 'Isn't that what everybody is saying? Only – you say it because you probably haven't thought about it very much – and Russell is saying it because it's the most obvious, elementary trick of all to decry the value of whatever it is that you want to buy... Don't tell me that EELS don't know what they want to do with Blimpton! – but even if they haven't made up their minds they want to be sure that nobody else gets it. They're not going to be left behind in the great game of seeing who can grab what first – '

'So you won't stay?'

'Indeed, I won't! I'm a skilled man. I can go out and get myself a job – '

'And,' now Gittins began to look like an old man, 'the rest of us?'

'Hm.' Morgan stubbed out his cigarette. 'They seemed to think that you'd like to take the opportunity to retire – '

'Retire!'

'The established civil servants will be sent to other factories. And the temporaries – they want to keep Parsons, and possibly Gower and Dr Aaron. Not Finch...'

Gittins rubbed a hand over his head. 'I can't believe it,' he objected. 'It just doesn't make sense...'

That night Morgan made a statement to the senior staff, and next day he addressed the workers over the factory broadcast system: to the morning-shift before they came off duty, and to the afternoon-shift during the mid-shift break. As far as he could discover they were taking it badly, grumbling, not knowing how to protest and not altogether certain what it was that they wanted to protest against. Some of the managerial staff seemed rather pleased, their sense that something had gone adrift outweighed by the reminder, repeated constantly from one to another, that big business meant efficiency, opportunity and, if one played one's cards well, a safe job after the war. Dinner at Mowbray Lodge was a melancholy occasion. Although the change would not be made for at least a month everyone was conscious that the break-up had begun, that though some would stay while others went, they would never again be united by the same discords, the same interests, the same sense of holding together in a world that they themselves had made.

Miss Creed's beads clinked against her coffee cup. 'How trying!' she exclaimed. 'How trying to think…' she broke off the sentence, not knowing how to continue because she had not yet made up her mind whether to go or to stay.

Dolphin said: 'I think I shall join the Army. Or the Navy… yes, on second thoughts, definitely the Navy…'

Finch looked at Ruth. 'And what are we going to do?' he asked.

Morgan jumped up. 'I must go and give my repeat performance,' he explained, and hurried out to go back to the factory to address the night-shift workers as they came on duty.

It was late when he returned, and the lounge was empty. He threw himself into one of the deep chairs beside the fire, his legs stretched out to the warmth, his body relaxed with fatigue. He smoked, throwing the cigarette ends after one another into the fireplace, looking into the fire, hearing the occasional drop of a cinder, and the distant sound of the wind, shattering a broken branch of the fir tree on the lawn.

He had been sitting there for perhaps an hour when Ruth came in.

'Hello,' she said, 'I didn't know that anyone was in here.' She looked nervous, her shoulders taut.

'Never mind. Come and sit down.'

She slipped into a chair.

'And what are you going to do with the rest of your life?' he asked.

'I – I don't know.'

'You don't, eh?'

'It's difficult to make up one's mind, isn't it?'

'Yes,' he agreed, 'I suppose it is… even if one knows what one wants, which most of us don't.'

'Do you know what you want?'

'Yes, I do. That's the devil of it – '

'Why – ' her face was averted, and she sat very still, her hands clasped on her knees.

'Ruth – '

Someone tapped at the door.

Ruth called 'Come in,' but before the words were spoken the

door opened. Standing in the entrance, lit from behind by the blue light of the hall lamp, was a woman, a woman in a mink coat. The fire flared up, lighting her face.

Morgan gave a violent start. 'Well...' he said, not attempting to get up.

Griselda took a step forward, and then stood still.

'Well...' Dan repeated, the jeering note creeping into his voice, 'if it isn't the Minister's daughter!'

She stood her ground, not speaking.

'And what can I do for you?' he asked. Now he rose, advancing towards her with mocking, belated courtesy.

Ruth said: 'I think I'd better go.' She scrambled awkwardly out of the cushions.

'No,' he turned to her, 'don't go. Why should you go? I think you know each other. Dr Aaron. Miss Green.'

Griselda took another step forward. 'I think we've met,' she said. She made as if to hold out her hand, and then, as the other girl's glance fell on her, she faltered. The lamp on the table caught the reflection of a square-cut emerald as her hand slipped again to her side. 'I seem to have chosen an awkward moment,' she said, looking from one to the other.

'You have,' Dan replied, his voice rough with a harshness which she had never heard before. 'This is a bad evening for people who care about Blimpton – '

'I know that,' she interrupted quickly, 'that's why I came – '

' – and it's already late,' he went on, ignoring her interruption.

'I'm sorry,' Griselda broke in again, 'I came as early as I could. I came to Dustborough to see – to see a friend of mine who's in difficulties, and while I was there I heard... about... I didn't know... I didn't think you'd be busy – '

'But I am. Very.'

Ruth said again: 'I must go.'

He lifted his arm in that familiar, eloquent gesture, motioning her to stay. 'When you came in,' he turned once more to Griselda, 'I was about to ask Dr Aaron to become my wife.'

'Oh!' Griselda sat down on the arm of an empty chair. 'And now

I'm here you're – '

Ruth jumped up and ran from the room.

The door fell to. Griselda took a cigarette from her bag and lit it. 'What a brutal, disgusting thing to do!'

'Yes. I shouldn't have – '

'Especially since you didn't mean it – '

'What makes you say that?'

'Because it's true. You know it's true, and I know it's true,' she flung off her fur cap and shook out her hair.

'Was that – ' he broke off, flinging his cigarette into the fire. A tongue of flame leaped up and subsided. The fire cast a faint glow over their faces, and beyond them to the dim, comfortable room. For a long time they did not speak, and then a lump of coal crashed into the glowing embers.

'What did you come here for?' Morgan asked at last, his voice harsh. 'Now? Now, of all times – '

'I have to talk to you.' She had slipped off her coat, and sat crouched forward, her face pale above the shadowy blackness of her dress.

'I'm listening.' Still he did not look at her. His hands, resting on the arm of the chair, were tense, the muscles tightening over the cretonne.

'I told you. I came to Dustborough this afternoon to see a friend of mine who needs help – '

'And what has that to do with me?'

'Nothing, unless you choose.' And then she looked at him.

'You remember that first day? The day when we came to see you in your office – ?'

'Yes. I remember.'

'And Norah? You remember Norah?'

He sat up, feeling in his pockets for his cigarette case. 'Of course I remember Norah... I saw her the other day... doing a fine job...'

'You have to help her.'

'Help her? My God! – '

Now she stood up, one elbow resting on the mantelpiece, looking down into the fire, her face averted. 'Listen. Norah's in trouble. Her young man was killed, just when they were going to be married; and now she's going to have a baby… she's terrified… really terrified… I didn't know that she could ever be frightened… She is, though…'

'Frightened of having a baby?'

'Not that. You must understand. She's frightened of what the world will do to her – '

'What more can it do?'

'Oh, don't be so – ' she turned towards him, and then, seeing his remote, shuttered face, sat down again.

'The people here – ' she indicated the empty, yet populated, room, ' – they'll never imagine… they'll make a disgrace out of what ought to be – ' she shook her head. 'Tom was a fine young man. And they loved each other – '

'What are you trying to say?'

'I've told you. I want you to help her… of course, as far as money is concerned – well, I can look after that. But Norah needs a place in the world – '

'And you want me to see that she gets her job back?'

'More than that… She should feel proud – '

The door opened and Finch rushed in. 'Oh, there you are!' he exclaimed flatly. 'I've been searching – ' Then he saw Griselda. 'I didn't know you were busy – '

'I'm not,' Morgan pulled himself out of the chair. 'What is it?'

'Hasn't anyone told you? They're calling protest meetings – all over the factory – in every canteen – '

'Who?'

'The shop-stewards. Parsons told me just now… he thinks you ought to go over – '

'To do what?' Morgan's voice was calm, laden with fatigue, 'I've told them – ' he shrugged his shoulders. 'Good luck to them: that's all I can say – '

'But aren't you going to – ?'

'I'm not going to do anything. I represent the management – I'm on the wrong side of the fence – now…'

'Well!' Finch pursed his lips, frowning. 'I suppose you know best.' Then he went out.

Morgan stirred the fire, and sat down. 'All right,' he said, 'I'll look after Norah. What else have you got to say for yourself? Or have you finished?'

'No.' Once more she stood up. 'I heard – in Dustborough – about – about what's going to happen to the factory. I didn't know. My father doesn't talk about these things... especially since... since the last few months... I know what it means to all these people here: to Ma and Kitty and Rose. To the shop-stewards and the politically conscious – '

'The what!'

'You didn't expect me to talk like that, did you? But I've been learning... anyway... And,' she turned, facing him, 'I think I know what it means to you, and what it is that you're going to do... But you can't. You can't walk out, now. You! You with your fine sense of social responsibility, with your eloquent Welsh phrases... pretending to yourself that because you've been running a state-owned factory you're building socialism... oh, it's a harder job than that. Where do you think you come in? What is it that you belong to? Paid by the state to fill shells, or paid by EELS – you're still powerless, as powerless – more – than Ma Venning or little Whitey... they know what they're fighting for, and you – you only know what you're fighting against... You refuse to see what the real issues are... You sit at a desk, and think and plan and talk, and they stand at the machines and turn the stuff out... but you haven't much more control than they over the general lay-out. Even your programme is given to you. You can say, yes, we'll do it, or, no, we can't. But you're not allowed even to appoint a foreman without getting permission from headquarters – yes, I've found that out! And whatever you may say, the final decisions on the big questions are made by... by people you hate – you know it... you've said so yourself. But you don't know your power... you and all the other workers – '

'Fine phrases!'

'No. I mean it. You know it's true, and you're uncomfortable. You should be... You can't stop at being a big-shot, sitting at a desk in your shirt-sleeves. There's much more of you than that. You're a great man.'

'I think you've said nearly enough.'

'Not yet. I've wanted to say this for a long time. And now I'm going to say it. You haven't begun yet. You've got something in yourself that you're afraid of. Perhaps you don't even know that you're afraid. You haven't run away from anything – '

'But you did!'

'Yes,' she put up her hands, covering her face. 'I... well, anyway,' she looked at him, and now her eyes were very bright, fierce and eager. 'But you – it's what you're running towards that frightens you... or that would frighten you if you didn't refuse to look at it. It's time you began to open your eyes. Feet on the ground, yes. But you've had your eyes on the ground for a long time. Too long. You see what's coming tomorrow. You get the next step right – '

'That's something – '

'But it's not enough. You never know whether it's in the right direction. It's not a beaten path... and if you're not looking forward you'll get bogged in the end... I don't like talking in metaphors or parables or whatever it is... anyway, this must sound very artificial and highfalutin to you – '

'No. Go on.'

'The difference between these girls and you is that you could look ahead and see the future. They can't. They haven't the knowledge. They don't know anything – or most of what they do know isn't relevant. You know. Or at least you have the means to knowledge. Access to the facts. And the power to think... It's much more than that, again. You have the right way of looking at things. If only you would look. There isn't anything that you people here at Blimpton couldn't do if you made up your minds to it... And you. It's time you stopped talking about leadership and began to lead – '

'What do you think I've been doing all this time?'

'I know. I'm not criticising the way you've been doing your job. But there's a world outside, and it won't wait – '

'But don't you understand – ' now he rose, towering beside her. 'We have to win the war first – '

'Of course.'

' – and we have made something in this factory. We've taught people much more than how to do their jobs... we've started to make a new world... and now it's beginning to fall down about our ears. First, EELS will take over, then the programme will be cut... people will drift off somewhere else... some will be unemployed. The politicians – men like your father – '

'But why should they always be men like my father? Don't you see that that's exactly what I'm trying to say? My father... he's only one sort... but the other sorts... they're well-intentioned... Some of them – the best of them and the worst of them – know which side of the fence they're on... but you – '

'Well?'

'You – you people who make the world... you don't understand that you've a bigger responsibility than merely doing the job. You say that you belong to the workers – '

'Belong to them! I'm one of them – '

Someone knocked at the door. A maid put her head through a narrow aperture. 'It's Mr – '

Gunn tore in.

'Evening, Morgan,' and then he saw Griselda. 'Well, I'll be – '

Griselda said: 'Get out!'

'Why! What – '

'Get out. You've done enough harm in this factory!' she turned on him, her arms at her sides, her fists clenched. 'Get out, or I'll – '

'Okay.' Meekly he turned, closing the door quietly behind him.

When she turned to look at Morgan he was laughing, silently, but with a sort of wildness. Then his face sobered. 'What harm did he ever do?' he asked.

'Why, he told me – ' she stopped, looked at him, hesitated. 'That night...'

'Yes?'

'When... when I got back to the hostel I found a note from him to say that you knew that...'

'Well?' his voice was frozen.

'That... that you knew that I – '

'My God!' rage burst out of him, shattering the stillness. 'You thought that I – ' he moved away from her, striding up and down the room. 'So that's what you think of me after all this – this fine, eloquent sermon that you've been giving me. That's the sort of man you think I am – ' He stood with his back to her, his hands thrust into his pockets, facing the curtained windows. His shoulders were squared against her, rigid with enmity.

'Listen!' she pleaded.

'Why should I listen to you?' he did not turn. 'Haven't I listened enough?'

'No!' her voice was so loud, so challenging, that he turned, involuntarily, to face her. 'It's true,' she said, 'that I ran away. But you must realise why – '

'I know. Because you couldn't believe in me – '

'No. Because I couldn't believe in myself…' her eyes were very large and clear as she looked into his face. 'I don't know whether I can make you understand… and perhaps it doesn't matter… I… I should have come back sooner.'

'Why didn't you?'

'Because – well, partly because I was afraid that you wouldn't give me a job again – '

'And now you've come too late.'

'Too late?'

The gleam of mockery vanished from his eyes. 'My dear, I can't give you a job. I've told you – or anyway you've guessed – that I'm getting out of here. I haven't any jobs to offer any more… even if you really wanted one.' He took a step back, watching her as she stood quite still before him, her face downcast. 'But you don't,' he finished, after a long pause.

Suddenly she looked up and smiled. 'But I do,' she said, speaking so softly that the words were only just audible. 'And besides – '

'Well?'

'You can't go. They need you here – '

'They?'

'Ma Venning. Norah. All of them. And there's the job that has to be done.'

'You've said all that.'

'Well, then – ' she began, and stopped. Her face was in shadow, and her arms, under the loose sleeves of her dress, made little swaying movements.

'Yes?'

Still she hesitated. From an open window above them the sound of music drifted into the silence. Miss Hopkins had turned on the radio in her bedroom.

'Listen!' Dan lifted a hand to the opening bars of *Eine Kleine Nacht Musik*. 'Do you remember that?'

She nodded, trembling slightly.

'Almost too much of a coincidence, isn't it?' he asked, still with an edge of irony in his voice. And then, abruptly, he turned towards her, his arms outstretched. She took a step forward, and his hands fell, seizing her by the shoulders, but holding her at arms-length. 'You know,' he went on, 'I used to think that you and I could do quite a lot together – '

'And now?'

'Now my world has come to an end – '

'No. It isn't an end. It can't be.' Her shoulders grew tense as the grip of his hands tightened. 'For us – '

'For us!' suddenly he grinned. Then his smile faded as he drew her to him. 'For us, perhaps, it's only the beginning...'

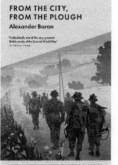

ISBN 9781912423071

£8.99

'Alexander Baron's *From the City, From the Plough* is undoubtedly one of the very greatest British novels of the Second World War and provides the most honest and authentic account of front line life for an infantryman in North West Europe.'

ANTONY BEEVOR

ISBN 9781912423163

£8.99

'Few other novels of the war describe the grinding claustrophobia, violence and lethal danger of being in a tank crew with the stark vividness of Peter Elstob... a forgotten classic that deserves to be read and read.'

JAMES HOLLAND

ISBN 9781912423095

£8.99

'Takes you straight back to Blitzed London... boasts everything a great whodunit should have, and more.'

ANDREW ROBERTS

ISBN 9781912423378
£8.99

'A highly unusual war novel with several confluent narratives; moving, interesting and of great literary value.'

LOUIS de BERNIÈRES

ISBN 9781912423156
£8.99

'When a man has been a soldier and seen action, he writes of war with true understanding, and with authority. When that man writes with with, elegance and imagination, as Fred Majdalany does in *Patrol*, he produces a military masterpiece.'

ALLAN MALLINSON

ISBN 9781912423088
£8.99

'A tremendous rediscovery of a brilliant novel. Extremely well-written, its effects are both sophisticated and visceral. Remarkable.'

WILLIAM BOYD

ISBN 9781912423101
£8.99

'Much more than a novel'

RODERICK BAILEY

'I loved this book, and felt I was really there'

LOUIS de BERNIÈRES

'One of the greatest adventure stories
of the Second World War'

ANDREW ROBERTS

ISBN 9781912423385
£8.99

'Brilliant... a quietly confident masterwork'

WILLIAM BOYD

'One of the best books to come out of the
Second World War'

JOSHUA LEVINE

ISBN 9781912423279
£8.99

'A hidden masterpiece, crackling with
authenticity'

PATRICK BISHOP

'Supposedly fiction, but these pages live
– and so, for a brief inspiring hour, do the
young men who lived in them.'

FREDERICK FORSYTH

ISBN 9781912423262
£8.99

'Witty, warm and hugely endearing... a lovely novel'

AJ PEARCE

'Evokes the highs and lows, joys and agonies of being a Land Girl'

JULIE SUMMERS